SWORD AND STARSHIP
BOOK 2: HARBINGERS

ELLIS MORNING

Harbingers (Sword and Starship Book 2)

Copyright © 2017 by Ellis Morning

Published by Ellis Morning
Pittsburgh, PA
www.ellismorning.com

ISBN: 978-0-9907573-5-1

Edited by RJ Blain
Interior layout by Ellis Morning
Cover art by Chris Howard
Cover design by Ellis Morning
Printed by CreateSpace, Charleston SC

Acknowledgements

Once again, I can't thank enough everyone who helped me in some way:

- Remy Porter, for initial editing and years of unfailing support
- RJ Blain, for her wonderful editing
- Chris Howard, for his amazing cover art
- Family and friends, for their encouragement
- My wonderful fans
- **YOU**, for giving this book a try!

Writing this book has proven an arduous but rewarding quest! I hope you enjoy reading it as much as I enjoyed putting it together.

-Ellis

CHAPTER 1

Before landing in the barony of Nidaros, I never would've imagined the army's headquarters would prove the safest place in the capital.

Few candles burned at this late hour. Healthy fires had diminished to embers within the hearths capping either end of the single-story wooden structure. Still, the barracks remained warm. Inviting, even. Dozens of soldiers had retired to their bunks in peaceful slumber.

Any knight errant with enough questing under her belt knew safety was fragile: always one decree, disease, or battle away from vanishing. Hundreds of people in the capital and out in the districts slept like these soldiers, unaware of the deadly threat lurking right beneath them — a threat I had to halt before it destroyed the planet, even if it meant losing my chance to save a dear friend and mentor.

I hurried toward the barracks' exit with urgency. The front door already hung open, swaying into darkness. Without bothering to find a lantern, I took a steeling breath and darted into the void.

My feet crunched through dead grass. Cold air stabbed into my lungs and ignored my coat to drill down to bone. Ahead of me, a man wearing a burgundy tabard over light armor sped down the side of the barracks, oil lantern in one hand and wooden bucket in the other.

Ingvar Leirfall, Captain of the Guard, rushed toward an iron well pump. Its handle had been tied off and adorned with metal charms, wards that were meant to keep evil—and people—at bay. They didn't deter the captain, who ran like he'd never noticed them.

They didn't impress me, either, as my mentors had cured me of superstition and belief in the so-called Unseen years earlier. With a mix of determination and dread that'd become familiar during my time in Nidaros, I chased after Ingvar. My side sword bounced against my back with each stride. I left it sheathed, as this wasn't the sort of emergency one solved with violence.

Upon reaching the well, Ingvar set down his burdens. He severed the leather ties with his longsword, then tossed the blade aside and placed his bucket beneath the spigot to work the freed pump. It was dry for a while at first before sputtering to life. Instead of water, out poured a ghastly purplish sludge.

Ingvar dropped to his knees. "Jayce." He choked out my nickname—Jess, really, but that was how he pronounced it.

Speechless, I stumbled to a halt beside him, eyes riveted to the bucket.

The mysterious substance—ichor, we called it—spread unchecked through the barony of Nidaros. In the presence of water, it created more of itself, destroying or contaminating the water in the process. Crops withered as a result, leading to dwindling food stores and a worsening shortage of flax, Nidaros' sole export.

Given flax's importance to their economy, the reigning sovereign Lord Catherwood and Madam Castor, Guildmistress of the Linum Dominorum trade guild, had taken note of the crisis. If her flax debt went unpaid, Madam Castor would surely stop shipping food and other supplies to Nidaros. Lord Catherwood might curse the barony, severing it from the galaxy and preventing its people from seeking help elsewhere. Either might send armed forces to "encourage cooperation" or extract their due in blood, all while the deadly ichor consumed the planet. Hundreds of Nidarans faced the gnawing agony of starvation — and who knew how all the other planets dependent on the flax trade would suffer?

Ingvar released the well pump and sat back hard on the ground. His tabard had Lord Catherwood's seal embroidered on the chest: a gold griffin devouring a snake. As he hunched over, the griffin looked to be struggling with a burden too heavy to bear.

"No wonder everything's dead." He braced his head in his hands. "If it weren't raining, we'd be dead, too."

Several full rain barrels stood nearby, a common sight throughout Nidaros. At least the emergency water supply was safe. But if it stopped raining — or worse, if it began raining ichor …

I shook off the thought and dropped to my knees beside the bucket, desiring a closer look. The flickering lantern light didn't dispel the shadows deep inside, but that wasn't a problem. My coat pockets played host to several ancient Shipbuilder light sources at the moment: my prized stick lighter, and the newly acquired light tile. Of the two, I understood the stick lighter's operation better, and it was more subtle. After a quick peek over both shoulders to confirm we were alone in the dark field, I retrieved it. Twisting the two halves of the small metallic wand aligned the components that activated its internal power source. One end glowed with a bead of heat and light, which charged the battery while active.

"*Skíta!*" Ingvar cursed, unfurling as though preparing to run. Midway through, he froze, frowning at the lighter. "Aye, that thing. Careful with it here, Jayce."

His fear lingered, but I got the feeling it was less for the lighter and more for the consequences I faced if I were caught wielding a "sacred" Shipbuilder artifact that the powers-that-be claimed I had no business touching.

"Don't worry." I cupped my left hand around the light to shield it.

Ingvar slowly sat back. He didn't run away or arrest me for witchcraft, which was better than most people on most planets. I longed to teach him more about the stunning technology and science the Shipbuilders had left behind centuries earlier—now largely forgotten, their artifacts hoarded among Lords and magic adepts. But the timing, and our moods, had to be better first.

I lowered my lighter into the bucket, tilting the container from side to side. Sure enough, no trace of water. The purplish ichor was odorless, slick and shiny like quicksilver, and seeped readily into the wood of the bucket. Imagining the entire *planet* overrun with the stuff sent a shiver through me.

For all the blights I'd fought elsewhere in the galaxy, I lacked the knowledge to ease this one. My ignorance hurt, almost as much as it hurt to see my one ally in this whole mess despairing. Was the ichor the result of some runaway chemical reaction? I didn't know enough chemistry to hazard a guess there. Maybe it was some kind of organism, like algae or bacteria? I'd seen plenty of such blooms before, but none that left bodies of water to race through soil. The ichor didn't seem to merely inhabit water, either. Whatever changes it made, the result was lethal to plants—and to people, as Ingvar and I had witnessed earlier.

With a stab of horror, I remembered the unidentified stains on my boots, trousers, and coat that'd accumulated over the past few days. I put down the bucket and checked them all over. They appeared to be splotches of ichor mixed with dried mud. Where possible, I examined my skin underneath, confirming it looked and felt normal.

I let out a quiet sigh of relief. This seemed further proof that physical contact with the ichor wasn't harmful. If any got *inside* a person, though … the thought filled me with uneasiness. I shut off and pocketed the stick lighter, then sat down hard beside Ingvar. The fatigue and pains of that long, dangerous day returned with a vengeance.

"The adepts blocked off all our wells weeks ago," Ingvar said, referring to the local practitioners of "magic" and guardians of tradition concerning the Unseen. "They've known of the ichor for some time, and yet, never a word of it to me or Baron Tristan." His furious, questioning gaze locked onto mine. "Is this their doing? What if this is some poison of theirs that got out of hand?"

It was frighteningly plausible. My trust toward magic adepts was middling to nonexistent as a rule, and the adepts in Nidaros had given me no reason to adjust my stance. That morning, some unknown number of them had sent me on a one-way trip into the dungeon beneath their keep to meet with a fire grenade. I'd fought my way out, but one of my attackers —Adept Knorr—had died in the process.

Despite all that, I had trouble believing the adepts had *made* the ichor. It seemed too powerful a creation from those who thoughtlessly aped tradition—and too lifelike, almost like it had agency. A drive to reproduce and spread, if nothing else.

"I think they discovered this stuff a while ago, but didn't know what it was," I replied to Ingvar. "So they kept it a secret, warned people away from it. It wouldn't be the first time adepts have covered up something they couldn't explain."

Ingvar's scowl shot toward the bucket. "Even if we take it to Baron Tristan and shove it under his nose, Ormyr will have a deflection ready!"

"I know," I said, tamping back annoyance. Master Ormyr, the chief adept in Nidaros, was hell-bent on steering us away from anything that had a whiff of progress about it. The local Baron was his all-too-willing accomplice in that regard.

Ingvar's eyes refocused on me, pleading. "What do we do, Jayce?"

With a deep breath, I gathered up my reassurance and determination. "We need to find out what this stuff is and how to get rid of it."

Though I had guesses about the ichor's nature, I lacked the means by which to test them. The proper equipment and know-how were hard to come by — but, to my continued astonishment, one woman in Nidaros possessed both. Anticipating Ingvar's reluctance, I brought up my next point gently. "Thordia's looking for answers. She may have them by now."

Ingvar slumped again, shaking his head downward. "Skíta."

Thordia Naustvik: the very "witch" accused of "cursing" Nidaros. In reality, she was an expert in botany and other Shipbuilder disciplines. She'd isolated the ichor on her own, but hadn't been able to do anything about it before Master Ormyr had come seeking her hide.

Earlier that evening, Ingvar and I had searched Thordia's home in the Low North district, hoping she was still evading the adepts there. She'd fled, however, leaving behind amazing specimens of ancient technology and a note intended for her brother Verahl. In it, she'd explained her intent to venture to some mysterious, far-off place called the Harbinger and seek a cure for the ichor there.

Ever since we'd made that discovery, Ingvar had avoided discussing it with me. My sympathy welled, a painful reminder of how much I'd grown to care about him against my own wishes. Longing to reassure him, I rested my hand on his back, close to his shoulder.

His head shot back up. Surprise flickered over his expression, but he didn't flinch or push me away.

Though my heart pounded, I managed to keep my voice level. "Why does Thordia think she'll find answers at the Harbinger? What *is* the Harbinger?"

Ingvar glanced askance. Silence stretched between us. Just as I was about to try asking again, he faced me, eyes full of trepidation. "The old ones say it presaged the fall of Lord Gyllenfeld."

The Lord who'd originally ruled over Nidaros decades ago, before Catherwood and several other Lords had swept through and conquered his holdings.

"'Tis how the Harbinger got its name," Ingvar continued. "Truth is, Gyllenfeld had fallen *afore* it struck."

I blinked at his choice of words. "Struck?"

"Ages afore any of us were born, this great *thing* fell out of the sky and drove into the ground like a tent spike." Ingvar swallowed around a lump in his throat. "The earth shook, forests fell, entire districts burnt up. Sky full of light one moment, ash the next. Hundreds died in the chaos."

My free hand rose to my mouth. "That must've been awful."

"The Baron of Nidaros at that time decreed that anyone who approacheth the thing should be put to death," Ingvar continued. "Every Baron since hath upheld the decree, not wishing to risk stirring up its wrath again."

It must've been *massive* to cause such turmoil. A meteorite, or an old Shipbuilder structure? Not just a single ship, but something vast. "Have you ever seen it?" I asked, curious whether he could offer his own experience and not just hearsay.

Ingvar nodded. "My family's farm lieth in the East, in a district spared its violence. I faced down the beast every day there wasn't a fog or storm. Always felt like it was watching us, waiting for the right moment to finish what it began." He glanced off into the nighttime void, sizing up a nemesis across an invisible battlefield.

"What does it look like?"

He swallowed hard. "A ringed spire towering in the distance."

My heart raced. Awestruck, I searched my feverish thoughts for the right words to explain. "A long time ago, the Shipbuilders built hundreds of stations in space — like spacefaring vessels, only much larger, and not faring anywhere. I won't know for sure until I see it, but it sounds like the Harbinger's one of those giant stations. Without the Shipbuilders there to take care of it, it must've drifted out of its proper position in space and crashed on Nidaros." I skipped the discussion of Lagrangian points and orbital decay. "That crash would've been very violent, like you said. Think of a stone sending ripples through a pond, only through air and land instead. It's amazing that it survived intact."

A testament to their ancient genius. Had anything inside the station survived impact? Thordia must've believed so. The mere thought of the incredible things that might lie in wait there sent chills through me.

Ingvar stared deep into my eyes, struggling to process my explanation. His apprehension killed my excitement, replacing it with dread. "Thordia must be seeking more powerful Shipbuilder magic to use against the ichor. But if she's not careful, she might unleash something even worse."

I bit my lip nervously. Was it possible? Adepts throughout the galaxy droned on about the awful dangers of mishandling Shipbuilder "magic," but they just wanted to keep everything to themselves and their masters. As for Thordia, I only knew her through notes, hearsay, and the artifacts left behind in her home. She struck me as someone who humored the local dogma far enough to satisfy the authorities while remaining true to herself behind their backs. Someone like me. I wanted to enlist her help. The only problem? It'd be sheer hell to search for a single woman on foot somewhere between Nidaros and the innards of a gigantic space station.

With wrenching agony, I wished my former mentor, Beguine Drea, were there with us. This discovery would've thrilled her, and she would've known exactly how to extract whatever knowledge the Shipbuilders had possessed regarding the ichor. But Drea was trapped in the frozen, adept-cursed town of Gules, millions of miles distant. Leaving Nidaros required the Baron's permission and the help of Master Ormyr, as Gules' coordinates had been erased from my ship's index. Even if I had those things, an entire planet depended on me, and might not have days to wait.

"Captain!"

The distant call jarred me from my guilt-ridden thoughts. I shook my head and glanced up, seeking the source of interruption.

A bobbing lantern revealed three soldiers clad in burgundy and gold tunics, approaching the barracks along a worn path. Lieutenant Pontus Grimsson, Ingvar's second in command, led the way: a shorter, stockier gentleman with a graying beard. Anyone who saw him next to Ingvar would assume Pontus was Captain of the Guard. An unusual arrangement, but it seemed Ingvar benefited from having a more experienced soldier at his right hand.

Behind Pontus trailed two younger soldiers, Ebbe Madsen and Magnus Holmvik. They stared at their feet, none of the usual rival banter passing between them.

"Over here, lads!" Eagerly, Ingvar sprang to his feet and offered me a hand up as well.

I accepted and stood with a nod of thanks, of two minds about the interruption. Our discussion was too important to shelve. At the same time, Ingvar had sent these soldiers on a mission of inquiry. They might've returned with valuable information—although, judging by their empty hands, physical evidence had eluded them.

The soldiers waved back, abandoning the path to make a beeline toward me and Ingvar.

"Thank the Unseen ye've returned, Captain. Dame Jessamine," Pontus greeted as he converged. He didn't explain why he spoke with such relief—probably because of the younger soldiers in earshot—but I knew it was because a part of him had feared we'd never return. When he'd learned of our intent to search the Naustviks' house, he'd all but pleaded us not to.

The other soldiers flanked their lieutenant. At Pontus' right, teenaged Ebbe smiled my way. Magnus stood at Pontus' left—closer to my age, and more reserved.

Ingvar gave a nod in greeting. "Any luck?"

"Some. We should talk." I assumed Pontus meant a private discussion, minus the younger soldiers—and maybe even me.

Ingvar lowered his head again. "Ebbe, Magnus, thanks for —"

"Sir! The well!" Ebbe gave a start and pedaled several steps backward, eyes riveted upon something behind us. One of his hands strayed toward his belt and grasped the loop of wishing beads suspended there.

With a stab of fear, I spun around. All that lay in wait were the freed well pump, the charms and ties littering the ground, the bucket of ichor, and Ingvar's lantern. Facing the soldiers again, I found Magnus and Pontus had joined Ebbe in clutching their own bead-loops with wide-eyed horror.

"We were supposed to steer clear of it, sir." A tremor went through Pontus' voice. "Who or what could've destroyed those wards?"

"We don't know," I intervened, fancying myself the quicker liar. "We're trying to find out. Don't worry, we're protected."

To prove it, I waved a hand toward Ingvar. My late mother's amethyst ring still dangled from the chain around his neck. I'd lent it to him earlier, a gesture that still made my heart jump when I thought about it. From there, I pointed out the mati amulet around my neck, which Master Ormyr had given me that morning; it resembled a blue human eye frozen in an unending stare. Ingvar had his own copy of the same amulet, hanging from his belt next to wishing beads that, to my satisfaction, I'd never once seen him grasp.

Neither Ingvar nor I believed that any of these things brought luck or protection. But, as the captain had mentioned earlier that day, they had their uses. For me, they helped with the show of conformity necessary to avoid prison cells, execution, and worse. These soldiers were friendly, but Ingvar was the only one with whom I had the luxury of total honesty.

The soldiers' worry eased, but didn't vanish entirely. "Could be a witch here in the capital," Magnus muttered.

"*Skíta!*" Ebbe cursed. "What if it's Thordia herself?"

"The real threat is what's coming out of the damned wells." Ingvar grabbed the bucket and brought it to them for inspection. "*This* is our curse! The adepts knew and never told us!"

Upon viewing the contents, the soldiers' jaws fell. Pontus' lantern looked like it'd fall next.

"The knight and I found more of the same in the Low North. The whole barony's infested." Ingvar proffered the bucket toward the nearest junior soldier. "Magnus, take this into the room left of my office. Ebbe, go with him. Don't show anyone, and don't speak of it yet. I'll brief you all soon. 'Til then, best not to let rumors run loose."

With dread plastered over their faces, neither young man moved to comply.

"Is it safe, sir?" Pontus pleaded more than asked.

"Don't touch it, and you'll be fine," I said. Prior experience led me to think physical contact was harmless, but it was best not to take chances.

At the soldiers' continued reluctance, Ingvar's demeanor softened. He placed the bucket on the ground again and glanced between them reassuringly. "The adepts aren't interested in solving this, lads, just locking it away. Our people need us to do better. If nothing else, we must make plans to warn everyone of this ichor."

I liked the idea of educating people. If they hadn't encountered the ichor yet, they would.

"Contained, the ichor's harmless." Ingvar gestured to the bucket. "Better we keep it contained than release it back into the soil, aye?"

Ebbe stepped forward, regaining lost ground, but his jaw quivered. "We don't know what kind of invisible evil's leeching from it, sir."

"With all the charms in the barracks, you have nothing to worry about," I said. Dozens lay before the hearths, not to mention the baubles each soldier carried on his person.

"Magnus? Your captain gave you an order," Pontus warned the soldier who had yet to move.

"Don't worry about it, lad. I'll take it in," Ingvar dismissed. "Just realize this isn't the last time ye've seen it."

"I'll take it, sir." Still grasping his beads, Magnus fetched the bucket with his free hand. "Come on, pup," he goaded Ebbe.

"Thanks, lad." Ingvar smiled faintly.

Pontus handed his lantern to Magnus, adding a clap on the back. "Wish hard for the Unseen's help."

"That's very brave of you, friend." I nodded my approval as Magnus started for the barracks.

"*I* could've done it, but he had orders." Ebbe nursed his shoulder as though someone had socked him there.

I bit my lip to conceal my amusement, then hit upon an idea. "Actually, there's something else we need help with, if you think—"

"What is it?" Ebbe asked eagerly.

I glanced toward the well pump. "It'll probably be a while before an adept can seal that off again. In the meantime, we should cover it with something. We don't want anyone to think it's safe to draw from." Or elicit more panic. I searched for anything useful in the perimeter of Ingvar's lantern-light. "Maybe we could upend one of the rain barrels over it?"

Pontus' stern expression made clear he wanted nothing to do with this venture, but Ingvar looked receptive to the idea. "The one we've been drawing against is low at this point," the captain said. "Let's pour off the remainder in one of the other barrels first."

I nodded. "Ebbe, here." I fished through my pockets, then handed him the hammer charm my handmaid Sigrid had given me when I'd first arrived in Nidaros.

Ebbe accepted it with a grin, then darted after Ingvar. I wasn't far behind. While Pontus hung back, the rest of us cooperated to lift a partially full barrel, drain it as Ingvar had described, then lower it over the well and its scattered charms.

"*Skíta!* Feel that?" Once it was in place, Ebbe jumped away from the barrel as though it'd shocked him. "Worst chill I ever felt in my life! An angry ghost for certain!"

It was all in his imagination, but scolding along those lines wouldn't help. "I don't feel anything," I said.

"Remember your control, lad," Ingvar urged him. "'Tis just as important here as on the battlefield. Let training take over and ground you. No matter what might happen, ye can address it as long as ye don't fall to panic."

Ebbe took a deep breath. "Aye, sir. It won't happen again."

Ingvar tossed his head toward the barracks. "Dismissed. Remember, not a word about this to anyone afore we're ready. Don't think it'll be much longer."

Ebbe moved to return my hammer charm.

"Keep it," I said.

"Thanks, Lady Knight." Galvanized, Ebbe took off toward the barracks.

I smiled to Ingvar with satisfaction. Once more, I admired his skill with his charges, striking a balance between friend and guide.

Ingvar smiled back, lowering his head bashfully.

Pontus remained entrenched in the secure glow of Ingvar's lantern, which lit the underside of his uneasy expression. As Ebbe ran past, he stared after like he had half a mind to follow, then faced Ingvar. "Ignoring wards? Hoarding the agent of a witch's curse? Unseen, what're we doing?"

"Narrowing in on what's truly plaguing us," Ingvar replied with conviction, stepping away from the barrel to retrieve his longsword from the ground.

"That's some hubris, lad," Pontus warned.

"The ichor stealeth our water to make more of itself," Ingvar explained as he straightened. "That's the reason everything's dried up and no seeds have taken root. The adepts can do *nothing* for it!" He thrust his sword-point into the ground for emphasis. "If Ormyr knew how to banish it, he would've done so already, then crowed about it 'til his boasts rattled Lord Catherwood's ears. Thordia may be no witch at all, just Ormyr's scapegoat."

Ingvar had found a clever way to propose Thordia's innocence without sounding heretical. I approached his side, lending my physical support for the possibly difficult conversation to follow.

Pontus' eyes narrowed. "Ye were just at the Naustviks' house. Surely ye saw proof of Thordia's guilt there?"

"We weren't there long," Ingvar replied, returning his longsword to his scabbard. The only way I knew he was lying was that I'd been out there with him. "We were set upon by a vinrake."

That much was true, though. A shudder went through me as I recalled our near-fatal struggle with the tentacled beast.

"A vinrake! In the districts?" Pontus' eyes widened fearfully.

"We took care of it," Ingvar assured him, "and we also happened upon Rigg's missing brother."

Another truth. A boy named Dag Nyvind had been lying low at the Naustviks' house, avoiding some bad situation at home.

"We brought him back here, got him billeted," Ingvar continued. "Rigg's keeping an eye on him."

This was the first thing Pontus was glad to hear from us. His expression brightened momentarily before sobering again.

Ingvar folded his arms. "All right, your turn. How'd ye fare at the keep? Obviously, ye weren't able to fetch the corpse from the dungeon."

Days earlier, Ingvar and I had infiltrated the adepts' keep to rescue Verahl Naustvik, whom Master Ormyr had imprisoned for aiding his sister Thordia's escape. Within the dungeon, we'd discovered the corpse of some long-dead prisoner, desiccated and coated in a strange purplish substance. The cause of death had been a mystery at the time, but no longer.

"Whoever they were, they probably died from exposure to the ichor," I chimed in.

"Aye, but we still don't know if it were murder, accident, or suicide," Ingvar said.

Pontus waved his hand dismissively. "Can't bribe my way down there right now, sir. The adepts are cleaning up after the day's events." His eyes narrowed. "Master Ormyr's avoiding me, or so it seems. Still feel like he's hiding something."

"No doubt." Ingvar's expression hardened. "Have a feeling there'll be no more corpse the next time we're allowed in the dungeon."

Over Pontus' shoulder, a flash of red light caught my eye, back toward the capital center. I doubted my own vision at first, but after a day full of odd lights like these, I was too twigged to ignore anything. I stepped sideways for a better view, examining the starry sky for any hint of recurrence.

"Something wrong?" Ingvar asked.

I felt foolish, as though I were admitting to seeing a ghost. "I thought I saw a red light, almost like a beacon."

Ingvar was at my side instantly. "Munitions?"

"I don't know, I didn't hear anything. It might've just been —"

A green flash, no bigger than a star, winked in and out of existence in the same part of the sky. The flash repeated, soon followed by an orange one that flickered against the darkness.

CHAPTER 2

Outside the barracks, Ingvar, Pontus, and I stared out into the starry night. Colorful flashes pierced a single point in the sky at irregular intervals—some strong, others flickering. Some were as short-lived as fireflies, easy to miss if one weren't looking directly at them. Most were green and orange, with the occasional burst of red.

I held my breath while puzzling over the matter. Stellar phenomenon, meteor shower? No, it seemed much closer than that. Explosives? But silence reigned in their wake. Ingvar and I had found the Naustviks' house full of Shipbuilder holograms and lighting devices. Could this be more of the same, wielded by adepts or others with adequate knowledge? But usually, such objects and knowledge were rare.

There was a more mundane possibility: fireworks. Metal salts like calcium chloride, ground into a powder and introduced to fire, burned up in a dramatic display of color. My mentors at the Enduring Flame Beguinage had introduced me to tricks like that, specifically labeling them tricks. Adepts performed such stunts, too, but called them "magic."

At my side, Ingvar frowned. "They seem to hover right over the capital buildings." He referred to the three Shipbuilder structures at the core of Nidaros' capital: the Baron's estate, the adepts' keep, and the storehouse.

"Unseen. Never thought ..." Pontus trailed off nervously. He stood ahead of us, his reaction invisible.

"Pontus?" Ingvar prompted. "Is there something I don't know about?"

The lieutenant faced us, fists clenched at his sides. The right one slowly ground his wishing beads into dust. "Last week, the boys on night watch whispered about a vision like this. They convinced the next night's shift to be on the lookout, but it never repeated itself. Forgot about it until now."

"Wherefore didn't anyone tell me?" Ingvar asked.

"We know not to bring you a ghost tale unless we have the ghost on a leash, sir." Pontus tossed his head over his shoulder. "Is that close enough?"

Ingvar scowled toward the flashing lights again, saying nothing.

I thought about the buildings Ingvar had mentioned, hidden in darkness from our vantage. All three stood dozens of stories high. The storehouse contained not just food and flax, but also plenty of munitions. The adepts' keep housed spell components along with most of Nidaros' remaining Shipbuilder artifacts.

The Baron's estate seemed the least likely source at first. But then I recalled a conversation I'd had with the kitchen servants a few days earlier. One of them had alerted me to unexplained shortages in the larder, and odd lights late at night. She'd feared these were signs that Thordia Naustvik had infiltrated the capital to rescue her brother Verahl from the adepts' dungeon.

"When I first got here, Alfrun told me about strange lights high up in the Baron's estate," I spoke up, leaving Thordia out of it. She was bound for the Harbinger, after all.

Two questioning frowns shot toward me. Then Pontus' eyes went wide. "Thordia must be casting against everyone in the capital. Propping up her curse!"

So much for keeping her out of it. "I think adepts are more likely," I said. They had the means and the freedom to practice their rituals as they deemed appropriate.

"But we can't rule out witches entirely," Ingvar said.

Indeed, witches were real. Not supernatural power-wielders, but people who either shunned or had been barred from formal adept training, which made their "unsanctioned magic" forbidden. Was someone performing witchcraft in the capital at the risk of their lives? What was worth the risk — more accurately, what did they *believe* was worth it? And did they mean harm to anyone? While I knew it wasn't Thordia, the possibility of unfriendly actors stuck in my head.

"We shouldn't leave this unexamined," I said, straightening with resolve.

Funny that I didn't immediately correct the "we" to "I." My questing elsewhere in the galaxy had inured me to dodging the local authorities, but here, I'd collaborated with Ingvar from the start. I could rely on his help. Moreover, I welcomed it.

"Agreed. It might well be visible all the way to the districts." Ingvar picked up the lantern resting on the ground. "People are frustrated enough over food. Rumors of a witch in the capital will only make things worse."

"Sir!" Pontus threw him a look that was part furious, part horrified. "Ye best one vinrake at a witch house, now ye think ye know something about facing evil magic? Ye haven't the first clue. Leave this to Dame Jessamine!"

Pontus had made a similar protest before we'd headed to the Naustviks' house. Again, I felt uncomfortable about being a source of friction between them. I glanced to Ingvar, biting the inside of my lip.

Ingvar faced Pontus, unmoved. "I have a duty to determine what's happening right over our Baron's head."

"Unseen, lad! Ye're being a damn fool!" Pontus cried.

"Tell me about it later." Ingvar faced me. "Jayce?"

I threw an apologetic glance Pontus' way. "We'd better move. If that's not adept magic, then any adepts who beat us there may bury the whole thing, just like the ichor."

Pontus' eyes went wide. "'We?' Unseen take me, I'll not go anywhere near that!"

"I'm not asking you to," Ingvar said. "Better that ye stay in the barracks tonight, just in case. We'll resume our talk later." He then jogged toward the worn path winding through the soldiers' practice field.

Pontus nursed his beads, looking on with helpless worry.

"We'll be back soon," I said with more certainty than I felt. But I had no trouble spurring myself after Ingvar, hurrying until I'd caught up to run at his side.

The path led deeper into the capital. Ingvar's lantern made sprinting impossible—unless we wanted a bath in burning oil —but we managed a respectable pace given the fatigue of a long, dangerous day.

As we drew closer, the mysterious lights continued to flicker among the stars. The looming silhouettes of the three capital buildings became distinct against the night sky, the last evidence of the Shipbuilders' original settlement in Nidaros. In the middle rested a structure that looked like a jagged fistful of straw: the adepts' keep. To either side stood twin buildings that resembled billowing sails on masts. The one to the right of the keep was the storehouse; to the left, the Baron's estate.

With the buildings in sight, it became clear that the sporadic colorful lights were indeed coming from the top of the estate. The inner capital's familiar cesspool smell returned, thankfully blunted by the cold. I scanned our surroundings for signs that anyone else might be mounting a response to the lights. Tiny fires bobbed in the distance, revealing soldiers on watch, but the routes they traced were relaxed and unhurried. There were no signs of activity around the keep, either. Only a few lights glared through its windows.

Close to the estate, one really had to crane his neck to even notice the oddity at the summit. That likely served to our advantage.

"No adepts. Maybe someone's begging to investigate right now, and Master Ormyr's telling them no," I quipped around short breaths.

A laugh escaped past Ingvar's worried demeanor.

I smiled back. "I have to say, I'm not used to chasing down so many *real* anomalies. Whenever I go back to Spectra and regale Lord Catherwood with my deeds in Nidaros, I won't have to embellish or make up a damned thing."

"Seriously had my fill of strange lights for one lifetime." Ingvar slowed to a halt, scowling up at the Baron's estate. "Afore we go in, we'd better figure out how we're handling this."

"Right." I stopped beside him, tamping down the instinctive urge to rush in and fix things—an instinct that'd burned me too many times in the past few days. "For what it's worth, that looks like the same material that goes into fireworks, but it could also be a Shipbuilder artifact. Remember the light tile Dag brought back from the Naustviks' house?"

I carried an identical device. Though it surpassed the lantern in convenience, it remained in my pocket. This close to the adepts' keep, there was too much risk of the wrong person spotting it.

Ingvar scowled upward. "Knowing what they are doesn't help much. If 'tis not an adept's doing, then someone's taking an insane risk. These lights are *meant* to be seen. Could be a signal, a warning—or a lure into a trap."

"True." Though I had to wonder who the target of such a trap might've been, if Pontus and Alfrun were right about this going on since before my arrival in Nidaros. "We'll be careful. Do you know a quiet way up there?"

"Only one stairwell leadeth that high," Ingvar explained.

"Stairwell?" I cringed at the prospect of climbing all those stories. "Does this building have any intact lifts?"

Ingvar frowned, puzzled.

"A Shipbuilder mechanism for traveling between floors quickly," I explained.

His confusion persisted. "Not that I've heard of."

Disappointing, but not surprising. As artifacts from the Shipbuilder era broke down over time, few people in the galaxy possessed the knowledge and materials to repair them. And in some places, like Nidaros, attempting a repair was enough to get you charged with heresy and killed.

Ingvar's expression hardened with determination. "We'll head up quietly, recon, then decide what to do."

I nodded my approval. "Side entrance?" Better to avoid panicking anyone in the estate before we knew what we were dealing with. We also didn't want to tip off our flame-wielder.

"I was thinking the same." Ingvar pointed toward the pitch-black gap between the estate and keep, which led to a familiar courtyard. "Follow my lead."

The courtyard housed another tied-off well pump, along with more rain barrels. Around the curving keep wall stood an entrance to the adepts' dungeon, guarded by a lone soldier. Fortunately, we didn't have to go near it. Our side-door was close to where we'd entered.

Ingvar slipped up to the door, put an ear to it, then tried the latch. It yielded, allowing him to open the door a crack. He peeked inside, glancing high and low. Finally, he beckoned to me, then slipped in first.

I kept close behind, content to follow, as the captain knew the estate better than I did.

Ingvar's lantern light revealed the now-deserted kitchen where I'd first met Alfrun and two other estate servants, Kofri and Lif. Kofri had mentioned sludge coming out of the wells. Alfrun had fretted over signs of a witch's presence. I wondered how many more of their outlandish claims would end up having some truth to them.

With the fire out, the kitchen was no warmer than outside. No smells lingered from supper, whatever watered-down concoction that might've been. The floor-to-ceiling larder held mostly shadow, a depressing reminder of how little everyone in Nidaros had by way of food, even Baron Tristan and his court. There was no sign of the food I'd gifted to the barony. Maybe it rested in the storehouse, awaiting distribution throughout the districts.

Ingvar crossed the kitchen without pause. As I followed, memories of the kitchen I'd all but grown up in flooded my mind, giving me goosebumps. If business at my mother's inn had ever slowed to this point, we would've stared starvation in the face.

We approached a door that led into the maze of estate corridors, through which Ingvar strode with purpose. His lantern remained valuable, as the candles mounted on broken artificial light fixtures had all been snuffed out. No light leaked past any of the wooden doors that'd replaced the malfunctioning Shipbuilder ones. Our muffled footsteps were all we heard.

Eventually, Ingvar honed in on a door that fed into a narrow stairwell. The winding staircase rose into darkness, seemingly without end.

"Aw, hell." My legs ached in anticipation.

Ingvar held up a hand to check my progress. "Listen," he spoke under his breath.

We paused a short while. The silent darkness persisted.

"It sounds like we got here first," I whispered.

"But the lights are gone," Ingvar replied in kind. "Mayhap someone beat us here after all."

Alfrun had seen them from the stairwell, hadn't she? I fought off a creeping dread. If the adepts weren't responsible to begin with, were they in the process of punishing the source this very moment?

"Let's move," I said. "Whoever's up there, they only have one way down, right? And that's through us."

Ingvar nodded with a strained look. "Hope we can assess the situation, then figure out what to do, but the situation might crash down on us first. I don't care to fight. Don't think ye do, either."

"Only as a last resort." But I was prepared for the possibility. Along with my weapons, I wore a nanofiber brigandine. The Shipbuilder armor was almost invisible beneath my coat.

"Also don't care to apprehend anyone over useless trinkets and hand-waving," Ingvar continued. "Anyone I take into custody over this will likely end up in the dungeon, at Ormyr's mercy."

Remembering my past experience with the dungeon brought on a shudder. "If it's not an adept, I'm hoping we can talk or scare them out of doing this again."

"Aye." As Ingvar glanced upward, his expression hardened. "But if they attack, or they're doing something awful up there—*whoever* they are—we'll have no choice but to stop them."

"Agreed," I said, glad we were on the same page. Normally, it would've surprised me to hear a soldier resolving to fight his own adepts if necessary. After the attempt on my life earlier that day, it no longer did.

Ingvar started upstairs, his free hand hovering beside his longsword's grip. I followed close, also leaving my sword sheathed. Craning my neck, I scouted the situation above and kept watch for pursuit, but everything remained quiet.

The air warmed the higher we climbed. Exertion warmed us as well; I was sweating before long. As the climb dragged on, our pace slowed. The continuing quiet made me fear we'd missed the show, that its source had already fled or been apprehended. Then a burst of green light flashed over our heads— faint, but real.

"*Skíta!*" Ingvar froze.

"They're still here," I murmured, galvanized.

The captain straightened with renewed vigor. "They won't be evading us now. Quickly."

We pressed on until, at last, only one more flight of stairs loomed ahead of us. Those stairs ended at a small landing that led to an open threshold. Panting with exertion, Ingvar darted up to said landing, then fell to his knees beside the threshold.

After dozens of stories, I was also sucking wind. I leaned up against the opposite side of the threshold, drawing and holding deep breaths in an effort to slow my racing heart.

A burning smell tinged the air, further evidence toward the metal salt theory. Another scent mixed with it, naggingly familiar somehow. Lavender? I couldn't recall its significance. A supplicating female tone murmured at the fringe of hearing. It sounded like the sort of chanting that accompanied "magic" rituals throughout the galaxy.

Once I'd recovered, I sneaked a glance past the threshold. Beyond lay a stub of a corridor, more like a cube-shaped room. The cramped space confused me until I recalled the billowing sail shape of building. This top floor was much smaller than the lower floors, where it billowed most. Left, right, and straight ahead stood doors. The left and center doors were open, their thresholds hazy with smoke. The door to our right was closed. Colorful bursts of light leaked out occasionally from around its frame.

I glanced to Ingvar, who by then had stood to survey the area himself. "It sounds like there's at least one adept or witch up here, but there could be more," I murmured. "Maybe we should check the open rooms first, get a better idea of what we're up against."

Ingvar nodded, quietly resting his lantern on the floor. "Go. I'll stay back and cover the exit."

The ominous chanting continued, rising and falling in intensity, seemingly oblivious to our presence. The captain drew his longsword to hold in a low, defensive guard. I reached for the dagger-hilt on my belt—only for my hand to close over air. Only then did I remember giving the weapon to Dag Nyvind as we'd left the Naustviks' house. I kept spare daggers aboard my ship, but had forgotten to take one. Carefully, I drew my side sword from my back baldric instead. These quarters were too cramped to wield it effectively, but if I were forced to defend myself, something would be better than nothing. Keeping the blade trained toward the ground for the moment, I slipped into the hazy corridor-stub. Behind me, Ingvar positioned himself to thwart any escape attempts.

I aimed for the open door to the left first, sticking to its threshold in hopes of avoiding detection. The opening led into a small, trapezoid-shaped room. Its entire curved back wall was made of a glassy material, revealing the stars and dark horizon. However, the cold breeze wafting through suggested the wall wasn't as solid as it looked. It reminded me of the window in my room several floors lower in the Baron's estate, which was similarly solid-looking and yet permeable.

No one lurked inside the room. However, green candles, braided loops of dried flax, scatterings of herbs and dried flowers, smoking censers, and a host of green and white ribbons suggested an earlier occupation.

It all seemed too homespun to be adept trappings. I also would've expected more of Lord Catherwood's colors, but burgundy and gold were absent here. The witch theory was gaining ground. Again, I marveled at how Alfrun's suspicions hadn't been that far off the mark. There could be a single witch or a whole coven up there, for reasons ranging from innocent to anything but. Unfortunately, nothing within the room spoke to those intentions. Then there was the possibility that this was all a frame-up job, something meant to get someone else in trouble.

I hoped the room past the center door might clarify things, but it was similarly festooned and deserted. Once I returned to where Ingvar stood guard, we retreated into the stairwell to discuss my findings.

"These don't seem to be adepts," I said. "The trappings are all green and white."

Ingvar's eyes went wide. "Lord Gyllenfeld's colors."

That's right, I'd forgotten. A shiver went through me. "Then these might be witches *and* dissidents."

Many people in Nidaros still harbored loyalty to Lord Gyllenfeld despite Catherwood's takeover decades earlier. Recent troubles had only stirred further resentment toward the Catherwoods. The Gyllenfeld dissidents, who'd never gone fully silent in Nidaros to begin with, expressed themselves ever more boldly. Maybe these were witches who meant their enemies active harm — those enemies being Baron Tristan and his court.

"Our answers are in that closed room." As I glanced over Ingvar's Catherwood tabard, worry seeped in. "Whatever they're doing up here, they probably won't take well to seeing you. Let me head in alone. I'll tell them they're endangering themselves and shouldn't gather here anymore."

Ingvar frowned. "Wherefore would they heed you, Goose? Gyllenfeld witches won't care that ye're Lord Catherwood's emissary. As a foreign sellsword, they'll like you even less."

He was right. I needed a solid way to appeal to them. Whom did witches trust most? *Other witches.* This burst of inspiration restored my confidence. "I'll pretend to be one of them."

Ingvar's jaw fell. "What?"

"People ask me if I'm a witch all the time," I said. "It's an easy sell." A boast my former master, Sir Mayweather Stark, had made constantly. His words slipped through my defenses—and just like that, the no-account braggart weaseled back into my thoughts. Mentally, I shoved him away in disgust, then refocused on Ingvar. "Pretending to be an ally is the most peaceful way to get this to stop. I'm not worried about trouble later. If they try to accuse me of anything, it'll be my word against theirs." And as a knight errant questing on behalf of Lord Catherwood himself, my word was orders of magnitude more credible than that of witches who'd been caught casting in the Baron's home.

Ingvar's surprise darkened. "I see your point, but I still don't like this. I'll guard the exit and keep an eye on you, in case ye need me." He braced my shoulder with one hand. "Careful, Jayce."

I rested my hand over his, took a deep breath, and nodded. Then I pulled away, angling for the last unexamined door.

The chanting continued, a single supplicating voice. It was impossible to know how many witches might be gathered around listening to it. Side sword held low, I approached the door, pressed down the latch, then opened it slowly.

Thin smoke wafted out, carrying more of the lavender smell. This third room was arranged like the others, except for one big difference. Along the transparent back wall, several scorched metal plates sat on the floor, with campfire-sized piles of burning firewood inside. Two more such fires flanked a slight, cloaked silhouette in the room's center, less than ten feet from where I stood. Her back faced me as she chanted on, oblivious.

She appeared to be alone, which was a relief. I anticipated a gentle heart-to-heart conversation in which I'd quietly convince her, from one witch to another, to pack up the show and find a safer place to conduct her business. Leaving my sword at my side, I slipped into the room, hovering at the threshold. "Sister witch? Don't be afraid, we need to talk."

Her murmuring halted. The witch whirled around, black cloak flaring with the movement. Fire- and candlelight revealed a familiar dark-haired young woman fairly drenched in green and white beads. A punching dagger adorned her right hand, its blade curved like a talon.

With shock, I recognized her as my handmaid. "*Sigrid?*"

Sigrid's mutual shock was written all over her face at first. Then her pretty features twisted into a hateful glare. Her hands darted toward belt-pouches, gathering up fistfuls of powder that she threw onto the fires flanking her. As they consumed the powder, the flames amplified in size and intensity, taking on bright orange and green hues.

Metal salts, for sure. The display was meant to intimidate me, but her punching dagger was more my concern. I put on a calm front, ignoring the chill spreading over my skin and the urge to raise my side sword in defense. It was crucial to stick to the game, reinforce I was a fellow witch and thus nothing to worry about. "Sigrid, I'm sorry I didn't realize sooner. I'm your kin!"

Her outrage didn't budge. "How dare you call me that!"

Words wouldn't move her. Fortunately, I had plenty of my own "magic" in my coat pockets. My left hand slipped into one of them, seeking something she'd respect.

"Lord Catherwood sent you here to murder my kindred!" Sigrid raised her fist, aiming the punching dagger at me like an accusing finger. Flashes of green and orange fire glinted off the blade. "But you've never gotten very far, have you? My magic freed Verahl Naustvik from the dungeon. Now it hides him and Thordia so no one will ever find them!"

My jaw dropped. What an imagination on her! She'd had no hand in those things whatsoever, but her eyes held complete conviction. Meanwhile, my searching hand closed around the light tile I'd found at the Naustviks' house. "Sigrid—"

"I painted you as an agitator, and now I've summoned you to die!" Eyes burning, she lunged toward me, dagger aimed at my chest.

As my sword-arm rose instinctively to block, my left hand brought out the square tile. A tap of my thumb caused its glassy surface to erupt with a cold, bluish light. Squinting against its intensity, I aimed the lit tile at Sigrid's face.

To the self-proclaimed witch, it must've seemed like a tiny star had just sprung to life in my hand. Sigrid screamed as though burned, then stumbled to a halt with an arm crossed over her face. Heedless of the fires and ritual objects strewn on the floor, she backed away from me, on course for the transparent wall lining the back of the room. The *immaterial* wall.

Dread seized me. "Stop!" I shut off the light tile with another thumb-tap, pocketed it, then darted after her.

One of Sigrid's feet slipped through the wall and outside, where there was no floor to support it. She shrieked and teetered on one leg, arms flailing as she tipped backwards.

CHAPTER 3

In the glow of the fires she'd lit atop the Baron's estate, Sigrid teetered over a dark abyss, half-protruding from a glass wall that looked solid, but wasn't. She screamed, arms flailing.

I couldn't let her plummet all those stories to the ground below, even if she'd meant me harm—even if she *still* meant me harm. Heart in my mouth, I dropped my side sword and sprinted across the room littered with witching materials. Once I was close enough, I reached for Sigrid's arm. My gloved hands seized the beads wrapped around her forearm, which rolled under my grip at first. With a stab of panic, I clamped down harder and yanked, pulling Sigrid free of the window.

As she stumbled to safety behind me, she helped cancel my momentum. I froze just short of the transparent wall and the cold void beyond. Eventually, I remembered to breathe and considered that it probably wasn't a good idea to keep my back to Sigrid for any length of time. I turned, primed for further emergency.

Sigrid had dropped to her knees beside a lit candle surrounded with lavender sprigs. She'd doubled over, hugging herself while trembling. The two fires in the room's center returned to normal as the metal salts burned away. Just past them stood Ingvar, longsword poised defensively. He'd darted in from the corridor, probably worried we'd both need help to avoid a nasty fall. Sigrid didn't seem to have noticed him yet.

Good. I wanted to keep this between me and her for now. Fearing his presence would spur Sigrid to violence again, I made eye contact with Ingvar and waved my arm, shooing him off.

He glanced between me and Sigrid, then retreated from sight.

Sigrid didn't react. The blade of her punching dagger poked over her shoulder, reminding me of her menace.

A chill ran down my spine. My handmaid wasn't just a Gyllenfeld dissident, but also a witch. When she'd refused to discuss the rumors surrounding Thordia, when she'd seemed nervous about what other servants might tell me, it'd made me suspicious, but not to this extent.

My eyes strayed to a loop of hair on the floor. I couldn't be sure, but it looked like *my* hair. Those times she'd insisted on braiding it, she might've taken some in hopes of placing curses on me. It spoke to a skin-crawling level of cunning. Then what was she doing at the top of the Baron's estate? Casting up here was the dead opposite of cunning. What was important enough for her to risk it?

I approached Sigrid from behind, glancing at my side sword on the ground nearby. Though I dearly wanted it in hand, it'd thwart the friendly impression I was aiming for. I ignored it to kneel at her right side, my left arm tensed to block any potential dagger-swings. "Are you all right, sister?"

Sigrid straightened and lowered her arms, but remained focused on the floor. "If I had fallen, I would've deserved it. Somehow, I never realized you were also a witch." Her voice broke. Tears rolled down her face, which she was quick to bat aside. "You kept asking me what caused the drought because you knew the Naustviks were innocent. You charmed your way

through Lord Catherwood's court and had yourself sent here to
protect Verahl and Thordia." She glanced up at me hopefully.
"Didn't you?"

Her conviction sounded deep. I marveled at how she re-
molded reality for herself as needed. "I have no love for Catherwood. I'm here to track down the real cause of the crop trouble
and keep innocents from suffering."

Sigrid glowed with tearful approval.

"What are you doing up here?" I asked.

"Someone has to address the curse," she replied. "The
adepts are going about it all wrong. It's the Unseen who've
cursed us, not any witch! Every year the wrong banner flies
over Nidaros, they get angrier."

"Lord Catherwood's banner, you mean?"

"Yes. So I must placate the Unseen, seek aid in visions …
and talk to my coven." Sigrid gestured with her dagger-hand
toward the transparent wall behind us. "They're out in the districts. I live here alone."

A coven—a family, maybe several families who believed
themselves witches, likely just as loyal to Lord Gyllenfeld's
memory as she. Had they helped to stir up trouble in Nidaros
lately, or was their impact entirely imaginary? Regardless, it
made sense they'd want one of their own in the capital, keeping an eye on things.

It had to be tough on Sigrid to live isolated from them,
though. Risky, too. She had to be doubly careful not to be outed
as either a witch or a dissident. Neither Ingvar nor Baron Tristan sought to punish people over their private allegiances, but
Master Ormyr gladly would.

I rose to my feet, helping Sigrid up as well. Despite our
rapport, I still watched her dagger. "What are you telling your
coven about?"

Sigrid kept her arms at her sides. Her eyes locked onto mine with intensity. "I had my strongest vision yet. People grow restless. Blood, fire, death — they'll be upon us soon."

Her conviction sent a shiver through me, but her words were vague, like most "prophecy." Of course people grew restless while their food dwindled and their futures became increasingly uncertain. I'd witnessed unrest at the capital gate several days earlier. Ingvar had his soldiers drilling constantly to handle whatever might go wrong in the near future.

Sigrid spun away to approach the transparent wall, her cloak trailing behind her. She picked up a rune-covered wooden bucket and moved from one fire to the next, pouring dirt into each of them. As the once dramatic light-show dwindled, we were left to converse by the candlelight distributed throughout the room.

The metal salts necessary for her fireworks required refinement, meaning they weren't cheap or easy to make. I'd only ever found them in large cities, earmarked for adept purposes. They might've been shipped to Nidaros along with the other munitions in their storehouse, or as magic components to be housed within the keep. No doubt Sigrid had stolen them from one of those locations. Even the firewood had likely been pilfered from the storehouse or kitchen.

So that was even more risk Sigrid had assumed to communicate with her coven. The doom-prophecy had to be something she was completely convinced about. Was there any truth to it beyond the barony's unrest? I retrieved my side sword, but kept my weapon hand lowered while facing her. "When will it happen?"

Sigrid placed her bucket on the floor, then straightened. "Soon. The tension is building, I'm sure you sense it."

Not good enough. "Have you heard or seen anything within the capital that supports your vision?"

The self-styled witch returned to where I stood and fetched a sprig of lavender from the floor. She twisted it in her fingers with a scrutinizing frown, then dropped it, lowering her head with grief. "I contributed to that tension. I sent Adept Knorr after you. I'm sorry."

Knorr? The would-be murderer I'd bested, who'd instead succumbed to his own lantern. I sucked in a breath, struggling to stay balanced atop weak knees. We didn't know who'd helped Knorr arrange the trap I'd fallen into — literally. Sigrid had never been on my or Ingvar's suspect list. It made me nervous about what else we might've been blind to. I had to keep pressing for details, though it'd be unwise to dawdle much longer. Anyone might've noticed the strange lights atop the Baron's estate. There was no guarantee that adepts, or some other brave party, wouldn't crash us at any moment.

"You sent Knorr after me?" I repeated. "How?"

Sigrid glanced up with remorse. "I cast a *galdr* over the keep to rile up the adepts. I like making trouble in their ranks now and then. I made them see you as a threat that had to be dealt with. Knorr rose up and did my bidding."

The unfamiliar word was probably Gyllenfeld dogma for "spell" or "incantation." I swallowed hard. "You never *talked* to Knorr?"

"No. I have to be careful about where I go and whom I'm seen with."

I forced a deep breath on myself to calm my nerves. It sounded like Sigrid had no involvement in my attempted murder after all, just like she hadn't done a damned thing to aid Verahl's escape. More self-delusion, claiming credit after the fact. The value of further questioning seemed uncertain, but even the kitchen servants' rumors had contained merit. Maybe Sigrid would also provide something useful despite her best efforts.

"At least one other person helped Knorr," I said. "Do you know who?" Any of the adepts could've been involved, even Master Ormyr himself, who'd been standing with me right before the trap had been sprung. Ingvar was skeptical of the possibility, but we hadn't ruled it out yet.

"No. But don't worry, sister, I'd sooner die than act against you again." Sigrid shook her head. "Knorr didn't need much goading against you. No one loyal to Gyllenfeld does."

The implication wasn't as shocking as it should've been, rather more vindicating. Ingvar and I suspected that there might be one or more adepts in Nidaros who secretly adhered to the fallen Lord Gyllenfeld despite their oaths to enforce Lord Catherwood's rule. We lacked conclusive evidence, though.

My grip on my side sword tightened. "How do you know Knorr was a dissident?"

"There was a time when my coven and our allies in the cloister worked together in secret: trading information, cursing the ruling Catherwoods and such. We're the reason why no line of succession has ever been established here," Sigrid answered with a note of pride.

That surprised me. "Adepts and witches colluding? That's ... I've never seen that anywhere in the galaxy."

"Lord Gyllenfeld's dogma allowed for it," Sigrid said. "Anyway, that all stopped after the last uprising."

I didn't need Sigrid to explain further. Ingvar had already told of the violence that'd erupted in Nidaros seven years earlier, when Baron Tristan had first arrived to claim his new title. A cabal of high-born soldiers and adepts had risen up to oppose him. Some had believed they'd possessed a stronger claim to Nidaros than the common-born Baron. Some had been charmed by the delusion of independence. And some had been Gyllenfeld adherents eager to overthrow Catherwood rule.

Sigrid glanced down at her tightly clenched fists. "Too many of our people were killed or imprisoned in the adepts' dungeon. Leif Eklund, Fastarr Jansson, a dozen more yet live. Their families plead for their release, but Baron Tristan refuses them mercy."

It had nothing to do with the Baron. They were Master Ormyr's prisoners. In his eagerness to rid the barony of dissent, he wasn't about to release anyone—but I doubted Sigrid wanted to hear this. I backtracked. "Are there other adepts like Knorr, secretly loyal to Gyllenfeld?"

"Several," Sigrid replied. "Adept Botvi, Adept Holsten—"

"Holsten!" I cried, unable to hide my surprise. "Master Ormyr's second?"

"Yes!" An evil glee chased off the last of Sigrid's grief. "His parents had been especially gifted, communing with distant contacts on our behalf."

Distant contacts? Just how distant did she mean? There were no other surviving settlements on the planet. The only people who cared about Nidaros resided in Spectra, many light-years away: Lord Catherwood himself, who had family here ... and the mistress of a trade guild whose entire supply chain stood to collapse if Nidaros' flax output faltered.

"Was Madam Castor one of those distant contacts?" I chanced.

Sigrid gasped in astonishment. "How did you know?"

"I figured someone outside Baron Tristan's circle must be passing her information," I replied, my pulse picking up again. "She doesn't seem the type to trust what the Baron tells her."

"Well, it stopped after the uprising," Sigrid said. "Holsten's parents were killed."

"I wouldn't be surprised if he took up their mantle after their passing." Losing family would've given Holsten more reason than ever to hate the ruling Catherwoods.

Sigrid blinked. "I suppose it's possible."

I'd run into Holsten a few times. On each occasion, he'd become fearful and anxious. Was it the strain of wearing a false front every day? Was it the knowledge that he and his collaborators would be murdering me soon?

Ingvar had to be listening in on this. I wondered what he was thinking. Though my heart raced, I cautioned myself not to get too excited yet. Sigrid was hardly the most trustworthy source. If only there were concrete evidence …

The Shipbuilders' interplanetary communications network had decayed centuries ago. These days, mail was the only way for people on different planets to communicate with one another. I'd conveyed a shipment of mail from Spectra to Nidaros, and may've unwittingly delivered my own death warrant in the process.

"Sigrid, you asked me before if there was anything you could do to help," I continued. "I don't know if you were sincere then, but—"

"Oh, of course, sister!" Sigrid cried. "I wasn't sure of your intentions before, but now? I'll do anything you ask."

"Can you help me look for evidence of Madam Castor and Holsten trading messages?" I glanced toward her smothered fires along the wall. "That vision of blood you had? I know for a fact that Madam Castor wants to dispatch mercenaries here."

Sigrid blinked. "But that's good. She'll help us overthrow the Baron. Once the Catherwoods are gone, Lord Gyllenfeld will return from Folkvang to rule over us!"

I shook my head. The entire Gyllenfeld family had been wiped out decades ago. They weren't hanging out in Folkvang, or any other alleged afterlife, waiting for an excuse to reappear. But I had to keep these thoughts private and speak in a way that better meshed with her ever-changing reality. "Madam Castor doesn't believe there's a curse at work in Nidaros, and she doesn't care about helping you escape Catherwood rule. Once Baron Tristan's gone, she'll impose her own will here. You're all just flax-makers to her. If you don't deliver, she'll whip you until you do."

Sigrid mulled this over with a worried expression, weaving her fingers through the beads strung on her left forearm.

"Can you help me find out whether Holsten's communicating with her?" I asked again.

"Why don't we seek the truth right now?" She turned toward the closest candle.

"No, not through visions," I said. "If we don't have physical evidence, Holsten will just decry you as a witch. Between you and him, whom do you think the court will believe?"

Sigrid paused, then glanced to me questioningly.

"Do you know the keep's layout?" If she'd stolen spell components from the adepts, there was a good chance she did. "Could you draw it out for me? I could search Holsten's belongings for any letters he may've received from Madam Castor."

If Holsten were smart, he'd burn them once finished with them. But if the messages were coded, as Ingvar suspected, maybe he'd been lulled into a false security.

"I know the keep." Sigrid shook her head with a strained expression. "It's hard to explain. There are so many little tricks and secret passages and keys you need to get very far. It'd be better if I went searching for you." Her eyes went wide. "Oh! But Verahl's escape, and Knorr ...? It'll be near impossible to get anywhere now. We'll have to draw them all out of there first."

I gaped. "Clear *all* the adepts from the keep?"

"You can do it," Sigrid assured me. "I'm sure it's within your power."

Her certainty hinged upon the light tile I'd surprised her with earlier. Somehow, I doubted the cloister would be as impressed with it. There was no way an evacuation was actually necessary, either. I was confident that I, Ingvar, or even Pontus could get by with a few well-placed bribes.

"I'll need time to ..." I trailed off, struggling to phrase an excuse that a witch would find acceptable. "Uh, there's a lot of spell components I'll need to — "

Sigrid gasped and flinched. Something over my shoulder had caught her attention.

"Hold still!" Ingvar called out behind me.

Not without my own measure of surprise, I defied the order to face the room's entrance, instinctively brandishing my side sword. The captain had planted himself before our only avenue of escape, his own blade raised.

"Thought there might be a witch up here." Ingvar scowled. "Never imagined there'd be two."

He must've decided the conversation had gone on long enough, but hadn't wanted to disrupt my ruse with Sigrid. Not bad. He'd lacked the skill for spontaneous play-acting when I'd first met him; maybe some of my foolishness had rubbed off.

I couldn't help grinning for a second. Fortunately, Sigrid was behind me and couldn't see it. Then I backed up to stand alongside Sigrid, mirroring her alarmed expression. My chief concern was preventing the handmaid-turned-witch from rushing Ingvar the way she'd done with me. I latched onto her elbow with my free hand, hoping to short-circuit any bright ideas.

"I'm not here to hurt anyone, but I'll defend myself if I must," Ingvar said. "Drop your weapons and slide them over here."

Keeping my grip on Sigrid, I knelt and complied with his request, all the while trying to look like someone who was putting on a brave front in the face of getting caught. By the time I stood, my fellow witch had yet to move. "Go on, sister," I nudged her quietly.

Sigrid stiffened in my grasp. Her expression had transitioned from surprise to devastation, as though her world was collapsing in on itself.

"Do it!" Ingvar pressed.

With clear reluctance, Sigrid unwound the green and white beads that secured the punching dagger to her right arm. She let the blade and beads clatter to her feet, then shoved them in Ingvar's direction. They skittered across the floor to collide harmlessly with his boot.

Ingvar remained braced for an attack, eyes darting about the room. "Never seen so much witchcraft—right over our Baron's head, no less. Ye're lucky ye haven't killed anyone or burned down the estate."

"So what're you here to do about it, Captain?" I challenged, happy to continue our impromptu play.

Ingvar faltered, blinking.

I realized he needed a hand. "I mean, all this magic gear. Don't you realize we could turn it on you in a second?"

"Ye'll dismantle it," he countered with resolve. "Then ye're coming with me to the barracks."

With that, I was pretty sure I knew what the captain was aiming for. He wanted to scare Sigrid out of repeat incidents, maybe also see if she had any other useful information, in a place where there'd be no chance of interruption.

"Unseen!" Sigrid cried. "You want to throw us in the dungeon, that's what you're really saying!" She looked to me with wide-eyed desperation. "Use your magic on him!"

I kept my grip on her and shook my head. "He could've attacked us by now, but he hasn't. Let's afford him the same courtesy. In most places I've traveled, we'd already be dead."

"Cooperate, and ye won't see the dungeon," Ingvar said. "We'll have a long talk early tomorrow. If all goeth well, ye'll be back here afore anyone noticeth ye're gone."

A dark, menacing glare settled over Sigrid's features as she clenched her fists. "I won't go!"

"Don't make this worse for us!" I begged, squeezing her arm hard in reproach. Plainly, she still needed a reason to trust Ingvar. I glanced toward him. "Do you really mean it, Captain? Are you willing to *give your word* that if we go along with what you're asking, we'll be safe? No one will find out about this?"

"Aye. Ye have my word on that," Ingvar replied.

Sigrid's glare faded. She looked to me with wide eyes.

I smirked a little. "Who knows, sister? He might just be a sympathizer."

The comment backfired. Sigrid's anger flared again. "Him! Sympathetic to our kind? He betrayed his own family to be here!"

Ingvar flinched, then scowled deeper than ever.

During the failed uprising, Ingvar had been one of the few Nidaran soldiers to remain loyal to Baron Tristan — much to the anger of his Gyllenfeld-sympathizing family, who'd disowned him as a result. Clearly, Sigrid only knew of his deeds, not the motivations behind them. Ingvar was no blind supporter of Catherwood rule. He was loyal to *Nidaros* and his people's survival. The barony was in no shape to even dream of independence. Farming was all they had, and most of that was geared toward flax. If they stopped receiving food and supplies from Madam Castor, they were lost. Not to mention, Baron Tristan was related to Lord Catherwood by marriage. Nidaros would've faced horrible repercussions had the Baron and his retinue been killed.

So I understood why Ingvar had acted as he had — respected it, also — and felt bad for his family's lapse in understanding. I also knew it was a wound that hadn't quite healed. It would've spurred me toward a compassionate gesture in any other setting, but right then, I had to be the witch who knew nothing about him, and didn't care so long as her hide remained intact. Hoping to calm Sigrid, I put up a composed, reassuring front. "He gives his word. I'm willing to give mine in return, as a sworn knight errant: I'll cooperate."

Ingvar hesitated. "Are ye knight first, witch second? Or the other way around?"

Good. A little more arguing would help sell this to Sigrid. I channeled the many earnest witches I'd come across over the years. "Magic is in my blood, Captain. It was the Unseen's will, and not something I asked for. But the mantle of knighthood, that I fought hard for and earned. I take my vow seriously. If I didn't, do you think I could've earned Lord Catherwood's confidence?"

In reality, I served as Milord's emissary because I'd been a convenient target, not because I was some great renowned knight errant. Ingvar knew it, but Sigrid didn't.

Ingvar's eyes narrowed. "Suppose not—but I'm watching you close from now on. Now what of you, Sigrid?"

"Promise you'll cooperate," I murmured to her. "Don't worry, I'll protect you."

With desperation, Sigrid glanced back at the immaterial wall that'd almost been her demise. "I'd sooner jump!" A moment later, she bolted to do just that.

I held fast to her arm. She managed to drag me several steps before I dug in and anchored her in place. Footsteps rushed up behind me; soon, Ingvar had Sigrid's other wrist in his free hand. The self-styled witch screamed and thrashed to no avail.

I thought fast about what she needed to hear. "That's exactly what your enemies want, Sigrid! What'll happen to your coven? What'll happen to Nidaros if you aren't here to fight the curse?"

Sigrid fell silent and froze, her arm tense in my grip.

"There's still so much we can do to help—and we will," I continued. "Trust me."

Her shoulders slumped. A moment later, a sob sent a shudder through her.

I motioned for Ingvar to step back. Once he withdrew, I put my free arm around Sigrid's shoulders. "We'll be fine."

Sigrid curled into me, weeping. Ingvar threw me a questioning look, probably wondering if I could continue to handle her alone. I nodded to him.

He nodded back. "Afore we leave, we'll go room by room. Ye'll put out all your fires. Leave everything else behind for now."

CHAPTER 4

Witchcraft flooded the top of the Baron's estate — and Sigrid and I were knee-deep in it, snuffing out fires while Ingvar shadowed us, his longsword primed in case of trouble. The mess had been necessary to fight Nidaros' curse and communicate with her coven, or so Sigrid had claimed. She was powerless now, though. Ingvar had confiscated her punching dagger, along with her belt holding metal salts and who knew what else. Trembling and weeping, she occasionally glanced over her shoulder as though fearing the wrath of someone or something other than the captain.

Meanwhile, I put up the front of a brave knight errant facing ruin unblinkingly. Ingvar and I were pretending to be hero and witch respectively, trying to remove Sigrid from the estate without violence or commotion before anyone else discovered us. Ingvar probably also hoped to scare her out of repeat spectacles — but with Sigrid, we had to be careful about how far we pushed.

Ingvar prodded us from one hazy room to the next. Worried Sigrid might make another suicide attempt or lunge after our captor, I stuck close to her at all times, shepherding her between fires. Whenever her gaze landed on me, I returned it as reassuringly as possible.

Only once did she speak, just before we extinguished the last few candles. "Unseen help me. Soon, everyone will know." Her expression was that of one facing down the gallows. Getting caught was the one thing she had to avoid at all costs.

"No, they won't," I whispered back. "The captain gave his word." If only she knew how lucky she was. Ingvar neither believed in her powers nor sought to punish her for them.

"But will he keep it?" Her eyes flashed with a sudden, desperate brainstorm. "Could you charm him? That *must* be within your power."

"Uh ..." I pretended to consider the idea while scrambling for an excuse. "It takes a lot of time and resources to pull off. We'll stick to our promise for now. If he reneges, we won't hold anything back." But I knew he wouldn't.

She sniffled, blotting tears with her sleeve. "I'll do what you ask, sister."

Her promise only halfway assuaged me, and I highly doubted it'd soothe Ingvar. In his place, I'd want physical assurance that my captives wouldn't attempt escape or mischief while being taken to the barracks. Neither of us had brought rope, but there were several Gyllenfeld-colored bead-loops lying around that could serve as makeshift bindings. I'd find a way to suggest it to him before we left.

Showing up at the barracks hog-tied. I couldn't imagine what Pontus would think.

Once we'd finished, Ingvar prodded us out into the stub-like corridor separating the three rooms. He closed up two of them, leaving the door to Sigrid's main witching-room ajar. It was obvious why: inside rested his lantern—now the only light at the estate's summit—and the weapons we'd surrendered to him.

Ingvar sheathed his sword, then unwound his beads from his belt. He used the loop to bind Sigrid's wrists behind her back. After that, he pulled out a handkerchief and tied it over her face.

Sigrid tolerated this without a peep or flinch. Meanwhile, I couldn't help smiling at my and Ingvar's similar trains of thought. The blindfold was an added stroke of brilliance. Sigrid would be completely dependent on Ingvar for navigation, and Ingvar wouldn't have to tie me up at all.

The captain then entered the open room to retrieve his lantern, my side sword, and Sigrid's talon-shaped punching dagger. The lantern, he set on the ground at our feet. Stepping behind me, he slid my side sword into its scabbard and looped my left arm through Sigrid's right, pressing my hand into the small of my back. Finally, he allowed me to take the dagger's grip in my right hand.

Once I had it, he picked up his lantern and grabbed Sigrid's left elbow. "Let's go."

I was confused at first, then understood: he didn't have enough hands to carry the lantern and guide us both downstairs. He had to chain his prisoners together, lest Sigrid start questioning our show. The dagger was for defense, if necessary. Ingvar could also use it as evidence against Sigrid.

Our awkward procession made slow progress down the stairwell. Though Ingvar did his best to steady us, it was challenging to remain in step with Sigrid, especially while maintaining the ruse of being bound. Wielding the punching dagger prevented me from reaching out for balance with my supposedly tied-up right hand. I split my attention between my next step and the handmaid-turned-witch. She was tense at first, gradually relaxing as we found a rhythm.

Upon reaching the ground floor, Ingvar backtracked us to the kitchen and into the cold night, blissfully undetected. From there, we marched down the worn path leading to the capital gate. Aside from our footsteps and the occasional rattle of beads, the capital lay still. No sign of activity issued from the adepts' keep. Even the soldiers on patrol seemed to have bunkered out of sight.

Ingvar's gaze remained locked forward, even when I sought eye contact with him. I wondered what held his attention, and hoped to pull him aside for a private talk once we reached the barracks. A *brief* talk. Most of me just wanted to collapse—onto a sturdy pallet, preferably, but even a dirt floor was tempting.

The glow of candlelight showed us where to leave the path. Within the barracks, a familiar smoky warmth banished the cold. Embers glowed at either end of the long structure, with mostly darkness and sleeping soldiers in between.

Mostly. As Ingvar shut the door behind us, Pontus hurried over with a candle in hand. "Captain! Thank the Unseen ye've returned safely!" he addressed under his breath. "Now what in their name is this?" As he processed more of the odd scene before him, his relief transitioned to bewilderment.

"I'll explain," Ingvar replied in kind, placing his lantern on a side-table. "Follow us." Keeping his hold on Sigrid, he strode through the barracks with purpose.

Sigrid and I had no choice but to follow. Pontus probably felt much the same way. He hovered at my side, frowning once he noticed the unusual weapon in my hand.

I wanted reassure him, but couldn't with Sigrid right next to us. Even if she weren't there, Ingvar knew best how to set his men at ease. He had to decide how or if he'd explain this to them. Once he did, I'd go along with it.

The captain stopped at a door that opened into a small room. A blanketed pallet rested against the far wall, just beside a shuttered window. Ingvar undid Sigrid's bonds, separated her from me, then steered her inside. "Get some rest. We'll talk in the morning."

Before Sigrid could react, Ingvar shut the door and dug through a pocket, extracting a key. "Need more than a few hours of sleep under me to deal with any more of *that*," he muttered as he locked the self-styled witch inside.

I sympathized, but kept it to myself, not wishing to disturb the young men sleeping nearby—or at least pretending to sleep. For the moment, I was happy enough with regaining the use of my left arm.

The flame Pontus carried guttered within his trembling hand. "Sir—"

"Come on." Ingvar slipped past us, aiming for another side-room.

The next chamber we approached was the same one where Ingvar and I had reviewed the ichor samples hidden within the Naustviks' home. Ingvar stepped aside and allowed us to enter first.

Pontus hesitated before the threshold. His candlelight revealed a single table inside, holding up mounds of soil, an empty canteen, and two buckets of ichor. Finally, he pushed through and placed himself in the corner of the room farthest from the table.

I followed. Cut off from the hearths, the room was almost as cold as the outdoors. While Ingvar secured the door behind us, I rested Sigrid's punching dagger on the table, then turned. To my left, Pontus warily focused on the spot where I'd placed the weapon. To my right, Ingvar faced us, remaining close to the door.

"This has gone far enough." Pontus' eyes flitted nervously between me and Ingvar. "What happened? Was Sigrid Asbjorn witching in the estate?"

"We found her thereabouts," Ingvar replied, voice and expression neutral. "She attacked when we approached her, which is why I brought her in. Is she a witch?" He shrugged. "Don't know. Never saw her cast any spells."

Part truth, part lie. I was glad Ingvar instilled doubt as to Sigrid's nature; it'd be easier to clear her later. As long as she cooperated and maintained a low profile, no one would ever know about her detention except us three.

Pontus gestured toward the dagger behind me. "I'd say *that*, and those lights in the sky, are telling enough. Hand her over to the adepts, sir. Something's rotten at the keep, but a suspect witch is beyond what we can handle. This is the cloister's mess to sort out."

"With torture?" Ingvar narrowed his eyes. "We have to be certain she's a witch afore I breathe a damn word to Ormyr."

"If she had the gall to attack you, lad, what's to stop her from attacking anyone else?" Pontus took a step in Ingvar's direction, spreading his hands in a supplicating gesture. "What if she's weaving witchcraft against us right now?"

Ingvar faltered with a strained look.

Here I spotted an opportunity to wield my bardic talent. Knights errant had to be ready to relate tales of their questing at any time. By custom, those tales were as outrageously false as the knight dared get away with. Years of practice had made me proficient at throwing together reassuring nonsense on an as-needed basis. I respected Pontus and felt guilty about lying to him, but we needed his cooperation. A small fib would hopefully set his mind at ease and earn Sigrid a reprieve.

"She isn't. It's impossible." I stepped forward as well, focusing on Pontus. "The witches I've fought in the past have all needed special components to channel their energies through. Crystals, totems …" I waved off further examples. "The point is, Sigrid's sitting in an empty room right now. Even if she is a witch, she lacks what she needs to cast spells."

Pontus studied me as I spoke. The worry in his expression gradually eased. "All right. At least those lights are gone, and ye've returned safely. What do we do with her?"

Relief flooded me. Still, it was safer to stand down here and let Ingvar control the discussion. Not knowing Pontus well, I had no idea when he might decide I, or even Ingvar, belonged in the adepts' custody right along with our suspect witch.

"The knight and I will give her a good talking-to early tomorrow. Based on that, we'll decide what to do with her." Ingvar folded his arms. "Let's get back to what we were discussing earlier. Pontus, ye were telling us about how he ye fared in the keep this evening. Ye couldn't bring back the corpse. What about any mail Adept Knorr might've received?"

"Wasn't able to get near his quarters or work areas, sir. Don't know if he received anything." Pontus frowned. "Now, what was this 'hunch' of yours?"

"Madam Castor was angry to hear of problems here." Ingvar glanced my way.

I nodded. This was as good a time as any to explain our suspicions to Pontus. "The Guildmistress doesn't believe there's any problem growing flax. She thinks you're all just being uncooperative, and Baron Tristan can't keep you in line. While I stood in the throne room in Spectra, receiving this quest, she asked Lord Catherwood about sending mercenaries in my place—to get you to show your Lord the proper 'respect.'"

Pontus' brow furrowed deeper. "That shrew. I have no trouble believing that."

"She didn't get her way," I continued, "probably because Lord Catherwood actually cares about your Baron and Baroness." The latter, Lady Amelia, was Lord Catherwood's aunt. "She doesn't seem the type to take defeat lying down, but as long as your Lord supports Baron Tristan, what can she do?"

"Disgrace him," Ingvar said. "We've always suspected she hath one or more informants here. What if she slipped a note into the mail Dame Jessamine brought us—to Adept Knorr, or someone else—ordering the knight's murder?"

He avoided mentioning Adept Holsten, who'd come up during my discussion with Sigrid. I supposed he didn't trust that lead. It seemed promising to me, but unless we came upon anything tangible, we only had Sigrid's word for it—and Sigrid frequently laced those words with the products of her vivid imagination.

For the present, I left Holsten out as well. "If I die here while acting as Lord Catherwood's emissary, Baron Tristan's responsible for that. Once he's removed from power, Madam Castor can 'establish order' here however she wants."

Pontus frowned toward the floor for several moments, then glanced to Ingvar. "Madam Castor would want her claws deep in someone here, that's for certain. But, the adepts? If Knorr weren't lying dead right now, I'd have trouble believing it. Why would any of them sell out to her?"

"The dissidents among them wouldn't need much goading," Ingvar said.

"Dissidents in *their* ranks?" Pontus' eyes went wide.

"Some of them came from pro-Gyllenfeld families, and lost family and friends in the last uprising. Maybe they hold a grudge," I said. "Or, hell, *anyone* in the cloister might have a grudge against Master Ormyr. If Madam Castor sweeps out the Baron, his court officials will probably get the boot, too. She'd want people she can trust or manipulate running the show here."

With worry knotting in my stomach, I threw a strained glance toward Ingvar. He was one of those court officials. For the first time, I considered whether he and Ormyr were also targets of this scheme, right along with me and Baron Tristan.

The other possibility was that Ormyr numbered among Madam Castor's trusted pets, and had been in on the murder attempt.

"Then it's starting to sound like *any* adept might've received orders from Madam Castor in the last mail shipment," Pontus said. "Knorr's still the most likely, but he might've acted on someone's behalf."

"Aye, agreed," Ingvar said. "We'll need to broaden our search."

"I *will* keep looking, sir," Pontus vowed. "I'm angry now."

"Tomorrow. Let that be your focus, and not the corpse."

Pontus nodded gravely, one hand reaching for the beads at his side. "We'd all do well to steer clear of the dungeon, anyway. The dead one won't be moving on to his next purpose until this business is resolved. Restless spirits are best avoided."

We still didn't know whether the corpse's demise had been accidental or intentional, but maybe it was best that no one disturbed it while more urgent business beckoned.

Ingvar heaved a sigh, lowering his arms to his sides. "'Tis late, we're all tired. Stay here tonight, Pontus."

"I'd prefer it, sir. With all the wild animals loose in the districts, I don't like my chances venturing home after nightfall." Pontus' gaze strayed toward the buckets. "But first, what'll ye be doing tomorrow—aside from sorting out suspect witches, I mean? Mayhap ye should come clean to our Baron about this ichor. People should be warned away from it, as ye said, and that starts with him."

Ingvar and I had a mandatory meeting at the keep every morning with Ormyr and Baron Tristan. Pontus' suggestion made sense, but there was a problem.

"I *want* to tell him," Ingvar said. "Only he'll entrust Ormyr to investigate—and Ormyr'll shut us out and bury it."

That was the same objection on my mind.

"We can visit the districts and warn our people, carefully," Ingvar continued. "Something to organize tomorrow after we're all back from the keep."

"That won't take long," Pontus assured him. "What other plans do ye have for tomorrow?"

This was still up in the air. Pontus' return from the keep, and Sigrid's interruption, had prevented me and Ingvar from discussing a course of action earlier.

"'Tis late," Ingvar repeated, deadpan. "Need to think on it more."

"We should wait to figure things out until after we've gotten some sleep," I chimed in. Ingvar had offered me a bed at the barracks earlier. With accomplices to my attempted murder still free, I had no interest in my room in the Baron's estate.

Pontus glanced my way. "Ye were both planning to fly off-planet after that wise woman. Is that still your intention?" His voice carried a note of suspicion, or so it seemed to me.

Ingvar soured at his lieutenant's prodding. Meanwhile, I tamped down a surge of grief. The "wise woman" was Drea. Ingvar and I had been granted permission to retrieve her, but Adept Knorr had intervened. Afterward, Ingvar had told me we couldn't leave Nidaros until the murder attempt was resolved. I wasn't sure if he still felt that way.

"At some point, definitely," I answered Pontus. "She might know how to deal with this ichor. But I don't know if we'll be allowed to travel." Not to mention, I still needed Gules' coordinates to even make the attempt, and only Master Ormyr could provide them.

Pontus nodded and continued in a reasoning tone, like one dispensing fatherly advice. "If I may, lass: whenever ye fly, it's best ye go alone. Ye've seen firsthand what problems we face. We can't afford to have our captain leave now."

Guilt seeped in, spoiling my certainty with doubt. Before, I'd only ever seen the upsides of having Ingvar along when I returned to Gules. I hadn't thought about how his absence might hurt the soldiers, maybe even Nidaros at large.

"Whether or not I go is *my* decision," Ingvar snapped before I could muster a response.

Pontus ignored him, his gaze taking on a pleading aspect. "Lady Knight, ye mean well, but our captain's not your squire."

These words provoked a flush that burned my face. I was grateful the room's dimness would hide it.

"Lieutenant." Ingvar's narrow-eyed gaze was as hard as tempered steel. Despite his calm tone, the warning came through clearly.

Pontus glared at him. "We've got unrest and unsolved murders to worry about, and ye keep running off playing crusader! Remember your duty!"

"Protecting Nidaros from all threats *is* my duty!" Ingvar countered.

"Our lads will hurt at your absence — assuming ye don't get yourself killed outright." Again, there was an air of fatherly concern in Pontus' appeal.

"Have some faith in them, aye? Ye act like they can't function the moment I turn my head," Ingvar returned. "I've trained you to depend upon no one, least of all me."

Pontus shook his head helplessly. "Don't know what else to say, lad. Ye're pushing your luck hard." His eyes then bored into mine. "And ye're encouraging it."

As my face continued to burn, a horrible dread closed off my throat. What if Ingvar were injured or killed while helping me? What if he landed in hot water with Baron Tristan or Master Ormyr? I could run away from Nidaros once my quest ended. He couldn't.

Ignoring Pontus, Ingvar beckoned to me. "I'll show you to a room."

With a deep breath, I pushed those awful thoughts into the huge pile just waiting to pounce on me during a quiet moment, then followed Ingvar out.

In the barracks proper, the captain stepped aside to take a candle sitting on a window-ledge. While waiting for him, I focused on a spot amid the bunks where open eyes regarded me curiously. Those eyes belonged to Dag Nyvind, the boy we'd rescued from the Naustviks' house.

To my astonishment, Dag had taught himself the use of some Shipbuilder artifacts within the Naustviks' house, like the light tile in my pocket. I worried whether Ingvar's protection would be enough to keep Dag out of trouble with the adepts. At some point, he'd likely need my help as well.

I nodded to Dag. His eyes darted between me and Ingvar with a discerning suspicion beyond his years. Judging by his scars, he'd had to grow up quickly. The same probably applied to his older brother, Rigg, who slept in the bunk above his.

Ingvar returned to guide me onward. The only other soldiers I recognized as we walked past were Fasolt and Logmadr, who'd unfortunately found themselves in the way of a panicking Verahl after Ingvar and I had sprung him from the dungeon. I'd been keeping an eye on Fasolt's head injury ever since.

The next room we stopped at was nearly identical to Sigrid's. Beside the pallet, a shuttered window only half-succeeded at keeping out the nighttime chill. My fatigue wasn't enough to overcome the guilt flooding my conscience. Just past the threshold, I faced Ingvar. "I don't want to cause fights between you and Pontus."

He stepped inside and shut the door behind us. "That was his own fear talking, nothing ye did. There's nothing wrong with disagreement besides." But his reassuring expression soon turned strained. "He may just have half a point."

Dread knotted in my gut as I worried what I might hear, but I had to ask. "About?"

Ingvar steered me toward the pallet, where we sat down beside each other. He set the candle on the floor, then straightened to arrest my gaze. "About Drea. I still want to help you rescue her, but after what we've found tonight, she's ..." He trailed off, then tried again. "She's not our priority."

The dread amplified. Somehow, I kept from doubling over.

"Thordia's aiming for the Harbinger," Ingvar continued. "We saw how her garden got out of hand. What if the Harbinger containeth living Shipbuilder magic — or whatever else ye call it?" he amended before I objected to the word "magic." "Even with good intentions, she might uncover something at any moment that destroyeth us all. Death penalty be damned, we must make sure she can't deal further harm than the ichor already hath. We can take Verahl and fly after her without having to beg anyone first."

His reasoning was sound. But Drea ... Conflicting emotions overwhelmed me. I didn't know where to start with a reply. The first thing out of my mouth addressed one of the last points he'd made. "Ingvar, the death penalty? As Lord Catherwood's emissary, I can probably worm out of trouble, but the risk for you may be too high."

"I'm prepared to die for Nidaros," he answered with calm determination.

As a soldier, he must've come to terms with that years ago. His courage, his willingness to confront something he'd feared all his life, commanded my admiration. I'd do everything possible to ensure he didn't suffer for it.

But someone else I cared about was suffering that very moment, if not already dead. What good was my resolve? A familiar soreness built up behind my eyes as warm tears coursed down my face. I brushed them away, annoyed at their appearance.

"Jayce?" A moment later, Ingvar's hand braced my shoulder.

"I'm not upset," I lied out of instinct, then corrected myself. "I *am* upset about Drea, but it's not your fault she's stuck on Gules."

"Not your fault, either," he said.

"Yes, it is! I was supposed to protect her until I could leave her with Branigan." My head dropped from the burden of shame, and my voice wavered. "Branigan's dead, and Drea's going to join him!"

Like Drea, Sir Branigan Cade had been a dear friend and mentor, someone I'd looked up to—and secretly loved. Upon reuniting with him in Gules, I'd planned to confess my feelings. However, Drea and I had found Gules cursed and ransacked. Frozen corpses, including Branigan's, had been strewn all over town. Branigan had been stripped of his gear, left to bleed out with a heretic symbol carved into his forehead.

Grief tightened painfully within my chest. I'd arrived too late to help Branigan or tell him how I felt. Shortly afterward, Lord Catherwood's forces had strong-armed me into marooning Drea and accepting their master's quest in Nidaros. Now I endangered Ingvar, as if I hadn't learned my lesson.

As I wept, Ingvar let go of my shoulder to embrace me instead.

Shock stiffened me at first, but there was no mistaking how my heart raced. Even more guilt piled on from there. I hadn't properly mourned Branigan yet. Goodness forbid, was I turning into my former master May, always dashing off to the next new thing—or person? Whatever the case, there was no denying I cared about Ingvar and was desperate for reassurance. I hugged back tightly, resting my head against his shoulder. He was lanky; even with armor, there wasn't much to him. Still, his embrace was strong and comforting.

"Ye're not the one who slew Branigan or left Drea behind," Ingvar spoke calmly. "They wouldn't want you carrying blame that belongeth to others."

They wouldn't. And Drea would want me to put Nidaros ahead of her. Remembering those things eased the guilt somewhat, but the grief remained. I clung to Ingvar like he was all I had left to lose, sniffling occasionally.

Ingvar clung back. "It may not be our decision to make. Sigrid may confess something tomorrow that changeth everything." He didn't sound terribly convinced on that count. "Or our Baron may forbid you from leaving the planet." This was far more likely. "In which case—"

"You're right. I know." Off to look for Thordia, shield her from harm, seek her help against the ichor. All worthwhile things, and yet I'd worry about Drea the whole time. I hoped she'd find a way to survive until I could return.

"I'm sorry, Jayce," Ingvar said.

"No, I understand. Drea would, too."

We remained in each other's arms for a while longer. The grief didn't go away, but with Ingvar's support, it was bearable. Though I'd been tired before, the thrilling novelty of our close contact kept me wide awake.

"I wish it weren't so late." I didn't detail what I would've wanted to do with more time.

"Aye. We have to be up early for Sigrid." Ingvar eased away from me, eyes focused downward. "I'll bet she's the one who planted that Gyllenfeld stone on you."

With surprise, I recalled the charm I'd discovered on my person earlier that day. If it'd slipped out in front of the wrong people, it could've landed me in serious trouble. "That's what she meant by that 'agitator' business."

Sigrid was a landmine: potentially helpful, potentially dangerous to friend and foe. Her magical thinking made me even more nervous. More so than with anyone else, we'd have to compare any information she provided against reality.

"You heard what else she said, right? About Holsten?" I asked.

Ingvar looked to me with a faint smirk. "Pretty sure 'twas but a fairy tale to please you, Goose. Master Ormyr's second, loyal to Gyllenfeld? He can't get through a blessing without flubbing the words. Keeping a secret like that would kill him."

"Every time I cross paths with Holsten, he acts like I'm a vengeful ghost," I said. "You should've seen when I asked for information about the dungeon, just before we sprang Verahl. He was about to faint! It's like he knew what was coming."

"Mayhap," Ingvar said. "Just as likely is a witch fearing for her hide. Sigrid would gladly deflect attention to an adept instead—or at least take one down with her."

His objections were valid. I shook my head. "Some proof of *something* would be nice."

"Aye. Hopefully Pontus fareth better at the keep tomorrow."

Silence fell between us. My eyes strayed toward my mother's ring, still hanging from Ingvar's neck.

Ingvar followed my gaze. "Here, this is yours," he said, chastened, then reached up to doff it.

"No, keep it," I blurted.

His wide eyes focused on me.

"I mean …" What *did* I mean? Blood rushed to my face, burning it, while my heart pounded out of control. Struggling for words, I bought time by lifting my back baldric off my shoulder, resting it and my side sword on the floor. "I mean, I'll want it back when my quest is over, but for now …" My rambling stopped, uncertain of its destination. I could spout off prattle to appease adepts and courtiers all day long, but I hadn't the faintest idea how to communicate my genuine feelings.

"That's … I'm honored." After a few moments of silence, Ingvar's eyes met mine again. "There's something I want to give you in return. May I?"

Despite his nervousness, he was genuine. Though I felt faint and could hardly draw breath, I managed a nod.

Obligingly, he leaned in close and kissed me on the lips.

I kissed back. This wasn't destined to end in a quick peck; we lingered on the moment and deepened it, slipping our arms around each other. Nervousness gave way to elation. For a while, I forgot everything else, soaring above it all like it no longer mattered.

Then, all too quickly, Ingvar drew back. "Leaving's the last thing I want to do right now, but 'tis time we slept, aye?" he whispered.

That was right: somewhere, some part of me was dead tired. I couldn't remember the particulars, and was supremely disappointed to learn of it. Still, I nodded again. "We'll continue this later?"

"I certainly hope so. See you in the morning." Smiling, Ingvar left my room.

CHAPTER 5

Once Ingvar left my room in the barracks, I remained seated on my pallet. The flame of the candle resting on the floor trembled, as did I—partly from the draft leaking through the shuttered window, partly from giddiness in the wake of our kiss. I couldn't recall the last time I'd felt such dizzying exhilaration.

Oh, you fool! The admonishment knifed through my brain, turning joy to panic. Had I just made a huge mistake, surrendering to the moment like that? It was only going to lead to trouble, wasn't it? But I hadn't met anyone like him in years. What was wrong with enjoying each other's company while we could?

Because I didn't know how Ingvar felt about all this, or what he wanted. What if he just liked the *idea* of me? What if I reminded him of someone else? After all, there was a lot about him that reminded me of Branigan. Were we just using each other to fill painful voids? What would any of this amount to, anyway? Another standard week and a half, my quest would be over, and I'd have to leave Nidaros in search of another. There was no future for us.

And why was I fretting over this while Drea, Thordia, and all of Nidaros remained in danger? What the hell was wrong with me?

An oppressive shame made me overly warm. I undid my belt, resting it and my first aid kit on the floor, then loosened my coat. The cigarillos in my pocket leapt to mind then, one of the worst old habits I'd acquired from my former master. As a teenaged squire, May's smoking had intrigued me, and he'd never discouraged me from it.

This is one of the only creature comforts left to pissants like us, he'd explained. *It'll be your friend when you need one, as long as you pay its bills and don't mind dying a little sooner.*

It was only at the beguinage that I'd learned the full health risks. The beghards and beguines were constantly after both of us to quit. There were times when I had no trouble abstaining for weeks at a stretch—like during long-haul flights across the galaxy—but at present, the call was too strong.

I doffed my coat and brigandine first, favoring my left shoulder, which had broken my fall into the dungeon earlier that day. Then I lit a cigarillo with my stick lighter, taking a pull with my eyes closed and holding the hot smoke in my mouth a while. Several more draws helped to banish the anxious thoughts that my brain would've churned over uselessly otherwise. My tense muscles relaxed.

While leaning down to tap ash onto the metal plate holding the candle, I noticed something unfamiliar jutting from my coat pocket. I pulled it out for a closer look: a thin, glassy rectangle about twice the length of the light tile, but still small enough to fit in one hand.

My heart jumped with surprise. Between the ichor and Sigrid, I'd lost track of this data carrier, one of the amazing Shipbuilder devices the Naustviks had secreted away in their cellar. Each data carrier held entire libraries full of information, and occasionally doubled as a communication device.

Drea owned an identical device. It was a long shot, but if enough of the right technology had survived between Nidaros and Gules, there was a chance I could transmit a message that she'd receive near-instantly.

Trembling again—this time with anticipation—I touched a finger to the data carrier's shiny surface. Much like the light tile I'd wielded earlier, the device flared to life, emitting a bluish-green glow. Shipbuilder symbols filled the screen and seemed to lift away from it, the same holographic interface I'd become familiar with during my study at the beguinage.

I pressed my finger to individual words and commands, digging for any communications information I could find. Eventually, the device showed me a tiny list: three other data carrier signals designated as "local" to me. In other words, they resided somewhere on the same planet. Nothing farther out than that.

I'd suspected as much, but still regretted I couldn't tell Drea to hang on, and that I loved her. That *any* carriers were detected was unusual, though. An active communications node had to exist somewhere on Nidaros. Maybe it resided within the Harbinger, lying dormant for the past several hundred years. Or maybe it sat within the adepts' keep among the other "relics" they safeguarded from the rest of the barony.

And what of those three local data carriers? Thordia had left two devices behind for Verahl, including the one in my hand. Did that imply she'd kept several for herself?

Despite my curiosity, I refrained from sending any messages to the other devices. It was impossible to know who, if anyone, would see them. I'd wait until I next saw Verahl, who was hiding from the authorities aboard my ship. Surely he could send a message Thordia would recognize and trust. And if she responded, we could arrange a rendezvous, avoiding a tedious search.

Then we could rescue Drea that much sooner. Hell, I hoped so.

—⁓⁓—

Minutes after I'd fallen asleep — or so it seemed — distant, unsettling noises nagged me from the fringe of consciousness. Crashes of wood on wood, doors opening and closing, agitated voices.

"We have a right to our prisoner!"

"'Prisoner' now? Whose word is that, yours or Ormyr's?"

"Adept Knorr's blood is on her hands!"

"Then mayhap he shouldn't have tried to kill her. What do ye want from us, anyway? She's not here."

"Impossible! We're not leaving until we've searched everywhere."

"Captain? Captain!"

The voices became louder and more spiteful with each volley. Then came a series of sharp, desperate taps that were louder still, practically in my ear.

"Sister? Sister!" a hushed voice pleaded.

Sigrid?

I flew up to a seated position and opened my eyes. My hair, loose from its braid, fell around my shoulders. This was still my room in the barracks. Ahead, the door stood closed. Behind, early sunlight peeked through the slats of the shuttered window beside my pallet.

The tapping returned, followed by rattling. Someone outside the window was testing the shutter. "Sister, come out here. Hurry!"

A large object, like a table or chest, crashed to the floor just outside my room.

I gasped. Someone, probably an adept, was tossing the barracks in search of me. And Sigrid was — wait, how the hell had Sigrid broken out of her room? Hadn't Ingvar locked her in? My own window's shutter looked sturdy, but not indestructible. She must've busted out that way—just like I'd have to if I wanted to escape.

I'd slept in my tunic and trousers, with the rest of my gear piled on the floor. It took only seconds to step into my boots and sweep everything else into my arms. Opening the window was merely the work of flipping some latches. I pulled the shutters open, admitting more of the morning sun, then slipped outside one leg at a time.

Sigrid knelt amid the parched grasses, spotting my progress with glowing relief. Once I was clear of the window, she grabbed my arm and pulled me down to her level, placing a finger to her lips.

I glanced left and right, desperate to orient myself. Sigrid and I crouched along the barracks' front wall. The entrance stood closed, and there wasn't a soul in the vicinity. A cool, dreamlike mist blurred the edges of reality.

"We must hide," Sigrid whispered.

Until I had a better idea, hers would work. Before I could tell Sigrid to follow my lead, she took to crawling down the wall, heading for the closest end of the barracks. She kept beneath a row of windows like the one we'd just exited and moved as quietly as I could've hoped for.

Satisfied for the moment, I followed her. Once we ran out of wall, I planned to steer her around the corner and grill her. And if my pursuer showed up mid-grilling? I wasn't sure yet whom I'd have to defend from whom.

Sigrid didn't need any prodding to round the corner in the wall. From there, she placed her back against it and sank to her knees, clutching her right forearm as though smarting from the loss of her punching dagger. Behind her jutted the wide stone chimney that made up one of the barracks' two hearths. Smoke from the morning fire curled into the air.

Kneeling beside her, I hurriedly donned my armor, coat, and weapons, ignoring the knots in my stomach. "What the hell is going on?"

"Those adepts are here to arrest you," she replied.

"Adepts?" Once equipped, I leapt up to my feet as though stung. That I'd been attacked by Knorr wasn't in dispute. Neither was the fact that he'd fallen victim to his own lantern. Baron Tristan hadn't brought charges against me yesterday. I'd thought I was in the clear.

A chill braced me. "Are they here on Ormyr's behalf? Or are they seeking revenge for Knorr?"

"I don't know." Sigrid stood as well. "But you're best off—"

"And don't ever let me catch you tossing my barracks again!"

Ingvar's voice rang out from the entrance with plenty of self-righteous ire behind it. A definitive door-slam followed.

The relief his outburst provided was only temporary. Whoever was looking for me, for whatever reason, they were now outside with us. I held my breath and tensed, listening for what came next. Sigrid stuck to the wall and mouthed something, her eyes glazing over in the process.

We waited for what felt like ages, but heard nothing to suggest my pursuers' position or status. When I couldn't tolerate the suspense any longer, I chanced a peek around the corner. The entrance to the barracks was closed, deserted. In the distance, three burgundy forms hastened down the path to the capital buildings. Their hooded robes obscured their features, but not the daggers and chains on their persons.

Dread crept down my spine. When it came to spells and premonitions, the adepts were full of it—but give them false charges, weapons, and carefully applied chemical substances, and they could make anyone's life hell.

"They're leaving," I muttered.

Sigrid snapped out of her trance to brace my elbow from behind. "You must leave too, sister. The capital isn't safe for you any longer. My coven resides in the South district, they'll help you. Go there and find the house with three ouroboros amulets over its threshold. Ask for Mother Birna. Tell her you're looking for a seamstress, and have heard she's very gifted."

Did she *know* I wasn't safe, or was she spinning tales for herself? I didn't plan on enlisting help from her coven, but I committed the information to memory anyway, just in case. Then I faced her and shook my head. "Captain Leirfall and I will head to the keep and straighten this out."

"But Master Ormyr won't be there," Sigrid said as though I should've already known.

I frowned. "He won't?"

She blinked. "Was it not your doing, sister?"

"What?" I demanded, short on patience.

Sigrid gestured behind me with a wave of her hand. "Look toward the keep."

I checked around the corner again. In the distance, the adepts' abode peeked through the mist. A knot of burgundy had gathered by the stables between the keep and storehouse. The adepts were saddling several of those wooly, bison-like animals called ulldyr.

My jaw fell. Now what was that about? There were no wagons, no ration deliveries meant for the districts. I saw nothing that explained their intent.

"They're all leaving! Whatever you did, it worked wonderfully!" Sigrid sounded delighted with the "magic" she believed I'd wrought.

It clearly wasn't *every* adept—the three who'd sought to detain me were still returning—but it might've been close.

"Now I can search for signs of Holsten's connection to Madam Castor, as you asked," Sigrid declared.

I faced her again. By then, my head spun; I placed my hand against the barracks wall for balance. That sort of search was better left to Pontus, who could be trusted not to create whimsical fantasies. Besides, it was no small risk on her part. "Sigrid, don't—"

"Don't worry about me, sister. Worry about staying hidden." Sigrid's gaze detached once more, and her voice took on the weight of a grim certainty. "The reckoning will fall upon us soon. I've seen how great a hand you'll have in it, provided the adepts don't break you." She refocused on me with a pleading look. "If they corner you, die fighting and go to Folkvang. Don't slink off to Hel in pieces from the dungeon!"

With that, she took off running toward the capital, black cloak trailing behind her.

Both of those mythical realms came from Gyllenfeld dogma. Folkvang was the afterlife one reached if one died in battle. Hel was different from the hell I'd been brought up to fear, an eternal void rather than eternal punishment. I didn't believe in any afterlifes anymore, but either hell seemed preferable to spending significant time in the adepts' dungeon. I hoped Sigrid didn't end up there, either.

Hastily, I braided my hair, not wanting it in the way during a potential fight. As my fingers flew, my brain churned over how and why I'd gone from esteemed guest to wanted killer literally overnight. Judging from what I'd heard, those three adepts wanted revenge. Was the sentiment confined to them, or did the entire cloister share it?

It also wasn't clear whether Ormyr or the Baron knew about this. It didn't seem likely that they'd changed their minds about Knorr. Was his death an excuse to lock me up for some other reason? Had they somehow learned about my and Ingvar's activities yesterday? The Naustviks' house, the fugitive aboard my ship, the ichor, Sigrid's witchery in the estate— any one of those send us to the dungeon.

But they weren't interested in punishing Ingvar, just me. Maybe Knorr's co-conspirators sought to finish what he'd started, hoping to discredit the Baron by murdering me.

It was time to find Ingvar, figure out our next move. Ignoring worry and dizziness, I darted around the corner to re-enter the barracks through the front door.

Between the hearths' unattended fires, tens of soldiers darted around a chaos of upturned furniture and unmade bunks. Their leadership was absent amid the bedlam. "Fasolt! Logmadr!" I flagged down the nearest pair I recognized.

The young men staggered to a mystified halt, as did several other soldiers nearby.

"Sir! Here's Dame Jessamine!" Fasolt called out.

"*Skíta*, we were worried they disappeared you somehow!" Logmadr cried.

Ingvar tore out from the room I'd slept in, clad in full gear. My mother's ring still jostled against his chest. His eyes locked onto mine with concern. "Are ye all right?"

A torrent of mixed emotions flooded me. Relief, longing, guilt—I shoved them aside. "Yes, but I'm damn confused."

"As are we all. Let's talk." Ingvar gestured toward my room with a toss of his head.

"No, outside. We may not have much time." I glanced around the barracks. "I'll help with this mess if I can, later."

"It won't take a second to set right," Ingvar dismissed. "Be back soon, lads."

We stepped out the front door together. My eyes riveted to the keep, where the adept gathering had yet to move.

"Someone'll be making up stories about your invisible armor afore day's end," Ingvar muttered, shaking his head.

"I climbed out my window," I explained. "So did Sigrid, I think."

"Aye, and left broken shutters in her wake. They were locked in place. Don't know how she managed it with bare hands." Ingvar scowled. "Any idea where is she now?"

"Heading to the keep. Where's Pontus?" I asked.

"Already there."

Damn. I would've wanted to warn him about Sigrid. Hopefully, they stayed out of each other's way. "What's going on over there?" I pointed into the distance.

When Ingvar caught sight of the adepts through the mist, his frown melted into concern. "Mayhap 'tis what Ulfarr's running up to report."

Confused, I scanned the empty field before the barracks, then finally spotted the soldier gunning for us about a hundred yards distant.

"Stay here." Ingvar ducked back inside the barracks, returning moments later with a longsword and quiver strapped to his sides and a strung bow over his shoulder.

A wave of nausea hit me. I needed Ingvar's support, without question, but what was he prepared to do here? *Fight the adepts* on my behalf? I couldn't bear to drag him down with me like that. I'd sooner turn myself in and let the adepts carry out whatever they had in mind. A protest rose to meet the bile at the back of my throat.

"Sir!" Ulfarr pelted to a stop before us, panting.

Ingvar focused on his soldier. "Report."

Ulfarr pointed behind himself, working up a few words at a time around noisy breaths. "Master Ormyr's taking adepts to Dame Jessamine's ship. For Naustvik."

"What?!" Ingvar cried.

Shock and betrayal shot through me like lightning. As if we hadn't had enough to worry about. Feeling weak in the knees, I glanced helplessly to Ingvar, who was equally stunned and not bothering to hide it.

"The adepts know Verahl's aboard my ship?" I managed.

"They weren't quiet about it," Ulfarr said.

"How'd they find out, lad?" Ingvar asked.

"Don't know, sir. I just ran when I realized what they were up to."

It was all I could do not to faint. How'd they found out? One of the soldiers must've tipped off the adepts, accidentally or otherwise. That explained the sudden change in disposition. And now they wanted Verahl back, and then hell only knew what they were going to do to him, me, and the soldiers who'd made Verahl's escape possible—Ingvar foremost among them.

The captain summoned a stern composure. "Thanks, Ulfarr. Head to the gate, then the port. Tell everyone along the way to run interference on the adepts."

"Aye, sir!" Ulfarr ran away.

"Who tipped them off?" Alone with Ingvar, the question tumbled out of my mouth. But it had to have been one of the soldiers, they were the only ones who'd known.

"Let's worry about that after Naustvik's safe, aye?" Ingvar frowned into the distance again, at the group of adepts who had yet to leave the stables.

"Can we hide Verahl somewhere else fast enough?" I asked.

"There's no time, especially if the adepts ride to the port." Ingvar looked to me with resolve. "We must fly, Jayce. Let's take Naustvik and head after Thordia."

Maybe Ingvar had gathered his weapons for searching the Harbinger, not for battling adepts. Still, Ormyr stood to uncover all the ways the captain had been abetting me. If the Harbinger itself wasn't a death sentence, breaking a witch's brother out of the dungeon almost certainly was. As much as I wanted his help, Ingvar would have to throw his whole life away to provide it—and that prospect killed me.

I couldn't jeopardize him any further. The only way to save him was to keep him out of future entanglements.

"Stay here, Ingvar." I looked him in the eye, ignoring heart-gouging pain to brace myself with cold determination. "*I'll* fly out with Verahl. For all Ormyr knows, you're trying to stop me. Got it? Don't worry—if I get caught, everything was my idea."

I took off running for the port before any grief could catch up with me.

Moments later, Ingvar was sprinting at my side. "Blood's oath! We see this through together!"

I'd forgotten how fast he could run—or maybe, subconsciously, I hadn't. "Are you crazy? Ormyr will fry you!"

"Once we save Nidaros, no one will much care how we did it," Ingvar returned. "Don't push me away, Jayce."

I didn't have enough breath to keep arguing while running—or so I told myself. With unimaginable trouble brewing behind us, and an uncertain future ahead, having Ingvar at my side was deeply reassuring.

But what if he loses everything because of me?

That sick feeling resettled in the pit of my stomach. I resolved to shield Ingvar at all costs. If that meant taking the blame—or taking him to another planet, like I planned to do with the Naustviks—then so be it.

CHAPTER 6

The sun rising in the yellow sky had yet to dispel the mist throughout Nidaros' capital, a mist that made the morning's chaos all the more surreal. I ran down the path leading to the capital gate, intent on reaching the port. Ingvar followed at my side with a determined expression, brooking no further debate about his presence. Behind us, Master Ormyr massed his forces to recapture the fugitive sheltered aboard my ship.

Fatigue and injury made the run a chore, however much it mattered to my continued existence. Between labored breaths, I doubted my own sanity. With hostile magic-wielders on our heels, we were prepping my flying machine to chase after a witch who'd fled to a lair that might be full of marvels and terrors, all because a mysterious poison was stealing the barony's water.

My life had turned into one of my damn fake quest stories.

Ingvar and I tore past the empty trade posts that made up the capital's disused commerce area. The worn capital wall loomed ahead. Its gate was open, revealing more mist beyond. Appropriate, given the uncertain fate ahead of us.

A glance over my shoulder revealed no sign of active pursuit. On foot, we had quite the lead, but the adepts had been saddling up those ulldyr. There was no telling how fast they could close the gap once mounted.

Ulfarr had briefed the gate sentries, as was clear by their nervous expressions. The soldiers manning the wall, usually hidden from sight, stood alert as we approached.

"Close the gate behind us," Ingvar called to them. "Hold up the adepts as long as ye can!"

A chorus of ayes rained down as we ran through the gate, then banked right for the port.

I nursed a stitch in my side while thinking about how we'd made this same run several days earlier in pursuit of Verahl. But this time, it wasn't just his hide at stake. The whole barony's future hinged on our success. And there I was, bruised and sucking wind—but it wouldn't matter as much once we reached my ship and got flying.

The watch post at the edge of the port came into view. Past it stretched an expanse of worn, cracked pavement, with a beacon tower standing in the center. No fire rose from it; Baron Tristan wasn't expecting visitors. At the tower's base stood Ulfarr, shouting to a soldier who hurried down a staircase to join him at ground level.

The tower presided over the perpetual funeral otherwise known as Nidaros' port. Most of the ships there would never fly again. Mist played through holes in their decayed hulls, all littered with flower garlands and charms like the ones Ingvar had removed from the well pump. There was no telling what serious or trivial flaws had condemned them to their fate. In Lord Catherwood's realm, ship repair was against the Unseen's will, a sacrilege that could land the offender in a dungeon or a noose.

The Baron's sleek yacht was the first able ship we came across. We passed her up in favor of the wreck I'd restored with my mentors' help: *Kepler's Law*. "Serviceable" was usually the most generous description she could garner, but with adepts on my tail, she rose from serviceable to a magnificence beyond description. It was a relief to see her intact, free of any signs of adept visitation.

We pelted to a halt beside her, bent double and gasping for air. As soon as I'd caught my breath, I took to pulling at the hatch, stubborn as always. Several firm tugs wrenched it open.

Two soldiers immediately filled the tiny airlock beyond. Ingvar had stationed men aboard *Kepler's Law* to guard and supervise Verahl.

"Dismissed, lads." Still recovering his breath, Ingvar tossed his head over his shoulder. "Go see Ulfarr, he'll brief you. Where's Naustvik?"

"He's in the hole under the floor, sir," one of them reported.

Ingvar faced me. "Prepare to fly. Then we'll explain things to him."

"She won't take long to warm up," I said. "We should get our gear and ourselves stowed first. Come on."

I vaulted into the airlock, then offered Ingvar a hand up. Once inside, Ingvar turned back to pull the hatch shut. I passed into the corridor beyond, turning right—aft. Even for my slightly less-than-average frame, the passage was narrow and cramped. Handholds poked out everywhere to aid passage outside of gravity, but became obstacles within it.

After a few feet, the corridor opened up into the galley. Closets and bolted-down containers ran along most of the bulkheads. A table and benches I'd unfolded from the deck remained standing, and the smell of our last meal lingered in the air—painfully enticing, as I'd been eating like a Nidaran since my arrival.

Verahl's blankets lay along the starboard bulkhead, but he wasn't lying on them. A magnetic tray rested on the floor, loaded with bandages and vials of antiseptic and painkillers.

He'd helped himself to my supplies. I was glad to see it, and hoped he felt better.

Toward the rear of the galley, the hatch leading to the engine room lay open. I supposed Verahl was having another look through the mechanisms that'd fascinated him before. He could stay down there while Ingvar and I got ready.

Ingvar shadowed me, eyes darting about with suspicion. However, his hands remained open at his sides, like he had yet to find any threat. It was a welcome change, but there wasn't time to comment on it. Working in tense silence, I helped him stow his weapons into a closet near the galley threshold, then placed my own baldric and side sword in with his. After that, I folded the table and benches back into the deck and put away the medical supplies. There'd be no gravity changes during this flight—at least I sure hoped not—but the ship's inertial dampening remained inactive when traveling at sub-light speeds. It was best to minimize what could go tumbling and crashing along the deck.

Heavy footsteps thudded up from behind. I turned to find Verahl climbing the engine room ladder, stooping over to fit in the galley once he reached the top. He was a tower of disheveled homespun; his size seemed necessary to contain the energy supply keeping him on his feet despite a chronic food shortage, a stint in the adepts' dungeon, and the wounds he'd earned during his escape. At that moment, most of Verahl's energy beamed from his eyes and burned through me. They were his most expressive features, as his full beard hid everything else.

Beside me, Ingvar reached for the hilt of the longsword he'd just surrendered, only to clutch at empty air.

"What's going on?" Verahl's deep bass rumbled across the deck.

I understood Ingvar's trepidation—Verahl had injured his men before—but we couldn't afford to let any distrust take root. I spat everything into the open. "Ormyr and some other adepts are on their way here. Don't worry, we're flying out right now to look for Thordia."

Verahl's jaw dropped. His wide eyes shifted between me and Ingvar several times. "What about Dag? Where is he?"

"At the barracks with his brother," Ingvar replied. "He's safe."

Verahl focused on Ingvar, his confusion turning into a frown.

Quickly, I turned to the starboard bulkhead and pulled down a chair from the wall. "Have a seat, Verahl. Once we're clear of the capital, we can talk about how we'll track Thordia down." Maybe we'd leverage those data carrier signals I'd detected last night, if any were actually hers.

As he faced me, Verahl's expression cleared. "I have some ideas. If she's reached the Harbinger, it might be even easier." He lowered himself into the offered chair, strapping himself in with the safety restraints before I could offer any assistance on that front.

I was eager to know what he meant, but the discussion was best left for later. With Verahl taken care of, I turned to Ingvar. "I need you to help me navigate."

Ingvar's eyes went wide. "Me?"

"Let's go." There was no time for debate. I took the lead back into the corridor.

The narrow passage ended at the cockpit. Sunlight streamed through the windshield, falling upon two of the wrecked ships outside. In the tiny command center sat two chairs surrounded with instruments and consoles. I squeezed into the familiar pilot's chair on the left. Ingvar gingerly slipped into the copilot's chair on the right, his hands avoiding everything that wasn't bulkhead.

Once I activated the warmup sequence, *Kepler's Law* hummed awake. The console lit up first, displaying lists of expired parts, missed maintenance checks, and other testaments to my neglect. In reality, those "expired" parts would hold up for another few decades at least. The maintenance warnings were programmed to show up at timed intervals, and I couldn't find anyone who knew how to shut them off. Fortunately, they wouldn't prevent our departure.

"Ornery little cuss," I couldn't help muttering. I rushed through the usual pre-flight checks, my hands and eyes moving as fast as instinct and adrenaline could carry them.

"Have a hard time believing ye ever raise this wreck off the ground, Goose," Ingvar remarked.

"She hasn't failed me yet," I said. "Which way to the Low North district? We should trace Thordia's entire path from there to the Harbinger, just to be safe." A ship flying low overhead would almost certainly rattle some nerves on the ground, but it couldn't be helped.

Ingvar pointed out the windshield, just left of the sun that had yet to burn with full intensity. His eyes scanned the horizon for trouble.

I wanted to acknowledge the huge risk he'd assumed for my sake. I wanted to thank him for his support, preferably with another kiss, but we weren't safe yet. I forced a deep breath past my pounding heart. "Do you know how to fasten those restraints?" He'd told me he'd flown on a ship before, but it'd been years ago. "We don't have to worry about punching through atmospheres, but you never know about the weather."

Still focused on the windshield, Ingvar reached for the straps. "I'll figure it out."

I fastened my own restraints before the magnetic thrusters kicked in. *Kepler's Law* cleared the ground, beginning a slow but steady ascent.

"None too soon." Ingvar didn't have to clarify his statement. We both saw the flood of burgundy coursing around the nearest wrecked ship.

My blood went from racing to freezing in place. The adepts, already? Even with the roadblocks the soldiers had thrown up? Those mounts were *fast*—or, Ormyr wasn't letting anything stand in his way. I forced another deep breath on myself. After all, the swarm fell out of sight as we climbed. We'd eluded them.

The engine cut in to supplement the thrusters. While gaining altitude, I oriented the ship in the direction Ingvar had indicated.

There was a violent thud. Movement flashed in the corner of my eye. Glancing toward the disturbance, I found Verahl behind Ingvar, his left arm encircling the captain's neck in a choke-hold. Ingvar struggled and clawed at Verahl's arm, seeking a position where Verahl wouldn't have as much leverage. Unfortunately, his restraints limited his movement.

Stunned at first, all I could do was cry out in alarm.

Ingvar couldn't make a sound. Meanwhile, Verahl maintained the deadly hold like a statue, eyes narrowed with cold purpose.

It didn't matter how desperate I was to help Ingvar, the ship was still rising. Outrage and adrenaline helped me focus on the console just long enough to pause us in mid-air. Then I undid my restraints, twisted around, and aimed a palm-strike at Verahl's face.

The blow connected with his cheek. Verahl winced, his head snapping back.

This gave Ingvar enough leeway to slip his right hand between Verahl's arm and his own neck, breaking the hold. Ingvar then threw his left elbow backward, driving it into his attacker's head.

As Verahl backpedaled out of the cockpit, Ingvar slumped forward, coughing hard, his face almost a match for his tabard. His restraints were the only thing keeping him from crumpling to the deck.

Worried, I grasped Ingvar's shoulders and eased him back against his chair. Fortunately, it was a strong cough. As scary as it looked, he hadn't suffered any serious harm. While Ingvar recovered from the untimely, uncalled-for assault—Verahl's second since fleeing the dungeon—I could *try* to figure out what had snapped in Verahl's brain and glue it back together long enough to flee the capital. From there? Hell, I didn't know yet. Why was this happening, at the worst possible time?

Struggling against terror and resentment, I faced aft. Verahl had retreated several steps into the corridor, doubled over with his head braced in his hands.

"What the hell was that for?" I demanded.

Verahl straightened as much as the corridor allowed, eyes burning. "He's been playing us this whole time!"

"*Ingvar?*" I blurted.

The captain and I traded a split-second look of alarm and disbelief. Then Ingvar clenched his teeth and clawed at his restraints.

My frustration toward Verahl intensified. "Ingvar helped you escape! You wouldn't be here if—"

"No!" Verahl cut me off. One of his hands fidgeted nervously within his pocket, making me fear the possible introduction of a weapon. "Don't you see? He and Ormyr *wanted* me out of the dungeon. They let you free me. Now they want us to lead them to Thordia. *He told the adepts to find us here!*"

At this, I froze. My old friend paranoia resurfaced, eating at my insides like acid. Was there anything to this? All throughout this quest, the adepts been just half a step behind me. They sure as hell hadn't managed it through "magic." How else but with help—from the soldiers? From Ingvar himself? Was it possible? Ingvar was loyal to Nidaros above all. He'd oppose anyone who threatened it—like some fool knight errant whose report to Lord Catherwood could save or sink everything.

Ingvar threw off his restraints, looking to me wide-eyed. "He's full of it, Jayce!" His alarm then turned into a fury that he cast over his shoulder. "Crazy arse! Are ye *trying* to get captured?"

"We're safe up here." Verahl seemed oddly certain about it. "But you have to go before we move another inch, or else the adepts will be able to track us."

"Ye're insane!" Ingvar cried.

A righteous conviction rose up in me, chasing off all doubt. Ingvar hadn't betrayed me. His care and concern, the way he'd risked his neck for me repeatedly? He hadn't faked that. Ormyr must've gotten his information from someone else. Pulling together as much composure as possible, I faced the threat in the corridor. "Verahl, we need to be calm here. You're scared, you're imagining things, and you're playing right into the adepts' hands. Thordia's more important. Let's get to the Harbinger, then—"

"We will." Verahl removed his hand from his pocket. Out came one of the data carriers I'd returned to him the night before. He tapped at its glowing interface.

The ship dropped, losing several feet of altitude. Ingvar and I winced as our heads bumped against the cockpit ceiling only a few inches above us. An alarm blared, punching through my eardrums.

"What the hell?" Once I recovered, I faced the console, desperately skimming the errors that scrolled past.

"What's happened?" Ingvar shouted to be heard.

"I don't know. Verahl must've done something with the data carrier." A chill went down my spine. Controlling the ship *remotely?* I hadn't known such a thing was possible. At least we still hovered a few yards above the port, out of reach of the adepts—for now.

"That light-square in his hands?" Ingvar gave me a look of angry determination. "Fix this. I'll fix him."

With that, he tore out of his chair and down the corridor.

My insides seized up with dread. Verahl was larger and stronger, but the captain had training on his side. Though I longed to help Ingvar recover the data carrier, all my effort had to go toward counteracting whatever Verahl had set in motion before *Kepler's Law* hit the pavement, or worse.

It was a struggle to think past the alarm and the worrying crashes that issued from the galley. The computer complained about several non-responsive engine components, but we were still airborne. In true nightmare fashion, none of the commands I issued through the console seemed to help. Had Verahl disabled these controls as well? Would I have to sprint to the engine room to resolve this?

I glanced over my shoulder, sizing up my prospects. Within the galley, Ingvar had pinned Verahl and reached for the data carrier in his hand—only to go flying once Verahl threw him aside.

Worry stabbed at my racing heart. *Damn it, focus,* I scolded myself, facing forward again. This seemed more like a computer problem than a hardware one. I ignored the console in favor of manual controls, hoping to climb and reorient the ship that way. "Come on, shrug it off," I urged her.

Instead, she pitched down *hard* of her own volition. I fell against the console and windshield, wincing from the blow. Behind me, Verahl and Ingvar tumbled out of the galley and down the corridor with their own startled cries. My ship's nose narrowly missed the hull of the wreck beneath us. Several adepts outside scattered away from the near-collision.

Before I could recover, *Kepler's Law* leveled herself out— then rolled even harder to port, until we hovered sideways in mid-air. I smashed up against the port bulkhead, an experience more frightening than painful. A loud slam sounded behind me. Something heavy had struck the airlock hatch.

The ship leveled out again. The errors vanished from the console, and the alarm went silent. We'd stabilized a few yards above the port. Below, the adepts surrounded us at a safe distance with arms raised overhead, probably casting ineffectual spells our way.

Untrusting, I held still, every muscle tensed. Hell and damnation, had Verahl's data carrier done all that? Who was in control at this point? The unsettling silence behind me seemed to indicate the fight was over, but who had prevailed? With my heart in my mouth, I glanced over my shoulder again.

Verahl clogged up the corridor, sitting beside the airlock entrance with his back against the bulkhead. He pulled in shallow breaths, sporting fresh cuts amid a sheen of sweat. The data carrier glowed in his hand, but he seemed unaware of its existence. There was no sign of Ingvar.

That slam against the hatch. When the ship had rolled onto her side, the airlock would've become more of a pit than a room. Had he fallen into it?

"Ingvar!" I cried, though I already feared the worst.

Terror propelled me into the corridor on weak knees. I fell against the airlock threshold and leaned inside. Empty. The thrice-damned hatch swung into open air.

Ingvar must've fallen out of the ship onto the rough pavement below. Now he lay there — maybe wounded, maybe even dying — completely at the adepts' mercy. The mental picture and the pain it brought were unbearable. I threw myself toward the airlock, intending to leap out after him.

Verahl's free hand clamped down on my wrist, anchoring me in place. His eyes lifted to meet mine, but were too glazed over to make contact. "He betrayed us."

"Like hell he did!" My loathing for Verahl rose up like an overpowering wave of nausea. I pulled hard against his grip.

He held fast. "It's true. I'm sorry," he continued without any change in tone. "Let's go. We'll reach Thordia together."

Though he could've probably set a course for the Harbinger with the data carrier, he didn't, apparently still too out of it.

Every instinct demanded that I break free and jump ship after Ingvar — but cold reason dictated otherwise. While Verahl was repulsive, Thordia hadn't done anything wrong. Most of Nidaros was equally innocent. I didn't know if we had minutes or years to act against the ichor before it was too late. Failure on that count would spell death for everyone in the barony.

Below, Ingvar stood to die much sooner — if not from injury, then from horrific torture in the adepts' dungeon. It was my fault he'd gotten into this mess. How could I let him mire in it alone?

What about *Kepler's Law*, though? My only means of travel, and my only hope of rescuing Drea? Surrendering her to Verahl was unthinkable. I had to take away his data carrier. But *could* I? Or would I just end up a pile of blood and bruises for my trouble?

As I agonized over my choices, an eternity of grief battered me in the space of seconds. Ultimately, it came down to the fact that someone I cared about — someone I *loved* — desperately needed my help. Everything else would have to wait.

There was precious little I could do while Verahl held me in place, though. I had to convince him to release me so I could gather up a few things. Swallowing my hatred, I faced him with resignation. "All right. I'm not thrilled about leaving him like this, but we … we have no other choice. Let me patch you up first."

"No," Verahl said.

"Thordia wouldn't want you running around the Harbinger bleeding and punch-drunk." Appealing to his sister was the best means I had of swaying him. "It won't take long."

He hesitated. Finally, he pushed himself to his feet, releasing my wrist in the process.

As I guided him toward the galley, the glowing data carrier held my attention. Unfortunately, it remained buried within his fist. It wasn't my priority, anyway. Far more important was leading Verahl back to the galley and lowering him into his chair on the starboard bulkhead. He sat back with a grunt, closing his eyes.

"Hold on." I backed up toward the closets, ostensibly for supplies, but my first aid kit was already on my belt. Instead, I aimed for where I'd stowed my side sword earlier. Blinking back tears, I took one last look around the galley of the ship that'd been my constant companion through years of questing. Aboard her rested everything I'd ever worked for.

Sorry, little cuss, I thought. *I know you understand.*

Drea would, too.

Righteous anger flooded back. This time, it was impossible not to vent it on Verahl. "I wanted to help you. I thought you were a kindred spirit. But you'd rather lash out blindly than make sense of things—just like the damned adepts. I hope your sister has a conscience!"

I grabbed my baldric and side sword from the closet, then sprinted to the airlock.

"Jayce!" Verahl cried behind me.

At the airlock's edge, I paused, assessing the scene a few yards below. Adepts and ulldyr clogged the port, snaking through the ruined ships. Some of the adepts encircled an insensate form on the ground.

Ingvar. He lay prone, his left arm tucked under himself, and made no move to recover.

My heart, tearing apart fiber by fiber, nearly killed me right there. Was he dazed? Had he struck his head off the ground? Had the adepts done something to him?

Then determination took over. Adepts be damned, I had to break out every bit of healing and fighting skill at my disposal. Ingvar wouldn't die or be captured. *I wouldn't let it happen.*

I tossed my baldric and side sword out the airlock. They clattered to the pavement, drawing the attention of several nearby adepts. One last breath, and I dropped down after them.

CHAPTER 7

Early morning sunlight outlined the port swarming with adepts, their mounts, and ships that'd never fly again. Ingvar lay prone on the pavement below, in sore need of aid.

I had no choice but to save him. I loved him. There was no use denying it any longer, no matter what it led to later.

The drop from *Kepler's Law* lasted only a few yards. My feet touched down first; I somersaulted, then came to a safe stop in a crouched position. Ahead of me rested the baldric and side sword I'd thrown down first. To my left, a ring of adepts surrounded Ingvar's motionless form — some clutching wishing beads in earnest, some facing me with wide-eyed apprehension. Overhead, the sweet coarseness of my ship's engine faded as she quit hovering to bolt into the distance, captive of the prisoner I'd rescued.

There was no time for despair. Ingvar had almost certainly been injured during the fall from *Kepler's Law*, to say nothing of the wounds Verahl and the adepts might've added. I hadn't seen any blood, but that didn't mean he wasn't bleeding. It also wasn't clear whether he was unconscious or just momentarily stunned. I had to stabilize him, then figure out our escape from the adepts. Somehow.

I drew my side sword from its scabbard, threw the baldric over my shoulder, then sized up the adept circle. Fighting wasn't my goal, but if that was what it took to reach Ingvar, so be it.

Before I could dart over, a host of adept hands latched onto my arms from behind, hauling me backward.

"No! Let me help him!" I thrashed with every limb, not caring whom or what I hit, but there were too many to fend off.

A hand shot toward my face. An unpleasant sting buried into my eyes like hot needles, and my vision clouded over in short order. Adept Knorr had used the same substance on me during our fatal encounter in the dungeon. The pain forced my eyes shut.

Taunting cackles mixed with wafting incense. A gob of warm saliva splashed across my cheek. Someone wrenched my wrist, forcing me to drop my side sword.

I cried out and struggled, still desperate to get to Ingvar. They could mess with me all they wanted afterward as long as I was allowed to treat him. It'd be hard to manage while blinded, but minor details like that didn't occur to me.

My left fist struck someone's cheekbone: a fortunate accident, but the adept crowd wasn't impressed. They pinned my arms behind me, then seized my braided hair and pulled hard, wrenching my head back. A blade pressed against my exposed neck, making me tense with alarm.

"Not so tough now, are you?" one of them barked in my ear.

"Knorr deserved better," a sinister voice murmured from the other side.

More of that vengeful attitude. I held still, fearing I'd cut myself before they got around to it, but it was probably too late for such concerns. A chill overtook me, sinking in deep enough to make me shiver. This was it. I'd failed everyone.

"What are ye doing? Cease at once!" The angry command boomed from a distance, its source unmistakable: Master Ormyr.

Ormyr! I'd never felt such a strange rush of relief and disgust in my life.

My tormentors fell silent but remained close, keeping me on my feet with my arms behind my back. I waited with them in nervous confusion. Why had their master told them to stop? He'd led this group of adepts to the port. He had to be directing, or at least condoning, their hostility toward me.

Hell, what if he just wanted the fun for himself? With horror, I remembered how much he'd enjoyed abusing Verahl in the dungeon. Was I his next torture subject? The thought made me want to thrash again, but the blade at my throat kept me still.

Rapid footsteps approached, bringing the scent of cloves I'd come to associate with Master Ormyr. Something whipped through the air, followed by a lashing sound and a pained whimper. The blade left my neck, clattering to the pavement.

"We're entitled to revenge for our fallen!" an indignant voice behind me cried.

"And seek it we shall—from the Naustviks, the source of our pain," Ormyr proclaimed, standing directly in front of me. "Dame Jessamine's actions were never her own. Forget it one more time, and I shall see your heads on pikes!"

What the hell did he mean by that? Forget it, his pet theories didn't matter. Ormyr was my lone source of mercy, and thus Ingvar's only hope. I straightened my spine as tears slipped past my burning eyes. "Master," I addressed the darkness with all the strength I could summon, "Captain Leirfall's hurt. It could be serious. Please, may I—?"

"Worry not, Dame Jessamine." Ormyr's voice dropped to a murmur. "He's being conveyed to the keep this very moment."

The keep! What would they do there, light some incense while Ingvar slipped into shock? And that was if they were feeling charitable. The *dungeon* was part of the keep, too, after all. With blind panic, I struggled against my captors again.

The adepts held fast. A hand—most likely Ormyr's—braced my jaw.

"Dame Jessamine Irless of Freemont. I know some part of thee heedeth me still," Ormyr continued in an encouraging tone.

Some part? "What are you talking about?" I begged.

"From the moment of thine arrival, thou wert enthralled by the Naustviks, forced into their bidding," Ormyr explained with a note of pity. "Their snares then fell upon Captain Leirfall."

Terror and disbelief froze me in place. He thought Verahl and Thordia had been controlling our actions all this time? I supposed that *was* the case, but not in the way he believed.

"Take heart," Ormyr continued before I could deny it. "Freeing thee is no simple process, but I shall be thy guide. Focus upon my words and do as I ask. When the Naustviks compel thee to ignore me, resist them."

Ormyr's hand fell away. A second later, a blunt object clobbered my jaw.

Pain exploded across my face. I winced, head snapping sideways and knees buckling. My captors ensured I stayed upright.

"Focus. Use the pain to clear thy mind of all else," Ormyr said, calm as ever.

I quivered with fear and revulsion while my jaw throbbed in time with my racing heart. *This* was his idea of merciful aid? Did he also think he'd been "helping" Verahl in the dungeon? It seemed ever more likely that this was the sort of "treatment" Ingvar could look forward to if I failed to stop it.

"I must know whither Verahl now fleeth," Ormyr continued. "He cannot conceal it from thee. Envision his destination in thy mind's eye. Canst thou see it?"

What was my best course of action? Talk? Stall? Make something up? If it'd spare Ingvar —

A second smack on the jaw blew up the other side of my face, my punishment for hesitating. I cried out again.

Someone picked at the glove on my left hand, pulling it off. Another hand clamped down on my left wrist and brought it around my back, shoving my bare hand toward Ormyr.

Terrified at what amputations were to follow, I forced my eyes open and thrashed desperately. I had to escape; anywhere not full of burgundy specters would be a good start. The tears pouring down my face did nothing to clear away the blur that'd settled over my vision.

The tip of a blade settled on my palm, just under my thumb.

"What are you doing?" I blurted. "I'm Lord Catherwood's emissary!"

The blade pressed down, then dragged along in a slow crawl toward my pinky finger.

Searing pain followed. A yowl got away from me. "Stop!"

The adepts kept my hand in play. Warm blood pooled in my palm, dripping down the sides.

"We've all worried for thee and Captain Leirfall the past several days." Ormyr sounded every bit as concerned as he claimed.

"Please stop!" I hoped my cries might reach someone in attendance, make them intervene, but my captors were made of stone.

"Baron Tristan and I were aware all along of thine affliction," Ormyr continued. "There was no foretelling the awful things the Naustviks would compel thee to do. First was Verahl's escape from the dungeon. The next day, the Naustviks whisked thee to the dungeon and employed thy hands in the slaying of Adept Knorr." A hint of pain betrayed itself. "Then they sent thee and Captain Leirfall chasing after monsters and

Shipbuilder relics. And now Verahl hath taken all he could and cast you both aside like refuse."

His sympathy grated on my ear. I bit my bottom lip hard in a bid to remain silent.

The blade lifted, only to start another cut diagonal to the first, meandering across my palm for what felt like miles. I couldn't think past the pain.

"Focus, Lady Knight!" Ormyr implored. "Help me apprehend the fiends who've endangered thee so! Tell me where Verahl seeketh Thordia. I shall chase after them at once, and thou canst return to my keep and recuperate."

"I'll tell you! I'll tell you!" I cried against my will.

The blade lifted from my palm. "Go on."

In that moment of reprieve, I trembled, fighting hard to think. May and my mentors at the beguinage had taught me plenty with regard to resisting torture. Laughing, singing songs, babbling nonsense ... the most potent defense was to attach meaning to the pain, make it a sacrifice you'd be willing to endure.

What was I suffering for here? *Nothing.* This was a waste of time. So what were my options? Stay and bleed out? No. Lie about the Naustviks' location, get taken back to the keep? Ingvar and I would probably rot in the dungeon from there, and Nidaros and Drea would be lost. The only way to help them was to stop the ichor and recover my ship. That meant going to the Harbinger and finding the Naustviks before they got it in mind to flee the planet. The adepts' mounts stood to cover ground quickly. I'd still have to protect the Naustviks from the adepts somehow, but I could figure it out later.

Thus settled, I hoped for a mental boost against the pain, but found heartsick agony instead. Ingvar would have to be on his own for a while. I didn't know if I'd return in time to save him from death or torture.

Still—like Drea—he'd want me to put Nidaros first.

To put my plan in motion, I had to re-elevate myself in Ormyr's eyes, return to being someone he had to impress. My stomach turned, anticipating the groveling to follow. I went limp in the adepts' arms, screwing my eyes shut as though in the midst of some great mental struggle.

"I must travel with you. *Please*, Master!" I didn't have to fake the intensity of my plea. "I've been living a nightmare the past few days, and now that bastard's stolen my ship! This is personal!"

A suffocating pause followed.

"Could it be vengeance is a better focus for thee than pain?" Ormyr mused, then fell silent again.

My left hand burned and throbbed while blood dripped to the pavement. I shivered uncontrollably as the wait lengthened, debating whether to keep begging.

"Very well, Lady Knight," Ormyr finally said. "I welcome thy sword. Quickly now, where doth vengeance lie?"

I crumpled further with relief. It took several steadying breaths to work up the answer. "The Harbinger."

Dread frosted around my words and pulled the breath from the adepts' lungs. They stood frozen amid my blurry surroundings, their silence lasting an eternity.

"The Harbinger, damn it!" I shouted.

"Gunnhilda!" Ormyr barked. "Return to the capital and inform our Baron of our purpose. The rest of you, prepare to embark at once."

"Wha- what of the standing decree?" someone stammered. "The Harbinger means death, Master!"

"We shall return the saviors of Nidaros," Ormyr dismissed. "What should that decree mean to us?"

"Actually, Master, I- I'm not certain the stars are favorably aligned for such a venture."

My attention snapped toward the fearful, reluctant voice. *Holsten*, Madam Castor's suspected informant. Was he merely afraid of the Harbinger, or did he have other reasons for objecting?

"Then adjust thy reading," Ormyr snapped while approaching to within inches of my face. Fingers pried open the lids of my right eye.

Oh, hell, not my eyes! I flinched and let out a preemptive scream.

"Hold still," Ormyr muttered.

Drops of warm liquid fell into the eye under inspection, then the other. As I blinked away the solution, my vision cleared, and the pain in my eyes dissipated.

The master adept resolved before me, his usual smug demeanor now tinged with worry. He'd switched from a conventional adept robe to a more travel-friendly belted cloak, with trousers and boots peeking out beneath. Crossbow and drawstring bag hung at his waist. His long dark hair, streaked with the occasional silver defector, had been pulled back. From his jeweled right hand hung a glass dropper.

I'd spent the last few days dodging this man, only to learn I hadn't been as dodgy as I'd thought. While staring my comeuppance in the face, I fought back a rising nausea.

Ormyr's expression held nothing but care and concern, as though someone else had been torturing me earlier. The dropper vanished, another display of his grudgingly impressive sleight-of-hand. In its place appeared his keris dagger, its long wavy blade edged with blood — my blood.

My hand was visible, too, a painful and bloody mess.

"Better?" Ormyr asked.

I could only laugh, cracking the tear-tracks that'd hardened along my face.

Ormyr frowned, maybe suspecting the Naustviks' influence. The keris vanished behind his back. In its place, he produced bandages, then seized my left wrist.

"I have a salve that some adepts from Turinger space gave me," I said. In my first aid kit was a bottle of antiseptic.

Ormyr ignored me and took to wrapping my palm, somehow avoiding getting blood on himself.

Damn. I also would've wanted to check whether the cuts needed stitches. Oh well, at least this was better than nothing. The absence of ritual surprised me at first, but then I realized I didn't rate such treatment. This was probably in line with how he treated torture victims: stop the bleeding, come back later for more.

It was comforting, in a sick way. This was proof that just maybe, the adepts had enough sense to treat Ingvar properly — if they wanted to.

Once finished, Ormyr tied off the bandage and dismissed the adepts behind me. I swayed on my feet as my support retreated. Ormyr steadied me, then spun me around and brought my wrists together behind my back. Rope dug into my skin moments later.

"This isn't necessary," I objected.

"Worry not, Lady Knight. 'Tis simply precaution," Ormyr soothed. "We know not when the Naustviks' influence may overpower thee again."

Hell. It'd take forever to shake off that enthrallment nonsense. As he bound my wrists together, I wiggled my fingers, ensuring there was no numbness or tingling from decreased circulation.

"Move not thy hand overmuch," Ormyr cautioned. "The wounds need time to close."

He was right. Even if I were free, I wouldn't be using my left hand any time soon. At least it wasn't my dominant hand, and the risk of bleeding out had been reduced.

Ormyr braced my elbow. "Come."

I held my ground. "My sword?" Fortunately, I only needed one hand to wield it — assuming I ever got the chance again.

"It shall be brought to us." Ormyr pulled me along.

In his grasp, I stumbled toward his caravan of wooly ulldyr. A dozen adepts adjusted equipment and checked provisions—preparing for a journey to hell, if their expressions were any indication. I had no idea who'd been trying to exact revenge on me before Ormyr had intervened, and who hadn't. Many carried crossbows as Ormyr did, including Holsten, already atop his mount.

The breath caught in my throat upon seeing Holsten again. In the past, he'd been the one reduced to quivering at the sight of me despite all the "magic" at his disposal. He didn't seem to notice me then, as he was too busy leaning down to reassure several adepts who'd approached him. His positioning revealed his prematurely balding scalp and exaggerated the hunch in his back. A pendulum swayed from his fingers, as always—a *green* stone pendulum, like the fallen Lord Gyllenfeld's colors.

Son of a bitch, I thought. Maybe he really was a dissident, hiding in plain sight. Physical handicaps helped with that sort of thing. I hoped like hell that Pontus was taking advantage of the adepts' absence from the keep. Maybe he'd also hear about Ingvar while there.

But what difference would that make? Pontus would almost certainly leave Ingvar's care to the adepts. Would they throw him in the dungeon and be done with it, or would they check for signs of shock, halt bleeding wherever they found it? If he'd suffered a head injury, could they spot a concussion? And fractures … did they know how to set bones? What if they just sawed off whatever looked broken? Missing limbs would be devastating to a professional soldier …

I forced tears and horror aside, and desperately redirected my thoughts. Ulfarr and the other soldiers who'd been on watch in the port—were any of them still present? I glanced about, but found no trace of them among the wrecked ships and adept caravan. Was there any chance they'd seen what had happened and were off rallying help? A slim hope that soldiers would arrive to bust up this caravan, but a tempting one.

And what about Sigrid? If she'd gone to the keep, would she learn about what had happened? What kind of wrench might she throw in the works? Maybe she could do something for Pontus or Ingvar—assuming her loyalty to me outweighed her loyalty to Gyllenfeld. Another slim hope.

Thus distracted, I fell out of pace with Ormyr, who continued to guide me with the serenity of a man who could never be wrong.

"How did you know to find us here?" I blurted. Ormyr was under no obligation to tell me anything, much less the truth, but I couldn't help myself.

The master adept halted and turned toward me, reaching for the chain around my neck. At first I thought he was aiming for my mother's ring; painfully, I remembered that Ingvar had it. Instead, his fingers closed upon the mati amulet I'd forgotten about.

"Embedded within this amulet is Shipbuilder magic that behaveth as a silent witness, relaying images of events as they occur to a receiver relic within my calefactory. I have similar devices seated throughout the dungeon as well." Ormyr passed his thumb over the blue glass eye, then looked to me with determination. "I watched over thee and Captain Leirfall, able to see but not hear. When Verahl called you to himself, he betrayed his hiding place aboard thy vessel. I've mustered a force to confront him, and now, I shall chase him to the blackest corner of the planet."

A fresh wave of sick rage left me dumbstruck and lightheaded. I'd worn that damned mati for days without a thought, sometimes under my collar, sometimes out in the open. Ingvar had kept his on his belt. I'd never suspected they were any different than any other adept tokens, and felt betrayed by my own assumption. Surveillance technology wasn't unknown to me, but I hadn't expected it here. For such a small and remote barony, Nidaros was shockingly full of Shipbuilder artifacts.

The mati slipped from Ormyr's fingers, thumping against my chest. I stumbled backward. My worry and longing for Ingvar intensified, smarting almost as bad as my throbbing face and hand. There was one consolation: my faith in Ingvar had been justified. Ormyr's technology-aided snooping had tipped him off to Verahl's whereabouts. The soldiers were innocent.

Ormyr steadied me. "At first I believed it best to leave thee behind. Now, methinks 'tis safer for everyone if thou remainest close to me. As we ride, I shall bless and wish for thee —and Captain Leirfall." He gazed into the distance. "'Tis a long journey. Let us tarry no longer."

Days long, at least by foot. The ulldyr would shorten our travel time, but would it be enough to return to Ingvar before something terrible happened? When Ormyr tried resuming our walk, I resisted his pull. "Couldn't we fly to the Harbinger with the Baron's ship instead? It'd be much faster."

By the look on Ormyr's face, I might as well have suggested swimming to the nearest neighboring planet. "We mustn't risk the loss of our only remaining vessel."

But none of the adepts in your party can be trusted. Any of them might be Gyllenfeld dissidents. I stopped myself from saying it. He'd just think I was spouting off lies under the Naustviks' influence.

Railroaded in Catherwood space—again. Anxiety tightened inside my ribcage, crowding out my heart and lungs. I worried whether I'd ever see Ingvar or Drea alive again. I worried what would fill the hours, possibly days, ahead.

CHAPTER 8

Within the port, I found myself surrounded by adepts and their mounts as they prepared for a journey to the Harbinger. My left palm throbbed with raw pain, and my wrists were tied behind my back. After failing Ingvar, losing *Kepler's Law,* and being tortured by the adepts, I had trouble staying my feet. This was my reward for giving Verahl Naustvik the benefit of a doubt.

Ormyr steadied me, looking on with concern. The master adept believed I'd been enthralled by the Naustviks and could succumb to their influence at any time. Surely he also day-dreamed of the good things I'd tell Lord Catherwood about him once he lifted my "curse."

Another adept ran over to us, proffering my side sword. Ormyr stepped behind me and slid it into my baldric scabbard. "Courage, Lady Knight. Thou shalt soon have thy vengeance!"

I was glad he couldn't see my expression, because I didn't know how much pain and frustration came through. The adepts were my quickest route to the Harbinger, not that I had much choice in accompanying them. It was either this or the dungeon. Hopefully, cooperating and stroking Ormyr's ego would con-vince him I could be freed. Then I'd have to track down the

Naustviks, my ship, and anything that might spare Nidaros from the ichor. All the while, I'd agonize over Ingvar and Drea, my loved ones languishing without anyone to help them.

Ormyr grasped my elbow and pulled me toward the only ulldyr that hadn't been mounted yet. The wooly animal resembled a bison, but had a horse's slim profile. On its back was an embroidered blanket. Packs of provisions had already been hitched in place. There was no hint of a saddle.

"I don't have much riding experience," I said. Every planet had their own favored mounts, bred over time to excel at whatever purpose they served. It was hard to gain proficiency with them all, and not much use when one owned a ship—or *had* owned a ship. *Verahl, damn you to hell,* I thought.

"Worry not, our mounts are well trained." Ormyr boosted me onto the ulldyr's back, then climbed on to sit in front of me.

The ulldyr didn't seem to mind the extra weight of two adult riders. I dug in with my thighs to stay balanced, longing to use my hands as well. That wasn't happening, but at least I could gently press my right hand against my left palm to assess its condition. The bandage felt dry, a welcome sign that bleeding was under control. Neither numbness nor tingling had set in, meaning circulation wasn't impeded.

Though the sun had risen since my and Ingvar's ill-fated run to the port, it was still early morning. I didn't know how long this journey would take mounted, but no one had skimped on supplies. Anywhere from hours to days seemed possible. I braced myself for the higher estimate, dearly hoping it'd prove shorter.

The other adepts exchanged worried, dreadful glances as they waited on us.

Once ready, Ormyr spurred our mount to a smooth trot, similar to what a gaited horse could do. Jolting stayed to a minimum, fortunate for my balance and the injuries I'd racked up.

The other adepts followed wordlessly. Behind us, the port became an empty graveyard again.

We rode back toward the capital gate, which stood closed and deserted. Ingvar must've been carried through there en route to the keep, and the soldiers on watch had probably insisted on escorting him. The scene played out in my mind, making my heart ache along with everything else. I had no idea how badly Ingvar was hurt, or whether the adepts only intended to add to his suffering.

Hang on until I can get back, I urged mentally.

Ormyr turned down the worn road leading away from the capital. Ingvar and Drea fell even further out of reach. If I lost them, as I'd lost Branigan …

My throat tightened. Hell, I couldn't bear to think down that path. To prevent the slow slide into misery, I sat up straight, pretending to be less a captive and more an integral member of the party. I'd still save my loved ones and the barony, just not quite the way I'd intended. *Side-steps,* as May used to say.

Guilt hovered at the fringe of my manufactured confidence, rattling the shackles of blame. Normally it would've barged through unchallenged, but Ingvar's words from the night before thwarted it. Granted, I'd misread Verahl, but *he* was the one who'd snapped and decided Ingvar couldn't be trusted. This wasn't my fault. All the same, I ached to set things right. For the moment, I'd have to be patient and watch for my chance.

The capital vanished behind us. In every direction stretched hilly brown prairie. We stuck to the roads, but took a different path from the one Ingvar and I had taken to the Low North district the night before. While Ormyr and I rode at the procession's head, the other dozen or so adepts hung back in clumps, some hooded against the sun. Their anxious whispering betrayed their reluctance.

Wariness had me glancing over my shoulder frequently. The rough treatment I'd received all morning made clear that at least some, if not all, of those adepts wanted me dead. Even Master Ormyr would think nothing of killing me if he could jam the deed amid one of the gaps in his personal mythos.

On Ormyr's back, I could plainly see the sheath holding his keris, the dagger he'd tortured me with. He was the last person in the galaxy I felt like talking to. Still, I had to reinforce my standing as an accomplished knight errant and Lord Catherwood's trusted agent. A fictional standing, but far better than the helpless thrall. Once we returned to equal footing, I could warn him about his subordinates.

Swallowing my disgust, I summoned an air of courage. "Master? Thanks for your intervention. It's been a horrible past few days."

"I can only imagine," Ormyr replied with the appropriate gravity, still facing forward. "I caught up with thee none too soon, Lady Knight. Any later, and thou might've been lost for good."

I nodded, even though he couldn't see it. "I told you when I first got here, I trust Catherwood rites dearly. I do, I truly do." In theory, Ormyr's rites should've kept me from ever being enthralled in the first place, but mentioning as much wouldn't help.

"Hold fast to thy trust." Ormyr sounded pleased. "Do precisely as I ask. Once the Naustviks lie dead, thou shalt be free."

Dead? Hell, my "thrall" label wasn't budging anytime soon. Maybe playing to his ambitions would help him overlook it. "I'll put in a good word for you in Spectra, supposing we make it back. Unseen willing," I remembered to tack on. "Lord Catherwood's cloister can always use more gifted magic-wielders."

Ormyr fell silent for several moments. "Nidaros is my native soil. I'm content with my standing here, but ultimately, I go where the Unseen require."

And if they insist on you being a big somebody back in Spectra, so be it, I finished mentally for him. "Is there anything I can do that might break this enthrallment faster?"

"Wishing would make a good start," he replied. "Though thou dost not carry beads, the Unseen shall note thy sincerity."

His phrasing carried a possible challenge. After all, since I'd claimed such faith in Catherwood dogma, where *were* my beads? Not that I was in any position to grab them, but still.

I thought fast. "I was traveling through Lagana space just before receiving this quest. It's not smart to flout Catherwood trappings there."

I honestly had flown through Lord Lagana's territory on the way to Catherwood's. While there, I'd learned of Catherwood's ongoing tensions with them. Their physical proximity sparked trade guild disputes, feuds between noble families, and the occasional border skirmish. I had no idea what, if anything, had started their bickering. It also wasn't clear whether it'd go on simmering like this or escalate into all-out war someday.

Their closeness also exaggerated the minor differences in their dogma. Lagana's people believed in the same Unseen, but appeased them with sacrifices and read their fortunes in fire. Catherwood wishing beads would stick out like a sore thumb there, drawing unwanted attention.

Ormyr seemed to accept my explanation. "I shall leave thee to thy contemplation."

Though I wanted to keep chipping at Ormyr's distrust, I had to remain silent while he expected me to be wishing. The process seemed to involve speaking to the Unseen mentally, similar to the prayer I'd been taught growing up in Lord Turinger's space. Those desperate pleas hadn't saved my family's inn from greedy adepts or saved my mother from dying, and they weren't about to save me here. I struggled to ignore the pain in my hand and push back the awful worry for Ingvar and Drea that was always there, threatening to consume me. Despair wouldn't save us, either.

Miles of countryside streamed past, surprisingly free from hazards. I wondered if the wild predators Ingvar and I had defended against were nocturnal. As the morning sun rose higher, so did our procession, up a long and gentle slope. Between the ulldyr's natural padding and smooth gait, the ride was as comfortable as I could hope for.

Ormyr's posture never flagged. Meanwhile, his trailing adepts hunched ever lower in their saddles.

When we reached the peak of a tall hill, Ormyr brought our mount to a halt. His arms twitched, their maneuvers hidden to me.

"Lady Knight, look now to the horizon," he bade with the same caution of someone creeping up on a sleeping bear.

I leaned sideways to glance past his shoulder. Misty and surreal on the horizon, an enormous axle jutted from the ground like a splintered onyx spike. Around its middle hovered an equally massive ring with no visible support structure to explain what held it in place. The whole assembly resembled a top leaning on its side.

The Harbinger. I gasped in shock and lost my balance. Digging in with my thighs saved me from falling off the ulldyr.

It should've burned up while plummeting through the atmosphere. Somehow, the massive Harbinger had survived to haunt Nidaros ever since. I'd read about orbital stations like these at the beguinage, but had never dreamed of seeing one—intact upon on a planet's surface, no less. A veritable Shipbuilder time capsule. Any other day or circumstance, I would've been half out of my mind with excitement. Right then, a hundred tormenting thoughts drowned out all hint of awe. What I wouldn't have given to be there with Ingvar and Drea instead. Hell, even May!

"I sense fear in thy silence." Ormyr glanced sideways, splitting his attention between me and the specter ahead. "'Tis an encouraging sign. The Naustviks' influence is weakening."

I nodded, pretending to relief at this bit of progress. "Do you know what we're up against in there? Is anything still intact—I mean, *alive?*"

Ormyr returned his attention to the horizon. "In the three generations since its appearance, none have approached the Harbinger and returned to tell thereof. None who've so tempted death were adepts of the arcane, however. We've studied closely the Shipbuilders and their relics. With that, our magic, and the Unseen's aid, we shall prevail."

The other adepts crowded nearby seemed less convinced, clutching their beads in white-knuckled hands. I was with them. Their lore could be pure fabrication, or fabrication with a grain of truth to it. There'd be no way to know until we needed it for something.

"Unseen, abide!" Holsten raised his voice. He'd gathered the most nervous of the group to lead them in an invocation. "Upon Death shall we unite, until our next purpose—"

"Holsten!" Ormyr glared at his second. "There shall be no new dead today!"

The targets of his reassurance flinched and wilted.

I bit back revulsion. Holsten's invocation was the same one I'd first read in Gules, written on a parchment scrap clutched in a woman's fist—a woman who'd frozen to death, likely hoping for that "next purpose" all the while. Unlike them, I didn't believe in reincarnation. Lying down and welcoming death? It seemed like a tragic, insane waste of the only life we knew we had.

Ormyr spurred our ulldyr to the hill's crest. The other side of the hill dropped steeply and leveled off at a fraction of the height we'd ascended. There sprawled another district similar to the Low North: meandering paths, thatch-roof houses, fallow plots. Glittering charms attracted sunlight, but nothing that might dispel the ichor lurking beneath the surface. Residents, wan and slow, lugged pails and kindling as though they weighed tons.

"The people need our blessing!" someone blurted behind us.

"We are but passing through," Ormyr objected.

One of the other adepts surged past us, waving to those below. His example inspired others to follow suit. Together, they edged down the hill.

"Very well," Ormyr called after them as though he'd ordered their descent all along. "See what provisions they might offer in exchange!"

I stifled my amusement. Friend or foe, it was irrelevant. They were probably tired of hearing "no" all the time, and welcomed the chance to stall given what lay ahead.

Ormyr and I waited alone atop the hill. Below, those who noticed the adepts' approach halted in their tracks, overjoyed at first. Then their faces fell. Maybe they'd believed the adepts had brought an extra allotment of food, but with no carts in sight, that clearly wasn't the case. Once over their disappointment, though, they brightened again. Most of the adepts left their mounts, exchanging hugs with the people who ran up to them. They might've made friends during all their trips to disburse rations. Some might've even grown up in this district.

I wondered why Ormyr held back. "You're not going to bless anyone yourself, Master?"

"I can better observe from here," he replied.

With that, I realized *I* was the one he wanted to keep an eye on. He probably didn't want to endanger the townspeople by bringing a "thrall" among them. A prudent move, if you believed in that sort of thing—and most people in the galaxy did.

The adepts who'd dismounted were literally pulled around to hold their beads and murmur over empty plots of land, sick people, and stubborn wounds. While Ormyr's head remained tilted toward the activity below, my eyes strayed toward the Harbinger again. Not knowing how far away we were, I had no concept of its size other than immense, rivaling a mountain. How the hell would we find a single woman—and a man and a stolen ship—amid that?

Something to worry about once we got riding again. In the meantime, I reluctantly considered how to resume my talk with Ormyr. Even as the other adepts' dread had melted into warmth, their menace had intensified in my eyes. They clearly didn't want to travel any farther. Some or all were dissidents, loyal to the memory of Lord Gyllenfeld. Ormyr didn't trust me yet, but I had to see if he shared any of my suspicion.

"Master?" I leaned forward, speaking as though we discussed private matters all the time. "Before you stopped them, some of your adepts attacked me at the port. I couldn't see well at the time. Who were they?"

"'Twas a mistake that shan't be repeated," Ormyr reassured me. "Prithee think no more thereof."

"But it *was* repeated," I replied. "Another group of adepts tried to root me out of the barracks this morning."

Ormyr turned my way sharply. This information seemed new to him, but whether he believed me was another matter.

"You've been concerned with the threat posed by dissidents," I continued. "Maybe they want me dead not just to avenge Adept Knorr, but also because they secretly hate Lord Catherwood. I'm his emissary, after all."

He met my gaze with a firm one of his own. "There are no dissidents in my cloister. I trained them myself."

Trained them how? Hurled a scroll at them and left the room? Holsten had always seemed more patient and nurturing than he.

"But some of your adepts had family members who were dissidents, didn't they?" I asked. "*Had* being the important word there." Like Holsten's parents, according to Sigrid.

Ormyr blinked and shrank, as though fearing the accusation I might level at him.

"I think it was good of you and the Baron and Ing- Captain Leirfall not to hold that against them," I hastened to add. "I'm sure in most cases, it's worked out in everyone's favor. But, don't you think it's possible — ?"

"Yea, of course!" Ormyr snapped, facing forward again. "I was no supporter of the mercy afforded them! After years away from Nidaros, I returned with Baron Tristan's retinue, only to be welcomed with fire and scythes. How was I to forget that?" Bitterness and pain leaked from his voice. "I sense the resentment lingering yet, ever festering in these districts — but not among *my* ranks. If it were there, I would've uprooted it."

"Your adepts don't want to be here and don't seem to like us much," I pressed. "We might be in a lot of trouble."

"I'm surprised the Naustviks haven't made thee to think we're *all* thine enemy," Ormyr dismissed. "Focus upon thy coming vengeance, and keep wishing for the Unseen's favor."

I stifled a frustrated reply. As I'd feared, anything he didn't want to hear was the product of enthrallment. How would I ever reach him? With the Harbinger still distant, I hoped I'd have time to figure it out.

-ᴎᴧ-

The adepts would've stayed to bless a thousand generations of farmers had Ormyr not finally ridden down and herded them on. Some carried back water that'd been gifted to them; if any had received extra food, they didn't mention it. We got going again when the sun had reached its zenith in the sky. The day was half over.

There were no more paths to follow. Everything of interest taunted us from the horizon: patches of forest, and of course the Harbinger. Ormyr resumed a confident lead through the dry grassland, seemingly untouched by anything I'd brought up.

I continued sneaking glances at the trailing adepts. They'd left their good moods behind in the district. Some rode alone, fidgeting or lost in thought. Most huddled in groups of flexible membership. Holsten seemed the most mobile, always whispering with someone new.

Paranoia raised my hackles. They seemed to be planning something, but there was no use telling Ormyr.

After the district, our progress was frequently disrupted by swarms of sverma — the dog-sized, insect-like creatures that'd attacked me and Ingvar on our way to the Naustviks' house. Though the adepts gave them a wide berth, several curious sverma broke from their formations and bounded after us. Fortunately, the adepts dispatched them with crossbows well before they reached our caravan. Impressively, Ormyr never missed a shot. While a crossbow was easier to handle than a bow, shooting from a mounted position added its own difficulties. I wondered whether Ingvar had any such training. Had he trained Ormyr?

In between attacks stretched quiet spells. I couldn't stomach talking to Ormyr. My legs became increasingly sore from maintaining balance on the ulldyr, my wrists chafed under the rope, and my nagging left shoulder returned to prominence, becoming a match for my left hand. I experimented with various ways of repositioning myself, but over time, relief became fleeting. I tried to focus on the Harbinger as it grew larger on the horizon, imagining what might've survived the impact and centuries of neglect. Still, nothing made up for Drea remaining stuck in Gules' harsh winter. And Ingvar — was he chained up in a dungeon cell, about to lose limbs, sanity, or life itself?

Grief lodged deep inside my chest. It should've been me and Ingvar exploring the Harbinger. We could've gotten right to work on saving Nidaros without any dangerous nonsense in the way. I could've taught him more about the Shipbuilders and their knowledge, too — after thanking him for his unwavering support and confessing the depth of my feelings for him.

Tears burned the backs of my eyes before rolling down my face. It was mostly Verahl's fault, but Ormyr had also played a huge part in this awful turn of events. He was right there ahead of me, the bastard, still parading me around like some sort of trophy. I slumped ever lower, but still did my damnedest not to lean against my riding partner for support.

Along with pain, hunger and thirst became more scathing by the hour. A cigarillo could take the edge off, but they were in my coat pocket. Inches away, completely out of reach. I would've traded the whole Harbinger to move my arms again …

"Clear terrain at last! Let us rest here."

I bolted upright, snapping out of a stupor I hadn't realized I'd fallen into. Had Ormyr actually called out to his men, or had I imagined it? How long had we been traveling? To my shock, the sun had descended more than halfway toward the horizon. A break was dearly welcome. Apparently, Ormyr didn't think sverma would be a problem on this empty stretch of prairie.

Behind us, the other adepts gladly dismounted and gave their ulldyr a chance to graze. Once we halted, Ormyr eased me to the ground. My legs felt numb and weak, and it took some time before I felt blood coursing through them again. It was unspeakably satisfying.

"Could you untie me for a little while, Master?" The question escaped past my resentment. "My arms need a break, too."

Ormyr studied my eyes, probably wondering who was asking: I, or the thrall. Finally, he turned me around and untied the rope. "I'll have to bind thee again ere we resume," he cautioned under his breath.

I almost didn't hear him past my immense relief. I rolled my arms and shoulders slowly, careful not to make any worrying movements. My wrists were red and sore. I flexed my right hand as blood returned to my fingers; my left hand had to remain still. Fortunately, I'd never bled through Ormyr's wrappings. Less fortunately, I couldn't dig through my first aid kit for painkillers without inviting unwanted questions. I opted for a consolation prize, pulling cigarillos from my coat pocket.

"Want a smoke?" I didn't want to share, but it'd be helpful to buy favor any way I could.

Still watching me carefully, Ormyr dismissed my offer with a wave of his hand.

With my teeth assisting, I extracted a cigarillo one-handed. Lighting the thing would be harder, since I couldn't use my stick lighter around Ormyr. Though I carried a tinderbox, it required the use of two hands.

The glow of fire nearby drew my attention. Without any prompting, Ormyr had conjured and lit a match. He cupped a hand around the flame and proffered it my way.

"Thanks." I got the cigarillo going, then took a mouth-filling draw. It didn't solve any problems, but provided a sorely needed morale boost all the same.

I didn't expect any more mercy from Ormyr—yet he also split his rations with me, unbidden. The dried leaves and stems, softened with water, didn't sate my hunger, but I was still appreciative. As we sat on the ground together, the other adepts threw us an occasional wary look, still keeping their distance.

"Dost thou fare any better?" Ormyr never strayed from arm's length, watching my every move.

"Yes." It wasn't a total lie. "How much farther?"

"Another couple of hours, by my reckoning. We should arrive before nightfall."

I brightened even more at the answer, then realized I had a lot of thinking to do. How would I keep the adepts from attacking the Naustviks on sight? What other difficulties might arise within the Harbinger? At that point, it was impossible to know.

Ormyr, however, looked sullen. "Our peril shall increase from here. The Harbinger's arrival corrupted the land for miles around."

I nodded—agreeing, not just humoring him. The Harbinger's landing would've been like a meteorite crashing into the surface of Nidaros. It must've been horribly violent.

Ormyr bound my wrists again once our break was over. I still couldn't say I was glad to be traveling with him, but at least I was feeling a little better.

Surprisingly, the ulldyr seemed content enough with their brief rest to continue at the same pace. As we pressed on, the sun sank toward the horizon, and the Harbinger sneaked closer like a predator slipping up on its prey.

Before I could start thinking about how to play things at our destination, fist- and head-sized rocks cropped up amid the grasses, forcing the ulldyr to veer around them. Ahead, another district appeared in the distance, one that seemed to sprawl endlessly. The houses were deformed, some much taller than others.

Strange. Every building I'd seen in Nidaros was single-story, with the exception of the Shipbuilder structures in the capital.

The grass gave way to smooth, sandy grit that bore no tracks. No one had ventured through here recently, or maybe ever. Larger rocks appeared, sporting veins of glass and crystal that gleamed in the waning sunlight.

Wait, that was *volcanic* rock. Where had it possibly come from? It must've been ejecta from the Harbinger's landing. The abandoned station had crashed into the rocky ground with enough energy to melt it, and had sent that melted debris flying everywhere. But we were still hours—and thus miles—from the Harbinger. The ejecta had flown that far?

Then I realized, that wasn't a district up ahead. It was a dense grouping of house-sized *boulders*.

The thought of such huge rocks flying miles through the air was insane and terrifying. Even as we approached the evidence, I couldn't picture it. Still trailing behind me and Ormyr, the other adepts had gone silent. It felt like we were approaching a cemetery.

We soon came upon the largest boulders. They towered over our heads, casting long, demented shadows over the ground. A wind kicked up and threw dust into our faces. Loose hair whipped into my eyes, defying my efforts to shake it away.

Ormyr guided our mount through gaps between the rocks while clenching the beads on his belt. "A district once stood here," he said grimly.

My jaw dropped in surprise. Our surroundings resembled the surface of a lifeless moon.

"When the Harbinger first appeared, it brought with it the fiery wrath of a sun," Ormyr continued. "The land quaked in fear. A great wind swept away whatever hadn't been shaken to its core. Then, these great stones rained down from the sky for miles in all directions."

This was similar to what Ingvar and Dag had told me, but hearing it while witnessing the aftermath left a knot in my stomach. Unbidden, my brain worked through what must've happened there decades earlier: people burned alive in the radiant heat, crushed under collapsing houses and ejecta, blown away by a violent air blast. And those were the lucky ones. Anyone who'd sought shelter had probably roasted alive inside it.

"The worst thing was that no adept foresaw the Harbinger's arrival." Ormyr steered around a tiny patch of grass daring to push up out of the rubble.

I couldn't speak around the lump in my throat. Who could've known when and how the Harbinger's orbit would decay? This tragedy had been completely unpreventable — and inescapable.

"Will- will you be paying respects here, Master?"

I bit back a gasp at the sound of a familiar voice, closer than it'd been in hours, and glanced in its direction. Holsten had pulled up beside us — head sunk between his shoulders, eyes flitting about in search of a threat.

"'Tis mine intent," Ormyr replied, not bothering to mask his annoyance. "None hath ventured here in my tenure. We shan't tarry long, however. I wish to reach the Harbinger ere nightfall."

"I- yes, Master." Holsten blanched and hastened forward, overtaking us.

Several other adepts followed his lead, streaming past without a glance in my or Ormyr's direction. They seemed eager to push through this stone graveyard as fast as possible.

Before I could imagine what sort of respects Ormyr might pay there, *something* pressed into my gloved right hand, still bound behind my back. In surprise, my half-numb fingers almost fumbled it, but I managed to hold on. It was hard and smooth, familiar somehow. A little more probing told me that I now held a dagger.

My hooded benefactor, slight of build, rode on without looking back. If Ormyr had noticed the transaction, he gave no sign.

A surge of adrenaline got my heart pounding. I grasped the hilt in my fist and contemplated the gesture. Was I supposed to free myself? And then what, escape? Attack Ormyr?

I glanced forward and back. The adepts had divided themselves, and both formations seemed to be tightening around us.

This reeked of a set-up. Whatever was to follow, I wanted my hands free for it. Ormyr had tied a figure eight around my wrists to bind my hands beside one another. I contorted the dagger to saw into the middle of the eight, then leaned forward and spoke in a hushed tone. "Master, your men are surrounding us. This looks like an ambush."

Ormyr was unfazed. "They are but forming a protective circle, Lady Knight."

"After a whole day lagging behind, they suddenly have a protective streak?" I challenged.

"The danger here is far greater than any realm through which we previously traveled."

Even when sverma were after us? I thought, but didn't bother to say it. He'd just think I was falling under "enthrallment" again. All I could do was keep watch—and keep sawing at the rope. I tried to slow my racing heart with deep breaths, but didn't have much success.

We rode toward what I assumed to be a memorial: a circular mound of dirt almost as large as one of the district's houses might've been. Unfinished stones of varying sizes stood along its circumference. Tracks told of how the monument builders had dragged over the most convenient slabs, then gotten the hell out of there. A faded, scorched banner fluttered from one of the stones, displaying an open white hand on a green background.

Lord Gyllenfeld's seal. It seemed we were the first visitors in decades.

Ormyr bore down on the banner like an unanswered insult. Once he'd steered us astride of it, he leaned over to pick up the fist-sized rock holding it in place. He drew his keris next, then sliced down the fabric, rending the white hand in half between the fingers. As the banner's remains fell to the ground, Ormyr cut a strip of burgundy and gold embroidery from the hem of his own robe, which he posted in the banner's place. That done, he lowered his head over his beads.

The long shadows of dusk enshrouded us. Another breeze stirred amid the silence. While cutting through my bonds, I kept watch on the other adepts. They maintained their distance, but had formed a loose circle around us. Several hands rested upon crossbows. When they weren't trading nervous looks, they threw murderous glances at Ormyr, as though he'd desecrated their mothers' graves.

Chills ran down my spine. "Master, I'm serious. We'd better punch through an opening now, or they'll have us."

No reaction from Ormyr, not even to scoff or dismiss.

"Master!"

An adept directly ahead of us—one of the first adepts to overtake us initially—broke from the formation, spurring his mount toward us with fear in his eyes.

"Master, you're in danger!" he cried. "They want to force —"

All around us, adepts hefted their crossbows. Instinctively, I leaned forward and shoved Ormyr from behind, bending him toward the ulldyr's neck.

Bolts whizzed through the space our heads had once occupied. At least one of them struck our ulldyr, which bucked and threw us off.

My hands weren't free yet, and couldn't break my fall. I cried out and dropped helplessly, eventually landing on my left side. Pain ripped through my already sore thigh and shoulder. As my skull bounced off the rocky ground, the dagger jolted out of my hands.

I lay there, stunned, while the world slid in and out of focus. Ormyr lay ahead of me, his back facing me as it had all day. Our mount tore off in a frenzy, heading deeper into the ruined district.

The warning adept's mount took off in the opposite direction. Its rider lay motionless a few feet away, bolt lodged in his chest.

"*Mir!*" Holsten screamed. In the distance, he scrambled to dismount from his own ulldyr.

The other adepts encircling us froze at this turn of events.

My brain felt like it was rattling inside my skull. I couldn't move. Ormyr remained motionless, too.

Get up, I urged myself. *Get up or you're both dead.*

But the other adepts behaved as though we were already no longer a concern. All eyes tracked Holsten as he hobbled over and dropped to his knees before Mir.

"Unseen. He's dead," Holsten pronounced a moment later.

"Slethi! You fool!" The accusation leapt from the circle, voiced by an unknown adept.

"It wasn't me!" a third voice answered. "Lafi must've done it!"

"Shut up! I would've hit Ormyr square-on if Mir hadn't … Unseen, why'd he do that?"

The dagger. Where was it? I rolled onto my angry left shoulder. My view shifted toward the darkening sky, away from the adepts. For an agonizing eternity, the fingers of my right hand probed through the dirt. It had to be close.

"It … it was me." Another voice confessed, then faltered. "I was aiming for—"

"Enough!" Holsten cut him off.

"I'm sorry!" The voice broke down into tears. "I didn't mean to!"

The dagger lay out of reach. Probably for the best; I wasn't feeling very coordinated. Was there any chance I could snap the remaining rope myself?

"The betrayer got what he deserved." The voice that'd answered to the name Lafi chimed back in.

"How dare you say that!" Holsten cried out, as pained as though he'd been the one shot.

"You can't avoid violence forever, Holsten," Lafi returned. "Blood must be shed for the cause!"

"No. We're above that."

I pulled hard against the rope's remains, and they gave. Galvanized, I rolled onto my stomach and pushed myself up to my knees. A wave of dizziness assaulted me, which I struggled to ignore. The dagger rested a few feet away. I seized it. Both hilt and blade were simple, familiar ...

It was *mine*.

How had it gotten there? I recalled surrendering the dagger, but couldn't remember the when or why. With survival at stake, I'd have to piece it together later. Unsteadily, I lunged toward Ormyr, who had yet to move. My bandaged left hand remained unusable. I looped my right arm through his and hauled him up to a seat. "Come on, we have to hide!"

The memorial in front of us didn't make good cover. The gaps between stones were too large, and the adepts had us surrounded. Our best prospect lay ten or so yards behind us, outside the adepts' formation: a cluster of boulders tall enough to cover standing humans.

Ormyr yielded to my pull and rose to his feet as I stood — fortunate, because I lacked the wits to argue with him. "Hide" was the most sophisticated plan I could muster at the moment.

"Lower your weapon! I said we're leaving them here!" Holsten cried, frantic. "They'll expire in time, Unseen willing."

Just as I pulled us behind cover, a crossbow bolt pinged off our rocky shield. I ignored it to settle Ormyr on the ground against one of the boulders. He sat up without assistance, but stared out at oblivion. A crossbow bolt stuck out of his thigh.

"Damn it," I whispered, my stomach dropping.

I couldn't treat him yet, not while the other adepts could storm around our cover and end us at any time. For some reason, Holsten wasn't having it. I left Ormyr to return to the nearest boulder edge, chancing a look back. The traitors remained in their ambush circle. Holsten was visible inside the ring of monument stones, hunched beside Mir.

Ormyr pushed himself up to kneel beside me.

"Stay put," I told him. "Leave that bolt where it is." With all the big veins and arteries in the legs, it was easy to bleed out from such wounds.

He swayed, but otherwise held still.

"Listen," another adept spoke, nervous. "I've never cared for Master Ormyr, but I'm not comfortable with killing him, either."

"Me either. I thought we were just going to leave them here!"

A chorus of affirmations followed.

"There's no guarantee we'll be rid of them that way!" a different voice protested.

"The Unseen are with us! Isn't that enough?" Holsten struggled to his feet, scowling. "Now, let's round up the ulldyr and leave."

The adept hefting his crossbow jumped down from his mount.

"I said *leave them*, Lafi!" Holsten darted toward the dissenting adept and tried to pull him back.

Lafi easily shook him off to advance in the direction where Ormyr and I hid. No one else tried stopping or calling after him. Some waited nervously. Others wound beads around their hands, shaking with repressed sobs.

I sheathed my dagger in favor of my side sword. Lafi would have to round the corner to reach us. Once he did, I was determined to give him hell.

However, the aggressive adept only managed a few steps toward us before he flinched and staggered with a yelp of surprise, grasping at the back of his head.

I missed what had happened. So had most of the adepts, who exchanged confused glances. Only one adept seemed to know what was going on. He or she had a knapsack on his back and a slingshot in hand, and sat atop an ulldyr a short distance from Lafi. A second later, the adept slipped from his or her mount, sprinted toward Lafi, then tackled him from behind.

Lafi ate dirt, crossbow skidding out of his grasp. The mystery adept pinned him to the ground and pummeled the back of his head with a fist wrapped in beads. Lafi screamed and bucked to no avail.

The hood covering the mystery adept's face fell askew. Twilight revealed a familiar young face set with fierce purpose.

"Dag?" I blurted.

Well, that explained how my dagger had resurfaced. I'd given it to Dag after Ingvar and I had saved him from the monstrous vinrake in the Naustviks' house. But how the hell had Dag ridden all this way with us undetected?

Dag leapt to his feet with an expression proclaiming that he'd thrash the rest of the adepts just as easily and enjoy it. While Lafi remained dazed or unconscious on the ground, Dag backed away in the direction where Ormyr and I sat in cover.

The other adepts were stunned, but their hesitation wasn't sure to last. Dag needed help, that was all I thought of. I darted out into the open and ran toward him.

"Stop him!" someone cried.

"Forget it!" Holsten shouted. "Grab Lafi and let's go!"

Several crossbows went up in spite of Holsten's order.

Dag backed up faster, glancing left and right. I darted ahead of him to push him back toward my hiding spot, shielding him with my body along the way. Bolts whizzed past us.

"*Skíta!*" Dag cried.

"*Stop!*" Holsten pleaded.

However, the adepts who'd shot at us were already reloading their crossbows. The other adepts hung back uncertainly.

Dag slipped in front of me, rummaging through his pocket to produce the light tile he'd taken from the Naustviks' basement.

Before he had a chance to use it, explosions erupted around the adepts, releasing clouds of thick smoke. Their coughs mingled with the sounds of their ulldyr bucking and circling in panic.

As I stood dumbstruck, staring at the unexplained spectacle, Dag activated his tile. Bright light burst from it, which he directed toward the tumult.

"Fall back!" Ormyr shouted.

I turned, surprised to hear him so close behind me. In defiance of my request to stay put, the master adept stood there in a guarded stance, his expression darkly determined. One hand hovered over his head, clutching several small smoke bombs. No crossbow; he'd probably lost it when the ulldyr had thrown us.

When I hesitated, Ormyr seized my arm with his free hand, tugging backward.

I shook him off and faced forward again. The light from Dag's tile danced amid the smoke Ormyr had deployed, creating eerie specters that further startled the adepts. I tucked my blade under my left arm, grabbed Dag's elbow, *then* fell back.

"Home! Now!" Holsten's voice rose above the mess.

No one disobeyed this order. Someone whisked Lafi from the ground. As the smoke dissipated, the adepts stampeded away.

"Aye, that's right! Run, bastards!" Dag was so jubilant, he tolerated my grip all the way back behind the boulders. Once there, though, he shook me off like my hand was made of spiders, then shut off his light tile.

Leaning against the rock, Ormyr watched his caravan flee without him, hiding his reaction.

I dropped my side sword to the ground and fell to my knees beside it, even though our trouble had only begun. My spinning head throbbed along with my left hand and shoulder. We were in a dire mess, but I had no way of reasoning out of it just then.

The ulldyr's hoofbeats faded into the distance. As the sun set, silence and shadow reclaimed the former district. A cold wind brought over trace amounts of the irritant Ormyr had cast, enough to sting my eyes and nostrils. Dag doubled over, coughing hard.

Worry cut through the fog in my brain. "Master, what was that stuff?"

Ormyr continued to stare out at nothing. His distracted reply took a moment to deliver. "It shall dissipate."

Shakily, I hauled myself up to approach Dag, looking for signs of an allergic reaction. He cleared his throat and straightened with narrowed eyes, discouraging me from getting any closer.

I relented, but couldn't stifle my curiosity. "How the hell did you get here?"

Dag brushed away the water streaming from his eyes with the back of his hand. "Heard Verahl was in trouble. Followed you and Captain Leirfall to the port. The adepts came in right behind me, so I hid." He glared toward Ormyr. "Convinced an adept to switch places with me. He was only too glad not to have to come out here."

"That was stupid," I blurted, then sighed. "And much appreciated."

"We're still going to find Verahl and Thordia, aye?" Dag urged under his breath.

"Yes, but not yet. Master Ormyr's hurt." I just hoped blood loss wasn't making Ormyr go into shock. While not in the best shape myself, I was the only qualified healer among us, which helped me focus. I approached the master adept, gently detaching him from his vantage point. "Let me have a look at your leg."

"Ye're helping him!" Dag cried in astonishment. "After what he did to you at the port?"

"I don't turn my back on anyone I can help," I replied.

Dag held silent. He was surely scowling at me, but I couldn't see it and didn't care. With my right arm, I lowered Ormyr to a seat against the rock again. His limbs obeyed, but he seemed absent mentally, eyes glazed over. I learned the hard way that he was still paying attention when his hand darted to the bolt in his thigh. He tore it out with one swift movement.

"Damn it!" I cried. It just figured he wouldn't listen. This bit of stubbornness might've cost him his life. Heart pounding and hands shaking, I dug into my first aid kit for bandages.

"I'm uninjured." Ormyr rested his head against the rock.

"I don't need your denial on top of everything else," I snapped, struggling to rein in my irritation. That, plus the fog and the dizziness? Not good signs, but I couldn't worry about myself just then. "Dag, turn on that light again. I can't see too well."

"*Gamla skíta*," Dag spat. "I'm not helping him!"

"No, you're not. You're *showing him the power the Naustviks gave you.*" There. Something to appeal to the kid's bravado and sate Ormyr's curiosity about how Dag had come to wield the Shipbuilder relic. But if Ormyr cared about such a thing at the moment, he gave no sign, his gaze remaining detached.

Dag edged over to my makeshift surgical arena. The bright light cut on again, which the boy aimed directly at Ormyr's eyes at first. The master adept's only response was to squint.

"Lower, Dag," I said.

He complied. Eventually.

I checked for a pulse on Ormyr's wrist. It was strong, and he showed no signs of shock from blood loss. In fact, there was a surprising lack of blood, both on Ormyr and the bolt itself. I wouldn't have expected much from the puncture, but ripping out the bolt should've upset nearby muscle tissue and blood vessels, unless Ormyr had been supremely lucky.

Not lucky, I realized. Through the puncture hole in his leg, something shimmered under the light. I glanced to Ormyr, wide-eyed. "Shipbuilder armor?"

"Like mail," Ormyr answered, still distant. "Imbued with magic to be nigh impenetrable."

It was probably similar to my nanofiber brigandine. You'd feel the blow, but you'd live. I slumped in relief, then worked on repacking my supplies—in darkness, because Dag revoked his light the moment he realized it was no longer needed.

As I worked, Ormyr used the rock behind him to reach his feet.

"Wait!" I said. "Maybe we should—"

Deaf to my words, Ormyr rounded the boulder and vanished. His footsteps headed toward the memorial where all the excitement had taken place. The timing sounded off, like he was limping.

Dag knelt beside me, his eagerness clear despite the encroaching darkness. "Let's run!" he whispered. "He'll never—"

"No one's leaving anyone behind. Got it?" I snapped, then immediately regretted my tone. I'd suffered some degree of concussion for sure.

Dag blinked, then leveled a blood-chilling glare at me. He jumped back up and stalked off alone.

CHAPTER 9

Nightfall cast a cold silence over the former district's remains. In the wake of the adepts' ambush, I remained kneeling behind a boulder, fairly certain my dizziness and irritation belied a more serious head injury. Ormyr's footfalls trailed away from me in one direction, while Dag's stalked off furiously in another.

Stranded in the middle of nowhere with people who wanted nothing to do with each other. This felt like a nightmare. If we separated, we'd surely succumb to dehydration, starvation, exhaustion, or predators. How in hell could I get everyone cooperating toward survival and progress?

From the shoulder down, my left arm was all but useless. I braced the boulder ahead of me with my right hand and struggled to stand, intending to call Dag and Ormyr back. I had no idea what to say, I just hoped to keep everyone talking long enough to reach an agreement.

Sore leg muscles and gravity fought against me. Blood drained from my head, making me dizzier than ever. My vision browned out, and I hit the dirt soon after.

At the fringe of consciousness, I heard a surprised cry—Dag's. His footsteps pounded back toward me. Bright light pierced my veiled eyelids. "Ye all right?"

I screwed my eyes shut, unable to respond.

"*Skíta*," Dag cursed in a hush. A moment later, hands latched onto my shoulder, shaking it.

"Get away from her!" Ormyr cried. More footsteps skidded to a halt nearby.

"Ye first, arse!" Dag released me and turned his light toward Ormyr.

The master adept had numerous weapons at his disposal to correct Dag's impudence, but I didn't hear any of them being summoned to the fore—yet. "Accursed whelp! This was all thy doing!"

"What? Like Hel it was!" Dag replied.

"Speak not of Hel! Thou shalt not invoke Gyllenfeld dogma before me, is that understood?" Then Ormyr's withering tone turned sullen. "'Twas the Naustviks' doing, truly. They poisoned mine adepts against me from afar. Thou art merely another of their thralls, obeying their commands against thy will."

"What in Hel's a thrall?" Dag asked.

"I said, *speak not of Hel!*" Ormyr paused, then continued in a softer tone. "Dame Jessamine sensed it was coming. She … she tried to warn me." Another pause. "Stand aside, whelp. Look at her. She'll die if I don't heal her."

"I'm still here," I managed to mutter.

"Unseen grace!" Ormyr cried with relief. "Stay awake, Lady Knight! Sleep is death, dost thou understand?"

Maybe, maybe not. But sleep was damned tempting, even on a bed of rocks out in the cold.

Someone who smelled of cloves dropped to his knees beside me. I forced my eyes open and spied Ormyr's outline. He took my right hand and slid under my arm. As he moved to stand us up, he winced and tensed, probably from where his leg still bothered him.

Dag stood by warily, casting light over the scene. At Ormyr's difficulty, he approached my left side. "*Skíta,* all this blood!"

At first, I had no idea what he was talking about. Then I became aware of a warm trickle past my left ear, down my neck. My head had struck the ground after the ulldyr had thrown me. In the heat of escape, I hadn't noticed any bleeding.

"I shall heal her," Ormyr grunted, still struggling with me.

Dag ducked under my sore left arm. Their combined effort got me upright. Though my head swam and pounded angrily in protest, I could place weight on my feet and lessen the burden for them.

Ormyr pulled us toward the monument that stood in memorial to the destroyed district. We passed through one of the ample gaps in the stone circle. "This is the best magic circle we could hope for, Lady Knight," he spoke encouragingly.

Nearby lay the body of Adept Mir. Poor Mir—victim of a hail of bolts that even Holsten hadn't wanted us to have. But Holsten's pleas against violence reeked of hypocrisy. Though he'd left us here alive, we stood to die in any number of ways.

"Away with thee, whelp." Ormyr's tone had chilled several hundred degrees. "I must lie her on her side."

"Thought she wasn't supposed to sleep." Dag voiced the words like an accusation.

"Dost thou prefer for her to bleed out?" Ormyr snapped.

Dag stepped back. Ormyr tried to lower me himself, but faltered with another wince. In response, Dag darted in again to help rest me on my right side, then knelt beside me with his light tile in hand. I screwed my eyes shut against the brightness and hoped Ormyr did something constructive.

A few moments later, something damp pressed against my left temple.

"Hail, Unseen!" Ormyr muttered. "Be her physician. Drive away her pain and suffering. Drive away the poisons that seep into blood and bone."

The healing spell continued. I rated magic now; good to know. While his ministrations did nothing for the dizzying headache, they would staunch the bleeding. Judging by the wounds and treatment he'd dealt me earlier, Ormyr was competent at that much.

Dag held his tongue for the spell's duration. Once it'd ended, Ormyr carefully wrapped a bandage around my head to secure the compress in place.

Not bad, I thought, placing my right hand on the ground and pushing myself up to a seated position. My head pounded, refusing to clear. While leaning on my right arm for support, I let my left arm go slack, cradling my bandaged hand in my lap.

"Ye all right?" Dag asked again. "Here, I got water."

"Take mine, Lady Knight." From behind, Ormyr offered me his own canteen. "He's another thrall, and I'm not certain how trustworthy he is."

"Gamla skíta!" Dag swore at him. "Ye're the one who can't be trusted! Ye just want to hurt my friends!"

Dag's bravado stunned me. Mouthing off to *the* master adept? Well, he'd just seen the other adepts throw Ormyr over, and he believed himself a powerful magic-user in his own right.

"Thou art even more a slave to them than I thought," Ormyr returned with contempt. "Doff that robe, whelp! Thou hast not earned it."

"Fair cop," said Dag, making no move to get rid of the adept robe that'd disguised him during the day's journey. "How *do* I earn it? Put a bolt in you?"

"We should rest," I blurted, hoping to defuse what promised to be an unending argument. Rest, take stock, figure out our next move, ponder how to get Ormyr and Dag cooperating. Nausea hit me, followed by an inexplicable urge to cry.

Ormyr braced my right shoulder from behind. "Rest now. Call out if thou needest me." He stood, rounding me to approach Mir's corpse.

Meanwhile, Dag's eyes and light tile shifted about as though sizing up his options for escape.

This one boy was more daunting than a whole throne room of courtiers. How'd I normally deal with children? I didn't. Like that young guide back on Spectra, the one who'd asked about my squire. If I'd told him I had no squire, he would've pounced on that and begged to serve me. I hadn't wanted to explain how I'd just repeat all the mistakes my master had made.

I took a deep breath around the pain and sickness. Maybe this didn't have to be hard. Dag cared enough about the Naustviks, and maybe even me, to come all the way out here. I had to show that I still cared about helping his friends. First things first, though.

"Do you still have your canteen?" I shifted my weight to free up my right arm, then dug through the first aid kit on my belt.

Dag proffered his water, blinking at the bottle of acetaminophen I produced. "What's that?"

"Medicine from a plant." Given Thordia's knowledge of botany, I figured Dag might be familiar with the idea. "Something to make my head feel better."

The boy watched closely as I helped myself to the medicine and washed it down, then leaned in to whisper. "The whole way out here, those other adepts talked about leaving you two without ulldyr or supplies, running back home."

By that point, I couldn't even raise an eyebrow at such news. Some of those adepts were Gyllenfeld loyalists, some had helped with my first murder attempt, and all had been forced to endure Ormyr's mentorship. It made sense. Once they rode home, they could spin a tragic tale about our ill-fated Harbinger excursion, and no one would question it.

If they could attack their own master, who was safe? As my thoughts returned to Ingvar, longing and worry crushed the air out of my lungs. *Recover and get the hell out of the keep*, I urged from afar.

Forcing myself to focus, I retrieved a clean compress and dabbed at my bandaged temple. To my relief, it came back with only faint smudges of blood. Head wounds tended to be gushers; I'd have to keep checking on it. At the moment, I lacked the coordination to address the wound more thoroughly. My dirty hands were the last thing I wanted to introduce to it besides.

"We have to ditch Master Ormyr," Dag whispered with a pleading look. "He just wants to hurt my friends."

I still had no interest in abandoning anyone. Knowing physical contact bothered Dag, I settled for eye contact. "I'm not in any shape to run away. Besides, it's better if we keep Ormyr close. His Shipbuilder knowledge will be useful in the Harbinger — and he still wants to find your friends. That won't change. If he finds them before we do? We won't be able to help them."

Dag frowned, thoughtful. "So we keep eyes on him. When we find Verahl and Thordia, he'll be outnumbered. Then we'll see what his magic amounts to against ours."

"Right," I forced out, already dreading that confrontation. At least I'd assuaged Dag; I had to get Ormyr cooperating as well. It was impossible to change his mind on the best of days, but I had to try — without Dag there to needle him.

"The other adepts left in a hurry," I said. "They may've dropped supplies we can use. Can you go look for anything like that?"

Dag nodded. "Ye'll be all right here?"

Not really. "I'll be fine."

The boy darted off, taking his light tile with him. Darkness fell over the stone circle, a darkness the stars above couldn't pierce.

To hell with it, I thought, and dug out my stick lighter.

The small light guided me to my feet. In protest, my head pounded hard. I ignored it to face Ormyr, who knelt at Mir's side with his head lowered over his beads. Testing my balance, I took slow steps in his direction. Not great, but good enough to cross the gulf without falling over.

Ormyr didn't react to my approach or the light I carried. Ground cloves now encircled Mir's head. Was this mourning? Guilt? Reality seeping into his fortress of denial? Ormyr remained part infuriating, part sickening … and yet, there were glimmers of compassion that ultimately made me pity him then. Head injury and blood loss probably had something to do with it as well. I knelt at his right side.

Expressionless, Ormyr withdrew a candle from one of his belt pouches. One wave of his hand later, and it was lit with no sign of how it'd been done. He must've palmed the match somehow.

I put away my lighter and tensed against the chill in the air. "I'm sorry about Mir." After a moment, I decided to inject more reality, hoping it might help him focus on actual problems. "Madam Castor may've gotten to your adepts. She might be trying to discredit your Baron, maybe even invade outright."

Baron Tristan's master adept was abroad, his Captain of the Guard was … out of the way. If Madam Castor still wanted to send mercenaries against Lord Catherwood's wishes, she'd set some fine ground work and caught several lucky breaks.

Another wave of nausea struck me. Despair was close behind, bringing tears that I fought hard not to shed. I shuddered, clenching my right fist at my side.

Ormyr studied the candle in his hands. "This was the Naustviks' doing."

I didn't even flinch at his denial, too used to such.

"I shall see them suffer—and free thee from enthrallment, with my final breath if necessary." His gaze finally met mine, the flickering candle casting grim shadows across his face. "For me, there is only one path. For thee and the boy, 'tis less certain. I don't wish to deny thee vengeance, but someone must warn our Baron of this treachery."

Retreat to the capital was more than tempting, but the unfriendly adepts would surely beat us there. What kind of reception would await me and Dag—assuming we survived the trip back?

"I worry about falling deeper under enthrallment and doing something terrible to the Baron," I lied, putting fear into my words. "My ship ought to be at the Harbinger. We should keep going together. Once we've dealt with the Naustviks, we'll return and warn the Baron. Flying back will only take minutes."

I hoped *Kepler's Law* would be easy to find, and that Verahl hadn't already fled the planet with Thordia.

"Vengeance is the only thing keeping me together out here," I added. "You welcomed my sword once, welcome it again."

Ormyr remained silent. After a moment, he set aside his candle to brace my head in his hands.

"What is it?" Had I bled through the bandage?

Across from Mir's remains, Dag appeared, skidding to a stop. My side sword, and a knapsack, fell to the dirt at his feet. The false adept then aimed his loaded slingshot at Ormyr. "Tearing her up again?"

"Put away that toy, whelp." Ormyr remained focused on me, speaking as though Dag wasn't worth the oxygen.

"It's all right, Dag," I said. "What'd you find?"

Dag remained poised to shoot, glaring at Ormyr. "Your sword, some food and water." He shoved the knapsack on the ground with his foot. "And ulldyr tracks. Might be *your* ulldyr, even."

At this, Ormyr detached from me to stare up at Dag. "In what direction?"

"Toward the Harbinger. If we're quick enough, we could catch up with it."

Ormyr blinked. "'Twould be a boon."

Yes, but could we really chase it down—at night, no less? "How far are we from the Harbinger?" I asked.

"Hours on foot," Ormyr replied, "but the ulldyr would make short work of that distance."

I stifled a groan. "I don't know. Maybe it'd be better if we rest here overnight, resume tomorrow."

"We can't!" Dag cried desperately. "He'll leave without us!"

"*I'm* the one who must worry about thee killing me in my sleep!" Ormyr retorted, then sobered. "'Tis unsafe to rest here, Lady Knight. We know not whether someone might return to secure our demise."

"Probably ghosts here, anyway," Dag said, finally swapping out his slingshot for his light tile. "Hear all that racket?"

I had no idea what racket he meant.

Ormyr waved a hand in dismissal. "The dead here have all gone on to other purposes by now."

"*He* hasn't." Dag glanced toward Mir. "Shouldn't we burn him?"

"If we're not resting here, we're not staying for that, either," I said, my patience toward ritual running thin. "The body will decompose over time, it'll go to its next purpose that way."

"Rot, ye mean?" This did nothing to assuage Dag.

"Thy native customs differ from ours, Lady Knight. That said, every moment we tarry is another moment the Naustviks have to prepare for our arrival." Ormyr retrieved his candle and settled it upon Mir's chest. "Let us track down the ulldyr."

My whole body ached in protest, but I steeled myself. After all, if we caught up to it, I wouldn't have to walk long.

Ormyr narrowed eyes at Dag's light tile. "Thou mayest keep thy trinket for now, whelp. We may as well exploit the powers the Naustviks have afforded thee. I shall do everything in my power to protect you both. Ye must do exactly as I command."

"*Nidstang!*" Dag spat the unfamiliar word with the force of a curse, casting another pleading look my way. "I'm not doing a damned thing he says!"

In no mood to join the bickering, I changed the subject instead. "Quick—before we go, how much food and water do we have left?"

Ormyr still had his canteen, but his food had vanished with his ulldyr. Dag had a more generous supply in his knapsack, no doubt bolstered by the preserves he'd been taking from the Naustviks' cellar. The second bag he'd found offered up another canteen and more dried plants.

It still wasn't much. Dehydration was the more immediate risk, but hunger gnawed at me like never before. I couldn't imagine it getting worse.

"We'll have to ration carefully," I said. "We don't know how long this will take."

"Everyone carries their own share," Dag proposed.

No arguments for once. Working quickly, we divided everything up between canteens, pockets, and pouches. Ormyr and Dag helped me stand. Finally, Dag retrieved my side sword for me.

My pain and dizziness persisted, but I could walk without tipping over. As we left the stone circle, Ormyr's robe-scrap remained there, fluttering with a sense of hollow victory.

"Where are the tracks, whelp?" Ormyr demanded.

"This way." Dag bounded ahead. If he still feared ghosts lurking about, he didn't show it. Eventually, he dropped to a crouch, his light tile highlighting a set of round depressions in the dirt.

Ormyr studied the evidence himself, then looked up with renewed purpose. "Let's make haste."

I was afraid he'd say that—but it really would be a relief if we found our mount. I could hang on that much longer.

We resumed our journey through territory devastated by the Harbinger's impact, with only rocks and stars for company. Our ulldyr had bolted from the adepts' ambush in a straight line, leaving tracks that Dag had no trouble following. Ormyr and I trailed behind, the master adept walking with a slight limp. I focused on one step at a time as my left arm and head throbbed, hoping the acetaminophen would kick in soon.

Only a few paces past the former district, a huge burst of colorful light consumed the horizon. The Harbinger, once invisible in the darkness, had returned to view thanks to hundreds of bright beacons along its hull.

Dag yelped. As we stopped and stared at the phenomenon, the breath froze in my lungs. Hell, it was last night with Sigrid all over again, only at mountainous proportions.

"Never seen it lit with those torches before," Dag managed.

"They are signs of health. The Harbinger liveth," Ormyr declared grimly, winding his beads over his hands.

Indeed, the colored lights pulsed in a way that seemed alive somehow, a giant taking its first breaths in centuries. Close to the horizon, a mysterious void blocked the lights and the stars. Maybe it was the edge of the Harbinger's impact crater.

"The Naustviks show no fear at our impending arrival—but they underestimate my resolve." Ormyr strode onward with only the Harbinger to light his path.

Dag darted to my side, fidgeting with his knapsack straps. "Mayhap that *is* Verahl and Thordia telling us they're all right. D'ye think?"

Was this some kind of message, like Sigrid's display? Given my violent parting with Verahl, I couldn't help putting an ominous frame around it. The message seemed less *We're here* and more *Keep your distance, we can do a lot worse.*

I shook it off. There was every chance that Thordia still had noble intentions. I hoped Verahl didn't talk her out of them.

"Maybe," was all I said to Dag while rubbing at my sore shoulder. "We'll get to ask them soon, won't we?"

"Aye, hope so." Dag glared at Ormyr's back. "Not too late to thrash him or leave him."

His cold determination pained me. "I can't fight or run. Stick to the plan." Not like there was much of one, but it'd worked so far.

"All right." Dag hurried off, passing Ormyr to resume the lead.

I pushed myself to follow, but my lightheadedness persisted and my legs quickly tired. My companions seemed too intent on the search to notice me lagging behind.

And then Dag halted, glancing this way and that with frowning confusion.

"Where is the trail?" Ormyr barked.

"I'm looking!" Dag's light beam swept off to our right. "*Skíta.* Veers off that way."

Away from the Harbinger. I slowed to a halt as my stomach sank with disappointment, threatening to pull me to the ground again.

"Keep going. I'll find him," Dag said.

"'Tis lost, whelp!" Ormyr snapped. "Don't run off!"

"I can get him!" Dag insisted.

"Let's just get to the Harbinger," I managed. Reaching the abandoned structure was only the beginning of our problems, but that was the goal my brain latched onto for sanity's sake.

Dag muttered a curse before hastening ahead again. The light tile waved about, maybe seeking monsters now that the ulldyr had been abandoned. Verahl was one monster for certain. Stealing my ship, lashing out at Ingvar ... Holsten was another. Who else was in danger once he and the other adepts returned to the capital?

Worry and frustration spread through my ribcage. I spurred myself on before hopelessness set in next. Ormyr kept pace beside me this time. I couldn't bring myself to look at him. After all, his foolish convictions hadn't helped.

The largest boulders fell behind us. The ground sloped upward, making Ormyr's limp more pronounced. I watched for any sign he might need help, but my own heart fluttered dangerously, warning me not to push myself much harder.

Then the terrain turned into mud, nearly ankle-deep at points, which filled in our footprints and erased all hint of our journey. Dag's light tile revealed a familiar dark substance mingling with the grit, creating a thick paste. He crouched, holding his free hand toward the mess.

"Don't touch it!" I stumbled to another halt, unable to run toward him. "It's the ichor we found in Thordia's cellar!"

Dag's gaze snapped to mine, eyes wide.

"'Tis not harmful to the touch." Ormyr stopped beside me, his words calmly reassuring.

Irrationally, they ate through what temper I had left. Blood boiling, I whirled on him—then staggered, but kept my balance. "This stuff has been coming out of your wells and spreading through your soil! Exactly when were you planning on saying something to the Baron?"

Dag jumped to his feet, bright with anticipation.

"When we'd fully uncovered its nature and purpose," Ormyr replied, unperturbed. "Any sooner would've invited unnecessary panic."

"So you started experimenting with it—like on that prisoner in the dungeon?" I glowered at him.

Ormyr stiffened with fists clenched at his sides, leveling a stern stare my way. "Let's be very clear about this, Lady Knight. That one killed himself."

"Are you sure? Maybe it was your murdering cadre," I snapped.

Ormyr flinched as though I'd pushed him.

Every bit of vexation he'd caused me over the past few days sprang to the fore. "I could've done something to stop the ichor, but you shoved me aside and walled me in like *I* was the danger. And then those killers under your wing kept me and Ingvar from rescuing the wise woman!" My voice rose to a shout. "She's stuck on Gules in the middle of winter. She'll die if I don't reach her!"

Stunned surprise overtook Ormyr's expression.

"Hell, for all I know, you helped them arrange that trap! What did Madam Castor promise you, huh?"

My words had outraced my sense. Once my brain caught up, it brought an anguish that drowned my rage like an ocean wave crushing a lit match. Ormyr hadn't known that Drea was marooned on a *cursed* planet. Now he'd never give me the co-ordinates I needed to reach her—assuming I ever got my ship back.

More and more things piled up to prevent her rescue. This latest one was squarely my fault. Shame and guilt staggered me, literally. I swayed on my feet.

Ormyr caught me before I fell into the ichor. Dag rushed over to help him. I was too dizzy, tired, and nauseated to wave them off.

Hell. This might be serious, I thought.

"Don't stop now," Dag piped up from my right. "Ye were really tearing into him."

"Let us find someplace to rest." On my left, Ormyr sounded too worried to concern himself with Dag.

Somehow, they agreed upon a rock to sit down on. Dag placed the light tile face-down in his lap, muting its glow. While keeping a hand on my right arm, he sat hunched, one leg bouncing up and down, eyes narrowed off at some intangible target.

"I shall set up a magic circle." Ormyr braced my left shoulder, causing me to shudder with pain. He withdrew his hand and leaned in close to my ear. "Lady Knight, if perchance there's any power the Naustviks have granted thee, anything at all, tap into it now. Normally I would caution against it, but 'tis a matter of survival. Worry not about their corrupting influence. I swear I shall pull thee back."

It sounded like I'd have more leeway to use Shipbuilder artifacts and knowledge from then on, if I didn't keel over. Was I going into shock? Probably not; if I were still bleeding, I would've felt it. This was probably concussion-related, plus all the other things working against me. A full day of riding, torture, days of rough questing beforehand ...

In the light of Dag's dimmed tile, Ormyr threw down a circle of ground cloves. Then Dag's canteen slid into my vision. I grasped it, drinking just enough to wet my mouth.

"Sorry about your friend," Dag murmured.

It was the nicest thing he'd ever said to me. Tears fell before I could suppress them. "Thanks."

Ormyr stepped inside the circle. His keris flashed into view as he balanced the dagger on his palm. "I look now to the favorable stars, who've guided us this far in safety ..."

"Hurts now, but ye'll be stronger for it," Dag whispered beneath Ormyr's incantation.

His brother Rigg must've reassured him with those words sometime in the past. It sobered me to consider why Dag might've needed such comforting.

"Which of those stars up there d'ye come from?" Dag asked.

I couldn't glance up just yet. "I don't know if you can see it from here. It's on the other side of the galaxy. I haven't been back in a long time."

"Sure are a lot of stars to visit," Dag muttered. "I'd be happy visiting *one*, just to see what it's like."

That was an opportunity he might get. As a known friend and "thrall" of the Naustviks, Dag would be in sore need of protection once this madness ended.

An upside-down hammer amulet floated into my view, proffered by Dag's right hand. His third and fourth fingers were fused together, and the tip of his index finger was missing.

"Mayhap ye need this more than I do," Dag said.

I was touched. "Hang on to it, I've got plenty." Not a lie. During quests, protective charms tended to accumulate like lint.

Once finished with his spell, Ormyr dropped to a seat on my left, bracing my elbow this time. "Dame Jessamine? Prithee stay awake." Alarm edged his words. "Tell us of one of thy former quests, perchance?"

"Aye, let's hear one!" Dag cried.

"Thy distinguished career —"

"Isn't," I cut Ormyr off bitterly. The last thing I wanted to do was spin ridiculous lies about dragons and witches. "I'm not great, or trusted, or anyone's court favorite. How's that for a story?"

"Oh," Ormyr said with dawning realization. It wasn't an *Oh, then I've wasted my time fawning over you.* It was an *Oh, you poor thing. I know what's really going on here.* "Fall not into despair, Lady Knight. It maketh one to believe all manner of untrue things. That I had anything to do with the attempt on thy life, for instance? I wish I'd foreseen Knorr's intent, but that was my only failing in the matter. Have faith that I shall see thee through this plight."

Enough of my senses returned to shut my mouth for me. The whole emissary thing was the only reason Ormyr showed me any kindness, and I'd nearly unraveled that. I nodded and separated from his grasp, preferring to lean forward and prop my right elbow on my knee. The mati amulet around my neck swung mockingly into view, hovering over the bandaged left hand that Ormyr had cut up earlier. I tucked the offending charm under my tunic.

"Lady Knight?" Ormyr prompted, strained. "About this wise woman—"

"That wasn't your fault," I admitted. "I'd just really like the coordinates for Gules if we survive this."

Ormyr's hand rested on my back. "If we have them, they're thine."

I stiffened at first, then gradually relaxed as relief sank in. More tears fell to the dirt.

"We shall spell here for a time," Ormyr said.

Good. I needed it.

"I can take watch," Dag said.

"I trust thee not, whelp," Ormyr smoothly informed him. "'Tis not thy fault per se. The Naustviks—"

"Ye like blaming everything on them," Dag snapped. "Truth is, ye're just a fool."

Ormyr turned into a simmering volcano beside me, but kept the eruption in check. "Methinks thou had best recall whom thou art speaking to."

I sat up straight, putting a physical barrier between them. My head spun in protest, but at least I was assured no weapons surfaced on either side. Dag and Ormyr settled on mutual death-glares.

"Be grateful I'm in no mood to see any more suffering this night," Ormyr said. "We may as well eat something." He began rummaging through his belongings.

Dag picked up his light tile again. Within seconds, he tensed. "The Hel is that?"

At the fringe of his light, yards off in the distance, lurked several dark figures. Most were slender, reaching skyward. Others tilted sideways, poised to fall on unwary passersby.

Ormyr froze, his errand forgotten. "Trees?"

"They can't be," I said, sitting up straighter. How could any living thing survive in the ichor?

Dag swept his light along a horizontal line. More silhouettes appeared, like the ranks of an opposing army, forming a line between us and the Harbinger.

"Frodi Fuldarr's haunting ground," Dag muttered.

The name was familiar. Oh, right, his ghost story. Frodi and his brothers had embarked on a failed excursion of the Harbinger. Now, their alleged spirits haunted Nidaros' alleged forests. Though I had my doubts, my heart pounded nervously. What *were* these things? We held still, but no further clues appeared.

Dag stood. "I'll have a look."

Ormyr jumped up and checked his progress. "Remain here with Dame Jessamine, whelp. I shall gauge the threat." His dagger appeared in his hand. "Ready a weapon, light my path, and remain silent."

To my surprise, Dag neither darted around nor blew up at him. His concerned glance toward me betrayed his willingness to cooperate for my sake.

"I can hold the light tile for you." He couldn't do that and brandish a weapon—not that I suspected a weapon was appropriate here, but I supposed it didn't hurt to be cautious.

Dag passed the light tile to me. Eyes narrowed, he retrieved his slingshot and scrounged through his pocket for ammunition.

As I trained the device ahead, Ormyr took his leave, trusting us thralls not to backstab him. Meanwhile, Dag found a smooth stone he must've harvested during our journey or sometime beforehand. Standing close beside me, he loaded the slingshot and aimed it ahead.

Ormyr approached the nearest "tree," pausing every so often with his keris primed. He safely closed to within a few yards, then a few feet. After another pause, he moved to arm's reach.

A ghostly rectangle of green light materialized before him at eye level.

The same current of surprise coursed through all of us. I gasped. Ormyr cried out and staggered back. His free hand shot forward, casting one of the steel throwing darts concealed up his sleeve. The last time I'd seen him use one was in the dungeon, against Verahl.

At the same time, Dag hurried forward several steps and fired his stone.

"Wait!" I cried. The glowing rectangle looked familiar.

Both missiles flew through the apparition and plinked harmlessly off the "tree" behind it. In response, the green rectangle rippled like a disturbed pond and disappeared. Then the offended "tree" uprooted itself and rose into the air to hover several feet above its former resting spot, dripping ichor back to the ground.

CHAPTER 10

At the edge of the mysterious forest, a single "tree" hovered in mid-air within the beam of light I cast toward it. Despite Ormyr and Dag's attempted assault, the rectangular object remained still in the nighttime silence, offering no retaliation.

Dag froze several feet away, his slingshot forgotten, craning his neck to follow the strange sight. Far ahead of us, Ormyr brandished his keris dagger, but was equally stymied.

I could only imagine their horror. Meanwhile, my initial shock turned to elation. This thing was *familiar*, not a threat. It was almost enough to make me forget how my head spun and throbbed in the wake of a concussion.

"It's a Shipbuilder construct!" I called out from the rock I sat upon. "And I'll bet that glowing rectangle was its command interface!"

I normally wouldn't have been so open in Ormyr's presence, but he'd granted me leave to tap into any power the Naustviks had granted me, their hapless "thrall." Shipbuilder lore could be one of those things. That'd be my excuse if Ormyr questioned it, at least.

Behind the hovering construct, dozens or maybe hundreds more constructs were rooted in the ichor-laced mud. I was used to seeing them in much smaller numbers and worse repair; at my mentors' beguinage, they'd taken in and restored constructs designed for all manner of tasks. Where had this construct forest come from? What was its purpose? The holographic interface might've offered a clue, but it had yet to return.

Dag ran toward the constructs, heedless of the ichor splashing onto his adept robe. As he approached Ormyr, the master adept lunged and hooked the boy by the arm with his free hand. "Reckless whelp! Hold still!"

"Get off!" Dag squirmed to no avail.

Ormyr returned his attention to the forest. "I've seen forms like these before in Spectra." A moment later, he raised his keris into the air. "*Apodrasi. Activate!*"

The first word he said, I didn't recognize. The second one was definitely Shipbuilder. In response, dozens of constructs — including our former antagonist — lit up with identical holographic interfaces. The forest glowed in their collective green light, its constituent "trees" looking even less treelike. Some were boxy, some were long and thin, some leaned or rested on their sides.

Ormyr's back faced me, and yet he seemed to glow almost as much as the interfaces before us. Dag flinched and stopped struggling, his slingshot dangling loosely from his fingers.

Captivated by the haunting display, I almost forgot to breathe. How long had these constructs waited for someone to revive them? The Harbinger seemed their most likely origin point. I couldn't imagine what had removed them from there and deposited them here, miles away.

The charm wore off as I considered what had made the display possible. "Voice command," I blurted, grudgingly impressed. Only a handful of my mentors could pronounce the Shipbuilder language well enough to make it work.

Dag blinked toward the master adept.

Ormyr stood a little taller. "In Spectra, I was granted knowledge of several universal words of power."

A common lexicon that worked across all devices. The chill in the air crept down my spine. First the mati amulet, now this. Ormyr had more *real* power at his command than I'd ever suspected. What if we found more intact technology at the Harbinger? Ormyr could potentially murder the Naustviks with a single word, and I wouldn't be able to do a damned thing about it.

Overwhelmed at the thought, I doubled over. The light tile in my right hand illuminated my bandaged left hand and ichor-stained boots.

"Lady Knight?" Ormyr called with concern in his voice.

"I'm fine. I just ..." My spinning head was in no hurry to rise.

"These constructs have the power of flight and can be shaped into many forms," Ormyr said. "I can command one to convey us the remaining distance to the Harbinger."

The suggestion cut through my malaise. "That'd be good," I managed. *Great,* really.

"I need time to fashion a construct for our purpose," Ormyr continued. "Whelp, go sit with Dame Jessamine."

Silence followed. I forced my head up to find Dag staring at the constructs. Then he glanced my way, and his reluctance turned into worry. He separated from Ormyr and walked back toward my rock. Once he sat down beside me, I returned his light tile to him.

As we looked on, Ormyr spread his arms wide and raised his voice to the forest, experimenting with one command after the next. Clever shifting and folding of constructs' constituent parts transformed them into cubes, ladders, and jagged stairs.

Their silhouettes stood out sharply against the ambient holographic glow.

Dag leaned toward the display, eyes wide, as though trying to absorb whatever power it threw off. His curiosity impressed me more than Ormyr's ability ever could. While the boy had dabbled with Shipbuilder devices in the Naustviks' cellar, it'd all been trial and error. No one had been there to explain how everything worked in accordance with universal laws.

Here was a chance to really teach him something. The prospect was so exciting, I all but forgot my pain and the usual worries about handling kids.

"Anyone can do that with the right commands." I gestured toward the ever-changing constructs ahead.

Dag's wide-eyed stare riveted to me. "Do ye know any spells like that?"

How to drive home that this was Shipbuilder technology, not magic? The two were surely tied together in his mind, as with Ingvar. I struggled against the fog in my brain to remember my own lessons. It hadn't been a bombshell revelation. My mentors had worked up to it gradually.

"Sort of," I said. "It's not casting, more like issuing orders."

Dag bounced in place. "Can ye show me? Please?"

If we approached one of the constructs, we could select commands through its interface. Though I dearly wanted to demonstrate, I dreaded returning to my feet and walking all those yards.

Then, with a jolt, I remembered the data carrier in my pocket. Verahl had used one to remotely control my ship. Could it also talk to these things?

The mystery gave me focus. Once I retrieved and activated the data carrier, Dag honed in on its blue glow like a moth toward flame. The device's interface displayed a list of nearby active constructs. Heart pounding, I swiped the top item with my thumb. A list of commands appeared next. Using that, and some quick experimenting, I managed to uproot a construct from the ichor and fly it toward our rock. As it sailed past Ormyr, he glanced sharply over his shoulder, following its progress.

Dag leapt to his feet. "How're ye doing that? Show me!"

For the first time in ages, I smiled. "Hold on." I landed the construct nearby, then glanced up. "The first thing you need to do is walk over to it."

Dag advanced toward the construct until its glowing interface lit up before him, displaying a command list identical to my data carrier's. He gave a start and shielded his face with his arm, but peeked over said arm inquisitively.

"Those are words from the Shipbuilder language. Descriptions of what this construct can do," I continued. "By touching the words, you tell it what shape and position you want it to take." How it registered touch, distinguishing it from accidental disturbances, was a mystery to me. But it worked, that was the important thing.

Dag lowered his arm. "I can't read."

Not surprising in the least. Adepts jealously guarded the Shipbuilder language. Few outsiders were both able and willing to teach it to non-adepts — and most of them were rounded up as heretics.

"I'll help you." I forced myself to my feet, ignoring the throbbing and spinning in my head to approach Dag's side. "Try … that one." I pointed to a command on the interface that seemed useful to our flying plan.

Dag swiped a finger over the indicated words. In response, the boxy construct morphed into a flat rectangular platform that hovered at his eye level.

"Not bad." I smiled again.

Dag glowed with a pride rightfully earned. Most people would've lacked the nerve to look at the interface, much less use it. Would Ingvar have done so? Maybe not right away, but after seeing me and Dag use it without creating trouble, he might've been convinced to try.

My heart lurched. I hoped I still got to teach Ingvar someday, if—

Movement from my peripherals cut my train of thought short. Dag noticed it, too, and aimed his light tile accordingly. From the forest, another platform flew toward us, with Ormyr standing at its center. Using voice commands, he lowered the platform to within inches of the ground. He still had his keris in hand, which he grasped tighter while glancing at my data carrier.

Dag's pride melted off into his default scowl.

Pushing heartache aside, I deactivated the data carrier and returned it to my pocket, not wanting to provoke Ormyr's wariness any further. "It seems you've gotten the hang of this," I remarked casually.

"Step aboard," Ormyr said.

"All right, but keep this thing low to start," I said. "Let's make sure it supports our weight."

We boarded the strange magic carpet, which didn't so much as flinch at the added burden. Ormyr raised his keris and called out a command that raised the platform skyward.

I lost my balance and dropped to one knee, screwing my eyes shut. "Slower, please!"

The pace dropped to a crawl. Dag was closer, and helped me stand.

Gradually, the platform rose over the forest, pausing in mid-air above the tallest constructs. Ahead, the Harbinger's pulsing lights bathed us in a rainbow of colors. Dag cried out in awe and rushed to the platform's edge, towing me with him, while Ormyr lingered behind.

Past the glowing forest beneath us, the hill we'd been ascending continued to rise, then stopped. On the other side, the terrain dropped sharply. It wasn't a hill at all, more like a bowl. A *crater*, several miles wide, and the mountainous Harbinger rested in its center in all its intimidating splendor. Beacons low on the structure's hull reflected off a mirrored surface. There was a lake inside the crater, and the Harbinger was partially submerged in it.

Only the lake wasn't made of water. The pulsing lights revealed a purplish sheen.

"Is that … ichor?" Another chill ran down my spine, causing me to shudder.

Dag glanced down at his boots, then shook the mud off one of them. "*Skíta.*"

For a while, none of us could speak. I stared helplessly at the giant crater-lake surrounding the Harbinger like a moat. Had it been water at one time, only to be contaminated? One drop of ichor was all it would've taken. But where had the ichor come from to begin with?

Standing there, the pieces finally snapped into place within my addled brain. Had the ichor escaped *from the Harbinger*, the way these constructs might've?

My knees nearly buckled again. It couldn't be. How? *Why* would the Shipbuilders ever create something so dangerous, something that had absolutely no good purpose?

"How'd Thordia make it through here?" Dag asked grimly under his breath.

"She could have manipulated these constructs as well," Ormyr piped up behind us.

True. Or Verahl might've spotted her from the air. But hell, the Harbinger was massive. The possibility of a days- or weeks-long search sank in then. I rubbed at my aching temple while fighting off a surge of nausea.

"On that note," Ormyr continued, "hand me thy Shipbuilder relic, Lady Knight."

I froze. There were dozens of reasons why I didn't want to surrender the data carrier. Most importantly, it could prove my only defense against Ormyr within the Harbinger. I struggled to come up with a plausible excuse. "Master, the Naustviks might sense if you take it away from me, and retaliate."

"I'm not so certain thou canst handle the power in thy state," Ormyr replied gently. "Better that it remain with an expert."

Light flashed in the corner of my vision: light from the Harbinger glinting off Ormyr's rings and keris. The master adept had seized Dag's shoulder and thrust his blade between me and the boy, holding it inches shy of Dag's throat.

Dag gave a start and yelped.

Burning with righteous anger, I spun toward Ormyr, reaching for my own dagger.

"Be still," Ormyr calmly ordered both of us. "I do not wish to hurt thee, whelp, but I shall defend myself if I must."

Dag glowered at Ormyr, but had no choice but to obey.

I braced my dagger hilt in my right hand, but kept it sheathed. I couldn't prevent my jaw from dropping, though. "It sure looks like you want to hurt him!"

"I'm simply preventing his interference." Ormyr focused on me and continued in that maddening, no-good calm and reasonable tone. "Thou art ill and enthralled, Lady Knight, but try to heed me: as we approach their hiding place, the Naustviks' influence may prove overwhelming. I need the relic in case ye both fall to them. With it, I may yet have a chance to save you. This is for all our safety. Prithee trust me."

"Don't give him a damn thing!" Dag snapped.

"Silence, whelp!" Ormyr returned.

"Jump off and break your neck!" Dag's eyes shifted my way, pleading with me.

I expected Ormyr to retaliate with the keris in some fashion. To my relief, he didn't. I trembled, struggling not to show it while also fighting hard to concentrate. What could be done? I was in no shape to challenge Ormyr. With survival in question, I preferred we kept working together. But in Ormyr's eyes, Dag and I were allies only up to a point. The moment we did something he didn't like, we were expendable thralls. The keris in his hand made that all too clear.

Ultimately, Dag was worth more than any Shipbuilder device ever would be. He probably wouldn't understand my actions; I hoped his resentment wouldn't last. Frowning, I raised a hand to my temple again, making a show of some great internal struggle. "Master? I … You're right. It's probably safer with you." I produced the data carrier and handed it to him.

With a look of grateful relief, Ormyr dropped the data carrier into a pouch on his belt and backed away, limping to the platform's opposite end. "I shall fly us along a path of my choosing. Neither of you shall be able to override or betray my course to the Naustviks."

My annoyance was hard to swallow. Just when we were starting to make progress, his paranoia had gotten the better of him—a less violent version of what'd happened with Verahl that morning.

Dag tracked Ormyr with smoldering rage, which soon swiveled from him to me.

"I'm sorry," I murmured.

He pulled his hood over his face, then retreated to the corner that put him as far away from me and Ormyr as possible.

Hell. I collapsed to my knees, screwing my eyes shut as my head pounded in protest. Our cooperation and everything else remained in jeopardy, but right then, I was glad not to be standing.

Obeying Ormyr's verbal commands, the platform spurred forward slowly—a good thing, or else inertia would've thrown us off—then picked up speed. I narrowed my eyes against the freezing night air rushing past, hugging myself with my good arm.

The glow of the construct forest faded behind us. Moments later, we passed over the lip of the impact crater to cross the massive lake, miles wide and endlessly deep. Its immensity was almost as dizzying as my concussion. A good thing I was off my feet.

On the other side of the platform, Dag had curled into himself, fidgeting with his slingshot. My heart ached, imagining the superstitious fear likely plaguing him the way it'd once plagued me. I debated whether to speak up, then finally decided it was better to clear the air sooner rather than later. I dragged myself closer to Dag's side, trying to speak loud enough to be heard over the rushing wind but not loud enough for Ormyr to eavesdrop. "The Harbinger's not that different from a starship, just—"

"Why'd ye surrender the relic to him?" Dag's incisive scowl peeked out from under his hood. "Now he'll ditch us, and then my friends are in trouble!"

I flinched. Part of me longed to shut up and retreat. The other part held me in check. "He could've ditched us already, but he hasn't. If I didn't give him the data carrier, he might've hurt you." My left hand was a sore, bloody testament to the measures Ormyr would take in the name of "helping" others. "We have to pick our battles. That one wasn't worth fighting."

"But it was the best weapon we had!" Dag insisted.

While a significant loss, it wasn't the end of the world. "What makes you think that?" I asked.

He faltered. "It's Shipbuilder magic. What could be better?"

"Being clever. Having tricks up our sleeves." I threw a furtive glance over my shoulder. Behind us, Ormyr stood poised for battle with his keris, staring out over our heads with the resolve of one who had to stay awake lest monsters come out. He seemed unconcerned by our exchange, if he'd even noticed.

"Ormyr will be even fuller of himself now," I continued. "That'll help us when a battle comes along that we *have* to win.

Like when we find Verahl and Thordia." Despite our differ-ences, I still had no desire to fight Ormyr, but depending on what happened in the Harbinger, it could become our reality.

Dag stared downward, scraping a thumbnail against his slingshot. It was clear he wasn't fully assuaged.

Several days earlier, protecting the Naustviks had been my priority. I wanted to reassure Dag that I'd do anything to help his wrongly persecuted friends, but couldn't. My anger toward Verahl had yet to cool off. As for Thordia, I still hoped for the best.

But when you assume the worst, people rarely disappoint you. May, my former master, had proclaimed as much constantly.

What might help Dag feel better? Hell, I didn't know. What would've reassured me at his age? The Unseen-fearing innkeeper's daughter was hard to reconnect with at that moment, but I was fairly certain that if she'd been there, she would've been pretty damn …

"Scared?" I blurted.

Dag's scowl returned. His whole body tensed as though preparing to tackle me.

"There's nothing wrong with that," I rushed to add.

"I'm not afraid!" he cried.

"Well, I am," I admitted.

Confusion overtook Dag's glare. "Ye have as much power as I do. More, even. Ye weren't afraid in the cellar."

"I knew those lights couldn't hurt me. But here?" I shook my head helplessly. "How can you *not* be scared when you don't know what lies ahead? Look at us, though, we're head-ing in anyway. *That's* bravery: being afraid, and telling your fear to go to hell. My friend, the wise woman, taught me that —except she used much nicer words."

Drea would've laughed at the way I'd employed her les-son. I hoped I got to tell her about it later.

Dag studied my expression, then squinted ahead. I wasn't sure whether I'd been forgiven, but at least he stopped fidgeting.

Looming thousands of feet high, the Harbinger's size impressed itself upon us more than ever. The mighty ring structure seemed to reach out and encircle us as we drew closer; we craned our necks in a futile attempt to take it all in. Hundreds of spokes, each dotted with beacons like dew on a spider's web, connected the ring to the main tower. They might not have been strictly anchor points. Transit vehicles might've run along those paths once, providing quick travel between the two sections.

As Ormyr steered toward the lower half of the structure, I lost all sense of scale. Between glowing beacons, the tower's dark hull masked whatever damage had been sustained during the crash. Luminescent Shipbuilder letters and numbers appeared, maybe labels for doors or sections.

Again, I marveled at how much had survived. The Harbinger must've made heavy use of the same materials employed in ship's hulls, materials that still withstood atmospheric stresses centuries later. Though concentration remained a struggle for me, I committed as much detail to memory as possible using my preferred mnemonic: storing pictures in a mental layout of *Kepler's Law*. My mentors at the beguinage would have lots of questions, supposing I ever saw them again.

"Where're we going?" Dag asked.

"Starships used to enter and leave the Harbinger all the time," I said. "Ormyr's probably looking for one of the doors they used."

Sure enough, we honed in on two massive rectangular panels outlined with beacons, scorched along their edges but otherwise intact. I pictured the grand armadas that'd once sailed through those doors, then wondered whether any Shipbuilder had ever imagined such a band of visitors in his distant future: half-starved, exhausted, most of them expecting monsters and foul magic.

Ormyr brought our platform to a halt just shy of the panels. I glanced over my shoulder as he threw his free hand forward. "*I ... bid ... you ... open!*" he called out in Shipbuilder, clearly enunciating each word.

The doors lurched into action, shuttling away from each other.

Dag gave a start. I was surprised, too. Sure, voice command was possible, but not out in the vacuum of space where these doors had once stood. A proximity sensor somewhere on the Harbinger's hull must've detected our arrival.

We hovered in mid-air, awaiting the doors' halting progress. After creating a generous gap, they ground to a stop.

The area beyond admitted no light, sound, or smell. No hint of what lay ahead. Trembling with anticipation, I forced myself to my feet. Dag stood with me, readying his slingshot.

"Steel yourselves," Ormyr said.

CHAPTER 11

I stood at one end of a platform floating hundreds of feet above a giant crater-lake, struggling against the injury, fatigue, and awe that wanted to knock me flat again. Beside me, Dag tensed with his slingshot primed to fire. Behind us, Ormyr was poised to steer us beyond parted doors and into the massive Harbinger.

A silence hung over us that, for once, wasn't the product of spite. I felt sure my trembling was more from the enormity of the moment than from my sorry physical state. The pitch-black interior had sat for decades outside Nidaros, and for centuries in space before that. Would we find a graveyard or a treasure trove? For the sake of everything, I hoped the latter.

Eventually, Ormyr found his voice again, using verbal commands to spur the platform into the orbital station at a cautious speed. The cold nighttime breeze fell away behind us, replaced by the warm staleness that canned air picked up over time.

Artificial lights surged on around us, banishing the darkness. We found ourselves entering an impossibly vast docking bay full of ships — resting on the *ceiling* of a chamber hundreds of yards long and wide.

I gasped.

Stone and slingshot clattered out of Dag's hands. He craned his neck, one hand hovering near the beads on his belt that he lacked the wherewithal to grasp. "What in Hel's keeping them up there?"

"Weight-of-earths magic," Ormyr muttered, apparently too shocked to chide him for invoking Hel again.

Active gravity plating in the Harbinger, powerful enough to overcome the planet's gravity. While not unheard of, it was hard to find intact. And those ships! They were sleeker and in better repair than any I'd ever seen before. Some sat upright, while others lay clustered on their sides or tops, still beautiful despite the indignity. Others had never fallen from the honeycomb-shaped chambers in which they'd been parked hundreds of years earlier.

Lords waged all-out war over fleets a fraction of the size. Nidaros could fetch insane prices for any that remained flight-worthy. Even damaged ships could yield valuable salvage, assuming the powers-that-be were willing to look the other way on the whole "repair is forbidden" thing. It was forbidden within Catherwood space, but most of the galaxy had no such qualms. Speaking of, there was a whole galaxy to escape to if the ichor proved incurable.

Maybe independence wasn't such a pipe dream for Nidaros after all. If only my friends, and Ingvar, were there to see this. Overcome, I dropped onto knees that could no longer support my weight.

Dag darted behind me as though to defend me from something. Meanwhile, the platform had paused in mid-air. I glanced over my shoulder and found Ormyr approaching. With lights rendering the place as bright as day, it was easy to see his worried look—and the ichor-laced mud staining our boots, my companions' adept robes, and my coat.

"I'm fine," I muttered. This time, it was definitely more emotional than physical.

Ormyr ignored me as usual, trying but failing to hide the limp he'd earned during Holsten's ambush.

Dag recovered his slingshot, loading it while leveling a vicious scowl at the master adept. I supposed he feared Ormyr's keris might wind up at someone's throat again, and I couldn't blame him.

The dagger remained lowered, though. Ormyr offered his free hand to help me up. Spacers were wrapped around the bands of the rings on his fingers, something I'd first noticed several days earlier. Nidaros' long brush with famine hadn't done Ormyr any favors, but whatever bothered him, he seemed compelled to hide. After all, he believed I could warn the Naustviks and Lord Catherwood of any weakness that leaked out.

If only he knew he didn't have to play such games with me. I'd tell him, but he wouldn't listen. He probably felt just as obligated to keep up the charade as I did whenever I talked to him or other superstitious types.

Surprise jolted me. Was Ormyr *always* putting on a show, even while berating his adepts or spouting confident prophecy to Baron Tristan? Did he ever wish he could act more like himself?

I couldn't tell him it was safe to let his guard down, but maybe I could show him. With as much reassurance as possible, I glanced up and met his gaze. "I feel better down here, Master. Don't worry, I'll be on my feet when I need to be."

The acetaminophen I'd taken had dulled the headache, but hadn't helped me regain balance or focus. My left arm, from sore shoulder to bandaged hand, remained all but useless. Accumulated aches and pains nagged at me all over. Hunger and thirst remained constant problems.

"How are *you* feeling?" I asked.

Ormyr's hand dropped to his side. He blinked at me, faltering.

"To Hel with him." Dag glanced between us nervously, slingshot primed. "Let's get away from these dead ships afore they fall on us."

"They cannot harm us, whelp," Ormyr scolded and reassured at once. "The same force binding us to our planet, the Shipbuilders could breathe into any surface at will. The force within the construct we stand upon is counteracting the force from above."

Right. Our platform must've detected the new source of gravity above and switched on its own gravity to keep us in place. The closest gravity field kept all others from interfering. Otherwise, we should've fallen *up* toward the ships and broken our necks.

Dag lowered his slingshot, frowning. "Why's the magic up there?"

"They probably treated the center of the Harbinger as 'down,'" I said. "Since this is the lower half of the structure, the floor looks like a ceiling to us."

Dag threw a bewildered glance my way.

I shook my head. "It's just a guess."

"A good one, however." Ormyr sounded impressed. "We shall gain a better idea as we explore—but first, let us take a moment to appreciate our surroundings. We may never again behold a scene of its like." He glanced high and low with a dreamlike reverence.

His fascination surprised me at first, but Ormyr was no charlatan adept. He possessed concrete Shipbuilder knowledge. From that, reverence followed naturally.

"It seemeth dead now, but this port once bustled with activity," Ormyr continued.

I had no doubt he was right. This port, as he called it— really more of a docking bay—would've rivaled the chaos of

Linum Dominorum's port in Spectra. People and goods moving freely, mechanics tending to maintenance without fear of persecution, dozens of constructs like our platform flying around, and other marvels we couldn't begin to imagine.

Ormyr pointed back the way we'd flown in. "A conjured barrier of specially arrayed energy prevented the air inside this chamber from escaping into space."

Mostly true, but it hadn't been magic. The Shipbuilders had developed containment shields that could be tuned to let only certain things in or out. I'd seen a few surviving examples, usually protecting settlements and ports from the hazardous environments surrounding them.

"Artificial minds monitored departures, arrivals, transfers —" Ormyr continued.

"Artificial *what?*" Dag interrupted.

Unfazed, Ormyr gestured to the platform beneath us. "In addition to constructs like these that require constant command, the Shipbuilders forged constructs which they imbued with the power of intelligence. Those constructs could act of their own accord — every bit as capable as the Shipbuilders themselves, if not more so."

Artificial intelligence. Most of it had resided within the giant computers that'd once managed entire bases and settlements. Drea was especially gifted with extracting data from whatever surviving examples the beguinage came across. Smaller devices like data carriers lacked AIs, at least as far as my mentors knew.

Dag's jaw dropped. "I want to see one." The boy seemed more awed than scared, as with the construct forest earlier.

Ormyr seemed to have completely forgotten he was on a witch-hunt. If this place captivated him so much, why hadn't he come sooner? Sure, there was a death penalty involved, but with as much sway as he held over Baron Tristan, he could've gotten the policy changed.

"There should be some place within this chamber where we can gain access to the rest of the Harbinger." Ormyr squinted about. "I shall summon a guide-spirit to aid us."

Guide-spirit? I had no idea what he meant. Prior experience warned me not to dismiss it as myth. I braced myself to see or learn something new.

Ormyr threw his arms out wide. "O great and ancient spirits of the Harbinger, I call upon your wisdom and guidance! By grace of the Unseen, aid these your weary visitors!"

His invocation echoed impressively, but silence met the call.

Ormyr's eyes narrowed. "The spirits must have long ago abandoned this place, or perished within the relics that housed them."

Dag glanced about warily.

I doubted there were actual spirits anywhere or ever had been, but maybe some voice-commanded system had once existed that'd since malfunctioned. Even if it were still working, Ormyr's spell was almost certainly not how one interacted with it. Unable to offer anything constructive, I kept silent.

"What now?" Dag prompted.

"We'll press on and keep vigilant." Ormyr spurred the platform forward.

Seconds later, we seemed to trip another proximity sensor. The chamber's bright light dimmed. Huge holographic rectangles lit up in mid-air on either side of our platform, flat in color, displaying messages like *"Error. No response from news service."* The Shipbuilder writing was oriented our way, even though we were flying upside-down through the docking chamber. An even larger, brighter rectangle splashed out across the far wall of the dock.

"Visitors, welcome!" A friendly voice issued from everywhere at once, and continued speaking in the sweetest, most effortless Shipbuilder I'd ever heard.

I gasped again. Unfortunately, her words were too fast for me to make out.

Dag flinched and raised his slingshot, but wasn't sure what to aim at. Ormyr also gave a start, then froze, frowning in concentration.

The voice stopped, leaving the holograms active in its wake.

"Was *that* your guide-spirit?" Dag whispered into the silence.

It'd probably been some sort of automated, pre-recorded message, but that was tough to explain right then. "She welcomed us," I piped up.

"Indeed, and described quite a few things that … are irrelevant at present," Ormyr added.

I took his faltering to mean the master adept hadn't completely understood everything himself.

"But, look there!" Ormyr pointed toward the far wall of the dock. The glowing rectangle highlighted a dozen vertical tube-like protrusions spanning across it. An even brighter aura fell upon one tube in particular.

"Are those lifts?" I asked eagerly.

"Indeed," Ormyr replied. "The guide-spirit hath allotted us that one. We may take it wherever we wish to go."

Hell, I hoped they still worked. The prospect of not having to navigate the Harbinger on foot was galvanizing.

"We must reorient ourselves to access it," Ormyr explained. "I shall have to lift us close to the ceiling, then dispel the weight-of-earths magic exerted by this platform."

Nervousness seized me, one I tried not to convey. "Let's do it."

Dag glanced uncertainly in my direction.

"We want to be on the ceiling with the ships," I explained.

The boy's eyes widened. "We'll have to walk upside down?"

"It won't feel upside down." I sighed helplessly. "I know it doesn't make sense, but trust me."

At Ormyr's command, the platform slid toward the high-lighted lift tube on opposite end of the chamber, rising toward a clear spot on the ceiling. The holographic displays to either side of us vanished as we flew past them.

"Lie upon your backs," Ormyr commanded.

This was smart. We didn't want to land on our heads, and this would better distribute the shock of the transition. For the first time, I noticed how big the chamber was in the opposite direction, how far there was to fall. Though it wouldn't be possible to fall in that direction, my brain couldn't be convinced otherwise.

After some hesitation, Dag put away his slingshot and followed my example until we were all lying down in a line.

Ormyr nudged the platform even higher. The glossy ceiling hovered inches above our faces.

"Dag? Arms up here." I placed my forearms against the ceiling with my head in-between. "Brace yourself like you're about to fall."

Dag's confusion persisted, but he complied.

Ormyr used one of the command words at his disposal to deactivate the platform's gravity. Once it was gone, the gravity on the ceiling was the only force we were subject to. We jerked upward. Only after every bit of me smashed up against the ceiling did my body make the disorienting switch to treating up as down. The platform now hovered over our heads.

Beside me, Dag cursed, then again, more bewildered than hurt or scared.

My head spun. I tamped down nausea to ask, "Are you all right?"

"Aye! *Skíta*, that was strange!"

On the ceiling—floor—beneath us, a thick layer of dust muted the shiny surface. Ahead, the faint outline of a footprint lay within arm's reach. A surge of excitement almost made me forget my disorientation. "Look," I prompted Dag, pointing. "That footprint must be hundreds of years old."

Dag's eyes went wide. "A man's boot, looks like." His tone contained surprise, as though not expecting the presence of people during the Shipbuilders' heyday. He pointed ahead. "There's another one. Running?" He slid out from under the platform and darted over for a closer look.

I remained where I was, trying to imagine what the person had been running toward or from. Hurrying to steady toppling cargo? Evacuating the station? What had the last of the Shipbuilders done here? Why had they left all these ships behind? Had they abandoned the Harbinger gradually, or had something catastrophic forced them out? Had it coincided with the Shipbuilders' decline?

An ichor-drenched hem and boots hobbled into view. Master Ormyr's jeweled hand appeared next, reaching for me.

With his help, I slid out from under the platform and slowly returned to my feet. "What part of your leg is bothering you?" I asked Ormyr under my breath.

He maintained his grip on my right arm with both hands. "Worry not for me, Lady Knight. Thy health is of greater concern."

I stifled the urge to object. No games, right? "I've felt better," I admitted.

"I wish we could spell a while, but I dread giving the Naustviks time to prepare for our confrontation. And if their influence should overcome thee ..." Ormyr trailed off, glancing askance.

It'd be better if you couldn't put up a fight, I finished mentally with a strange mix of bitterness and acceptance. That seemed like where the thought was going. I didn't care for Ormyr's reasoning, but couldn't fault it, either. He was just trying to figure out how to survive in his enemy's staggeringly intact lair.

"Focus upon thy vengeance. 'Tis nearly at hand," Ormyr resumed. "It shall save thee."

I lacked the energy to chip at this charade just yet. Wordlessly, I pulled free of his grasp and glanced back the way we'd come, sizing up the docking bay from our new perspective. A thick maze of ships crowded our rear view, with the honeycomb stacks towering throughout. The ships' hulls were iridescent, maybe some advanced alloy developed after *Kepler's Law* had already lapped the galaxy several hundred times. In the short-term, one of them might be useful for returning to the capital and rescuing Drea, if I couldn't find *Kepler's Law*. But the longing for *my ship* tugged at my heart. This was just one docking bay. How many more existed? Which one had Verahl used, if any?

"I shall attempt to summon a lift car." Ormyr's voice broke through my thoughts.

I glanced toward Dag—still following his footprint trail, gradually nearing the closest vessels in the shipyard. "Go ahead. We'll be right behind you."

The master adept hesitated with an uneasy expression, then turned to approach the highlighted lift tube.

I called Dag over to explain what Ormyr was up to. "Lifts carry equipment and people—like ulldyr, but faster."

Dag frowned. "Where're we going?"

"We still have to figure that out," I said.

"What happens when we find Verahl and Thordia?" he murmured, narrowing eyes at Ormyr.

"I'm not sure about that, either," I admitted. "But Ormyr won't get to hurt them."

Dag's eyes remained narrowed. Nevertheless, he followed me toward the highlighted wall without complaint. There, Ormyr puzzled over a new holographic interface that displayed a three-dimensional schematic of the Harbinger. The orbital station was divided into dozens of levels, with dozens of locations upon each.

Ormyr glanced to us. "Do you sense where the Naustviks reside?"

Dag scowled in reply.

"No." Once I said it, a sickening dread fell over me. If we didn't cough up an answer, would Ormyr torture one out of us? I braced myself for the worst, vowing not to let him lay a finger on Dag.

To my relief, Ormyr turned back to the map. "They are most likely in a command center wherein they might assume full control of the Harbinger's surviving aspects."

Thordia's note to Verahl returned to mind. She hadn't sought power, rather a cure for the ichor. "I think they're more interested in …" What should I call it? "Research," I finally said.

Dag remained scowling and mum.

"Perchance I should set up a circle and scry on the matter," Ormyr suggested.

I shook my head, not bothering to hide my distaste. "We don't have time for—"

Dag whirled back toward the shipyard, eyes wide. "What was that?"

Ormyr and I shared a confused glance before following his gaze. Several nervous seconds ticked by in silence.

"'Course it won't go again while ye're listening," Dag whispered.

Ormyr returned his attention to the directory.

Listening? "What did it sound like?" I asked.

Dag faltered. "I don't know."

I had my answer a second later. Whatever had startled him repeated itself somewhere deep amid the pile of ships. Little wonder Dag couldn't describe it. Pistons and gears formed it in part. At its core was the screech of metal dragging across metal.

Ormyr turned again, his expression betraying equal bafflement.

The noise repeated — louder, picking up pace. One of the stacked ships at the rear of the bay tumbled to the floor. Another followed, then a couple more, tracing a meandering line toward our position.

A chill slid down my spine. Something was coming for us, pushing ships out of its way to reach us. I struggled to imagine what it could be, aside from huge and powerful. And there we stood, most of us weak and injured, carrying only blades and stones for defense.

Hell.

CHAPTER 12

Mechanical clunks and scrapes filled the large docking bay. Something hidden from sight pushed its way through the sleek starships piled up like toys in a spoiled child's playroom.

On the opposite end of the bay, I stood with Ormyr and Dag before the entrance to a lift. The sounds gained momentum, drowning out our bickering. We fell silent, staring back.

Adrenaline got my heart pounding and cleared some fog from my brain. This had to be some kind of construct. Maybe a cargo mover, or part of a security system? Given the way those ships slid and toppled in its wake, *indifferent to its surroundings* was probably the best we could hope for. It certainly wasn't what to plan for.

I glanced back at the lift and its holographic interface. "Pick any location, Master," I whispered. "We can adjust course later."

No argument, for once. Ormyr turned to choose a destination.

Dag kept watch, his expression full of dread. He took two steps forward and armed his slingshot.

"*A lift car ...*" The friendly disembodied Shipbuilder voice returned briefly. I didn't catch the rest of her message past the din of sliding, tumbling ships.

Ormyr faced me with a grim expression, brandishing his keris. "There's no lift car here. We must wait for one to journey to us from deeper within the Harbinger."

Damn it, I thought, tensing. "How long will it take?"

"The guide-spirit did not say. She seemeth unaware of our plight." Ormyr advanced to stand with Dag, assuming an offensive posture.

We'd found many functional systems, but that was no guarantee the lift was also working. I scoured our surroundings for an alternate escape route. There didn't seem to be any other exits left or right of us. How were there were no stairs? One could usually count on Shipbuilder structures to have both lifts and stairwells. Maybe orbital space stations had been designed with different assumptions in mind. Oh well, I wouldn't have fared well on a climb anyway. With all the abuse I'd taken, it was hard enough keeping myself upright and awake.

I checked the lift's interface again, hoping to get an idea of when the car might arrive. Numbers and letters swished past, none of which held any significance. Reluctantly, I turned back around to stand at Dag's opposite side, adding my dagger to the line. It was more of an instinctual move than anything. What could the little blade do against whatever was knocking entire ships around?

"It doesn't have us yet," Dag muttered, poised to shoot. "Still sniffing us out."

"Quiet, whelp!" Ormyr chided.

Its progress was haphazard at first. Then the clunky, lumbering noises smoothed out, as though our pursuer had needed a little time to shake off centuries of rust. It glided straight toward us like a shark, parting ships in its wake, closing to within a hundred yards. Small flashes of shadow appeared through the gaps between ships.

I sucked in a breath, having a hard time not assuming the worst.

Ormyr raised his arms. "*Apodrasi. Deactivate!*"

Unfortunately, the verbal commands that'd worked so well amid the construct forest had no effect on our pursuer.

Dag darted forward and shot. His stone sailed toward the left-hand side of the docking bay, out where the thing clearly wasn't.

"Fool!" Ormyr cried. "What—?"

I shushed him, fairly certain what Dag was up to.

The stone plinked and rattled to the ground. Our hidden pursuer halted and went silent for a few seconds. Then it cut a new course, angling for where the stone had fallen.

"Decoy!" I whispered, indulging in a moment's relief. "Good work."

Galvanized by success, Dag reloaded his slingshot.

Ormyr looked on with understanding. A handful of smoke bombs appeared between his fingers. After waiting several moments, he hurled one toward the right side of the shipyard. It cracked open, sending plumes of reddish smoke curling into the air.

Our pursuer plowed toward it next, its form still hidden, then went silent again—likely poking around more carefully in that vicinity. It had to be hunting based on sound. *Was* it part of a security response? If so, why weren't we hearing alarms? Why were we allowed to leave the area via lift? The Harbinger at large didn't seem to consider us intruders. Something was probably malfunctioning here, but what?

I glanced over my shoulder. Still no telling when a lift car would arrive.

"We can't do this all day," I muttered. "We'll run out of things to throw." Or worse, our pursuer might catch on to our game before that. My mentors had owned constructs that could learn simple things like the layout of a room they were placed in. With what little we'd seen of the Harbinger, I assumed more advanced examples of machine-learning existed.

Escape seemed our best hope. Was the lift really our only option? Unconvinced, my searching eyes landed on the platform we'd ridden to the Harbinger, hovering a few yards away.

An idea breathed new life into my limbs. "I'll be right back." I sheathed my dagger, then spurred myself toward the platform.

"Hold!" Ormyr cried.

I ignored him, dropping to my knees beside the floating construct. Its glowing green interface appeared obediently before me, right-side up despite the platform's orientation. I dug through the command list, seeking gravity control.

Ormyr appeared at my side in short order. "What art thou doing?" he demanded, part worried and part accusatory.

Footsteps skidded to a stop behind him: Dag, slingshot loaded.

"We can fly back out of here and find a safer entry point if we need to," I replied. If Ormyr had let me keep the Naustviks' data carrier, I could've arranged for it safely back near the lift—but I kept that to myself.

"*Skíta!*" Dag cried in protest. "Not leaving now!"

"*If we need to,*" I repeated for emphasis, reorienting the platform's gravity controls. "For now, let's stand on this thing while we wait for the lift. If it doesn't show up, we'll fly out the way we came."

Ormyr boarded the platform, then turned to seize my elbow and pull. "I shall tend to its flight. Come, whelp!"

Once I'd crawled onto the platform, I turned and reached back for Dag. He darted away from me with a hurt expression.

However, a ship sliding along the floor nearby spurred him aboard soon enough.

Using voice commands, Ormyr steered the platform back toward the lift tube, hovering inches shy of it. He and Dag crowded the platform's front end, each launching new projectiles for the construct to chase after. I remained toward the rear, kneeling beside the lift with bated breath.

Finally, a door in the wall shuttled open.

"It's here!" I cried with relief.

But then I found myself staring at a squat cylinder with shimmering glass walls — and no door.

"Is it?" Dag asked over my shoulder.

I hesitated, stymied. This didn't look like any lift car I'd ever seen. Was a security system locking us down in the docking bay after all?

Maybe not. There were seemingly solid glass windows at Baron Tristan's estate that air — and people — could pass through, after all. The Shipbuilders had been able to manipulate the empty space between atoms as easily as they'd commanded gravity.

I held my right hand toward the transparent cylinder. My fingers plunged through the wall, into the lift car beyond. The feeling of touching a live wire coursed through my hand, making me flinch in surprise, but the sensation was too weak to do any harm.

A crash from behind jarred me away from my discovery. I turned to find another large ship sliding along the ground, hurtling toward our platform.

There was no time to explain. I grabbed Dag and Ormyr by the elbow, then fell back toward the glass wall.

We passed through the permeable surface together. The same jolting feeling spread through me, vanishing fast. Then we were inside the boxy lift car, taking up half of its space.

My strength gave out. I released the others and staggered backward until I landed on my backside, my bandaged left hand screaming in protest. Thankfully, the floor was solid, but just as transparent as the walls. Below me stretched a dizzying view of endless darkness.

Dag screamed in terror, the sound amplified by our small confines. He lunged toward the wall we'd just passed through.

Ormyr sheathed his dagger, then threw both arms around Dag, anchoring him in place.

The lift car descended from the docking bay, leaving our pursuer a mystery. Its glowing transparent walls showed us plummeting past layers of metal, insulation, and other sub-stances I could only guess at. There was no sensation of move-ment. Gravity plates were most likely at work, canceling out inertia.

Dag thrashed against Ormyr. "Get off!"

"My pleasure, whelp!" Ormyr released him and backed away. "Canst thou not spare one moment to observe and think before panicking?"

Upon glancing outside, Dag froze, forgetting to badmouth Ormyr back.

"We're inside the lift car, Dag," I muttered from the floor. "It's taking us away." It looked like we were dropping fast enough to reach hell in minutes, but we'd flipped upside down earlier. That meant we were traveling *up* the Harbinger's axle.

Ormyr glanced my way. With a look of compunction, he limped over and knelt at my left side, checking the bandage he'd placed over my temple.

I sat there, too lightheaded to reach my feet. Though my left hand and shoulder hurt the most, my concussion and fatigue hadn't lifted. I savored the excuse to rest, maybe eat and drink something if the break proved long enough.

Dag remained frozen as he stared outside, facing away from me.

"Any idea what that thing was?" I asked Ormyr. He'd been so knowledgeable earlier that I actually believed it worth-while to ask. Or hell, maybe I was banged up worse than I thought.

"Most likely a defensive mechanism that now seeth us as a threat," Ormyr replied, intent on his examination. "The Naustviks know of our arrival. They've sensed it through you."

Somehow, I doubt that. But thanks for making it our fault. I managed to keep my mouth shut.

Dag spun around to scowl at Ormyr. Then he noticed me and, with concern, darted over to kneel at my right. "Why would Verahl and Thordia try to hurt us?" he challenged Ormyr, gesturing between me and himself. "Aren't we their servants or something?"

Nice, I thought, appreciating how Dag used the master adepts's own logic against him.

Ormyr remained focused on my skull, speaking in an apologetic tone. "The Naustviks care nothing for thee, whelp. They are but using thee."

"They're my friends!" Dag glowered at him.

"Where are we headed, Master?" I asked, hoping to defuse the argument.

"I chose at random."

Ormyr probably wanted to keep the destination secret, lest we warn the Naustviks. I didn't press the point, too focused on keeping myself together.

Before any of us had much chance to relax, the lift car and our view beyond blacked out entirely. The disembodied voice of our female guide returned—less friendly, more matter-of-fact. The only word I picked up was *"Failed."*

My eyes went wide, even though there was nothing to see. Dag muttered something, his words lost amid the announce-ment. He'd probably cursed. I wanted to reach for him in the darkness, but with all the tension filling the lift just then, I stood to lose my hand doing that.

The lights surged back on, showing our car had stopped somewhere amid the Harbinger's mechanical innards. Dag looked out with worry, grasping his hammer amulet.

Had the lift just malfunctioned? Shoving aside the fear of being stuck in a glass coffin forever, I glanced to Ormyr, hoping he'd understood more of the announcement. The master adept's expression was pale and worried.

I forced myself to be calm for Dag's sake. "Master, what did she say?"

"I … 'tis difficult to explain." He fidgeted absently with the beads at his side.

"It's all right if you don't know," I said. "You're allowed to admit it."

Ormyr faltered, blinking.

"Not as smart as ye think, aye?" Dag narrowed his eyes at Ormyr.

"Not knowing something doesn't make anyone stupid. You can always fix not-knowing," I corrected Dag gently, then refocused on Ormyr. "Are we stuck? Should we be looking for an escape?"

Ormyr glanced high and low. "I—"

The lift car started back up again—moving *diagonally*, if the material streaming past us was to be believed.

I gasped, startled. Was there a diagonal lift shaft here, or was our car passing *through* floors like a ghost? Using some combination of electromagnetic fields, gravity manipulation, and permeable materials, might it be possible for the lift car to travel anywhere it wanted?

Ormyr still seemed troubled by the recorded announcement.

"We're moving again," Dag said.

"In a different direction," I managed past my surprise. "The, uh, *guide* said something failed earlier. Maybe we can't go to the original location for some reason, so we're being rerouted." Not a problem, given we'd been traveling to a random location to begin with.

"But how this came about is uncertain." As Ormyr got slightly closer to admitting he didn't know something, his worry intensified. "Are we being swept along by the guide-spirit, or the Naustviks? We may be bound for some manner of detention facility, or some other trap of their design."

Dag glanced to me with a bit of hopefulness. *"Are* they are bringing us to them, d'ye think?"

Unlikely. How would the Naustviks know we'd arrived, much less how to override our lift's destination? Still, what if we *were* about to come face to face with them? It was possible —and I'd never really planned past *find the Naustviks.*

My guts dropped. What would we do? How would I prevent all hell from breaking loose? Struggling to think, I glanced to Ormyr. "If we are about to see the Naustviks, it'd be best if Dag and I approach them first while you hide. They'll lower their guard. You'll have the element of surprise." And I'd buy more time to figure out how to keep things peaceful.

Dag's hopeful look turned strained.

"They know I'm here with you." Ormyr rested a hand on my knee, apologetic. "I appreciate that thou wishest to help, Lady Knight. Unfortunately, thou may'st lose control of thine actions at any time."

Dag seethed at Ormyr as though sizing up someone he'd soon be killing.

"Don't distance yourself from us," I urged Ormyr. "We helped each other this far, we have to keep working together."

"To Hel with him! We don't need him!" Dag snapped. "We know enough Shipbuilder magic to do this ourselves!"

Dag's words sent a chill through me. Anywhere else in the galaxy, they would've gotten us killed. Here, Ormyr just studied me with a questioning frown.

"That's not true," I blurted instinctively. "How could we know more than an adept?"

Ormyr's expression didn't change. After probing my gaze a while longer, he looked away.

My sense of relief was fleeting. Despite his Shipbuilder knowledge, Ormyr remained dangerously out of touch with reality. Dag and I had avoided retribution thus far, but if we survived to return to the capital, it'd be a different story there. I hoped we could dodge witchcraft allegations by blaming our "enthrallment."

The lift car changed direction again to move upward, then slowed, carrying us up through a solid floor and into an area bathed in soothing colors. The air took on a mysteriously sweet smell.

On either side of me, my companions jumped to their feet, readying weapons. I moved slower, but there was no way I *wasn't* standing to have a look around. My vision browned out and my head spun, but I powered through it to remain upright.

Our lift car had halted in the center of a circular room ten or fifteen feet across. A waist-high counter surrounded us, stocked with drills, clamps, and saws. Side-rooms branched off from the main chamber like flower petals. These rooms contained cabinets, wall-mounted consoles, and empty metallic beds shaped like half-cylinders, with probing instruments hovering over each one.

The harsh implements suggested a sinister purpose, but the soothing lights implied otherwise. Some sort of medical facility, maybe?

One bed in one of the petal-shaped rooms was occupied. A man lay there blanketed and sleeping, oblivious to our arrival.

Surprise, fury, and horror seized me at once. "Verahl," I blurted.

Ormyr and Dag froze, processing the sight of their respective enemy and friend.

My heart pounded with anticipation while also burning with resentment. Verahl. *Here*. We'd discussed the possibility, but I still couldn't believe we'd found him so fast. Maybe he'd tracked down his sister, and Thordia had talked him into resting. He wouldn't have stood still, much less gone to sleep, if she remained missing.

Kepler's Law couldn't be far off. Same with Thordia. We could cure the ichor, then race back to the capital, save Ingvar, thwart Holsten, and hasten off to Drea. Beyond my anger toward Verahl, there shined the tiniest glimmer of hope.

Dag's face broke into relief. "Mate! Ye all right?" He put away his slingshot and bolted toward the lift car wall.

"Stay back, whelp!" Ormyr darted ahead of me and grabbed Dag's arm.

My stomach sank. If things devolved into chaos here, Nidaros and everyone I cared about would be lost. All I could think to do was move toward the conflict, try to break it up.

Dag thrashed like a wild animal desperate to slip a snare. Upon breaking free, his elbow flew up and struck Ormyr in the face. Ormyr stumbled backward into me.

I lost my balance and fell backward, crying out in pain as I hit the floor.

CHAPTER 13

I fell backward within the glassy lift car, my reward for trying to keep Dag and Ormyr from fighting each other over Verahl. As I hit the floor, my tailbone and back absorbed the brunt of impact; my skull took a mere tap in comparison. The air rushed out of my lungs along with a wince. I lay there with my scabbard poking into my spine, biting my lip and screwing my eyes shut against the pain.

A startled cry rang out—Dag. Two sets of footsteps quickly approached. The scent of Ormyr's cloves bloomed around me again.

"Don't fall asleep. Ye can't fall asleep!" Dag pleaded as a hand latched onto my right shoulder, shaking hard. Then his tone turned angry. "Cast a healing spell that *works* this time!"

"What dost thou think I've been doing?!" On my left, Ormyr's voice trembled. "If thou wouldst see her live, whelp, start wishing as hard as thou canst."

Dag's hand lifted from my shoulder. I opened my eyes to find Ormyr kneeling beside me with a furrowed brow, rummaging through his belt pouch for spell components. Dag, meanwhile, had shut his eyes over his beads.

A wave of guilt sent tears spilling down the sides of my face. It wasn't rational in the least, but it hit me powerfully all the same.

Ormyr's gaze latched onto mine. "The Naustviks may attempt to sacrifice thee for the sake of diversion," he said, voice still wavering. "Remember thy vengeance, Lady Knight. Speak to us. The words matter not."

I tried to think of something to say, but couldn't. Past Ormyr, Dag, and the lift car's walls, I saw the soothing lights of the room I suspected might be a medical ward. Verahl Naustvik slept just a few feet away—assuming this commotion hadn't awakened him. Worried, I tried to sit up.

Ormyr pushed on my sore left shoulder. "Stay down. 'Tis serious."

Maybe it was. Having already sustained a concussion during Adept Holsten's ambush, I was hardly the best judge of my own condition. But it didn't matter. If I stayed down, the ichor would spread through Nidaros unchecked. Dag, Ormyr, Ingvar, Drea, *everyone* would die.

I forced myself up to a seat. Dizziness and a pounding headache overwhelmed me for a few seconds, then subsided to a tolerable level. I glanced around to see if we'd been discovered, but the circular counter surrounding the lift car blocked my view. No sight or sound past the counter indicated that Verahl was awake, at least.

Dag opened his eyes, then blinked.

Again, Ormyr tried to push me back down. I shrugged him off. There was no time for spells and wishes. We had to approach Verahl, get him talking—and ensure Ormyr didn't harm him.

"Master?" I struggled to come up with the words I wanted. "We need to find Thordia, and my ship. Dag and I will ask Verahl where they are. Stay here and keep low."

Dag's hand returned to my right shoulder, clenching down tighter than before.

"Nay. Thordia already knoweth we're here together," Ormyr replied, his expression uneasy. "Didst thou not see those constructs surrounding Verahl? She's watching. Concealment shan't aid any of us."

I racked my brain for a good-sounding excuse. "There may be traps here, though — traps that only target you. It's best if you stay put."

Ormyr drew into himself, frowning while rubbing at one of his beads with his thumb. Finally, he looked me in the eye with determination. "Very well. I trust thee, Lady Knight, but the whelp less so." He focused a hard look on Dag. "Remain with me. Dame Jessamine hath fought valiantly against enthrallment this whole way, but thou hast not shown her strength. Against thy will, thou may'st yet betray us all."

"Ye'd deserve it!" Dag snapped, scowling.

I wanted Dag with me. Less chance of fireworks erupting behind my back that way. Besides ... "Verahl's more likely to open to up to Dag than to me," I pointed out.

Ormyr sighed, glancing about nervously. "Then take him. I shall remain here — for now. But be careful. Thordia could come to *us*."

Unlikely. She either had no idea Verahl was here, or had thought it was safe for him to be here alone. But, she might've set up surveillance, as Ormyr had within his dungeon. I supposed we'd find out. I took a collecting breath, then glanced to Dag. "Ready?"

The boy sprang to his feet and reached down to help me up. "Let's go."

My hide protested being vertical and mobile again, but to recover my ship and save everybody, I could power through it a while longer. Beyond the waist-high circular counter rested petal-shaped rooms filled with cabinets and mostly empty beds.

Verahl slept undisturbed on one of them — or at least faked it. Relief overpowered the many questions I had about our surroundings, and about how we'd stumbled upon Verahl so easily within the vast Harbinger.

While Ormyr remained in the lift car, keris in hand, Dag and I slipped out together. Passing through the permeable wall wasn't as jarring the second time. We walked through a gap in the circular counter, Dag spotting me until convinced I could keep my balance. Then he separated to dash toward Verahl.

When he reached the room's threshold, one of the empty beds nearby tilted into a vertical position, hovering not unlike the first forest construct we'd run into. Bars extended from its sides like a spider's legs, poised to snatch up an unwary fly.

"*Skíta!*" Dag cried out, backing away.

Instinctively, I wanted to run to him, but my body wouldn't cooperate. For the best. I approached at a calm pace instead, emphasizing there was no emergency here. Dag could handle this himself.

"Check for its interface," I reminded him.

After a moment, Dag inched toward the construct. When its holographic interface appeared, he let out a cry of triumph, straightening to his full height with a rare grin.

I halted beside him and indulged in a moment of pride — until some of the construct's bars reached toward me.

Dag yelped, then raised his arm to bat them away.

At first, I flinched, but the bars stopped short of physical contact. "Hang on," I said, putting up a hand to block Dag. "Let's see what happens."

A short time later, a new readout cluttered the construct's interface. The bars retracted and vanished into the construct's sides.

"What in Hel was that?" Dag asked.

Good question. Maybe a diagnostic of some kind? I scrolled through the Shipbuilder text with a finger, finding several recognizable things like temperature and heart rate, but most of it made no sense to me. The things I understood best were the many errors about missing components and other needed repairs.

The interface offered no further options. It probably needed someone to resolve those errors first, and I had no way of doing that.

"I think it just tried to figure out how hurt I am," I finally said, my heart jumping at the thought. My mentors at the beguinage had told me of constructs that'd once worked alongside healers, performing triage and patient transport among other things, but I'd never seen one. If it could be repaired, it'd be wonderfully handy to have around.

Dag blinked up at me, then stared at the glowing interface. "Is that why it went after you and not me? It knows ye're hurt?"

"Maybe," I replied. Then my pulse sped up as I recalled how our lift car had been rerouted there. "Maybe the, uh, *guide-spirit* realized we were hurt, too." I used Ormyr's pet name for the disembodied voice that filtered in and out on occasion. Its announcements had seemed like prerecorded messages at first, but maybe it was actually the voice of a still-functioning AI.

I struggled to keep my voice down. "This looks like a medical facility—a place for healing. The lift car might've brought us here so we could recover. Verahl was hurt from all that time in the dungeon." And fighting his way out of it, and stealing my ship. "Maybe the same thing happened to him."

Dag swallowed hard with a look of compunction, then spun away from the construct to finish his run to Verahl's bedside. "Wake up, mate!"

All that time, Verahl had remained motionless under the blanket covering him. It wasn't a bed he was resting on, rather another of the medical constructs. He'd cleaned up since I'd seen him last. Several smaller constructs hovered over him, their purposes unknown.

Dag ignored the floating devices as he approached, latching onto his friend's shoulder. "Verahl?"

Still no response.

Good. I hope you're messed up. The cruel thought flashed uncensored through my punch-drunk brain. A twinge of guilt followed, but it was lost amid the crushing heartache I nursed for Ingvar, miles and centuries removed from this medical ward. Most likely, he lay on a straw pallet in the keep while some traitorous adept hovered over him with spell components that were useless at best, harmful at worst—unless they'd decided on bloodletting, amputations, burning him alive in the dungeon, or something even more horrible than I could imagine.

Worry and longing tore at my insides, doubling me over. Tears came to my eyes. It wasn't fair. Ingvar deserved to be resting safely in recovery, not Verahl. This was the first time I'd ever seriously regretted sticking out my neck for someone— and things stood to get even worse. When Holsten and the other Gyllenfeld-leaning adepts returned to Nidaros, what plans might they set in motion while Ingvar and Ormyr were out of the picture?

"He doesn't look good."

Dag's words pulled me back. He tugged at the collar of his adept robe, eyes darting uncertainly among the cryptic readouts surrounding Verahl like a halo.

The faster we handled this, the faster we could return and save everyone. I dabbed at my eyes with my sleeve and approached the construct-bed. Rage and despair closed off my throat. I could've choked Verahl where he slept.

Dag glanced nervously my way. "Feeling all right?"

I nodded, unable to speak without losing it. For Dag's sake, I fought for control. We needed answers.

Unfortunately, Verahl remained unconscious, or at least pretended to be. Reaching for his wrist, I found his pulse easily. Next, I flicked my forefinger against his cheek, under his eye. To my surprise, not one muscle in his face twitched.

"He's sleeping," I said. "And it's a deep sleep."

It looked more like sedation. But really, *sedatives?* Exhilaration bolted through me, which I dismissed. Viable drugs in the Harbinger? That was impossible. Organic compounds broke down over time.

Nothing within view explained how Verahl had been treated. It reminded me of his stay aboard *Kepler's Law:* brief, neat, respectful of my space. Even through my anger, I had to grant him that much. Had he tended to himself? Had Thordia done it? Or had they learned how to use the medical constructs?

"He won't wake up?" Dag's worried frown deepened.

"Not just yet, but he seems fine." I swallowed my mixed feelings on that count. "He probably needs the sleep. Let's try to get our answers another way." I backpedaled from the bed and glanced downward. "The floor's a good place to start. People don't think about what they leave there."

Dag crouched beside me, then laid himself flat against the ground. "There's our footprints ... and more there!" He pointed to a spot nearby. "One set's big, the other's like yours. A little bigger." After a moment, he darted up and hurried around to the other side of Verahl's bed, oblivious of the gray streaks of dust on his adept robe.

That sounded like Verahl—and maybe Thordia. Excited, I kept quiet and followed him at a distance. While Dag studied the trails, he missed what I saw: a pair of worn boots propped between the bed and the waist-high drawer flanking it.

Galvanized, I knelt carefully before the discovery, then seized both boots with my right hand. They were Verahl's, all right, the ones he'd worn throughout our acquaintance. I twisted my wrist, inspecting them from every angle.

Dag abandoned the footprints and slipped up beside me, leaning in curiously.

I pointed to the darkened soles. "There's ichor in the adepts' dungeon. That's where Verahl picked this up."

He pulled away something stuck to the side of one heel, then shoved it toward me: a green, leafy stem fragment. "Flax! Only a few weeks old!"

My jaw dropped. I took it from him for a closer look. "Are you sure?"

There was no doubt in his jubilant expression. "Thordia's growing flax here!"

The more I thought about it, the more I succumbed to Dag's excitement. It seemed improbable that Verahl would just happen to run into young flax. There wasn't any growing in Nidaros, and certainly not anywhere on the way to the Harbinger—but there'd been plenty of exotic plant matter at the Naustviks' house, suggesting Thordia could cultivate whatever she set her mind to.

There'd been no flax at her home, though. Coupled with the footprints, this was strong evidence that she'd survived, reached the Harbinger some time ago, and found someplace to raise another astonishing garden. Had she also found a cure for the ichor?

"But where is she now?" Dag cast a strained glance my way.

There was still a long search ahead of us. A sobering thought. Unless … "Maybe something in this drawer will tell us."

I set aside the boots to check the storage space at Verahl's bedside, and found the knapsack Ingvar had prepared for him days earlier. It contained all its original contents—bread, canteen, candles, tinderbox, cloak—plus more food and first aid supplies skimmed from my ship's supply closets.

The food was all I had eyes for at first. Without a thought, I broke off a hunk of hard bread for Dag, then devoured some on the spot myself. After a swig of water from my canteen, I noticed something else within the knapsack that made me gasp: the second data carrier. The one Verahl had used to take control of *Kepler's Law*.

I picked up the device, forgetting all else in a moment of mixed sorrow and vindication.

"Hey, another one!" Dag glanced back toward the lift car, likely making sure Ormyr hadn't witnessed our find. He'd taken the other data carrier from me, after all. Fortunately, the master adept remained silent and out of sight.

"Ye can control constructs with that!" Dag spoke under his breath, bouncing on his knees.

"And plenty of other things," I murmured. "It might even tell us where Thordia and my ship are."

"How?" Dag asked.

"These devices contain records of every action they perform." They logged notes about each computer, construct, and instrument they communicated with, and when. "We can find out what Verahl has done in the Harbinger up until now." Provided he'd passed through areas that functioned as well as the ones we'd seen.

"Well, go on then!" Dag said.

I struggled to recall what Drea had shown me years earlier about tracing the history of a given device. Sometimes, it was a just matter of historical curiosity. In other cases, one could hunt down a missing friend. If Branigan had brought a data carrier with him to Gules ... well, it didn't matter; it would've been stolen along with his other possessions, and he would've been killed all the same. But Drea would still have her data carrier. I'd be able to track its signal—assuming I ever made it back to Gules.

Later. I pushed away worry and grief to start up the device and dig through its interface. Eventually, the steps came back to me. With trembling fingers, I scrolled through the most recent entries. The first one to grab my eye was of Verahl entering a location described as a docking bay. That had to be where *Kepler's Law* was. Elated, I continued scrolling. "It looks like he traded messages with another data carrier somewhere in the Harbinger."

"How d'ye mean?" Dag asked.

It wasn't easy to explain. "Verahl wrote a message on this device, then the same message appeared on the other device. Then the person with that device wrote a message back to Verahl."

Dag frowned, but seemed to understand enough. "Who else could he be talking to but Thordia?"

"Right, that's what I'm thinking," I said. "He traded messages with Thordia, then summoned a lift car and rode it to a place called, uh …" I trailed off. The individual Shipbuilder words meant "joy" and "union," but I wasn't sure if there were some special context in stringing them together.

"Are ye all right?"

Ormyr's concerned voice sounded behind us, far too close for comfort.

Surprise jolted me, followed by annoyance. He just couldn't sit still, could he? And I was about to lose another data carrier to his paranoia. What if he refused to follow its leads? What if he insisted on using magic to hunt for Thordia, thus delaying our return to the capital? No one needed that, least of all Ingvar. Our situation offered one saving grace: Ormyr was directly behind us. My body hid the data carrier from him. I moved to tuck it inside my coat, up against my nanofiber brigandine.

"I see the glow of the device in thy hands, Lady Knight," Ormyr spoke calmly. "There's no need to conceal it."

Damn it. Worry knotted in my stomach.

Dag jumped up and whirled around. "Ye're not taking this one!"

"Nay," Ormyr replied. "Nay, I'm not."

At his calm insistence, I frowned. Turning, I found Ormyr standing at the foot of Verahl's bed, keris in hand, with an oddly accepting look on his face.

"'Tis the second time the Unseen have conspired to place such a device in thy hands," he continued. "I shan't dispute their will."

My surprise intensified, but then I recalled that Ormyr still had the data carrier he'd confiscated from me previously. With that, and his voice commands, he could potentially override anything I did. That was probably where his generosity came from — but I also wanted to believe that maybe, he trusted me a little more. In return, I was more willing to trust him. He'd hung back as requested — mostly — only rushing our way out of concern. And although Verahl was right there before him, fully vulnerable, he hadn't paid the fugitive any attention.

While I remained kneeling, Dag had armed his slingshot, poised to defend us if necessary.

Things had to stay peaceful. After taking a deep breath, I slowly reached my feet to stand beside Dag. "I may have figured out where to find what we're looking for."

Ormyr blinked, then gestured toward the data carrier with a jeweled hand. "Show me."

"Nay, don't!" Dag protested.

"We have to stay together, remember?" I asked, hoping he remembered our plan of being with Ormyr when he found Thordia. "That's how we keep everyone from getting hurt — or hurt *worse*."

After some hesitation, the tension left Dag's shoulders.

"That toy is useless against me anyway, whelp," Ormyr muttered.

Dag stiffened, glaring, and raised his arms again to fire.

I placed myself between him and Ormyr. "Dag, you're better than that. Take a deep breath and put it away."

"Not 'til he disarms first!" Dag cried.

A reasonable request, given Ormyr had held that keris to his neck earlier and tortured me with it before that. I faced the master adept, who calmly put away his weapon. I was thankful — until I recalled how easily he could make it reappear.

Dag complied as well, smoldering at Ormyr.

The boy had never taken that deep breath. In my relief, I wound up taking it for him, then thought about how he might remain occupied while I talked to Ormyr. "Could you keep an eye on Verahl?"

Without hesitation, he glued himself to his friend's bedside, grasping his beads.

Keeping the data carrier firmly in hand, I approached Ormyr and showed him the records I'd discovered. To my pleasant surprise, he didn't interrupt me once.

The name of the location Verahl had visited still didn't make sense to me. "How would you translate that?"

Ormyr appraised the words. "Wondrous Unity."

"All right," I said. "It seems to be the name for an entire level. Verahl landed my ship in a docking bay, went to Wondrous Unity, then came here." *With Thordia,* I thought, but didn't add. "He found flax somewhere in between." I proffered the stem from Verahl's boot.

Ormyr snatched up the evidence as Dag had. "Thordia," he muttered, then glanced to me with amazement. "Where within Wondrous Unity did Verahl travel?"

"The logs don't say." I let him read as much for himself.

After skimming the records, he narrowed his eyes. "Of course, this may be a trap."

I frowned while considering the possibility. "Can these records be forged?"

"I put nothing past Thordia," Ormyr replied. "Perchance I should scry a while on the matter."

I normally would've objected, but I had reason to drag my feet a little. "We could use some time to rest and heal, like the guide-spirit wanted us to." I worried about any delay that might keep us from averting disaster in the capital, but there was no denying that with some recovery, we'd be more effective there and in the Harbinger.

Ormyr reached into his belt-pouch for a handful of cloves that he scattered at the foot of Verahl's bed. It seemed he had no further interest in Verahl himself, probably because Verahl had been little more than an obstacle in Ormyr's way to begin with. Thordia had always been his real prize.

"Have a seat within the circle," Ormyr offered.

I struggled to dismiss my cynical thoughts. "There might be more here that can aid healing." It was worth a look. Anything I found, I could claim the Naustviks had given me the power to use. "Dag, want to help me search?"

"I'll stay here." He scowled toward Ormyr.

With the lingering tension between them, and Verahl right there, I decided not to stray far. As Ormyr entered his circle and lowered his head over his beads, I geared down and piled my weapons, armor, and coat on the floor next to Verahl's knapsack. While carefully rolling both shoulders, basking in the relief of being fully unencumbered for the first time in ages, I scanned the rest of the petal-shaped room. Cabinets, dormant constructs, and the occasional flat panel of unknown purpose lined the walls. Two basins stood on opposite sides of the room, each with silvery mirrors and promising-looking taps installed above them.

Water? Could there still be *purified running water* here?

I pushed the thrilling thought aside momentarily to rifle through the nearest cabinets. Among unfamiliar devices sat compresses and bars of soap, two welcome sights. I examined one of the wall-mounted panels next, and discovered a small built-in niche. A holographic display appeared, presenting a dizzying list of chemical compounds. The interface described *synthesizing* these items, not just dispensing them.

It produced medicine. On demand! The realization left me breathless. I backed away until my spine found a construct to collide with.

Footsteps hurried over. Dag latched onto my arm with a worried look. Farther away, Ormyr glanced up warily from his ministrations.

"It's all right," I assured them. "Just, hell. If this works …"

My mentors knew how to make simple medicines, and knew of even more fantastic, impossible formulations — impossible because the ingredients were no longer manufactured. I ordered several medicines I knew by experience and reputation — some topical, others housed in dermal injectors — to go with the armload of cabinet supplies. Then I camped myself at the nearest mirrored basin.

Dag followed at my side, brow furrowed.

My reflection held no interest to me just yet. Breath held, I tried the faucet. A stream of perfect running water rewarded my curiosity. I let out a happy cry.

"*Nidstang!* Don't have to pump for it or anything!" Dag leaned into the basin, astonished.

I handed him a bar of soap. "Here, wash up."

He shoved his hands and face under the stream without hesitation. Once finished, he leaned to within an inch of the mirror, studying his scarred reflection. No doubt he'd seen it before, but maybe never as clearly as in that silvered surface.

I avoided looking at myself as I washed up, then filled the basin to soak my left hand, bandage and all. The fabric had scabbed over the wounds beneath. With Dag watching, I slowly peeled off the bandage, biting my lip against pain. For the first time, I saw the screaming red cuts across my palm, forming an X.

"Master Ormyr did that?" Dag asked, blinking up at me with concern.

I nodded, avoiding further discussion. The cuts weren't deep, and my fingers had never gone numb. There seemed to be no nerve or circulatory damage to worry about.

"I have to clean these, then keep them clean so they don't fester." After another careful washing, I grabbed one of the bottles from the synthesizer. This was suture gel, which was supposed to be an antiseptic and bandage all in one. I applied some to my hand, spreading it around with a compress. Once dry, it formed a surprisingly tough seal over the wounds. Flexing my hand, it seemed I could enjoy a full range of motion as long as I didn't mind the pain.

Dag looked on with wide-eyed interest. "Can I have some of that stuff?"

"Oh, we're keeping some, all right," I replied.

"What about your head?" Dag asked, pointing to my left temple.

"That's next." Ormyr had staunched the bleeding back in the district ruins, and as far as I could tell, the wound had never reopened. The mirror showed me for the first time the blood that'd streamed down my head and neck before the cut had been addressed. Head wounds tended to bleed a lot.

With damp compresses, I wiped away the dried blood first, then unwound the bandage from my head. Leaning in toward the mirror, I parted my hair and tried to assess the damage from the corner of my eye. It appeared to have closed up well enough on its own. I applied suture gel all the same.

So much for superficial injury. A depressing number of joints and muscles still ached, and I'd suffered a concussion of unknown severity that'd take rest and time to heal—neither of which I had in ample supply. But I could patch over it. Some of the dermal injectors I'd requested housed dosages of stimulant and general painkiller.

Despite my excitement at having real medicine to work with, I hesitated nervously. Assuming the medicines were viable — Verahl's sedation lent me confidence on that count — I knew their effects, but wasn't sure how the drugs might interact. They might work perfectly, they might cancel each other out, they might make me feel worse or kill me outright. It'd be safer to only take one or the other. But for what lay ahead, how could I possibly choose between a clear head and a body that could fight or flee as needed? The fate of the planet might rest on how we approached Thordia. Then Ingvar and Drea would need my help. For all the lives at stake, this was a risk I was willing to take.

Bracing myself, I placed the painkiller against my arm first, then pulled the trigger. The painless injection was powerful enough to penetrate clothing and skin. Then I followed through with the stimulants. They'd probably take a while to kick in. I'd hope for the best while trying to keep my mind off the worrying parts.

"What was that?" Dag asked.

"More medicine," I replied, turning to him. "Let me have a look at you now."

He reared as though I'd jabbed a knife toward his eye.

"All right, never mind." He still shied from physical contact — more specifically, contact initiated by others. I found myself wanting to treat *that* as much as anything else, but where would I even start? At least Dag nursed no obvious injury. Thanks to the stash of food in the Naustviks' basement, he'd also been eating better than anyone else the past several days.

Dag turned to the basin, dug out his canteen, and opened the tap to fill it.

"Could you fill mine, too?" I left it with him, then returned to my gear to don it again. Not one shred of guilt burdened me for taking Verahl's knapsack, leaving the remaining food, water, and cloak behind. In what space remained, I crammed Shipbuilder medical supplies, things we'd likely need before our adventure ended. If not, they were earmarked for Ingvar and Drea.

Hang on, I urged them around a sore heart.

I added some supplies to my first aid kit as well, hedging my bets in case we lost the knapsack.

Within his magic circle, Ormyr had fallen silent. He watched my progress with wide eyes, his beaded hand hanging forgotten at his side.

Once he'd refilled our canteens, Dag returned to Verahl's bedside, maintaining a vigil with beads clutched in his fists. I understood their history together, but for some reason, his concern toward Verahl hurt. If he only knew what Verahl had done to Ingvar … but I couldn't bring myself to speak ill of his friend. Later, maybe, once all the trouble was over.

We knew where to find my ship. The option of rushing back to the capital was awfully tempting — but Ormyr wasn't leaving the Harbinger without Thordia. In his mind, she'd caused Holsten's ambush and still had Dag and me under her sway. My reasons for reaching her were entirely different. First, to shield her from Ormyr. Second, to see if her flax might help Nidaros pay its future obligations to Madam Castor's trade guild. Third, to seek her help in dealing with the ichor before it consumed the planet.

My head felt a little clearer, the aches all over a little less persistent. With renewed purpose, I approached Ormyr's circle. He picked up my left hand, examining the sealed cuts in amazement. "Where didst thou learn this?" he whispered.

"I get in fights often enough." Without further explaining or fabricating, I set down Verahl's knapsack, then rifled through it for one particular dermal injector. "Here. Once I take the edge off your pain, you won't have trouble carrying it."

Ormyr froze, hesitating.

I cracked a faint smile. "It's safe. If I wanted to kill you, I'd take out my sword and do it."

He hesitated a moment longer before shutting his eyes, clutching his beads at his side. "Very well."

I took hold of his tensed arm and administered the medicine.

Ormyr shook it out nervously. "Let's not hesitate a moment longer. Thordia awaiteth us."

"Wondrous Unity is a good start," I said. "Maybe back at the lift car, there'll be an interface we can use to narrow down her location further."

Ormyr lowered his head, then shouldered the knapsack. "We shall see. Come, whelp," he beckoned without glancing back.

Dag hurried up beside me. As he handed me my canteen, his expression turned worried.

"Verahl should be fine here," I spoke under my breath. "Let's keep Thordia safe."

He nodded, forgetting his anxiety in favor of purpose. We followed Ormyr back to the lift, and I was gratified to see the master adept walking without a limp.

Inside the lift car, Ormyr brought up a schematic of the Harbinger, narrowing in on the Wondrous Unity level. No scale was provided, but the level seemed huge given the dozens of points of interest marked out on the map. It was as though we hadn't narrowed down our search window at all.

Ormyr studied the glowing interface with narrowed eyes. "Where might we find a place capable of housing flax?"

I skimmed the labels attached to each point of interest. Libraries, schools, commercial areas ... hydroponics? I pointed. "How about this?"

"A bay of hydroponics!" Ormyr cried. "Indeed! 'Tis where the Shipbuilders reared plants for consumption using naught but water. We shall venture thither first."

"Wait! How do we approach Thordia?" I asked.

An uneasy silence followed, stretching taut between each second. Finally, Ormyr spoke up again. "Perchance we should journey to a point outside the bay to scout, then determine our course."

"That sounds good," I said. "Dag?"

"Aye, s'pose it's all right." He pulled the hood of his adept robe over his guarded expression.

Fortunately, no weapons came out, but the same tension lingered with or without them.

CHAPTER 14

Ormyr, Dag, and I stood inside the lift car sitting within the Harbinger medical ward, primed to depart in search of Thordia. Remarkably, we'd just gotten through finding Verahl without bloodshed. I hoped our cooperation held up, and that no one's misgivings or superstitions flared up at a bad time.

The master adept used the lift's holographic interface to select our destination, a spot just shy of the hydroponics bay on the level called Wondrous Unity. As the lift car descended through the floor like a ghost, I threw one last glance toward the bed where Verahl slept—for now. If we came up empty-handed, we could return and raise hell with him. It'd be a struggle to remain civil after he'd stolen my ship and threatened Ingvar's life, but for the sake of Thordia and everyone endangered by the ichor, I'd find a way.

Our lift car plunged downward through layers of metal and glass, too fast for me to tell whether we were traveling inside a network of lift shafts. If not, then maybe some combination of permeable materials and repelling gravity fields allowed the lift car to fly wherever it wanted. Across from me, Ormyr balanced his keris' hilt in his palm, steeling himself for our confrontation with the "witch" who'd "enthralled" me and

Dag. At my side, Dag bounced on the balls of his feet. I imagined he was eager to reunite with Thordia and safeguard her from Ormyr, somehow.

I took a collecting breath, feeling less pained and more focused after treatment. My anticipation reached trembling highs at the prospect of finally meeting Thordia Naustvik, the brilliant mystery I'd been chasing for days. Upbringing and circumstances had put incredible Shipbuilder knowledge in her hands, knowledge she'd never wanted to reveal. She'd done it anyway, had been decried as a witch for her trouble — yet here she was, trying to save Nidaros and who knew how many other dependent settlements in Catherwood space. The sprig of flax we'd found convinced me of that. What else could she be raising it for except to help Nidaros meet their future quotas, which in turn would keep Lord Catherwood's economy afloat?

Was Thordia also growing food here? Had she found any remedy for the ichor? I resolved to help her, to do everything possible to protect her — even if it meant opposing the well-meaning but dangerous adept in my company.

Though a fight was the last thing I wanted, Ormyr and Dag would both be primed for one. And what might Thordia do at the sight of us? What limitations or advantages would our meeting place provide?

As I considered these things, our view abruptly changed to a starry night sky. Some of the stars hovered at our altitude, while some seemed to shoot past within arm's reach of the lift car.

Dag and I gasped, jarring Ormyr from his concentration.

"What in Hel!" Dag clamped onto my arm as though it were his last shred of sanity. "We're back outside?"

"Nay, impossible. The stars' positions are wrong!" Ormyr craned his neck, gripping his wavy dagger before it fell to the floor.

My knees weakened again, threatening my balance. It was almost tempting to believe we'd been swept off to some distant corner of the galaxy, but I'd never heard of teleportation devices. When in doubt, go with the simpler explanation: artificial lights and holograms.

"We're still in the Harbinger," I managed past my surprise. "They're probably just—"

"Unseen grace!" Ormyr cursed.

His gaze had shifted downward. Dag and I followed it, peering through the transparent floor. Beneath our feet spread acre upon acre of glassy, luminous towers. We hovered over a city that seemed to sprawl for miles.

Overcome with shock, I dropped to my knees. Dag yelped and dropped beside me, still grasping my arm.

"This must be Wondrous Unity," Ormyr murmured above us.

It felt like we were dropping out of atmosphere with a starship, but there was something different and special about Wondrous Unity. Many surviving Shipbuilder cities still looked impressive in daylight—like Mizu with its massive waterfall sculptures, or the spires that made rainbows out of sunlight on Spectra—but all that splendor vanished after nightfall. Small, infrequent splotches of firelight became the only signs of civilization.

My heart raced. This vibrant nocturnal city had no surviving equal that I knew of. Seemingly every building was outlined in light and held dozens of sparks, like a million firefly jars. It was as if we'd gone back in time to a Shipbuilder city in its heyday, but time travel wasn't any more likely than teleportation. We were still inside the Harbinger. Reflections of light, or some manner of holographic illusion, probably made Wondrous Unity seem as large as it was.

Stunned silent, we kept staring outward as our lift car descended toward the city. The tallest spires curled, twisted, and swooped in gravity-defying shapes, glowing with a multitude of colors. Even the most modest specimens outdid the trio in Nidaros' capital. Wide thoroughfares snaked through them like water dripping down a block of crystal.

All of this was still intact, *alive*. Tears of awe sneaked past my defenses, which I was quick to bat aside.

Wide-eyed and slack-jawed, Dag made an attempt to reach his pocket, maybe looking for his beads, but his hand never made it that far.

"'Tis more beautiful than Spectra," Ormyr muttered, still standing behind me and Dag. "Only here, there's no air or ground traffic."

His words shattered the illusion of life. Empty skies and streets usually meant a settlement had fallen into decay, or had been cursed and left for dead. I bit the inside of my lip. Beautiful, maybe, but Wondrous Unity was more of a time capsule than a thriving metropolis.

"Is this what cities are like?" Dag managed.

"Yes," I replied. "They all started out like this, at least. But over time, the lights and structures have been falling apart. Few people have the knowledge or materials to restore them." Not to mention, in Catherwood space, adepts took a dim view toward repairing anything of Shipbuilder origin.

"What in Hel d'ye put in such big buildings?" Dag asked.

"Everything you can think of," I said. "Schools, libraries, homes. Thousands of people could've lived in places like that. *Thousands* of thousands."

His eyes glazed over. Imagining hundreds of people was likely tough for him, never mind thousands.

"Art thou a student of antiquity, Lady Knight?"

Ormyr's question sounded more curious than suspicious. All the same, I kept my guard up while answering. "When you fly ships around long enough, you get curious about the people who built them."

"*People* didn't build any of this," Dag muttered.

"Of course not, whelp," Ormyr said. "The Shipbuilders were magicians with unrivaled mastery over nature and the Unseen."

"What happened to them?" Dag turned and frowned up at Ormyr.

"Some claim the Unseen punished them for hubris," he answered. "Others claim that they *became* Unseen. Whatever the reason, the magic that held the galaxy together faltered, and the planets became disconnected. Many worlds could not endure alone, and so perished; the rest struggled for survival. Small alliances came and went, but the planets were not truly united again until the rise of Hegemon Zander. 'Twas his adepts, and their understanding of the Unseen, that restored the galaxy and revived the Shipbuilders' magic."

One heard roughly the same story throughout the galaxy, amazingly free of local embellishments. Unseen-related parts aside, Ormyr was mostly right. According to my mentors' best understanding, the Shipbuilders had succumbed to numerous civil wars, most likely resulting from the failure of the technology that'd once facilitated instantaneous galaxy-wide communication. A divided empire, unable to speak with itself, had fragmented and fallen.

However ... I leaned toward Dag and spoke under my breath. "The Shipbuilders *were* people."

Dag shot me a dubious look.

"The things you've learned so far haven't made you any less of a person, have they?" I asked.

"Nay." Dag's brow furrowed as he clenched his fists. "Mayhap when I'm more powerful ..."

I waited for him to finish the thought, but he didn't.

"You'll always be a person," I said gently. "There's nothing you can learn that'll take away your humanity. You'll still have all your feelings, all the same strengths and weaknesses."

"I'll get above that!" Dag insisted.

"Not with a wave of your hand, you won't. You have to do it through hard work — in *here*." I tapped at the side of my temple.

Glowering, Dag returned his attention to the massive buildings outside.

Disappointment left me with a sinking feeling. I reminded myself that the message needed time to resonate. May, my former master, had stressed something similar as I'd embarked upon the path of shedding superstition. *Your parents won't rise from the grave. Lord Turinger's adepts won't give back your inn. And none of that pain will budge an inch until you budge it yourself. When and how, that's on you. Don't expect anything you learn from me to do it for you.*

Later, Drea and Branigan had expressed the same sentiment in their own gentler terms. Learning the Shipbuilders' ways didn't make a god or monster out of anyone, and though it was important to understand how the world worked, it was no substitute for personal development.

In the meantime, there was something else Dag might appreciate more. "It works the other way around, too," I continued at a near-whisper. "No matter the title, the uniform, or the power wielded by anyone you meet, there's a human being underneath who makes mistakes, gets scared, and deserves a break once in a while. That's important, don't forget it."

Dag looked dubious, but at least his frown eased.

The boy's Shipbuilder knowledge had been almost entirely self-taught — all show, with none of the underlying wisdom. The Naustviks hadn't given him any, fearing he'd be persecuted. It was crucial for Dag to understand the power he wielded. I was willing to provide guidance and shield him from any resulting trouble. Unfortunately, I wasn't nearly as wise or as Drea or Branigan, hence much of the difficulty I'd run into before and during this quest. I'd have to try to be better, set the best example possible.

Our lift car strayed toward the ground, eventually landing in the center of a street lined with tall metal posts. Glowing buildings loomed impossibly high on either side of us. Having grown up in Freemont, Lord Turinger's capital, this urban setting felt like a reassuring embrace to me.

Dag's shoulders tensed as he glanced upward. More accustomed to open ground, he probably felt daunted and confined.

A sense of longing tightened in my chest like a clenched fist. I wondered what it would've been like to explore Wondrous Unity with Drea or Branigan. Even May might've proven tolerable given the circumstances. But I yearned for Ingvar's company the most. His curiosity would've pushed him past any apprehensions he might've harbored, rewarding us both in different ways. I hoped it wouldn't be much longer before I could save him from injury and punishment. Drea as well.

Ormyr's hand rested on my shoulder, breaking me out of my thoughts. I accepted his help to reach my feet, thankfully, suffering no dizziness or head-pounding along the way.

There was a nervous reverence in Ormyr's eyes that I sympathized with as a former believer. To him, this was sacred ground, and he didn't know yet if he were welcome or a trespasser. He kept hold of his keris like it may be needed at any moment.

Dag stood, his light tile back in his hand again. He swept the beam around our vicinity, most likely scanning for threats.

More curious than wary, I didn't bother preparing a weapon. I wasn't sure how effectively I could wield one, anyway.

We exited the lift together, stepping onto smooth pavement. The warm air had no smell to it, a blessing when one visited a city. I'd expected deserted vehicles, wrecked constructs, and other debris to litter the streets, but our lift car was the only object on the road in either direction. It was as though Wondrous Unity had been cursed and picked clean, like Gules.

I banished the unpleasant thought and focused on our goal: the hydroponics bay. We had to be close. However, none of the surrounding buildings had signs on them.

"I see no bay of hydroponics," Ormyr spoke before I voiced my confusion. He raised his arms. "O wise guide-spirit, show us where to find Thordia Naustvik!"

His voice boomed impressively through the street. No response followed.

Ormyr glanced to me with another glimmer of uncertainty. "Thordia must be interfering with our progress."

"Maybe," I said, less convinced. Even if the disembodied voice we'd heard earlier was part of some AI, it probably couldn't parse his spells. "Then again, we can't expect everything in here to work perfectly."

"Let's consult the map aboard our lift," Ormyr proposed.

Dag whirled around to face said lift—then gasped.

Ormyr and I spun around, too. Behind us, there was nothing, a worse shock than if there'd been something. Dag's light pointed like an accusing finger at the spot where our lift car had once stood.

My heart jumped to my throat, cutting off my breath.

"What happened, whelp?" Ormyr asked.

"How would I know?" Dag snapped. "I just looked back when ye mentioned it, and it was gone. Didn't see it leave."

"It stayed with us within the infirmary. Wherefore should it vanish now?" Wariness seeped into Ormyr's demeanor. "This *must* be Thordia's doing. Now we're in the wrong part of the city with no conveyance!"

Dag scowled, shining his light tile in the master adept's face. "Mayhap we don't need it anymore."

Ormyr raised an arm to shield his eyes from the onslaught. "Without a map, how can we be certain?"

"Hold on. Maybe I can pull up a map on this." I retrieved my newly recovered data carrier from my coat pocket.

Ormyr drew closer to my side, his expression hopeful. Dag forgot his resentment.

Upon activating the device, I carefully examined each option presented, drilling down through whatever made the most sense. Eventually, I was able to display a map of Wondrous Unity with our current position marked out, then compare that to the hydroponics bay's location.

"There's no scale noted here," I said. "We'll have to walk the rest of the way—however long that is."

Nervousness crept up on me. Wondrous Unity's size might or might not be an illusion. If the lift car seemed to defy reality, couldn't the city? That meant *miles* of unfamiliar terrain might lie between us and Thordia, a hike none of us were prepared for. Though the painkillers and stimulants Ormyr and I taken at the medical ward seemed to be helping, I didn't know how long they'd last. We carried more, but were multiple doses a good idea? I still wasn't even sure whether I'd suffer some consequence of drug interaction. If we didn't find Thordia quickly, we faced difficult choices.

"The path is simple, at least," I said, struggling to push worry aside. "We head down this street, make the first right, then go straight." I faced the direction we needed to travel. Our path curved gently left, hiding much of what lay ahead.

"Let's go!" Dag's enthusiasm for finding Thordia returned. He sprang ahead several paces, assuming the lead.

Before Ormyr and I could follow, blinding light exploded around us.

Fear and instinct seized me. I shut my eyes against the painful glare, crossing an arm over my face, then turned and ran from whatever hellish agony or instant doom would surely accompany such light.

It took several strides before I registered that no such horror had come to pass. With stabbing guilt, I turned back, forcing my eyes open a sliver. My companions' cowering outlines were frozen in place up ahead. Around us, the once calm building facades now displayed blaring lights and unfamiliar symbols, the chaos of a tumbling kaleidoscope.

My tense muscles relaxed. It was actually quite pretty, just unexpected. Was it artwork? I couldn't imagine it'd been active at all times. Even from one's peripherals, the light-show was intense and distracting, impossible to ignore.

Then—as though to show me I had no idea what distraction was—a host of disembodied voices filled my ears, friendly and oblivious of one another. I couldn't pick out a single word amid the commotion.

Dag faced me and Ormyr, agape and fearful. Between us, Ormyr assumed a fighting stance, keris brandished at the air. Smoke grenades appeared between the fingers of his left hand. He held them overhead, but didn't throw yet.

I approached Ormyr, straining to be heard. "Can you make out what they're saying?"

Brow furrowed, Ormyr pointed the tip of his dagger toward one of his ears, signaling that he was trying to parse the mess.

Dag edged closer to us. "What do these spirits want?"

Ormyr's expression gradually turned to confusion. "They're … solicitations."

"Solicitations?" It was my turn to frown. "Like a market full of criers? *Really?*"

"Precisely that!" Ormyr replied. The grenades vanished from his hand, and his stance relaxed. "During my study in Spectra, I saw all manner of wondrous artifacts. I recall now one of the more senior adepts possessing a box with spirits like these trapped inside. The spirits repeated the same words over and over, their intonation ever the same, imploring all who listened to partake of goods and services."

Recorded advertisements? Then the light show probably went along with them. I glanced over the chaos again with disappointment. I'd always imagined the Shipbuilders as above things like slimy sales pitches. Then again, what had I just got done telling Dag about humanity?

"The spirits want us to buy something?" Dag asked. "But we only barter. Don't think they'd want anything I got here." He shrugged his shoulder, gesturing to his knapsack, then looked to me curiously. "Is this what a real market's like?"

"It's noisier and more hectic, if you can believe that." I shook my head.

"But safer." Gravity descended upon Ormyr's demeanor. "These spirits heed us not. They remain forever captive in some past moment. Not even the greatest adepts of Spectra could aid them." He glanced high and low with pity. "Thordia hath stolen our lift, and now she employeth these hapless souls against us. I fear she shall continue summoning everything she can to antagonize us — like the beast that troubled us upon our arrival."

My guess was that some automated system had detected our presence and activated the display in response. It was much harder to imagine Thordia leering down at us over some massive switchboard. I kept quiet, having no desire to start up that profitless debate.

"Our peril shall only worsen from here," Ormyr continued. "Keep alert."

"Ye're wrong, and ye'll be sorry soon enough," Dag threatened with narrowed eyes.

"Thou art too far gone to see it, whelp." Ormyr stated it more as fact than reproach. "Remain close to me and Dame Jessamine."

I wanted to explain the reality of the "spirits" to Dag, but there wasn't time to go into detail. Something to tend to later, without Ormyr listening. "Let's keep moving."

Dag seemed happy to retake the lead. Ormyr beckoned me on next. "Stay with him, Lady Knight. I worry." Surprisingly, I got the sense he was more worried *for* Dag than *of* him. "I shall keep watch from the rear."

Maybe he just wanted an eye on both of us. Whatever the case, I nodded and followed after Dag, glad for the chance to sneak him more information about our surroundings.

CHAPTER 15

The advertisement display only infected a handful of nearby buildings. As Dag and I walked down the curving street, with Ormyr trailing, bright lights and marketplace "spirits" faded in our wake. Wondrous Unity's staggering splendor rose toward the starry night sky above—also a fabrication, but no less breathtaking. Again, I couldn't help noting the absurdity of hunting down a "witch" within this mind-blowing technical marvel.

Dag set a fitful pace as he stopped to examine one shadowy corner with his light tile, then hurried to the next. Keeping half an eye on my data carrier's map, I followed close, answering any questions he posed and occasionally prodding him along. I was torn between digesting every detail and reaching the hydroponics bay as fast as my legs could stand it.

Behind us, Ormyr kept his keris in hand, glancing about the empty city with concern. With aid from painkillers, he no longer limped.

The same medicine had taken the edge off my pains as well. Stimulants provided energy, but a fuzz settled over my brain that made concentration difficult. Still, I was determined to come up with some plan for meeting Thordia without violence. Our success with Verahl gave me hope that it was possible if we put aside grudges and cooperated against our common threats: the ichor, starvation, Adept Holsten and the others who'd ambushed us.

"Look there!"

Dag's cry startled me out of my thoughts. He'd frozen before one of the narrow gaps between buildings, aiming his light tile toward the cramped alley. A short distance away, a cube-shaped construct rammed into one of the alley walls, backed up, then repeated the process. It'd been at this mysterious task long enough to put a square dent into the wall.

I pondered the scene. Finally, a construct in Wondrous Unity—but what was it up to?

"What's it doing?" Dag wondered the same.

I checked my data carrier. "I'm not getting a command interface for this one. It might be broken."

"I'll summon it." With that, Dag crept up on the construct as though approaching a wounded animal.

I shadowed him, biting the inside of my lip. While I normally would've held back, there was no telling what this construct might do once approached.

"Leave it be!" Behind us, Ormyr's nervous words accompanied the sound of his footsteps pelting to a halt. "Canst thou see 'tis dead?"

Dag pushed on, deaf to his command. I stayed with him, unwilling to pull him back unless danger actually reared itself.

Uninterested in our presence, the construct kept butting into the wall. Once within arm's reach, Dag paused, but no holographic interface appeared. He turned to me with an anxious frown. "Can we heal it?"

I shook my head in apology. "I don't know much about repairing constructs—and repair's forbidden in Lord Catherwood's realm anyway." With an adept right behind us, it wasn't smart to say otherwise.

"Adepts may attempt resurrection on occasion," Ormyr affirmed. "However, in most cases, a perished relic is allowed to rest peacefully. Come, now."

Dag scowled toward Ormyr. I maintained a neutral expression, more used to hiding my true thoughts whenever superstition reared itself. I'd restored *Kepler's Law* from scrap and kept her running. That was a *good* thing. Most of the galaxy didn't bat an eye at ship repair. I couldn't imagine how much longer Catherwood's domain would survive without fixing the ships they already had.

Then again, we'd just stumbled upon that huge fleet in the docking bay. The Harbinger had at least one more docking bay that we knew of, if not dozens.

I pushed aside the thought in favor of the present — or the past, as it were. "These constructs haven't had caretakers for centuries. I really expected more to be broken here."

Dag faced the construct again, no less assuaged, maybe because his "power" had failed. Did he also feel bad for it? Having a soft spot for machinery myself, I could relate. Compassion in any form was worth encouraging. Unfortunately, I was forced to couch it in terms acceptable to Ormyr.

"The Naustviks have granted us a lot of power as their thralls," I said. "Maybe we'll find a way to restore constructs while we're here."

"We've no time for diversions," Ormyr pressed. "Thordia awaiteth."

Dag's gaze hardened. He peeled away from the construct and hurried back to the street.

We ran into more constructs as we continued: geometric shapes of different sizes that lay motionless, twitched, or dragged broken "limbs" behind themselves. They defied our attempts at communication — even Ormyr's voice commands failed — leaving Dag that much more frustrated and determined on the next encounter. Meanwhile, the master adept's uneasiness increased until he wore a look of permanent worry. He likely feared Thordia was suppressing his power, but wasn't about to admit it.

Our progress toward the hydroponics bay slowed, which also delayed our return to the capital, but we were learning more about Wondrous Unity and the Harbinger in the process. If the knowledge helped us with Thordia, the ichor, or something else later, it was an acceptable tradeoff. I offered Ormyr reassuring looks and kept Dag moving toward our goal.

On our left, a gap appeared amid the tall buildings, revealing the remains of what might've been a garden. Several graceful, glowing tree sculptures shed light on the barren plots, fallen trunks, and pools of stagnant water surrounding them.

The decay sent a tingle down my spine, even though it shouldn't have. In most cities, decay was everywhere.

Dag abandoned our path to dart toward the enclosure. He might've lost patience with us, or spotted something of interest in the rotting garden.

"Come back!" Ormyr called in vain.

"Dag, let's stay together!" I tried, also unsuccessful.

A chill seized me. This was like the Naustviks' house all over again. What awful creatures might lurk in these shadows, ready to pounce on the unsuspecting boy? I drew my dagger and went after Dag at the quickest pace I could muster, prepared to escalate to a run if necessary. After my concussion, I hoped it wouldn't be.

Ormyr followed, gripping his keris as though expecting a fight.

At the garden's borders, the stench of rot burned my nostrils. Ormyr and I both stopped, coughing and retching. Ahead, Dag ran on unfazed—squelching through mold, fungus, and hell knew what else—toward one tree sculpture in particular. Beneath it sat a large crystalline bowl filled with scummy water. A shiny sphere a foot in diameter rolled along the lip of the bowl, rounding it over and over. It was another broken construct stuck in an endless cycle.

Struggling for a breath I could hold without gagging, I forced myself after Dag again, still worried about a potential threat. Ormyr was at my side again soon after, his expression strained.

Dag halted at the fountain's edge. When the sphere circled around to him, he picked it up in both hands.

"Put it down!" Ormyr called.

Again his warning went unheeded. Dag lifted the sphere over his head to inspect it on all sides. Its mirror finish reflected the colors in its vicinity.

While Ormyr held back, I approached Dag's side. A quick scan of our surroundings revealed no trouble yet. I spoke as calmly as I could, pulling breaths through my mouth to avoid the stench. "That's a nice construct, but running over here alone wasn't very safe. Remember the vinrake?"

Dag stared down at the sphere in his arms, scowling and silent.

"It's all right, I think the smell's the most threatening thing here. Why don't we head back to the street?"

"Can ye control this one?" Dag asked, not budging an inch.

I sheathed my dagger and checked the data carrier. "No."

His shoulders crumpled in disappointment.

"Leave it be, and let us return to our path," Ormyr beseeched.

Dag hesitated, obviously not eager to give up on yet another construct.

I sympathized. "Keep it for now if you want, but it may be tough to carry and have hands free for other things later."

He hesitated a few moments longer. Finally, he returned the sphere to the fountain's edge, where it balanced in place.

"Maybe we'll come back," I murmured, unable to help myself.

Ormyr led us away from the fountain. A moment later, something thudded behind us. We spun around, weapons primed—only to find the sphere had fallen from the fountain to roll along the ground toward us.

While the master adept retreated several steps, Dag and I held still with breathless anticipation. I was in a good position to bat the thing away if necessary, but I wanted to see what happened first.

Somehow, the sphere picked up none of the muck on the ground, remaining shiny and flawless as it rolled right up to Dag, bumped against his ankle, then stopped.

Galvanized, Dag picked it up, once again studying it all over.

"No way," I blurted. "Try that again!" It had to have been a fluke—but what if it wasn't?

"Nay! Come along!" Ormyr urged us.

Dag hastened back to the fountain to place the sphere there, then backpedaled away, eyes trained on the construct. We all watched the sphere leave its stable platform, seemingly of its own volition, to follow Dag as he retreated.

"Are you kidding me?" I murmured in amazement. It was like a duckling following its mother—or whatever it'd decided was its mother, anyway.

"Stay!" Dag held out a hand toward the sphere, backing up several more steps. "All right, come here!"

This made me think Dag had owned a pet at some point, but I didn't ask. With the food shortage, and predators invading the districts, a lot of kids had probably lost their pets of late. It was a thought I dropped entirely when the sphere obeyed Dag's commands, even though he wasn't speaking a language it understood. It had to be cluing in more than just words, maybe also sound and gesture.

I had no words. My jaw fell.

As the sphere rolled up to him, Dag picked it up and hugged it to his chest, cracking the biggest grin I'd ever seen on his face. "I'm keeping this one!"

"Nay, whelp!" Terror had overtaken Ormyr's expression. "What if Thordia meaneth for us to keep it? It may be a grenade, or some other threat that shall turn upon us when we can ill afford it!"

The boy's excitement vanished behind a fierce scowl.

"By that logic, we shouldn't be in Wondrous Unity at all," I intervened before Dag exploded. "Anything might be rigged to kill us instantly at any second. It's the risk we're taking to reach Thordia, right? I'm willing to let him keep it, especially since he can control it."

Ormyr stewed silently, for once not shamelessly plowing past the fact that he was outnumbered. More and more, the Harbinger humbled him. Would that aid our cooperation or stoke his resentment? From what I knew of him, resentment seemed more likely, but he'd been surprising me a lot lately.

Dag glanced my way with gratitude before returning the sphere to the ground. "Come on, Flekka!" As he rejoined me and Ormyr, it lapped at his heels.

"Is that its name?" I asked, gesturing to the sphere.

"*Her*," he corrected.

Taking his cue from *Kepler's Law*, maybe, which I stubbornly feminized? I found this ridiculously amusing, but stifled my grin. I didn't want him to think I was laughing at him.

The boy radiated pride over his discovery. I was happy for him, too—finding a healthy construct at last, and a cute one at that. If he took it from the Harbinger, he'd need a good hiding place for it, which was something I could help him with depending on where he ended up. It seemed increasingly certain that he couldn't return to his former life. Probably for the best.

We left the garden and returned to the street, resuming our course. Flekka rolled out to wherever Dag pointed his light tile, always returning to his side within seconds.

Ormyr walked beside me, still seemingly convinced something would leap out from the shadows at any second. "How much farther?"

"That's our right turn up there." I pointed, maybe a hundred yards off.

We converged upon a dark and silent side-street. Dag's light tile revealed a huge pile of debris crowding the alley, knee-high in some places and towering above our heads in others. He and his little sphere ran right up to it.

I dug out my own light tile for closer inspection. The pile was a jagged, tangled mess of metallic and ceramic scrap. Every so often, there were patches of flesh tones ranging along the full human spectrum.

The skin patches assumed shapes I recognized. A hand jutted out from beneath a twisted, broken leg.

Dag screamed and dropped his light tile, scrambling away from the pile of human limbs.

CHAPTER 16

Within the dark alley, Dag screamed and backed away from the pile of scrap and body parts, plowing right into me with Flekka at his heels.

. I stumbled, but kept my balance. Wrapping one arm protectively around Dag, I aimed my light tile forward. A man's head emerged from the pile, his vacant gaze staring back at me.

I gasped.

A flash of silver—one of Ormyr's throwing darts—sliced through the air past my shoulder, then pierced the man's brow. The head rocked and tumbled to the ground, its frozen stare rolling skyward. There was no sign of distress, blood, or decay. A black cap neatly truncated the neck.

My tensed muscles relaxed slightly. These weren't actually body parts, but the remains of constructs. My mentors had told me stories about androids and gynoids, which had excelled at things humans were specifically good at: companionship most of all. These days, their remains tended to be buried away in adepts' cloisters and, occasionally, worshiped publicly. Beghard Joachim had spoken of one village that claimed their damaged android was the vessel in which the Unseen resided when they spoke to humanity—which didn't happen often, I imagined.

Dag shivered against me. I pulled him into the tightest embrace my sore left arm could stand. "It's all right. These aren't people."

Unlike prior occasions, Dag didn't protest our close contact. He remained with me, still shaking, while his sphere-construct Flekka traced worried circles at our feet.

Ormyr hurried up beside us with his keris brandished, poised to cast another dart if needed.

"If they were people, they would've rotted to their bones by now," I continued. "These are constructs—or they *were*."

"Unseen!" Ormyr's jaw dropped as his arms went limp. "The Shipbuilders *did* shape magic in their own image!" He sheathed his keris, then strode up and knelt before the dislodged head, studying it closely. "The legends are numerous, but I had never seen it for myself ere today," he muttered with awe.

"Me either," I admitted. These particular constructs were all dismembered, but what if others survived elsewhere in the Harbinger, quietly waiting out the centuries? Was that why things still mostly worked around here?

The possibility chilled me all over. I held fast to Dag, whose trembling continued.

Ormyr stood and looked over the entire scrap heap blocking our path. "Some say this was the final hubris," he murmured, reaching for the fingers of a hand that stuck out toward him a short distance away. "The creation that brought the Unseen's wrath upon the Shipbuilders."

Humanoid constructs were one of dozens of innovations I'd heard blamed for the same thing. It didn't matter, I was more concerned about Dag. Thankfully, Ormyr hadn't called out his fear. I wasn't about to, either, not wanting him to pull away in angry denial.

While waiting for Dag to gather himself, I panned my light tile over the scrap heap, wondering why the parts had been gathered in this particular location. Maybe it was the work of another construct we had yet to run into. None of the taller masses looked stable enough to climb; sharp jutting pieces threatened to make a painful ordeal out of any such attempt. However, the knee-high sections seemed navigable.

Ormyr remained in a silent reverie while wrapping his beads over his hand. Eventually, Dag separated from me and flipped his hood over his face.

"Are you all right?" I asked.

Without a word, he retrieved his own light tile to survey the heap as I'd done. Once finished, he picked up Flekka, then started for the spot where the scrap was shallowest.

Dag's movements seemed confident, not angry. I supposed he was ready to move on. "Master?"

It took a moment for Ormyr to snap to attention. "Yea, let us proceed carefully. While captivating, I fear 'tis a bad omen."

"When *he's* afraid of something, ye know it's fine," Dag tossed over his shoulder.

"Go to, whelp!" Ormyr snapped. "I'm highly attuned to these matters!"

"We'll keep an eye out for trouble," I intervened.

We steered through the shallower sections of the heap, testing each step before placing full weight on it so as not to sink and get stuck. Even with this care, my coat and my companions' adept robes got snagged on scrap a few times. Humanoid limbs, heads, and torsos were visible, but never any whole specimens. Had the Shipbuilders meant to salvage this material or dispose of it? I hoped to take an armful back to the beguinage someday, once the ichor and Holsten were no longer threats.

At one point, I stumbled and had to catch myself with my left hand to prevent a fall. This put painful pressure on the cuts Ormyr had carved into my palm. Fortunately, the suture gel kept the wounds from reopening. My shoulder wasn't happy with the jolt, but it could've been worse without painkillers. I was grateful for our medical ward detour. It hadn't cured my ills, but it'd certainly dulled them.

"What now?" Dag asked, the first of us to jump clear of the pile.

Once Ormyr and I joined him, we stood deep inside the alley, dark except for our light tiles. I pulled up the map on my data carrier again. "Keep going straight. It shouldn't be much farther."

My old friend paranoia crept back up on me. This seemed like the right time for Ormyr to knock us out, tie us up, and run off alone. After all, Thordia could turn us "thralls" against him at any time.

Ormyr's keris appeared in his hand once more. "Onward, then."

No problem yet, but I remained wary.

The alley continued in quiet darkness for a while before ending at a huge clearing, like a lake amid the city. Its still black surface—water, glass, or maybe something else—reflected the artificial stars above and the glowing skyline on the horizon.

Within the clearing, about a hundred yards from us, sat a circular island lit up as bright as day. Multiple glass towers rose from its core like the points of a crown. Foliage spilled out from their sides, and constructs hovered around the greenery like bees. Around the towers stood a ring of coniferous forest stolen from some foreign planet. Finally, a ring-shaped meadow circled the forest: a field of blue flowers perched atop green stalks.

We stood stunned and agape at first.

"That's the hydroponics bay," I managed around the heart lodged in my throat. Again, I wished my friends and loved ones were there to see it. The blue flowers reminded me of the Linum Dominorum trade guild's seal. "Is that flax?"

"Aye! Must be three harvests at least," Dag replied.

We had no proof Thordia was there, only that Verahl might've visited earlier. But the chance that flax would grow in the Harbinger of its own volition was miniscule.

Dag hurried up to the clearing's edge, Flekka lapping at his heels. The toe he dipped toward the surface failed to sink through. It wasn't actually a lake, rather solid ground.

Ormyr's demeanor turned grim, likely in anticipation of a life-or-death magic battle ahead. "Come back, whelp! We should bless and steel ourselves first."

"We could use it," I agreed. In reality, my fuzzy brain needed more time to figure out how to prevent all-out bedlam if we found Thordia.

Dag tramped back toward us with clear reluctance. His narrowed eyes searched mine, possibly wondering if this was the time to cross Ormyr before he crossed us.

I didn't like *any* betrayal scenario. As Ormyr dug through his supplies, I stepped forward to meet Dag partway and whisper in his ear. "No fighting. Let me handle this."

Dag hesitated, then nodded.

Ormyr threw down a quick magic circle of ground cloves. "Lady Knight, hast thou any sense of Thordia yet? The whelp seemeth convinced we'll find her ahead."

I faltered. "I'm not sure." Desperately, I considered what might convince Ormyr not to attack Thordia. No amount of pleading would move him to compassion for her, but whatever his reasons, he cared about me and Dag. Could I leverage that? There seemed only one way: more lies. Reluctantly, I dug through my mental index of quest-story nonsense.

"I'm feeling nervous, and a little ill. I think ..." I trailed off, placing a hand to my head.

Ormyr came up beside me. "Go on."

I faked a shiver and avoided eye contact, biting back an untimely sense of guilt. "Sir Roman Banks of Greenvale. Have you ever heard of him?" I'd just made him up. If Ormyr had heard of him, I would've been impressed. "He ... he was a knight errant I met in passing. He told me of an awful quest of his in Lord Baranek's space. A witch there, like Thordia, had dozens of people under enthrallment. When he drove his sword through her heart, every single thrall dropped dead with her." Dramatically, I doubled over like I'd been punched in the gut after finishing a marathon. "Thordia didn't want me telling you," I gasped.

Ormyr steadied me. "Your life force must be tied to hers," he murmured soberly.

Dag refrained from coming to my aid. He seemed to understand where this was going.

I pulled in a deep breath, working on my false recovery. "You may not have much choice, Master, but if you can avoid hurting her—"

"Indeed. I shall incapacitate her first," Ormyr soothed. "Then I shall force her to lift this spell from you both, along with the spell over mine adepts and the curse over Nidaros."

Holsten and the other Gyllenfeld-leaning adepts who'd attacked us in the district ruins weren't about to have a change of heart with Thordia gone, but there was no use bringing it up. Better to keep reinforcing that Thordia was best kept alive.

"It'd also be useful to find out how she did that." I tilted my head toward the waiting hydroponics bay. "You could use the flax."

"*Witchcraft* is how she did it," Ormyr returned with certainty. "But if she can exert such mastery within the Harbinger, I should be able to learn the same. Dost thou feel well enough to seek vengeance?"

Not really, I thought. "Yes," I said, easing myself from his grasp. "How about you?"

"I'm ready," Ormyr said, "but I shall feel even better once this blessing is cast." He launched into it.

For all his jabs at Ormyr, Dag seemed to take the invocation seriously. He stood with us inside the circle, gripping his hammer amulet in his disfigured right hand while glancing longingly at the hydroponics bay.

I stood there with an uncomfortable mix of relief and shame. Part of me wondered if Ormyr only humored me because he planned to betray or abandon us soon, but Ormyr did nothing but bless.

A stunning reluctance braced me when I considered the possibility of opposing the master adept. I had to remind myself of what he'd done to Verahl in the dungeon, what he'd done to me at port, and what lay in Thordia's future if he got his way. Once he dealt with her, would he consider Nidaros' "curse" broken, or would he keep cementing over the truth and punishing scapegoats? No amount of human suffering would make the ichor go away, so it seemed the persecution would only continue.

All this simply confirmed there was nothing to be gained from letting harm come to Thordia. Whether or not she could do anything about the ichor, I had to keep her safe ... even if it meant killing Ormyr.

I bit my lip and focused on my feet, unable to look at any-one. Once the blessing concluded, I consulted my data carrier for a map of the hydroponics bay itself. It showed little detail, only that the facility was arranged in concentric rings. This was supported by what we could already see: a ring of flax, then one of forest, covering whatever lay at the center.

"Dag and I should go in first," I suggested to Ormyr. "It'll prevent her from attacking you right away." And vice-versa.

"Very well." Ormyr prepped his keris again. As much as he would've denied it, there was doubt in his otherwise hard expression. Maybe his inconsistent success with "magic" inside the Harbinger wore on him, along with the many lives he believed lay in the balance of this encounter. To save them, he'd have to best someone whose powers outmatched his.

Dag, meanwhile, bounced on the balls of his feet. If Thordia were ahead, this marked the end of his quest. He'd have found his friends — and then what? I doubted he'd thought that far in advance.

"I shall do my utmost to protect you," Ormyr said, glancing between me and Dag. "You have my thanks."

I couldn't stop my eyes from going wide. In the wake of shock, I struggled to return the most honest sentiment possible. "This wasn't ideal, but I'm in your debt. Yours too, Dag." Certainly, I wouldn't have made it out of the district ruins without them.

"There's no debt between us," Ormyr said. "Let's finish this."

"Come on!" Dag took off across the clearing at a brisk pace, Flekka following.

Biting my lip again, I spurred myself after him. Ormyr followed at my side.

As we drew closer to the hydroponics bay, the burbling of water fountains reached us. The waist-high flax stalks swayed as dozens of butterflies flitted among them.

Had insects survived within the Harbinger? Had Thordia brought them with her? Or were they yet another Shipbuilder marvel of some kind? My knees weakened with each new discovery, making progress even more difficult.

Upon reaching the flax meadow, Dag pelted to a halt and ran his hand over the stalks surrounding him. There he waited for me and Ormyr to catch up.

As we surveyed the meadow with wonder, half a dozen constructs — formless wraiths that resembled billowing smoke — rose up through the flax, encircling us from a distance.

My hackles stood on end. Perimeter defenses? Whatever the case, we each tried to gain control of them in our own way. Ormyr called out verbal commands, I checked my data carrier, and Dag ran up to one in hopes of coaxing out its holographic interface.

None of us succeeded. The wraiths closed in, forming a tighter circle—but only around me and Ormyr. They slipped past Dag and left him behind in their pursuit.

Dag whirled to follow their progress with a frown. "What do they want?"

"Thordia sent them!" Ormyr cried. "Fight, or we're finished!"

Before I could venture any guesses, the wraiths encircling me and Ormyr lashed out in unison with whips of metallic rope.

We both hit the floor, avoiding the onslaught. As the whips receded, we scrambled to our feet and instinctively placed ourselves back to back.

Dag remained outside the circle—unharmed, ignored, frozen with confusion.

I wasn't in the best shape to fight, and these constructs were likely forged of materials I'd never heard of. Still, I drew my side sword. As I'd learned with the sverma in Nidaros' countryside, my blade was tougher than it looked.

A metallic clink sounded behind me, maybe Ormyr retaliating with a dart. The wraiths hovered too far out of range for his keris.

Dag recovered his senses, attacking one of the wraiths from the rear. The rock he shot glanced off the construct harmlessly, and it didn't retaliate.

Why were they ignoring Dag? There wasn't time to think, as the wraiths launched another coordinated assault against me and Ormyr. I dodged the whips aimed at me, then slashed twice, cutting an X in the air. My side sword went through the whips with surprising ease, sending lengths of metallic rope to the ground.

Upon hearing Ormyr wince, I turned. One of the whips had ensnared his forearm. He struggled to lever it off with his keris.

"I'll get it!" I said, raising my sword.

Another whip shot past my right shoulder to wrap around Ormyr's right arm. The keris fell from his grip.

Then the wraiths began dragging Ormyr through the flax meadow, aiming for the dark forest beyond.

CHAPTER 17

A pair of wraith-like constructs dragged Ormyr through the flax meadow like demons bearing a damned soul off to hell. The master adept thrashed and dug his heels into the dirt, to no avail.

"Ormyr!" In panic, his name slipped out of my mouth, not his title. Any other time, he might've issued a haughty correction, but not then.

Dag gave chase as the constructs headed for the dark forest past the flax meadow.

"Nay, whelp! Spare thyself!" Ormyr cried.

As usual, Dag paid him no mind. I was right behind the boy, side sword in hand.

The other four wraiths slipped between us and Ormyr, forming a semi-circular barrier. Dag cried out and skidded to his knees just short of colliding into them. As I slowed, a mass of whip-like arms shot out toward me, which I was forced to bat aside and dodge past. I fell to my knees in the process, and was sure I'd be caught up from there—but I wasn't. They didn't seem interested in capture, just diversion.

It worked. By the time the four broke away and fled from sight, Ormyr and his captors had disappeared into the forest. Past that lay the hydroponics bay, and who knew what else.

I remained on my knees, breathing hard, struggling against a nauseating sense of failure. Why Ormyr and no one else? They hadn't made a single move against Dag, even when he'd provoked them. What had protected him?

"Come on, we have to move!" Dag shook my shoulder urgently. Flekka rolled back and forth at his feet, almost like a person shifting her weight from foot to foot. "What if Thordia's in there with more of those things?"

Panic jolted me at the thought of Ormyr *and* Thordia in danger. I pushed it aside. "We will—but we have to be smart about it. We're no good to anybody if we get caught."

Ormyr wasn't totally defenseless. I could only hope he held out long enough for us to reach him. Same with Thordia, if she were there.

Dag wavered with a strained expression, glancing toward the forest. I feared he'd run off before I could gather myself. Fortunately, he didn't, and instead helped me stand.

I nodded my thanks, keeping my relief to myself. Nearby, something glinted in the artificial light: Ormyr's keris, lying amid the flax stalks. Using my side sword as a crutch, I leaned down to retrieve it. Flecks of dried blood stained the wavy blade—probably my blood, from when Ormyr had "questioned" me in Nidaros' port.

A mix of frustration and grief came over me as I studied the weapon. Ormyr had the capacity to be kind. Maybe leaving Nidaros' court, being away from power and responsibility, had allowed that side of him to surface past his dogmatic and sometimes cruel exterior. Could he be convinced to nurture that kindness—assuming we saved him?

Dag glanced about our surroundings warily, a wariness that only intensified when he glanced at the keris. "There's magic bound up in that blade," he assured me. "Only he can wield it."

Spying a chance to chisel further at his superstition, I held the dagger out to him. "It's just a weapon, Dag. Anyone can use it. Here, keep it."

Wide-eyed, the boy hesitated, then lifted the keris carefully from my hand. After studying the dagger all over, he tucked it under the belt of his adept robe.

I was satisfied that he'd kept it. "All right, let's go after them—carefully. We don't know how those things found us, and there may be more nearby." The constructs might've used infrared scanning or some other form of biometric detection. There wasn't a damn thing we could do about those. But sight and sound, we had more control over. "We should sneak until we know what we're dealing with."

Dag nodded, then brushed aside an armful of flax to reveal drag-marks through the soil. "We got a path to follow."

I nodded back. "Take the lead, but stay close to me."

He silently prepped his light tile. I kept my side sword in hand. Though I wasn't feeling terribly energetic or quick-witted, and dreaded the prospect of another fight, adrenaline would help me a little while longer. With so many lives at stake, I could keep pushing myself. I just hoped we found what we were looking for beyond that forest.

Worry knotted up my insides. A deep breath only partially dismissed it.

With Flekka shadowing Dag, we slipped through the fortune of flax, then entered the dense clutch of trees beyond. A bumpy expanse of dirt and pine needles rolled out beneath our feet. Only the smallest patches of artificial light broke through the foliage. It was easy to imagine we'd left Nidaros and the Harbinger behind for another planet. Forests like this didn't just spring up in days. It was more likely that these trees had survived the lonely centuries with help from the hydroponics bay.

Then again, while I was no flax expert, the knee-high stalks in the meadow seemed mature for plants that'd only been growing for days. Something unusual was at work here. I'd investigate after Thordia and Ormyr were safe.

Dag shielded his light tile with his other hand, carefully following the traces of Ormyr's resistance. Nothing unusual caught my attention within the forest—fortunate, as my side sword would've been difficult to swing there. Switching to my dagger, however, didn't feel safe enough.

As we advanced, more artificial light pierced openings between the branches. The forest thinned out, then transitioned into gleaming floors and rows of tables bearing lab equipment. The circular hydroponics bay was like one of the research facilities at my friends' beguinage, only huge, sitting open to the artificial night sky. Glass towers clustered near the core. Several constructs hovered around them, nursing the plants they housed.

Ahead of me, Dag froze. "There he is!"

In the chamber's center, tens of yards distant, Ormyr knelt between two flanking wraiths. With his back facing us, there was no telling whether he remained conscious or alive. Given his restraints, both were likely.

Relief and worry hit me at the same time. This felt like bait for a trap. "Do you see or hear anything off?"

Dag looked around. "Nay. No Thordia, either."

Nausea crept up on me again. Before I could ask Dag not to tear off in search of her, he glanced over his shoulder at me. "Let's free that arse."

My eyes went wide with surprise. After Ormyr's constant scolding and unwavering hostility toward the Naustviks, I'd thought Dag would bid him good riddance. Hell, he *had* tried to lose Ormyr back in the district ruins. This was a welcome

sign of compassion—but was it smart? I bit my lip in delibera-
tion. If Thordia were there, wouldn't it be better to leave Ormyr
tied up so he didn't do anything foolish? Cold logic said yes,
but my conscience tugged at me too hard.

"I want to help him, too, but we can't control those
wraiths," I said. "They could take him away again—and more
might show up while we try to free him."

"They listened to your sword, and they paid me no mind."
Dag put two and two together. "If ye give me your sword—?"

"Not a chance," I cut him off. Dag was a head shorter than
me and had zero training. At best, he'd wield my sword as a
cudgel, not a cutting machine. "I'll work on freeing him, you
keep an eye out for trouble."

Dag swapped out his light tile for Ormyr's keris. "Aye,
let's go!"

We hurried out of the forest toward Ormyr. While the boy
ran across the shiny floor, Flekka just behind, I struggled to keep
up. Close to the towers, unfamiliar fragrances spilled down
over us.

Ormyr glanced over his shoulder, maybe alerted by our
approaching footsteps, then glared. "Get away from here! Find
Thordia and end this!"

Strange that he thought we'd have a choice as Thordia's
"thralls." Unmoved by his plea, Dag and I closed to within
striking distance. Instead of fighting with the restraints around
Ormyr's arms, I brought my side sword down on one of the
wraiths directly. Though it looked immaterial, it felt solid
against my blade, and fell to the ground without rising up again.

More wraiths appeared all around us, darting out from
behind towers and lab tables. This time, there was no finesse,
just dozens rushing in to suffocate us like a black cloud.

I cried out as my arms were wrapped up and pinned behind my back. My side sword fell who-knew-where. Despite

my thrashing, the wraiths drove me to my knees beside Ormyr, who no longer had an arm free.

Then the storm-cloud subsided. As the majority of wraiths flew off, I caught sight of Dag, still trying to free Ormyr's left arm with the keris. The wraiths continued to ignore him for some reason.

"Dag, my sword! Grab it!" I cried. It lay only a few feet away.

"*Skíta!*" Upon noticing my duress, Dag stuck the keris under his belt and lunged after my side sword, picking it up with both hands to test its heft. It was lightweight, somewhere between a longsword and a rapier.

"It's all right now, Dagfin."

From out of nowhere came an unfamiliar feminine voice, world-weary and hoarse.

Recognition dawned on Dag's face, which then turned into a worried frown. He stood with my sword half-raised, Flekka at his side, eyes darting about. "Thordia?"

My heart took off racing. Ormyr and I joined Dag in seeking the voice's source.

"Step away from them and come here."

She was behind us, at a distance. Sheer force of will allowed Ormyr and me to spin our captors around to face her — or maybe they'd spun us. Either way, there she was, a homespun-clad woman at the forest's edge.

The real Thordia Naustvik defied my mental picture of her. I'd imagined someone warm and delicate with quiet strength, like Drea. This woman stood a good foot taller than me, with a faded gold plait spilling over one shoulder. Her world-weary expression had enough lines in it to make her seem decades older than Verahl, but it lacked the pinch of long-term food shortage. Like Dag, she'd remained well fed during Nidaros' crisis, probably thanks to those preserves in her cellar.

But these were her least surprising features. Her missing left sleeve revealed a chrome-finish robotic prosthetic stretching from shoulder to fingertips. Days earlier, I'd heard estate servants gossiping about Thordia having only one arm. Somehow, amazingly, she'd coaxed the Harbinger into giving her another. It was probably just as useful as her natural arm, if not more so.

Thordia's left eye was a withering blue. Her right eye was a silver orb, no doubt another prosthetic. Swollen purplish splotches surrounded the artificial eye. I thought they were bruises at first, maybe the aftermath of such tricky surgery, but they really looked more like —

Ichor. *Under her skin.*

A fist-sized knot hardened in my stomach. I summoned every ounce of control to keep the horror off my face.

Dag stepped past me and Ormyr, carrying my sword low in both hands. Flekka trailed him as always.

Goosebumps crawled over my skin. I feared he might be obeying her summons. *Why* did I fear that? Hadn't Thordia and Verahl sheltered Dag whenever he'd needed help? Wasn't Thordia on our side? Was I reacting unfairly to her appearance?

No, it was something else. Something was very wrong. The first clue was that Ormyr and I remained bound up like prisoners while no wraiths attacked Thordia. Had Ormyr been right all along? Had *she* summoned them to protect Dag from me and Ormyr?

"Stay here, Dag," I whispered, almost begging. I'd believed all along that Thordia and I had common intentions. At that moment, I had no idea what her intentions were.

Whether due to my plea or his own uneasiness, Dag planted himself in front of me and Ormyr, keeping my sword in both hands.

"Well done, whelp! Resist her!" Ormyr whispered his own encouragement.

"Dagfin," Thordia tried again, as coldly calm as before. "I'm not sure what you're doing here, but you're safe now. Come here." A lift car rose up through the ground beside Thordia without a single word or gesture on her part.

What the hell? I wondered. How was she commanding constructs and lifts with no commands at all? She wanted to take Dag away from here—for what? And what plans did she have for me and Ormyr once Dag wasn't around to see?

"Dag, no." I struggled fruitlessly against my bonds, hoping he'd stay away from her until her motives were clear.

To my relief, Dag held still, Flekka at his side.

"Thordia Naustvik! How dare thou enslave these two!" Righteous anger straightened Ormyr as much as his bonds allowed. "I'll make thee suffer for all thy sins against Nidaros, thou monstrous—!"

Another lift car rose up around Ormyr, its walls silencing his words.

Dag spun around when Ormyr went silent, then jumped, wide-eyed. Helplessly, we both watched Ormyr go from talking to shouting, giving no indication that he realized what had happened.

Meanwhile, Thordia's cold stare turned hateful as she observed Ormyr the way anyone else might look at an annoying insect trapped in a bottle.

A chill ran down my spine. I had to state my case before I wound up in my own soundproof cage. "Thordia?" I swallowed around the lump in my throat. "Please, I'm not here to hurt you. My name—"

"Dame Jessamine Irless of Freemont. I know who you are," she cut me off, then continued with a note of warmth. "Thank you. My brother owes you an apology once he wakes up."

In shock, I stopped struggling. Did she consider me an ally? Then why the rude welcome? It didn't matter. If she were willing to listen, I could get her to stand down and focus on our mutual problems.

"We have a lot to talk about, Thordia," I continued as calmly as possible. "It'd be nice if I weren't tied up for the conversation."

"Soon." Thordia's gaze shifted back to Dag. "I'd prefer to speak with you first, but not here." Her metallic arm gestured toward the lift car beside her, demonstrating the prosthetic's graceful articulation.

Dag faced her again, trembling all over. "Nay, Thordia, just spit it out. What gives?"

Disappointment flickered over Thordia's expression, which then returned to cold purpose. "I'll explain. But first ..." She squared her shoulders and advanced toward Ormyr's cage.

Dag tensed from head to foot. A similar dread coursed through me. I felt what was coming next in my bones, and railed against my restraints, but they held. To spare Ormyr's life, words were all I had at my disposal. "Let's talk about the substance you found in the soil, Thordia! What have you learned about it?"

She ignored me. Meanwhile, Ormyr's soundless tirade continued. As Thordia drew closer, the lift car slid through the floor, exposing the master adept.

"Thou shalt not destroy Nidaros!" Ormyr shouted. "By the Unseen—!"

Thordia chambered her robotic arm and delivered a brutal backhand to his face.

Ormyr's head snapped back. The wraiths ensured he neither defended himself nor got away.

Dag flinched and paled as though he were the one struck. I felt sick to my stomach. "Stop!" I shouted, still struggling in the vain hope of darting between them.

Thordia glared down at Ormyr's dazed form. "None of this was necessary! You and your backward, childish cult! Verahl's only crime was shielding me. That's a *crime* to you! It was easier for you to torture him than face the truth."

Blood and saliva dripped down from Ormyr's hanging head, but he remained ever insistent upon the last word. "Release them."

Thordia frowned in confusion. "What?"

"Do what thou wilt with me, but release them." He raised his head toward me and Dag.

Ormyr was reaping what he'd sown, but there was no pleasure to be had from it. My heart wrenched with compassion when his eyes met mine. It hadn't been so long ago that I'd felt like this for Verahl, at Ormyr's mercy. How things had changed.

"Thordia, this won't help anything!" I tried again, desperate to stop her. "Leave him alone and let's talk!"

Dag looked on silently, almost as dazed as Ormyr.

"I'm not done with you yet, Adept. You won't ignore the truth any longer." Thordia seized Ormyr's jaw, forcing him to come eye-to-eye with her. "Look at me! It won't be long before everyone is dying as I am!" She pulled back her robotic arm to punch Ormyr across the face.

Ormyr's head flew aside, blood spurting from his nose. Then he dangled limp in the constructs' grasp, looking an awful lot like Verahl when I'd first found him.

Dag flinched again.

I doubled over like I'd been punched as well. *Dying*. My brain, seeking distraction, latched onto that word. If the ichor were literally under Thordia's skin, then yes. In fact, I couldn't see how she hadn't already succumbed like the corpse in the dungeon. At that moment, though, my sympathy went to Ormyr. I longed to separate everyone and start fixing things, but I was pinned down, unable to reach pockets or weapons, and my words couldn't breach Thordia's anger.

Dag, on the other hand … she wouldn't hurt Dag. At least I dearly hoped not.

The boy remained paralyzed, his gaze detached. This ugly encounter seemed to be teaching him something he hadn't known about his friend.

"Dag?" I muttered. "Pull her away from Ormyr."

His gaze shot to mine, fearful and incredulous.

"You have to. Please." I was sorry I couldn't do it for him.

As Ormyr hung limp and insensate, Thordia wound up for another devastating strike.

At first, Dag did nothing. Had he frozen up from fear? Would he just let his friend tear into his adversary?

Before I could repeat myself, Dag dropped my side sword and darted toward Thordia's arm, wrapping both arms around it and wrenching it backward.

Surprise, more than anything, sent Thordia reeling away from Ormyr with a gasp.

Mentally, I praised and thanked Dag for his courage. There was no time to express it out loud. "Thordia, listen!" I begged. "You have every right to be angry, but this isn't the way you go about making things better!"

Once they were several paces away from Ormyr, Dag released Thordia and positioned himself behind her, Flekka following. He shook all over, but seemed ready to interrupt another attack if needed.

Thordia whirled on me, metal fist clenched at her side. Her remaining eye took on the same wild quality I'd seen in Verahl's when he'd fought to expel Ingvar from *Kepler's Law*. "What am I supposed to do? Complain to Baron Tristan?"

My heart pounded out of control. "You're safe here in the Harbinger. What's the point of this?" I tossed my head toward Ormyr, still motionless.

"I must send a message," Thordia replied. "I don't want any more of the Baron's men here."

"Is that it? It looks like revenge to me," I returned. "Revenge won't heal Verahl or give you your old life back. It's just making things worse for you. Meanwhile, people in Nidaros are still starving."

"Because everyone looks to fools like him for answers!" Thordia turned back to Ormyr.

Fear braced me, both for Ormyr and Dag if he intervened. "If you kill his master adept, the Baron will retaliate!"

"He won't die," Thordia said. "He's going to suffer."

Damn it. Somehow, I had to pull her away from revenge and back to what had drawn her to the Harbinger in the first place. It could be the one thing that saved us all.

"There's a better way, Thordia." I hoped the tremor in my voice wasn't noticeable.

"No, there isn't! After what he's done …" Thordia trailed off, shaking.

"Is that really how it works?" I challenged. "Then I should've fouled up Verahl for stealing my ship."

Thordia faced me again with simmering rage, like a lioness whose cub I'd just messed with. "You'll get your ship back. Our lives are over!"

"No, they're not," I said. "You came here seeking a cure for the ichor — whatever you call the poison in the soil, the lake surrounding the Harbinger. Let's work together to get rid of it. You'll save the barony! No one will hunt you anymore!"

"Thordia, listen to her," Dag pleaded.

She regained her composure and straightened, throwing one hand aside in a wave of contempt. "I'm not interested in Nidaros anymore. Let them chase their witches and curses until they rot."

Anger washed away what sympathy I still harbored. "Then maybe you are a witch after all."

It wasn't a smart thing to say. I just hoped it'd take the heat off Ormyr.

Thordia gaped, then glared. Sure enough, she forgot Ormyr to lunge toward me. Dag tried to hold her back, but was shoved aside. Her robotic hand latched onto my neck, lifting me off my feet and over her head. The wraiths pinning me in place unfurled just enough to permit my change in altitude while also preventing me from lashing out with any limbs.

I didn't flinch as the metallic fingers dug into my throat. I only gaped noiselessly when my body demanded air.

Dag threw himself at Thordia again, wrenching her right arm behind her back. "Let her go! She's a friend!"

Thordia cried out and dropped me. The wraiths released me, too, then retreated from the scene. I collapsed to the floor, hurting all over but gratefully pulling in air. *Friend.* A nice word to hear at a time like that.

Thordia whirled on Dag, cutting the pleasant reflection short. Terrified that she'd lash out at him, I forced myself to my knees. My side sword lay in arm's reach, where Dag had thrown it down. I grasped the hilt, then glanced up.

"Dagfin," Thordia pleaded.

Thank goodness, she wasn't hurting him. Still, I moved to a crouch, intent on tackling her if I had to.

"What happened to you?" I couldn't see Dag past Thordia, but the panic in his voice came through clearly. "Ye're not the same!"

"Do you mean …?" She trailed off. "I hurt my eye on the way to the Harbinger, but I was able to replace it," she explained. "When I did, the surgical constructs also gave me this arm."

"Nay." Dag replied, haunted. "Since when d'ye *hurt* anyone?"

Though he didn't like Ormyr, he didn't care to see him suffer at anyone's hands, even Thordia's. He was also sticking up for me.

Keep it up, young man, I thought with a welling sense of pride. No more "boy" for him, he'd earned it.

Thordia hesitated. "You saw what they did to Verahl, didn't you? We tried to help, and that was how they repaid us."

It was Dag's turn to falter. "We came here to help you, aye?"

"I know you did, but Master Ormyr didn't. And I'm not so sure about her anymore." Thordia turned, finding me crouched with my side sword. Her eyes went wide with shock.

"She rescued Verahl from the adepts," Dag half-informed, half-pleaded.

"And then Verahl stole my ship and reunited with you here." I stood slowly, keeping my weapon at my side. "I'm here to help you — *and* Nidaros. You're all victims. You seemed to get that once, but not anymore." I couldn't help venting further bile on that point. "It's a good thing Dag followed me out here. If he hadn't, you would've left him to rot with everyone else."

"*Nidstang,*" Dag cursed at barely above a whisper.

"No!" Panicked, Thordia whirled to face Dag.

"How many others like him are back in Nidaros?" I pressed. "How many infants and children? Do they deserve to rot, too?"

Thordia swayed and collapsed to her knees. "Dagfin," she pleaded.

A blinding light erupted around us. I cried out and screwed my eyes shut, averting my gaze. Thordia let out a pained cry as well.

No heat, fire, or explosion followed. When the light subsided, I recovered fast, my heart in my mouth. Thordia had curled off to one side, shielding her head with an arm. Dag stood over her, wielding his light tile, which he must've set off in her face.

Relief washed over me. Dag's emotions were less settled. His eyes passed from Thordia, to Ormyr's insensate form, to the lift car behind his shoulder, then finally to me—overwhelmed, pleading for help.

Hoping to calm him and provide focus, I gestured toward Ormyr. "Go steady him."

Dag ran off to do just that. Placing my side sword on the ground, I approached Thordia to grab her arms and pin them behind her back. As I leaned toward her ear to speak, I noticed a small device resting in the canal. Was that what she'd been using to control things without a data carrier?

"We're all heading to the medical ward to patch ourselves up," I said. "After that, we'll have a long talk about the ichor, and about keeping you safe. *No one hurts anyone else from now on*, understood? I'm your only hope of keeping the Baron's people away from this place, so don't test my patience."

"Fine," she muttered. "Let me go."

"Release Ormyr first," I said.

She hesitated. A few seconds later, the wraiths let go of Ormyr and flew away. As the master adept sank to his knees, Dag grabbed his shoulder and kept him upright.

I released Thordia, then approached Ormyr's opposite side, readying my first aid kit.

A lift car appeared around all three of us—*four*, as it turned out. When I glanced back, I found Thordia propped against the far wall. From a pocket, she pulled a wad of cloth that she pressed against her metallic eye.

"The medical ward," I repeated firmly, forcing back the dread that she might just do whatever she wanted.

Thordia wiped her prosthetic hand upon her apron, streaking it with Ormyr's blood. "Exactly my thoughts," she murmured.

CHAPTER 18

Our lift car rose out of the hydroponics bay and into the artificial sky over Wondrous Unity, but I didn't pay much attention to the scenery. Dag and I knelt on either side of Ormyr, keeping him steady. To my growing anxiety, his heavy-lidded eyes seemed to look out at nothing.

With compresses from my first aid kit, I staunched the bleeding from his nose and mouth. There was damage I could see and feel—lost teeth, fractured bones—and who knew what internally. A single well-placed punch from a normal person could potentially kill, never mind two from a super-strong prosthetic.

Thordia's prosthetic. The object of our grueling search leaned against the lift car's far wall, holding a compress against her metallic eye.

I ignored her, having nothing kind to say. Strange—before coming out here, I'd never dreamed of the scenario where I'd favor Ormyr over her. I'd never anticipated Verahl stealing my ship and throwing Ingvar from it, either. The Naustviks were Ormyr's scapegoats, but were far from the innocents I'd first imagined. Yes, they'd tried to help Nidaros and had suffered as a result. But that was no excuse to throw aside conscience and pretend the planet's troubles weren't theirs.

For the moment, my companions had my full sympathy. Ormyr had shown his compassionate side. Dag had grown up years in a matter of hours. He'd even defended me against his good friend Thordia, which floored me to think about. We'd actually reached our goal, and while the end result was far from perfect, no one lay dead, either. I just hoped Ormyr didn't slip any further.

Wondrous Unity disappeared beneath layers of metal and glass. That was when Thordia broke the silence. "What was that light you used, Dagfin?"

The desperation in her voice made me glance up. Thordia leveled a searching blue eye at Dag, who faltered while Flekka hovered at his side, bumping against his knee.

"Think ye saw it well enough," he finally said.

"Where did you find it?" she demanded.

He didn't answer.

"From our cellar? You went down there?" Thordia sounded pained, betrayed. She pushed away from the wall and straightened to her full height. "Didn't we tell you not to? Don't you realize what kind of trouble you've brought on yourself?"

"Glad I did," Dag replied, eyes narrowed at the floor.

"Are you? Master Ormyr will never let you leave this place alive." Thordia gestured toward Dag's robe. "Why are you wearing his colors? Why are you *helping* him?" Her pain came through clearer than ever.

"Ye could've asked sooner, but ye'd rather hit things," Dag replied flatly.

Thordia fell silent, defeated.

My heart ached for Dag. Seeing his friend behave with the cruelty he'd feared from Ormyr must've hurt, but he wasn't denying or making excuses for it. Thordia owed *him* explanations, not the other way around. I threw Dag an approving look, which I hoped he'd notice past his sadness.

Dread crept over me as I refocused on Ormyr. I lacked the skill to patch up everything myself, but Thordia knew how to use constructs to perform advanced procedures. Though I could possibly figure out the constructs on my own, it'd take trial and error that Ormyr might not have time for.

I couldn't help glancing toward my side sword, lying on the ground between the three of us and Thordia. I was nervous enough about whether she'd keep her word about steering us to the medical ward, speaking to me about the ichor, and not harming Ormyr further. Could I possibly get her to *heal* Ormyr?

For the master adept's sake, I swallowed my reluctance against working with her. "Thordia? You said you used a surgical construct before. Can you show me how?"

Thordia's good eye blinked, then narrowed in Ormyr's direction. She remained silent for several moments.

"Thordia?" Dag prompted. "Please?"

I felt sure Thordia would refuse. Finally, she glanced downward. "You saved Verahl's life. For his sake, I'll help you."

As surprise wore off, tense silence reclaimed us. Our journey continued for what felt like another hour, but it was probably shorter. We entered the medical ward the same way as before, rising up into the flower-shaped chamber. Everything was just as we'd left it—or so I thought.

"Thordia?" Verahl called out, groggy.

Still on my knees beside Ormyr, I seized up with dread and anger. The circular counter surrounding our lift car shielded me, Ormyr, and Dag from sight. Fearing the breakdown of our truce, I held still, primed to defend Ormyr if needed.

"Yes, dear? How are you feeling?" Like a doting mother, Thordia slipped through the lift car wall and hurried toward his bedside. Her voice gave no indication that anything unusual had happened while she'd been away.

Unlike before, Dag seemed uninterested in greeting his friend. He remained crouching with me and Ormyr, eyes lowered.

I didn't know how long our reprieve would last, but damned if I wouldn't use the distraction. With Dag's help, I smuggled Ormyr to the petal-shaped chamber on the opposite side of the ward, as far from Verahl as possible. We sat the master adept upon one of the bed-like medical constructs. I found privacy curtains and set them up, hiding us from sight.

"Get back to Nidaros. Warn our Baron." Ormyr's words were nearly inaudible past the compresses around his nose and mouth.

For once, I was desperate to do as he asked, but couldn't. "Not just yet. The three of us came this far together. We're going back together, too."

"Lady Knight," Dag piped up.

I turned. Thordia stood at the privacy curtain: arms folded, cold stare back in place. Over her shoulder hovered a small construct with multiple appendages and a glowing screen.

"Come here," she beckoned me. "I'll show you how this works."

Once I'd coached Dag on keeping Ormyr upright to avoid blood running down his throat, I approached Thordia. Dispassionately, she demonstrated loading the construct with a fresh pack of surgical tools and initiating a diagnostic scan.

If this worked, it'd spare Ormyr a lot of agony. That was what I focused on to avoid any further negative thoughts. "I think I've got it. Thanks."

Thordia stayed put to observe, folding her arms again.

Her bitterness toward Ormyr was understandable. It was less understandable why mine had subsided. Ormyr's penchant for torture, his ingratiating behavior, always treating his pupils like garbage and imposing his will ... I hadn't forgotten about these things. For the moment, though, I wasn't dealing with the opportunistic courtier. I was dealing with someone in pain, someone who'd stayed true to me and Dag when I'd feared betrayal. Ormyr really had tried to look after us "thralls" in his own way. This was a chance to return the favor.

As I led the construct toward Ormyr, he cried out and nearly tumbled off the bed. Dag held him in place, eyeing the construct curiously.

I grasped Ormyr's opposite hand and shoulder. "Sorry about this." Anyone would be scared to have that spidery construct directly in their face while it contemplated replacing a tooth, setting fractured bones, and tending to internal injuries.

Ormyr clutched my hand hard, trembling.

The construct's readout listed recommended procedures and medicines. I could scroll through both lists and get explanations for everything. Fortunately, it didn't look like Ormyr was as hurt as he could've been. The construct could address his wounds without having to leave metal wiring or other nastiness behind. The recommended medication was largely to prevent pain, inflammation, and vomiting. No sedation was required.

"It sent that list of medicine to the nearest synthesizer," Thordia explained. "Once they're administered, it will start the procedures."

"I'll get them." I didn't trust Thordia to do it. "Dag, stay with Ormyr."

"Aye."

Thordia glanced to Dag, primed to say something—after I left.

My defensiveness spiked, but there was nothing I could do to stop her. Besides, after what had happened in the hydroponics bay, I trusted Dag's ability to detect and resist her nonsense.

No one's expression had changed much by the time I returned. The construct got to work once Ormyr was numb and lying down. The master adept screwed his eyes shut, fumbling in vain for his beads.

I remained at his side, wanting to be of further reassurance. Remembering the mati amulet he'd given me days earlier, the one he'd use to track me and Ingvar, I doffed it and pressed the blue eye into his palm.

Ormyr's hand formed a fist around it.

"Thordia, can ye help Dame Jessamine next?" Dag asked. "Ormyr tortured her, too, then she got thrown from an ulldyr."

Thordia focused on me, eyes wide.

"I'm fine," I dismissed reflexively, avoiding eye contact. In truth, I felt increasingly worn down as adrenaline subsided.

"These constructs are a better judge than you are," Thordia said.

"That's all right." I didn't trust her. I had to look after Ormyr. Ingvar and Drea needed me, the sooner the better. As I thought of them, longing and anguish seeped painfully back into awareness.

Thordia's gaze burned holes into my hide, but she said nothing.

With a sigh, Dag dropped to a cross-legged seat on the floor. There, he took up a listless game of pushing Flekka away, then waving her back.

"Could I take one of these constructs with me when I leave the Harbinger?" I asked Thordia — checking for feasibility, not asking permission. Who knew what it could do for my loved ones?

"They can travel to different parts of the Harbinger, but I'm not sure to what extent they're tethered here," Thordia said. "They may stop working outside of a certain range."

I was concerned about that myself. My eyes strayed to the little sphere Dag played with. I hoped Flekka would remain functional once we left.

"You'd also need spare surgical tool packs, and medicine." Thordia narrowed her eyes. "And how could you possibly use it without getting thrown in the dungeon?"

"I'll figure that out later." Once Ingvar was safe, I felt confident of talking myself out of any residual trouble.

"Go ahead and try. I can't stop you." Thordia turned and left.

While the construct operated on Ormyr, I lowered myself beside Dag on the floor, biting back a wince in the process. My legs were sore, and the throbbing headache had returned with a vengeance.

"Thanks for all your help," I said, hoping not to let on.

Dag pulled Flekka into his lap, wrapping his arms around her. His dejected stare fell toward a corner.

"I'm sorry," I said. "We found your friends, but it wasn't what either of us expected, was it?"

Dag blinked up at me. "Is Thordia really dying?"

Pain welled in my chest. This had gotten difficult in a hurry. "I don't know."

His expression turned haunted and distant. "She's changed. Verahl, too. Saw what happened to you and Captain Leirfall at the port. Been trying not to think about it, but ..." He trailed off.

An invisible knife stabbed into my gut. Dag knew Verahl had betrayed us? It hadn't seemed like it the first time we'd come through the medical ward. He'd been glad to see Verahl, concerned about him. Maybe he'd been in denial then. The business with Thordia must've driven it home for him.

"Never saw them snap like that," Dag continued. "They'll do it again, won't they?"

Probably. I strained to be more diplomatic. "I hope not." Not very reassuring, but what would be? I wasn't about to lie to him.

Dag gave me a pleading look. "Helping Verahl and Thordia now ... is it a *bad* thing?"

While I wanted nothing more to do with them, that wasn't realistic. "I guess it depends on what we help them with. I'm hoping that once we all focus on helping Nidaros, they'll go back to being more like the friends you knew."

This seemed to assuage Dag a little. He pulled Flekka out of his lap to restart their game. I watched, prepared to field further questions, but he kept quiet.

"It's time I talked to Thordia about the ichor." As much as I dreaded the prospect, I had to finish what I'd started. "Do you want to come with me or stay here?"

"Come with." Dag straightened.

The only hard part was reaching my feet again. I had to fight against pain and a growing reluctance toward being upright.

Dag spotted me with a worried look. "Let Thordia help you. I won't let her hurt you."

I glanced toward Ormyr, whose operation seemed to be proceeding smoothly. "Once we take care of everyone else, it'll be my turn."

Dag's gaze focused on the floor.

Slowly, we rounded Ormyr's privacy curtain and stepped out into the open. Across the ward, Verahl lay in bed alone, eyes half shut. Another privacy curtain stood beside his bed. That was likely where Thordia had disappeared to.

The fight with Verahl aboard *Kepler's Law* replayed in my head, pushing me to the verge of throwing up. It'd been so unnecessary. Ingvar, Verahl, and I could've flown to the Harbinger in minutes and found Thordia without anyone getting hurt.

But would Ormyr still have insisted on chasing us down, in that case? Would Dag have sneaked along if I hadn't been in danger? Would Holsten and his co-conspirators have pulled the same stunt, leaving Ormyr stranded without any help at all?

Hell. I couldn't in good conscience claim I'd swap the hypothetical mess for the one that'd unfolded.

Dag and I crossed the ward with Flekka following alongside. At the halfway point, I asked Dag to retrieve my side sword from the lift car, which I then returned to the scabbard over my shoulder. While approaching Verahl's bed, I couldn't bring myself to look at him. In my weakened state, my frustration and anger reached dangerous highs.

"Dag!" Verahl greeted him once we'd reached the foot of his bed, relieved and astonished. "I never expected you here, but it's a nice surprise."

"Hey, mate," Dag returned weakly, staring at his fidgeting hands.

"What's got you down?" Verahl asked. "Did Thordia — she didn't yell at you over the lights in our cellar, did she? We were just talking about that." He sat up straighter, lowering his voice. "Listen, don't feel bad. I knew you were sneaking down there. I left those Shipbuilder devices out for you to find."

Alarm bolted down my spine. My gaze snapped toward Verahl. "What?"

Dag glanced up, too, no longer fidgeting. "Ye did?"

Verahl leaned toward Dag. "I want to teach you everything. It's wrong to keep it to ourselves. I mean, once Thordia and I are gone, what's going to happen to it? We need someone to follow in our footsteps. Someone like you."

Dag's jaw loosened. Meanwhile, my blood boiled. That irresponsible manipulator! He'd handed Dag raw power without any wisdom or context. What kind of person would that have molded him into over time?

"I can teach you more—" Verahl began.

"He'll learn more, definitely," I cut him off. *Just not from you*, I thought.

"Jayce?" Verahl faced me for the first time with a contrite expression, squirming under his blankets. "I—"

"Don't call me that!" I clenched both fists, driving my fingernails into my palms in a failing bid to hold back my wrath.

"Dame Jessamine — sorry." Verahl hesitated. "How ... is Captain Leirfall — ?"

"I don't know." *You'd better hope he's still in one piece, or I'm coming back here with every soldier I can muster.*

The guilt in Verahl's eyes deepened. "I'm planning to restore some ships when Thordia lets me. If you check back before you leave Nidaros, there may be a ship or two ready to fly."

"I like my own just fine," I said.

"Just ..." Verahl fumbled for words. "I want to do something to make up for — "

"A ship doesn't make up for turning on people who risked their lives to help you!" I couldn't restrain myself any longer. This reminded me too much of how May, my former master, apologized with lavish presents — then went right back to doing whatever had hurt me in the first place. "It doesn't make up for stealing *Kepler's Law* or for the hell I caught from the adepts, either. But I can overlook all that. It's Ingvar I'm worried about. He might be suffering in the keep or rotting in the dungeon because of you. He may even be dead by now. If you've taken him from me, Verahl, I'll *never* forgive it!"

Tears spilled down my face as I shook with rage. I glanced down at my fists and fought for composure, only facing Verahl again when I could speak in a level tone. "You know what you can do for me? Work on keeping that damnable temper in check before you hurt someone *you* care about."

Verahl had paled. Dag glanced between us, tense. I didn't want to leave him with Verahl, but Thordia and I had to level.

"Dag, I'll be right back," I promised, blotting at tears with my sleeve.

Behind the privacy curtain beside Verahl's bed, Thordia had gathered a towel, a mug full of steamy water, and two empty buckets. As I approached, she was bent over one of the buckets on the counter, irrigating her sinuses with a bulb syringe. The discharge flowing out of her nostril was shockingly purple.

I darted toward her with alarm. "That stuff converts water into more of itself!"

Startled, Thordia doubled over the bucket, gagging and coughing. She still had the wherewithal to reach back with one hand and shove me away. Then she put down the bulb and reached for the towel to muffle her coughs.

"My sinuses fill up regularly," she eventually managed, setting aside the towel for the mug without a glance in my direction. "I can't leave it sitting in there."

Horror gripped me. "But—"

"Warm water is harder for the substance to convert. That's how I get away with this." Thordia rinsed out her mouth, then spat into her discharge bucket. "There's a larger container I pour this off in. Not very pleasant, but I don't want to risk contaminating the Harbinger's water supply." She dropped the mug and bulb into the other bucket, presumably for later washing or disposal.

"This is how you've kept yourself alive?" I asked.

"It's one measure, yes. I've also been taking immune response-boosting drugs." Thordia kept her back to me. The ice-layer had reformed over her voice.

A shred of sympathy for her plight returned. "How'd this happen?" I asked.

"While I was traveling here, some of the substance splashed into my eye. It can't penetrate skin, but the eyes, mouth …" She trailed off.

"Mucous membranes in general, I guess." There was an astonishing amount of water in the body.

"I tried to stem the damage." Light glinted off her artificial eye, surrounded by ichor-bruises, as she turned to look down on me. "I wasn't fast enough. Now all I can do is fight the spread. I don't know how long I have before it spreads too far." A sliver of fear broke through the ice in her voice.

I bit the inside of my lip. "Can't the surgical constructs do anything?"

"Replace more body parts, cut out parts of my face? Even then, there's no guarantee." Thordia shrugged a shoulder, but the gesture wasn't as dismissive as she might've hoped. "For some reason, the constructs here don't recognize the substance as something harmful. There must be some function or scan I don't know about yet."

"I'm sorry," I said, and meant it. "I wish I could help, but this ichor's a mystery to me, too. I know it's consuming Nidaros, and I know you came here to find a way to stop it." She now had plenty of motivation to figure it out.

Thordia glanced downward, silent for a while. "Are you really serious about that? You're not here to drag me back for punishment?"

"I never had any intention of witch-hunting," I said.

"Then why is Master Ormyr with you?" Her gaze returned to mine, intense.

"He dragged me out here, and Dag followed, after my attempt to fly here failed," I said. "You can ask your brother about that."

Thordia's eyes narrowed. "What Verahl did was wrong, but you're here now. Your ship is safe. Don't hold his fear against him."

"I wouldn't, except he seriously wounded the Captain of the Guard — the man who helped me spring him from the dungeon and hide him from the adepts." I struggled to keep my voice from revealing too much. "Did he tell you that?"

Her gaze hardened further. "For someone who claims to want to help us, you're very eager to judge and condemn."

And she was eager to condemn Nidaros in turn, which didn't endear her to me. Regardless, I had to steer the conversation back on track. "I'm more interested in the ichor than in either of you. You've done some research. What do you know about it?"

Thordia glanced askance, sullen. Finally, she beckoned me toward a part of the counter not taken up by buckets. The metallic fingers of her left arm tapped against the wall, between the counter and the storage cabinets above. "Look here."

Before my eyes, the wall turned transparent, exposing little vein-like structures throughout. Ichor filled every last one of them.

My head spun, while my knees weakened. I grabbed the counter for balance. Ever since we'd found the huge lake, I'd feared this possibility and hoped it wasn't true. At that moment, it became stark reality. I had no choice but to accept it.

"The ichor came from the Harbinger," I muttered.

"Yes. It's literally everywhere you look in here." Thordia folded her arms. "The walls, the constructs … it's like the blood of this station. It must've escaped containment when the Harbinger crashed, and has been spreading through the soil ever since."

I kept my hold on the counter, trying to think around my lightheadedness. "Why would the Shipbuilders create something that'd cause such an ecological disaster if it ever got free?"

"The Harbinger was in permanent orbit over this planet," Thordia replied. "They probably never imagined the day when they'd be gone, and the Harbinger would fall out of orbit to crash-land amid peasants who believed it was a punishment from invisible forces."

Probably not. "What's the ichor for?" I asked.

"I still don't fully grasp its purpose, but here." From one of the storage cabinets above, Thordia retrieved a device that looked familiar based on similar models I'd seen at the beguinage: a microscope. She then produced an ichor-stained slide from her apron pocket, which she slid into position. After focusing the device, she stepped back and folded her arms again. "Have a look."

I lunged toward the device to do just that. Under magnification, the "ichor" was more a pile of tiny creatures tumbling over one another. I gasped. "Organisms?"

"No. Machines."

My head shot up. I stared slack-jawed at her detached expression.

"They break down water and trace minerals to build more of themselves," Thordia continued. "They never stop. That's how they spread."

Dazed, I stumbled back, bracing my temple. "Little machines inside walls and constructs, like blood." I was pretty sure I'd read about something similar once. "They might be part of a maintenance system, like *real* blood. Maybe the ichor's why so many things here still work."

"Perhaps," Thordia said.

"Do you have any idea how fast it spreads?" I asked. "At what point is Nidaros beyond help?"

Thordia paused for a deep breath, grim. "It took at least sixty years to reach the barony, but the spread hasn't been consistent all that time. It gains bursts here and there from groundwater and heavy rain. The more it accumulates, the faster it spreads. It won't be much longer before the soil is completely broken down and consumed. That would be the point of no return. More people will fall ill as I have, Nidaros will never grow flax again, Linum Dominorum will stop delivering supplies."

"The guild might send troops, or Lord Catherwood's adepts might curse Nidaros and take everything you have," I continued, heart racing. "And who knows what happens to the other planets that depend on your flax." I looked to her desperately. "It can't be unstoppable. The Shipbuilders always put contingencies in place. There must be a failsafe!"

"Trust me, I've been looking." Thordia's eyes narrowed. "It's difficult finding safety and medical data when I don't even know what the Shipbuilders called this substance, never mind that most such data is barred from public access. I'm no computer expert."

Drea! I bolted to my full height. "I know someone who is."

At this outburst, Thordia betrayed a rare glimmer of surprise.

"A friend of mine on a nearby planet. She's spent decades studying Shipbuilder computers. She might be able to dig up more about the ichor, if she's still … if I'm not …" I trailed off with pained remorse.

Thordia, less than optimistic, returned to her default coldness.

Saving the barony would take more time and effort than we could spare at present. More urgent matters waited back in Nidaros. Rescuing Ingvar, first and foremost. Ensuring Holsten and his friends didn't go unpunished for what they'd done to me, Ormyr, Dag, and the dead adept Mir. Warning Baron Tristan about how Madam Castor might've manipulated all of us. Seeing what Sigrid and Pontus might've discovered in the adepts' keep. Making Ormyr make good on his promise for coordinates to Gules, then flying off to save Drea.

And sleep. I supposed I'd have to fit sleep in somewhere.

What would happen to the Naustviks in the meantime? How far would they be willing to cooperate? Given our short history, it seemed collaboration would have to be bought or forced.

The immediate future was best planned between me and Thordia, then communicated outward. Though we hardly liked one another, we could at least get along. I couldn't imagine sitting Verahl and Ormyr down in the same vicinity.

"I need to head back to Nidaros," I began.

Thordia pulled a data carrier from her apron pocket, tapped at its surface, then handed it to me. The screen showed a map with a docking bay highlighted, high up in the Harbinger's axle.

"There's your ship." Her piercing gaze loomed over the display. "What will you tell the Baron?"

I paused, gathering my thoughts. "I'll show him the ichor and tell him it came from the Harbinger—not you. *You're* looking to stop it, and I'm doing everything I can to help you."

"Tell him if he wants to see his master adept again, he'll keep his men away from here," Thordia added.

The unspoken reason she'd consented to treating Ormyr. My protectiveness spiked. "Ormyr's coming with me."

"He's my only leverage!" Thordia clenched her fists at her sides.

"No, your flax is," I countered. "And everything else you've raised in that hydroponics bay. You can keep Nidaros alive in exchange for being left alone."

Of course, people would eventually get curious about the Harbinger's wonders. The spacefaring vessels, in particular, would be tough to ignore. And I reviled the idea of leaving the entire Harbinger to just two people—especially if those two were the Naustviks, and especially if the ichor proved incurable. There was a whole city beneath us that could sustain evacuees. Countless people throughout the galaxy could benefit from the food, medicine, artifacts … but that was a fight for later. We still hadn't resolved the current one.

"You've helped your neighbors in the past," I continued, recalling the preserved food in her home that Dag had said she'd shared openly. "You want to continue that."

"My neighbors." Contempt smothered Thordia's words. "If we weren't sick and hurt, Verahl and I would be pouring all our effort into fleeing this planet."

"Really?" I challenged. "Why did you grow all that flax if you didn't mean to help Nidaros meet quota?"

"We … could've sold it abroad." Thordia faltered, glancing aside.

"No one trades in raw materials but the guilds," I said. "And the guilds would be really interested in where you got it—like, throw-your-hides-in-prison interested."

Thordia let out a weary sigh and didn't speak again for several moments. "I should return with you, plead my own case before the Baron."

The "witch" was willing to deliver herself into enemy hands. *That* was how much she didn't trust me to speak for her. I tamped down my annoyance. Were our positions reversed, I'd probably want the same, but it was still surprising given her desire to remain hidden away in the Harbinger.

I looked her hard in the eye. "I'll take you back with me and keep you safe, if you promise not to harm *anyone* unless in self-defense."

Thordia nodded her acceptance. "Verahl will remain here, he's in no shape to travel. Dagfin will stay with him."

Again, my protectiveness flared. I stood as tall as possible —still shorter than Thordia, but I was used to being the shorter one in a confrontation. "Dag's with me."

Terror flickered over Thordia's expression. "It's not safe for him in Nidaros. His parents beat him at the slightest whim, and now everyone will know he's associated with witches and magic!"

"I'll look out for him." My heart pounded with conviction. With an education and some training, Dag would be capable of amazing things. Besides, both Naustviks had exposed their devastating tempers and callousness. I'd hang before I let Dag remain with them.

Thordia hesitated, eyes narrowed. "Dagfin should be the one to decide."

"I'll ask him, don't worry." It would hurt if Dag didn't want my patronage, but I'd never force it on him. "I want to talk to his brother first, though—Rigg." He, and the army, would be a much better alternative for Dag than the Naustviks.

This seemed to assuage Thordia, fractionally. I turned away, slipping past the curtain.

On the other side, Dag and Verahl paused mid-conversation. Were they reconciling? The idea raised my hackles, but I forced worry aside. I couldn't tell Dag whom to associate with. He had to obey his instincts, even as I helped to hone them.

Dag darted to my side. Trembling all over, I regarded him with new eyes: a potential partner in questing. Hell—was I ready for a squire? Could I be someone's master without repeating May's mistakes? I'd have to figure it out if he agreed, but I couldn't ask without speaking to Rigg first.

Thordia appeared and sat down at Verahl's side, calmly explaining what she and I had planned.

Verahl looked devastated. "You can't go back!"

"I have to plead our case personally." Thordia draped her arms around his neck.

He hugged back like she was his universe. "They'll kill you before you get the chance!"

"I swear I won't let that happen," I said. "It's unlikely, given what she'll be offering."

Thordia pulled Verahl's head against her shoulder. Again, I had the sense that this was a mother with her son. Given their age difference, she must've helped raise him. Or maybe she really *was* his mother, and had hidden the fact for some reason?

I had no idea what she might be hiding. If Nidaros received a steady source of flax and we made progress against the ichor, that was good enough for me.

CHAPTER 19

While Thordia comforted Verahl, I turned and crossed the medical ward as fast as my legs permitted, with Dag and Flekka shadowing me.

Revulsion and worry settled in the pit of my stomach. Could Thordia keep her temper in check long enough to strike a deal with Baron Tristan? Would reason and compassion prevail? I hoped so, because I couldn't enforce them with my sword. Stress, pain, and disorientation slowly crept back up on me as well.

Behind Ormyr's privacy curtain, the surgical construct continued its work. Ormyr remained awake through the procedure, clutching the mati I'd given him. As badly as I wanted to return to Nidaros, I'd have to wait until he was ready to move.

"What'd Thordia say?" Dag piped up behind me.

I turned and spoke under my breath. "The ichor's coming from the Harbinger. Remember the lake we saw outside?"

"*Skíta!*" Dag cried.

"Thordia doesn't know how to stop it," I continued. "We'll work on that later. For now, she'll return with us to the capital. Once we make sure Captain Leirfall's all right—"

And Drea. Rescuing her was a necessary battle in the war against the ichor, but I'd explain that to Dag as it happened.

" —she'll offer her crops to Baron Tristan in exchange for her and Verahl's freedom."

"Baron Tristan?" Dag's eyes went wide.

"Stick with me, young man. We're going places." I smiled, then sobered upon remembering one of Dag's earlier questions. "Those bruises on Thordia's face are really ichor. If it's not removed, it'll kill her eventually. It's another reason for us to work toward a cure."

Dag blinked a few times, sullen, then glanced downward. "I want to help."

"I'd welcome that. For now, though, we have to wait." Gingerly, I lowered myself to a seat on the floor near Ormyr's bed, resting my back against the wall.

My worry for Ingvar and Drea mingled with pain, hunger, and thirst. I reached for my pockets, instinctively seeking comfort from a cigarillo — then froze, considering Dag with a pang of guilt. Didn't I want to be a better influence than the Naustviks, or May? It wasn't enough to indulge and refuse to give Dag any; that reeked of hypocrisy. I had to abstain so he never got tempted.

Hell. I might've finally found the reason I needed to quit. Wouldn't Drea be thrilled? For the moment, though, I had to endure the strain and irritation of doing without.

Dag watched me for a few moments, then turned and left our curtained refuge.

Panic braced me, but wasn't strong enough to return me to my feet. Dag wasn't my squire. I had no right to boss him around, but I hoped he remained wary of the Naustviks.

Faint murmuring from deeper in the medical ward gave me goosebumps. Eventually, Dag returned — with Thordia and a surgical construct looming behind him.

Thordia narrowed her eyes at me, then approached my side.

Apprehension chilled me all over. It wasn't the treatment I feared, rather the supplier. My back was already against the wall, but I braced myself as if to retreat even farther. "Let's do this later."

"After you're dead?" Thordia offered me her prosthetic hand. "Come, let's get you to another bed and assess your condition properly."

"Please, Lady Knight?" Dag inched up toward my other side.

I sighed in defeat, resting my head against the wall. "All right, but do it here." With both Naustviks willing to kill, I *had* to keep watch over Ormyr. Besides, I truly had no inclination to return to my feet just then.

Thordia knelt, putting the construct to work. Dag stood over us while fidgeting with his beads.

Once the construct finished its initial scan, Thordia appraised its readout. "Multiple contusions and muscle strains, lacerations—" she glanced at my patched-up left hand, the most obvious example "—and mild traumatic brain injury, not to mention evidence of overexertion and deprivation." Her real and artificial eyes focused on mine. "You need food, water, and rest. A few hours off your feet at least."

Hearing it all laid out like that drove home everything I'd been fighting against. I swallowed around a lump in my throat. "As soon as we can move Ormyr safely, we have to leave. The Captain of the Guard ..." I trailed off, too pained to finish the sentence.

"Thordia?" Dag pleaded.

She glanced between us. "I can administer something to counteract the pain and concussion symptoms. It'll be a cover, though, not a cure." Her gaze settled on me. "You'll probably hurt yourself worse."

"That's a risk I have to take." For Ingvar, I'd crawl through hell. "You'd do it for Verahl, wouldn't you?"

Thordia flinched. I feared some form of retaliation. Instead, she left without further protest.

Nearby, Dag paced fitfully.

"Thanks," I told him. "I promise I'll rest after Ingvar's safe." Then on to rescuing Drea.

He said nothing. A few moments later, Thordia returned with several dermal injectors in hand.

My distrust plagued me as much as ever. Could I really let her do this? I reminded myself that I was her best bet for a good future. She wouldn't want to endanger that.

Thordia administered the medicine, glancing up dispassionately when done. "I have to ready a few things for the capital. I'll meet you at the docking bay."

I nodded my gratitude.

"Thanks, Thordia." Dag was sincere, but couldn't bring himself to look at her.

"Of course, Dagfin." She glanced to him wistfully before she left, the medical construct following her.

Dag dropped to a seat beside me, resuming his game with Flekka. Over time, I began feeling less pain and more focus — or at least I thought so. Even if it were a placebo effect, I'd take it.

Some time later, Ormyr's surgical construct lifted away from him. Once Dag helped me stand, we approached his floating bed. Stunningly, the construct had cleaned up the blood and done its work without leaving marks or bandages. One would never think Ormyr had been hurt. He'd just have to be careful about his nose and jaw for a few days. Though we hadn't placed him under sedation, he lay with his eyes closed.

"Hey, arse!" Dag greeted. "I have your fancy dagger. Ye can have it back once ye get off this slab and take it from me!"

Ormyr opened his eyes, weaving the mati nimbly through his fingers. "Tempt me not, whelp."

"How do you feel?" I asked with an irrepressible smile.

He laid the mati aside to reach for my hand and squeeze hard, like it was his turn to reassure me. "Better, although there's no feeling in my face." He reached toward it.

I held his hand back. "That's on purpose, so you won't feel any pain from the surgery. Don't worry, it won't be permanent. Rest here a bit longer, we'll head to my ship soon."

His eyes went wide. "Thou hast recovered thy ship?"

"Yes." Unless Thordia had lied. But if she had, she only hurt herself. "Dag, come with me."

I felt better on my feet—not perfect, but functional. Once Dag helped me pack up extra surgical tools and medicine, I rigged Ormyr's surgical construct to follow me around. I'd have my own super-useful Flekka, at least for a little while.

As we worked, Ormyr sat himself up, then tested his weight on his feet. He seemed steady enough to walk, but fortunately remained still, throwing me a questioning look.

"There's a lot to explain," I told him.

Ormyr lowered his head in assent. "Thou and I, indeed, away from prying ears."

In other words, without the Naustviks *or* Dag listening. "All right. On my ship." It was the only place in the Harbinger where I could hope for privacy. "Let's get going. Don't look at or talk to any Naustvik you happen to see past this screen."

We stepped out into the open. Thankfully, another privacy curtain had appeared around Verahl's bed, masking all sign of the Naustviks. We took a lift car to the docking bay indicated on Thordia's data carrier: another cavernous chamber loaded with jaw-dropping ships. I feared it might take extensive searching to find my harpy among those goddesses. As it turned out, the familiar blocky, segmented chassis rested only a few yards away.

Kepler's Law, the galaxy's most beautiful eyesore. Overpowering joy and relief sent me to my knees; I felt like a mother reunited with her lost child. Once my companions helped me up, I took one lap around her, scanning for any new structural issues. Dag and Ormyr flanked me; Flekka and the surgical construct trailed behind.

If there were any problems, I expected the evidence to appear low on the hull. The most damage Verahl could've dealt her was with a rough landing. However, the ship's scorched and unpolished exterior seemed no worse for wear. Satisfied, I glanced around the docking bay. No sign of Thordia yet. I hoped her preparations wouldn't take much longer.

After yanking open the ever-stubborn hatch, I waved Dag aboard first. I followed him, then turned to give Ormyr a boost into the airlock. "Welcome aboard, Master."

We filtered into the corridor. Unlike Ingvar, the master adept walked with no sense of fear. Upon reaching the galley, Dag raided the closets, digging through the available rations.

I turned back, confirming the surgical construct had followed us aboard, then rigged it to remain in the galley. "Are you hungry?" I asked Ormyr.

The master adept appraised our surroundings with a dubious expression. I supposed that on the rare occasions he flew places, he did so aboard much nicer ships. "Not whilst more dire matters loom before us."

He had to be lying about his appetite, but I understood the sentiment. I beckoned him to follow me farther aft, toward quarters. It was more private there, and besides, Thordia would show up eventually. To preserve the peace, I'd have her stay in the galley.

In quarters, I lowered a bunk, then gestured for Ormyr to have a seat.

He braced my shoulders and sat us both down, his voice hushed as though to confess a dire secret. "This whole time, I was mistaken."

Quite the admission from him. The words, and his gesture, made my jaw come loose. "What do you mean?"

"Thou wert never truly enthralled." His gaze bore into mine. "Thou art a witch in thine own right, who pretended to be enthralled long enough to approach our common foe."

My initial annoyance gave way to fear. Everything that'd occurred the past few days had been the result of Ormyr accusing Thordia of witchcraft. If he believed the same of me, I could only imagine what he'd do about it once we returned to the capital. "I—"

"As thou saved my life, I shall spare yours." Ormyr cut off my attempted denial, his grip on my shoulders tightening. "Unseen as my witness, I swear I shan't tell a soul!"

I felt relieved at first—until I began to worry about what Ormyr wanted in return for his silence.

"With such talent, thou couldst easily join a cloister and become a full-fledged adept." Instead of pivoting to the favors he expected from me, Ormyr offered this suggestion for my own good. "Thou wouldst never again risk the penalties of witchcraft."

I recoiled at the idea, but didn't get far, as Ormyr held me in place. When I was younger, I'd lacked the money, connections, and desire necessary for adept training. I'd been set to run the family inn, after all. Now, I had no interest in spreading lies and superstition.

"Master—Ormyr—listen." I shrugged out of his grasp and dodged the matter. "Thordia's coming with us to the capital."

His eyes went wide.

"I don't care for her, either, but she can keep Nidaros alive while we look for a way to stop the ichor. You saw all those crops in the hydroponics bay."

Ormyr frowned. "How can we trust her?"

"If she gets the safety she's looking for, she'll cooperate. Besides, she needs a cure for the ichor more than anyone. It's killing her."

He lowered his eyes, maybe debating whether further protest was a waste of time. Of *course* I'd defend a fellow witch.

I held in a sigh. "Stay here. We'll leave as soon as Thordia arrives."

When I stood to depart, Ormyr stood as well, grasping my elbow. "Mine adepts remain under Thordia's sway. Wilt thou help me free them?"

Again, I gently freed myself from his hold. "They're under Madam Castor's sway, not Thordia's." I'd told him the same thing right after Holsten and the others had attacked us. "Either way, I'll help, after I … ensure Captain Leirfall will recover as well as you have." I nearly spoke of saving Ingvar, then remembered that Ormyr's custody was one of the things I wanted to save him from. I swallowed hard. "Will you still give me the coordinates for Gules?"

"Indeed," Ormyr answered without hesitation. "If I have them, they're thine."

"Thank you." I bit my lip to force back tears. "The wise woman—Drea—she knows more about the Shipbuilders than I do. It'll be to everyone's benefit."

"May it be so. Unseen guide us." Ormyr grasped his beads and sat back down.

I turned away, relieved about certain things and anxious about others. Ormyr harbored a spark of compassion for me and his adepts, but I feared the self-serving courtier might return once we reached Nidaros. He could undermine me in front of Baron Tristan, when it'd really count, and fully exploit my "witch" status for personal gain. How would I defend myself? Probably by appealing to my status as Lord Catherwood's emissary. Were they really willing to persecute one of their Lord's trusted agents? Never mind that I *wasn't* a trusted agent. Baron Tristan didn't know that.

In the galley, Dag had helped himself to watered-down tack and dried meat. I aimed for the airlock, intending to wait for Thordia outside—but from the corner of my eye, I noticed the hatch leading to the engine room lay gaping open.

Paranoia dripped like ice-water down my spine. Had Ver-ahl caused all that chaos solely with his data carrier? Or might he have tampered with something during the time he'd spent down there?

He wouldn't get the better of me twice. I approached the ladder and slowly climbed belowdecks.

The cramped, windowless engine room housed the systems that kept me flying and breathing in space. When it came to physical tampering, a subtle approach required tools that Verahl would've lacked. If he'd sabotaged anything, there'd be obvious signs. I inspected the stuffy confines carefully, especially the casings and conduits that housed and fed into the computer. Nothing looked, smelled, or sounded off. There was some relief in that, but I wouldn't completely relax until our safe return to the capital.

My sense of balance still a bit off, I took my time ascending the ladder. Dag waited at the top of the hatch, observing curiously.

"Everything looks good for takeoff," I said. "I'm going to wait for Thordia outside."

"Aye." He followed me out into the docking bay.

Eventually, a tall wraith appeared, wearing a light-colored cloak with flowing sleeves and a veil that covered her head. Her gloved hands clasped a bundle of flax stalks tipped with blue flowers. Satchels hung from both shoulders, while baskets of fruits and vegetables sat on a large platform floating beside her.

"Thordia?" I prompted, surprised at the bounty accompanying her.

"I need people to listen. My appearance would prove a distraction at best." No resentment or shame tinged Thordia's voice. It was a matter of practicality.

There was plenty of room aboard *Kepler's Law* after I'd given away most of the supplies Linum Dominorum had given me. With Dag's help, I loaded Thordia's cargo quickly. We returned aboard, and I seated Thordia in the galley.

"Unseen!" Ormyr cried, bolting to the threshold of quarters. "What is this apparition?"

"Thordia," I replied. "Have a seat, Master."

He fixed her with a stare that was deservedly suspicious. Fortunately, he backed away and sat down, but looked ready to defend himself if needed. Meanwhile, Thordia paid him no mind.

I herded Dag toward the cockpit. He all but leapt into the copilot's chair, forgetting the half-eaten snack in his hands as he examined the console instruments. Flekka sat in his lap. For one about to leave the only home she'd known for centuries, the little sphere seemed to be taking it well.

My climb into the pilot's chair took longer, but collapsing into it had never felt so good. I kissed the console, which proved wonderfully responsive this time. Again, I shunned the data carriers I'd racked up in favor of manual piloting. We lifted off and aimed for the first set of docking bay doors we spotted. They slid open slowly at our approach, bathing us in blinding daylight.

The bright warmth fueled a new sense of optimism. A lot of work awaited us in the capital, then Gules. But once Ingvar, Drea, and the Naustviks were safe, we'd be on our way toward real progress against the ichor, just as I'd always intended.

Dag squinted, holding an arm up to shield his eyes. "Wonder how long we were in there?"

"I don't know," I replied. Hours or days seemed plausible. According to my ship's chronometer, I'd landed in Nidaros over five standard days ago, but I'd never learned how Nidaran days compared to standard.

I called Thordia to the cockpit to confirm which way to fly. My assumption was straight ahead, and I was right. When he'd reached the Harbinger, Verahl had simply shot straight toward the first docking bay he'd spotted.

As we emerged from the docking bay, the picture we flew into was breathtaking in all the wrong ways. Shadow smothered the landscape out to the horizon: the vast ichor-filled impact crater. I wanted to ask Thordia how she'd crossed all those treacherous miles herself, but she'd already retreated to the galley.

I pushed *Kepler's Law* up to her maximum speed within atmosphere. The occasional creak conveyed her protest, but she held. Dag stared out in disbelief at the miles melting away beneath us. Closer to Nidaros, the ichor dwindled, then vanished — or seemed to. It lingered under the surface, still a threat.

We flew over a few districts. I wondered if anyone noticed our passage, and what they thought of it. Then the tall capital buildings finally peeked over the horizon. The anxiety I felt toward the ichor vanished as determination took over. In a few minutes, things would start getting a lot better for everyone.

As we neared the capital, huge clouds of dark smoke appeared in its vicinity. It wasn't mist or morning fires. "What in hell?"

Dag looked out slack-jawed.

My heart pounded nervously. I decided to skip the port and shoot straight for the capital.

No further detail resolved until we hovered over the scene — the battlefield, really. An insane number of ships had landed in a scattershot pattern within the wall, close to the capital buildings. Smoke billowed from dozens of small fires burning around and inside the ships. Bodies littered the ground. Some wore Catherwood colors, but the majority were irregulars in white tunics.

With a growing sense of horror, I noticed the ships bore the seal of a white field with three blue flowers.

"Linum Dominorum!" I cried.

Madam Castor had sent an invasion force.

CHAPTER 20

From the safety of my cockpit, Dag and I stared down help-lessly at the trade guild ships crowded outside the capital build-ings. Flames and smoke were everywhere.

"Those don't look like harvest ships." Dag clutched Flekka, eyes wide.

"No. It's an assault." Horror crushed my heart and tight-ened my throat, preventing further words.

Through the occasional gap in smoke, bodies littered the ground, some wearing white while others wore burgundy. The main event seemed to have occurred earlier. Most of the invad-ing force was now elsewhere, probably the Baron's estate. A few packs of white-clad stragglers combed the area around the ships.

Ingvar and I had feared this might happen, but we'd never imagined Madam Castor would act so quickly. Harvest, in an-other standard week or so, would've given her a plausible ex-cuse to send ships. The officials aboard those ships would've learned about my murder and blamed Baron Tristan. It all would've gone to hell naturally from there. Apparently, Madam Castor was confident I'd be dead by now—and if not, that it'd be quick enough to arrange.

Once shock ran its course, a sickening worry overtook me. Who was still alive? Was I too late to save Ingvar?

Footsteps rushed toward the cockpit. Thordia emerged, sticking her veiled head past my and Dag's shoulders to take in the scene.

More footsteps issued from the galley. "What is the matter?" Ormyr called.

"The trade guild has invaded the capital!" I replied.

Ormyr had no reply at first, likely too stunned to offer one. For him, history repeated itself. He'd returned to Nidaros and his seat of power, only to be met with violence.

Instinct screamed at me to land and look for survivors, but dropping into the middle of a battlefield risked drawing attacks from both sides. There was also no telling what was in that smoke, either; it might've been poisonous. Ingvar remained foremost in my mind — but, with wrenching agony, I realized he could be anywhere at this point.

"Our Baron," Ormyr finally said. "We must report to Baron Tristan, safeguard him and Lady Amelia at all costs."

Not a bad thought, if they needed safeguarding. Before entering the fray, we needed to learn more about the situation on the ground. Where to land?

In my mind, the barracks remained the safest place in the capital. The soldiers would have the best idea of where things stood, or so I hoped. The Baron and Baroness might also be there directing troops, for all we knew.

I steered *Kepler's Law* away from the invasion ships. "Let's try the barracks. The soldiers should know where Baron Tristan is." And Ingvar. "If this doesn't work out, let's be ready to fight or retreat."

Thordia withdrew to the galley. Once she did, I could see Dag's expression, which mirrored my worry. He was almost certainly thinking about his brother Rigg, among other soldiers he might've befriended.

I suppressed the horrible what-ifs threatening to distract me. *Damn it, everyone, be alive,* I thought.

The barracks stood intact, thankfully, with no guild ships in its vicinity. Smoke rose from its chimneys, but there wasn't a soldier in sight. I couldn't decide if this were a good or bad sign.

As *Kepler's Law* descended, smoky haze dimmed the sun. The moment we touched down, Dag tore out of the cockpit to the galley. I couldn't summon his energy, but anxiety and purpose breathed some life into my limbs.

In the galley, Ormyr and Thordia ignored one another admirably while wishing over beads and slinging heavy satchels over her shoulders, respectively.

"Speed and safety are more important right now," I warned her, slipping on my baldric.

"These things *are* my safety." She packed the flax bundle so that the blue flowers stuck out prominently from one satchel.

It wasn't worth arguing further.

"Hand me my keris, whelp." Ormyr held out his hand expectantly.

Dag returned the weapon, then prepped his slingshot and knapsack in silence.

"Leave Flekka in one of the closets," I told him. "Otherwise, someone might confiscate her." We had to be careful with Shipbuilder artifacts again.

Dag frowned. "Would rather have her help, but aye, better not to lose her." With care, he stowed her in one of the closets he'd raided for food earlier.

"How're you feeling, Master?" I would've preferred for Ormyr to continue resting after surgery, but we didn't know yet how safe that prospect was.

Ormyr hitched his knapsack over his shoulders, meeting my gaze with resolve. "Well enough. And thou?"

"Fine." *Déjà vu* niggled at me. We'd performed a similar check before confronting Thordia. Once again, I had no clue what lay ahead or how quickly it'd exhaust the boost I'd gotten from medicine. Fighting for Ingvar and Nidaros would keep me going a while, though.

Thordia's earlier warning rang in my ears. I probably *would* make things worse for myself in the process. So be it.

"Let us assess the situation outside," Ormyr said, dragging me out of my grim thoughts. Some of the old courtly certainty had returned to bolster him. It might quickly prove unbearable, but he probably needed it here.

I considered how we might scout with minimal risk. It seemed best for me to go alone, but Dag and Ormyr would surely object. As for Thordia, she no doubt carried at least one more data carrier in one of her satchels. She might do anything with *Kepler's Law* if she felt desperate enough.

We'd *all* scout, then. Few others in the barony could steal my ship, and most of them were adepts. There weren't likely to be many of them at the barracks.

"I'll open the hatch," I said, glancing between the others. "Keep low and quiet. Speak up if you see a problem." I pulled the dagger from my belt, then headed for the airlock.

When the hatch finally gave, smoke wafted inside. It carried the awful odor of burnt flesh, along with a host of other burning smells. Hair, leather …

That bad omen soon faded against the three faces staring up at me from outside: Fasolt, Logmadr, and Ebbe. They surrounded the hatch with swords and axes hefted, sweating from exertion. At my appearance, they lowered their weapons.

"Thank the Unseen, Lady Knight!" Ebbe cried with a hint of his ever-present smile. "'Tis ye and not that brute Naustvik!"

A few coughs escaped Fasolt.

"Is it ever good to see you!" I sheathed my dagger, dropping to my knees with relief. "I saw this mess from above and didn't know what to think. I'm glad you're all right."

"We have no right to be," Logmadr said, "but we learned the guild was coming afore they landed."

I gaped. "What? You did?"

"Pontus told us everything, had us prepare an ambush," Ebbe said.

Pontus! Maybe he'd found something incriminating within the adepts' keep after all. I wondered whether Sigrid had had any luck herself.

"Been holding them off longer than we have any right to, unaided ..." Fasolt trailed off when footsteps and angry shouts sounded in the distance.

My gaze snapped toward the noise, landing on nearly a dozen white-tunic mercenaries charging through the haze with an assortment of melee weapons. All were older, well fed, and better armored than the poor boys they bore down upon.

As the breath halted in my throat, the Nidaran soldiers whirled to face the onslaught.

"C'mon, lads! We defend this vessel!" Ebbe cried. He, Fasolt, and Logmadr hurried forward with weapons hefted, forming a line before *Kepler's Law* that was tight enough to net the oncoming force, but loose enough to avoid hitting each other.

Adrenaline and righteousness coursed through my blood. There was no way I wouldn't defend my ship and friends. I dropped from the airlock and drew my side sword, adding it to their line.

To my surprise, I had a shadow: Dag, eyes narrowed and slingshot primed.

"Stay close to the ship," I spoke over my shoulder. "Fire at will."

That made things closer to two-to-one. Still not great odds, but better. As far as I could tell, Ormyr and Thordia remained aboard the ship, which was for the best. Thordia couldn't fight —not without staking her prey down, anyway.

The mercenaries closed. Lacking ranged weapons, they used taunts instead.

"Four infants and a woman!" one shouted. "Looks like we have ourselves a ride home!"

"Fine talk, geezer!" Ebbe called back. "C'mere, we'll take care of that last tooth for you!"

"We'll try to knock the ugly off, too, while we're at it," Fasolt chimed in.

"Gamla skíta!" Logmadr's eyes shone eagerly.

Like hell you're taking this ship. I just got her back! I said nothing, as the soldiers had me covered.

Before the mercenaries closed to melee distance, gas clouds erupted around them, causing them to falter. Once the gas took effect, they stumbled and coughed blindly.

Glancing over my shoulder, I caught a flash of burgundy in my ship's airlock just before the hatch swung home to protect against retaliation.

Thanks, Ormyr, I thought.

The Nidaran soldiers exchanged surprised looks at this turn of good fortune.

"Stay back," I said. "Let them come to us."

Fortunately, there was no wind to blow the caustic smoke our way. It proved a good screen; many of the mercenaries retreated. Dag harried the remainder with rocks, sending several shots into eyes and noses. The soldiers and I finished them off, depending on whoever was closest.

Restraint was a deadly waste of time. It wasn't hard to summon the bile necessary for lethal force. Who knew what these sons of bitches had done to Ingvar, the Baron, and countless others? I exploited the gaps in their armor, occasionally smashing my sword's pommel into their faces as well.

When the last mercenary fell, I remained tensed while panting hard, looking out for reinforcements. No further danger presented itself.

"Stand me up, I'll walk it off!"

My gaze snapped toward Ebbe. He sat on the ground, eyes screwed shut, clutching the inside of his thigh. Fasolt and Log-madr had sheathed their weapons to pull him to his feet.

"Leave him there!" I hurried over.

The pair yielded, kneeling to either side of Ebbe. They'd seen my healing in action before.

I knelt with them, tossing aside my sword to dig through my first aid kit for compresses. This was a part of the body with serious blood vessels; I had to get the bleeding under control fast. "Keep putting pressure on it."

Blood flowed around Ebbe's fingers. "Not quite a splinter this time, is it?" he asked with a nervous laugh. "Have I bought my trip to Folkvang?"

"You'll be fine. You still have that charm I gave you, right?" The hammer-shaped charm I'd offered him just before Ingvar and I had discovered Sigrid's "witching." It felt like ages ago.

Relief relaxed his expression somewhat. "Aye. In my pocket."

"Leave it there." I sensed a shadow hovering behind me. "Keep a lookout for trouble, Dag."

"Aye," he replied.

I gathered up a wad of compresses. "Lift your hand."

Ebbe did so, revealing a disturbingly deep gash. I pressed the compresses against the wound, struggling to hide the guilt and worry that tore at my heart. We had to press on, fight off the invasion and find Ingvar, but I couldn't leave Ebbe in mortal danger.

For once, I had more at my disposal than just a first aid kit. Normally I would've worried about bringing it out in the open, but this was a special case. I'd stabilize Ebbe, then lie my way out of trouble later.

A quick glance toward *Kepler's Law* revealed Ormyr framed in the wide-open airlock hatch, watching us with concern. Thordia's veiled form loomed behind him. I couldn't call her over, as her name would spark a panic.

"Dag, come here!" Once he dropped beside me, I leaned over to whisper. "Get Thordia, have her bring the surgical construct."

The young man nodded, then ran off.

Fasolt and Logmadr exchanged nervous looks as blood seeped through Ebbe's compresses. I layered more on top, trying to look reassuring while mentally urging Thordia to hurry.

"Speak quickly, men! We must know what transpired here."

Ormyr's voice startled me. Glancing up, I found him standing over us with an air of authority.

The soldiers' gazes riveted toward the master adept, then soured.

"Thanks for nothing!" Fasolt snapped.

Ormyr glared. "Show the proper—"

"Your adepts received these bastards with open arms!" Fasolt leapt to his feet, scowling. "The guild mercs who escaped our ambush are all holed up in the keep now!"

Ormyr gaped, the color draining from his face.

I felt sick as well, wondering if Ingvar were trapped in the keep with them. "Madam Castor never believed there was any crop trouble here," I managed. "She thought you were resisting Catherwood rule again, and the Baron lacked the spine to straighten you out. She wanted to invade Nidaros even before I got involved, make sure her flax supply would be safe. Holsten and his friends are probably helping her."

The master adept was speechless for once.

"Move aside."

A new voice entered the fray: Thordia. The veiled specter approached with her surgical construct and satchels at the ready.

The soldiers flinched and stared at her in horror.

"*Skíta!*" Fasolt backpedaled several steps.

Logmadr and Ebbe remained on the ground, trying to crawl backward.

"Hold still!" I cried, grabbing Ebbe's arm. "This woman can help us."

They froze, but looked less than convinced—even as their stares shifted toward the flax she carried.

"Let's move him somewhere safe first," Thordia said. "Your ship?"

"The barracks!" Fasolt snapped.

"But we've got more wounded there!" Ebbe seemed reluctant to let a ghost near them.

"You do?" I asked uselessly. Of course they did. How many more were in serious trouble? Could I leave them behind in good conscience to pursue Ingvar?

"It's safer at the barracks," Logmadr reluctantly agreed.

"Let's head in," I said. While treating Ebbe, I could learn more about what had happened. I'd figure it out from there.

Ebbe glanced between everyone present—uneasy, but convinced enough for now. "Come on, lugs, help me up."

While I ensured Ebbe kept pressure on the compresses, Fasolt and Logmadr lifted him upright. Ebbe then hopped on his good leg as his friends guided him toward the barracks' entrance. Ormyr followed right behind them, with Thordia and the construct trailing after.

With spare compresses, I wiped the blood from my hands, then glanced around for my side sword. Dag had picked it up; he could keep it for now. He and I brought up the procession's rear.

As we walked, no one had anything more to contribute, aside from Fasolt's grumblings concerning Madam Castor's questionable virtue.

Inside the barracks was not the usual happy home. A grim field of casualties took up entirely too much floorspace. Burns, cuts, fractures ... some minor, some serious enough that others had taken up vigils, hunched over beads and charms.

Every capable eye in the room fastened on the odd group streaming through the entrance. My stomach knotted up as I thought of the violence we'd missed, and the violence yet to occur. I recognized most of the young men, and desperately wished I could tend to them, but it'd be better to end the fighting first.

Fasolt and Logmadr laid Ebbe down by one of the fires, then remained near his head. I dropped by Ebbe's feet to elevate his wounded leg. Meanwhile, Thordia and Ormyr knelt on either side of the wounded soldier. While one loaded her surgical construct with tools, the other grasped his beads and recited a spell.

The soldiers nearby who could shudder and back away from Thordia and her floating minion did so. Others were too stunned to react. A few seemed less nervous about the spectacle since an adept was present, but most of the looks Ormyr attracted were loaded with mistrust and resentment.

"You on our side, Master?" a soldier piped up. "Might want to tell your cloister to stop shooting at us."

Ormyr continued reciting without pause.

While the construct assessed Ebbe's wound, Thordia fished out a dermal injector from her satchel. Lying down, Ebbe didn't have a full picture of what was going on, but saw enough to make him nervous again. "Don't let these ghosts kill me, lads," he muttered.

Fasolt and Logmadr sent uncertain looks my way.

"Trust me, friend. I wouldn't let anyone hurt you." I patted Ebbe's foot reassuringly.

Standing behind me, Dag rested my sword-point on the ground and raised his voice. "Anyone seen Rigg?"

"Defending the storehouse, last I saw," another soldier replied.

I hoped Rigg was still on his feet somewhere. "Who's in command right now?" I asked with the goal of distracting the soldiers and learning more about the current situation.

"Pontus is in charge," Ebbe answered, eyes screwed shut as the construct tended to his injury. "He and our Baron took shelter within the dungeon."

"Unseen be praised, our Baron liveth," Ormyr muttered, weaving it into his spell.

This was good news on several fronts. The dungeon was relatively secure, having only two public entrances to guard— assuming the enemy even thought to search down there. I clenched my fists, steeling myself for the question I was both dying and dreading to ask. "What about Captain Leirfall?"

"Stuck in the keep, along with our Baroness," Fasolt answered. These words seemed to pain each soldier worse than his wounds.

"Hell." I struggled against an inconvenient surge of nausea and tears. The enemy had him, along with Lady Amelia, Lord Catherwood's aunt and heir presumptive. As desperate worry overwhelmed me, I couldn't think through the full implications. "Are they still alive?"

"As far as we know," Logmadr said.

They probably wouldn't harm such valuable hostages. I clung to that hope to stave off an emotional breakdown.

"We're dying to break the captain out, but our Baron won't allow it," Fasolt said. "Not with Lady Amelia in there."

"I'll see if I can't convince him otherwise." These words escaped my mouth despite the fact that Baron Tristan's hesitation might've stemmed from some unknown legitimate factor.

"Fasolt, Logmadr? Escort our Lady Knight to the dungeon so she can meet with our Baron," Ebbe said.

They brightened at the prospect.

"You shan't go anywhere without me!" Ormyr insisted.

"Or me." Thordia's veiled head turned my way. "This won't take much longer."

I blinked at her. "You should stay here and tend to the wounded." I'd feel slightly better about leaving them that way.

"I'm safest wherever the Baron resides, so I'm coming with you," Thordia replied evenly.

She was still primarily concerned with her own hide. I swallowed my resentment. "Do you have anything to defend yourself with?"

"Yes." She made no move to prove it. It was probably a Shipbuilder device hidden in one of her satchels.

I left it at that, focusing on Ebbe. Under Thordia's supervision, the construct sealed his wound and cleared away much of the shed blood. Whatever medicine Thordia had administered seemed to numb and relax him. As his condition visibly improved, the soldiers nearby gradually de-tensed in the presence of the wraith and her construct. A few noticed the flax in her satchel, and pointed it out to each other.

However, the occasional poisonous glance still fired Ormyr's way. The master adept pretended to blindness.

Once Ormyr and Thordia had finished their administrations, I patted Ebbe's boot again. "My ship's well stocked with food and other supplies. Take whatever you need, and place wounded in there if you have to."

Ebbe propped himself up on his elbows to nod my way. "Hurry up and send those bastards packing." He then focused on Dag. "As for ye, little Nyvind, pretend-time's over! Get out of those adept rags and grab some bench!"

Dag darted up beside me, scowling, and looked ready to drive my sword through him.

"Mr. Nyvind's with me," I said.

As the soldiers focused on Dag in bewilderment, Dag straightened, meeting the attention with defiant pride. This little moment of triumph was more reassuring than any platitudes I might've offered concerning Rigg. He'd also forgotten to kill Ebbe, which was good. I suppressed my relieved smile, not wanting Dag to think I was mocking him.

"Well then," Ebbe said, lying back, "Unseen guide you all."

Fasolt and Logmadr wished him well before stepping away from the fire. Thordia stood, the construct trailing obediently. I was about to suggest she leave it behind, but it seemed someone had to supervise its work, feed it fresh tools and administer medicine. It couldn't tend to the soldiers without us. Once everything was settled in the capital, I resolved to bring it back.

Ormyr rose and faced Fasolt and Logmadr with stern determination, beckoning with a jeweled hand. "A crossbow. Quickly."

Fasolt glared, unmoved. Wide-eyed, Logmadr broke away to head for the storage chests.

Dag handed back my side sword after I stood. I nodded my thanks, keeping it in hand.

Our group returned outside. I recalled one last thing I wanted from my ship, and returned alone to the galley. One of the closets still housed Ingvar's longsword, bow, and quiver. He'd left them there in preparation for our ill-fated Harbinger trip.

Upon reclaiming the weapons, a crushing grief seized me. At that moment, Ingvar could be in chains, in agony, or both. I'd do everything possible to reach him quickly — but, he'd want me doing the right thing for Nidaros first. I loved him too much to ignore that.

Heart racing with dread and anticipation, I hurried back outside.

Dag and the soldiers kept their distance from Ormyr and Thordia, who in turn remained distant from each other. Unfazed, Ormyr launched into an invocation. "Hear me, Unseen! Breathe strength into our limbs for the battle ahead ..."

Fasolt and Logmadr grudgingly wound their hands through their beads, but reserved their reverence for the weaponry I carried.

"I think your captain would want you to put these to good use," I murmured.

They exchanged a glance. Then Logmadr sheathed his sword in favor of the bow, strapping the quiver around his waist.

"Nyvind!" Fasolt offered his hand-axe to Dag. "Think ye can handle this?"

Dag gladly relieved him of the weapon, allowing Fasolt to take Ingvar's longsword.

"How are you on ammunition?" I asked Dag, prepping my own sword with a flourish.

"Fine," he replied, donning his hood. "We walked past lots of rocks, aye?"

That we had. I glanced over my shoulder at Thordia, who looked more ghostlike than ever among the mist. She had yet to produce a weapon; I didn't prompt her to.

Ormyr stepped to the fore, surveying the hazy field of invading ships with narrowed eyes. "Very well. We shall—"

"'Tis *our* lead ye follow!" Fasolt cut him off. "We'll circle around." He drew a C-shaped arc in the air with his pointer finger. "Some mercs linger among the wreckage, as ye saw."

"We ambushed them when they landed. Reduced their numbers afore they got organized," Logmadr chimed in. "Their commander escaped into the keep, though."

Ormyr whirled on him, aghast. "Commander Savidge is here?"

"Aye," Logmadr replied.

This news seemed to strike Ormyr almost as hard as the invasion itself.

"Who's that?" I asked, vaguely remembering the name. I must've heard it somewhere in Spectra while receiving my quest.

The master adept loaded a bolt into his crossbow. It gave him an excuse to lean over and hide his face. "The leader of Madam Castor's mercenary force. He involveth himself in only her most important missions."

Invading another planet was pretty important business. For Ormyr to openly show fear of someone was even more serious.

"Stay together and stay quiet!" Fasolt cautioned. "We'll use the smoke for cover, go undetected as long as we can."

CHAPTER 21

We left *Kepler's Law* and the relative safety of the barracks behind. Ahead, sunlight played through the smoky battlefield between us and the capital buildings. It was almost pretty, but the nostril-burning scents in the air told of the horrible suffering that'd occurred before we'd flown in from the Harbinger.

I worried about everyone trapped behind that mess. The guild mercenaries wouldn't care who lived or died, only whether they got paid. We had to reach the adepts' keep and infiltrate the dungeon, where Baron Tristan and Pontus hid. Then we had to figure out how to rescue our loved ones and end Madam Castor's invasion.

The soldiers took the lead as they'd insisted. Logmadr held multiple arrows in his shooting hand, the same way Ingvar did, while Fasolt held Ingvar's longsword in a low guard. Side sword in hand, I stuck close to Thordia and the surgical construct, feeling like she was the most vulnerable—even though she towered over me, and chances were good she could level the battlefield with whatever was in her satchels. Dag shadowed me with his new axe. Ormyr brought up the rear, crossbow hefted.

We moved quickly and quietly—not an easy prospect for me, even with drugs dulling the worst of my symptoms. But with so many lives at stake and Ingvar's fate uncertain, I spurred myself on. The haze thickened, as did the nauseating smell of burnt flesh—lending cover, but also hindering our shooters. We arced around the scattering of trade guild ships to avoid detection. Flames flickered and burned throughout. Blackened corpses, contorted in agony, clogged ship hatches and spilled out onto the field.

Madam Castor had sent a force capable of overwhelming all resistance from Nidaros, but they clearly hadn't anticipated Pontus' ambush, which seemed to have relied heavily on incendiary weapons. The Baron's storehouse contained Greek fire grenades, among other munitions. They'd likely been hurled inside the ships before the mercenaries had disembarked.

It wasn't all fire, though. Judging by the smell, some had fallen victim to phosphorous.

Revulsion hit me like a gut-punch. Those who survived phosphorous exposure carried reminders of the attack for the rest of their lives. A vendor I'd met in Spectra came to mind: scarred, missing an arm. It surprised me that Pontus had resorted to such a measure. When I considered how young, under-nourished, and outclassed the Nidaran army was, how little time they'd had to prepare—without any adept "magic" to aid them, no less—it made more sense, but remained awful.

Was shooting and hacking them to pieces all that much better, though? Rationally, no. Still, it bothered me, as did the question of where the phosphorous had come from. It took big, expensive effort to harvest and assemble the materials properly. Maybe Lord Catherwood had supplied it to Baron Tristan in case of future popular uprisings.

The sight of Nidaran casualties in the field jarred me out of my thoughts. Friendly young men days earlier, now cut apart and shot through because some obscenely rich woman on a far-flung planet hadn't finished getting richer.

My disgust shifted away from the defenders and back toward Madam Castor and her minions. I had to avert my gaze, keep moving forward.

The soldiers maintained their pace, ignoring the gruesome sights. There'd be time for mourning later. Hell, were we ever racking it up. Dag focused ahead, likely eager to see whether his brother was indeed at the storehouse. Thordia held silent and betrayed nothing, while Ormyr had paled. This was probably all too reminiscent of the time he, Baron Tristan, and Ingvar had put down a misguided bid for independence.

We reached a small clearing, a no man's land between the burned-out guild ships and capital buildings. Catherwood soldiers guarded the twin sail-shaped buildings, the storehouse and the Baron's estate. In between them rose the adepts' keep, unprotected from the outside. Enemy territory. Ingvar's and Lady Amelia's prison, assuming both still lived.

For a moment, my anger toward the adepts overshadowed pain and worry. If they'd helped the army resist the invaders, this might've been over already, with fewer casualties. Unfortunately, Madam Castor had gotten to them — almost certainly through Holsten. I wondered if I'd be seeing him again soon, and paying him back for all those murder attempts.

A bolt sailed past Logmadr's shoulder, shot from the cluster of ships behind us. He turned and fired several arrows while pedaling backward. Another bolt struck Thordia in the arm she'd raised over her head for cover, deflecting harmlessly. It'd hit her prosthetic arm, which remained invisible under her cloak. A lucky break, indeed.

Fasolt pointed toward the familiar rain barrel-strewn clearing between the estate and keep. "Run! Stop for nothing!"

We sprinted toward safety. Ormyr hurled gas grenades behind us, flushing out several staggering mercenaries. He and Logmadr then shot down some of the exposed targets. Arrows sailed overhead from the Baron's estate, picking off more.

Among the high walls and shadows of the courtyard, mercenary bodies littered our path. The angle of the arrows lodged in their corpses suggested an attack from above. The kitchen door was closed; I hoped Lif, Kofri, and Alfrun had sheltered somewhere safe.

The soldiers wound to a halt, Fasolt succumbing to a coughing fit. Logmadr remained vigilant, breathing hard himself.

My head pounded in protest of exertion. Dizziness sent me to one knee. While catching my breath, I glanced over my shoulder to ensure the rest of our group made it to safety. A hint of Ormyr's limp had returned. He leaned over his crossbow to reload it, conveniently hiding his exertion. Dag and Thordia, meanwhile, seemed unaffected.

I planted my sword-point into the ground, but couldn't quite pull myself to my feet. Ormyr and Dag appeared on either side to help me stand.

"Did you see Rigg outside the storehouse?" I asked Dag.

"Nay." His gaze settled on his feet.

My sympathy welled. "He might be *in* there."

"Let us not lose sight of our goal." Ormyr glanced to me uncertainly. "Lady Knight—?"

"I'm fine." In reality, I was tired and hurting, but I had to keep pushing until Ingvar was safe and the invasion was over.

Once recovered, the soldiers led us around the keep to the dungeon entrance, then unlocked the doors built into the ground. Another wave of sickening smells greeted us, a reminder of how I'd nearly burned to death down there.

"Who removed the wards within the dungeon?" Ormyr asked, frowning.

"Not sure," Fasolt replied. "Just know it isn't a problem."

The darkness ahead prompted Dag to pull out his light tile.

"Keep that hidden here," I whispered. Granted, we'd brought the surgical construct, but I wanted to keep any and all witchcraft suspicion off Dag.

"Aye. Forgot." He shrugged. "Doesn't feel like magic after a while."

Logmadr called into the depths. Soon after, lantern-light illuminated the bottom of the ramp, carried by a soldier who lowered his weapon with relief. "Come on, mates!"

This time, Ormyr insisted on being first behind the soldiers. I followed with Dag, and Thordia brought up the rear. We tromped down an all-too-familiar muddy corridor. I'd since learned the mud was laced with ichor, which made me worried for the prisoners mired in it—but their cells appeared to be empty. Just an effect of the meager lighting? Something to worry about later.

The soldiers led us to a cell at the dungeon's far end, close to where Verahl had been imprisoned, and unlocked it for us.

Ormyr pushed his way in first. "Your Grace!"

Dag and I entered next.

The cell had been converted into an impromptu strategic command. Soldiers lined the room. A table on the far wall supported candles, smoking incense, and parchment scrolls. Baron Tristan huddled over the clutter, still in plainclothes, but with a sword at his side. His head was lowered as the young woman to his right chanted softly.

Sigrid?

Shock paralyzed me beside Ormyr, who had also frozen before the spectacle in slack-jawed astonishment. Dag halted on my other side, shooting uncertain looks between me and the Baron.

Pontus stood to the Baron's left, turned away from him and Sigrid—arms folded, frowning with contempt. He was the first to witness us burst into the room. His arms dropped to his sides, and he mirrored Ormyr's expression.

Sigrid and Baron Tristan faced us soon after. The Baron clutched his hammer amulet with a bewildered gaze. Sigrid raised her familiar punching dagger into a defensive posture.

When her eyes found mine, though, she grinned, clapping her hands together before her chest.

How had she recovered her weapon after Ingvar had confiscated it? More importantly, why the hell was a self-styled witch casting in Baron Tristan's presence? Having lost his adepts' support, the Baron might've grown desperate for magical aid, but I never would've imagined *that* desperate.

Habit trumped shock. I passed my sword into my left hand and slowly lowered myself to one knee before the Baron, using my right hand to pull Dag down with me.

Behind me, Fasolt's and Logmadr's shifting armor betrayed their kneeling. I had no idea whether Thordia joined them.

Ormyr remained standing. "Your Grace—"

"Silence!" Baron Tristan stomped Ormyr's address into the ichor-laced dirt. "Arise!"

I'd never heard the Baron shut Ormyr down like that, and wasn't sure whether to cower or applaud. Despite my mounting confusion, I obeyed, barely noticing how my head pounded and spun.

The soldiers lining the room stared at us like we were ambulatory corpses. Sigrid and Baron Tristan, meanwhile, looked relieved. Encouraged, even.

"Lady Knight!" The Baron detached from the table and, to my continued astonishment, stepped forward to seize my free hand in both of his. "Thank the Unseen thou art alive and free of whatever evil influence once plagued thee." He sobered with concern. "But it seemeth thy freedom came at great cost."

I surely looked much worse for wear since the last time we'd met. Also, Ormyr had told him about my "enthrallment." Did he also know we'd gone to the Harbinger? Was all of this relief about to turn into an angry *Off with their heads?*

Behind the Baron, Pontus snapped out of his surprise, settling into a stern look. I could only imagine his worry for Ingvar, his soldiers, and his family. He also hadn't been thrilled with me the last time we'd talked.

Sigrid remained silent, looking on in triumph.

"By the Unseen, what happened?" the Baron asked.

I could ask you the same question, I thought. "There's a lot to explain, sir. Let's leave it for a safer time."

The Baron's gaze shifted to Dag. "I know thee not, Adept. Art thou yet loyal to me?"

"Uh …" Dag trailed off. I considered speaking up for him, but he rose to his full height—up to my shoulder, if lucky—and pulled back his hood to look the Baron in the eye. "Not an adept, Your Grace. Dagfin Nyvind. But aye, I fight for you."

Baron Tristan glanced past my shoulder. As if we all hadn't endured enough surprise already, his jaw fell.

Behind me, Thordia's veiled form hovered in the threshold, still looking awfully wraithlike. Blue flax flowers stuck out of one satchel, while the surgical construct hovered at her side.

"What is this apparition?" the Baron muttered.

"Someone you need to speak with later," I answered.

"I … should say so." He looked nervous, but determined.

Meanwhile, Sigrid basked in unrestrained joy. She'd connected the dots in a way no one else had yet.

"What's the situation here?" I prompted before anyone else realized Thordia Naustvik stood among them.

"We've been awaiting augury," Baron Tristan continued, looking me in the eye. "Thou art our sign!"

"We've had a long and harrowing journey, Your Grace." Ormyr spoke before I could respond. "There's much to discuss concerning our barony's future. For now, we must—"

"Thou never foresaw this!" the Baron cut him off, scowling. "Nothing thou might propose can reverse that, or restore the lives lost!"

The soldiers and Dag stared wide-eyed. I flinched despite myself. The Baron's reaction startled me as much as a slap in the face would've.

The words cut Ormyr deeper than any sword. After a moment of silence, he forged ahead. "Your Grace, at least permit me to ask what *she* is doing here?" His heated glare focused on Sigrid, melting her triumph.

"Performing thy function, whilst thou ran off chasing specters." The Baron released my hand to clench his fists at his sides.

Ormyr's eyes went wide. "Your—"

"Silence! Speak no more unless I bid it."

Stricken, Ormyr had no choice but to comply. Sigrid melted again, this time with relief.

My side sword almost fell out of my hand. Sigrid's secret was out, she was still free, and the Baron defended her against the master adept he'd never once gainsaid in the time I'd known him. How had she won such immense favor? Did it have something to do with succeeding where Ormyr had failed?

Baron Tristan glanced to me again. "We shall cower here no longer. 'Tis time we stormed the keep!"

Now that was an idea I could get behind. But—

"Your Grace? Much as I'm raring to do just that, we'd better have a plan first." Pontus stepped forward to join our huddle.

"I agree." And I meant it, but my heart pounded with dread at what I might hear. "How much do we know about the situation upstairs?"

The Baron took a deep breath. "Lieutenant Grimsson, start with yesterday morning and explain events as they happened."

"Aye, Your Grace. Well, about the time Master Ormyr carried you off to the Harbinger—" Pontus' bitter gaze flicked toward Ormyr "—I was in the keep, unknowing of all of it. We'd talked the night before about that strange ichor in the ground and your suspicions against Madam Castor. I was determined to find anything that might shed light on those problems. Most of the adepts were out of sight; I thought they were off attending to some ritual." He tossed his head toward Sigrid, eyes narrowed in distaste. "Ran into that witch snooping around, looking for the same thing I was—and she found it, all right."

The withering stare Baron Tristan cast about the cell snuffed out any witch-related protest before it occurred.

"A note to Holsten from Madam Castor," Sigrid piped up for my benefit, triumphant once more.

I gaped, then swallowed hard. Just the evidence Ingvar and I had been hoping for. Sigrid *had* outdone Ormyr, all because I'd sent her to the keep to gather the proof sitting in Ormyr's own sanctuary.

"The note was sealed and ciphered, but Holsten had worked out the cipher directly on the parchment and hadn't yet destroyed it," Pontus explained. "It said a trade guild invasion was imminent—and it ordered Holsten to kill you, Lady Knight."

I nodded grimly. This was less troubling and more vindicating.

"Had to leave the keep and warn our Baron, make plans to meet the invaders immediately," Pontus continued. "Once I returned to the barracks, I found it in chaos. That's when I learned what happened to you and Captain Leirfall." He lowered his guilt-haunted expression. "Wanted to extract our captain from the keep, but feared it would rouse suspicion. I didn't know which adepts might be colluding with Holsten, and I didn't want them to know we were wise to them. We prioritized invasion planning—a good thing, as their forces showed up within hours."

My heart ached for Ingvar, wounded and stuck behind enemy lines all this time. "And the guild mercenaries who survived your ambush fled into the keep," I spoke around the lump in my throat, repeating what I'd learned earlier. "Including their leader, Commander Savidge."

"Aye," Pontus said.

"How'd they capture Lady Amelia?" I asked.

"At the time of their landing, she was wishing in the calefactory. Amidst our planning, I hadn't realized swiftly enough." Baron Tristan cast a painfully anxious look downward.

Beside me, Dag listened with a deepening scowl. Meanwhile, Ormyr's strained expression made plain his own worry. Even Sigrid had sobered, nursing the green and white beads wrapped around her arm.

I sympathized deeply with Baron Tristan. Unfortunately, this led us to the most urgent and dreadful questions of all. "Has anyone confirmed that they have her and Captain Leirfall alive?" I forced out. "Have they made any demands?"

"Not yet," Pontus replied. "We shook them up bad. I don't think they planned on engagement, just to scare us with sheer numbers. They believed you'd be dead; Savidge would've marched into our Baron's estate, demanded to speak with you, and arrested His Grace when your live body never turned up. Instead, they're pinned down in that keep now. If it were my mess to dig out of, I'd be attempting to take inventory and regroup."

Less than satisfied with the uncertainty, I tried to reassure myself. It made sense that Lady Amelia and Ingvar would be alive, if the captain hadn't already succumbed to injury or abuse. They'd make great hostages in a pinch. For their sake, I hoped Savidge was smart enough to see it.

But was Savidge even calling the shots?

"What about Holsten, and the other adepts who rode out with us to the Harbinger?" I didn't bother tiptoeing around the Harbinger, as Pontus had already mentioned it. "Halfway through the journey, they left us to die. Have they returned yet?" If not, this would be a great time to bolster gate defenses.

Pontus' gaze hardened. "We couldn't count on anyone coming back from the Harbinger. Needed every last man on the invasion, so gate coverage wasn't what it could've been. Heard Holsten and a group of adepts made it back some time ago, and succeeded in returning to the keep."

Dread and nausea crept back up on me. If Holsten were in charge, and relied upon the Unseen for guidance in this fight, then trying to guess the enemy's most rational moves would be a waste of time. They might do anything, *anything*, with Ingvar and the Baroness. Torture and sacrifice leapt to mind first. I choked back a retch.

"We've waited here for some time, wishing that the Unseen might tell us when to act," Baron Tristan said. "Clearly, thy return is our sign."

"It's just as I envisioned." Sigrid glanced to me with certainty. "Blood, fire, and death are upon us, but you'll have a hand in turning them back."

"Let us storm the keep before they have a chance to regroup!" Baron Tristan declared.

I was eager to forge ahead on that topic, shift from worry to action.

"There are several concealed passageways from dungeon to keep." Pontus was no less impatient. "The enemy can't guard them all. Master, can ye open one for us?"

"Indeed I can." Ormyr found his voice again. "Then I —"

"Once inside the keep," Baron Tristan cut him off, "we shall seek out Lady Amelia and Captain Leirfall, moving quietly to avoid detection. I care not about Holsten or Commander Savidge yet. Let us remove their leverage first."

I had no objections to this plan. The Baron's reasoning and priorities were reassuring.

"Aye, Your Grace—but should we get the chance, we should capture and return their leadership here," Pontus said. "The mercs won't have any more reason to fight once their commander's out of play. I suspect the same goes for Holsten and the adepts helping him."

"Verily." The Baron nodded. "Killing is to be avoided. We need witnesses to question regarding Madam Castor's plot."

Pontus' confidence faltered at a new consideration. "How'll we defend ourselves from the adepts' magic? Wards and curses are sure to be everywhere."

"Master Ormyr's got us covered—right?" I glanced his way, certain this would lead to his redemption in the Baron's eyes.

Ormyr stood resolute. "I shall—"

"Thou shalt open our path, then remain down here to mire in ignorance, as I've had to!" Baron Tristan cried.

Stunned silence consumed the entire cell.

A cringing sympathy braced me. It was difficult to watch "friendly" Ormyr being punished for "cruel" Ormyr's sins. I considered protesting—we could use all the help we could get—but the master adept had just weathered surgery. Besides, the look on Baron Tristan's face brooked no challenge.

Ormyr's renewed shock masked whatever he was thinking or rationalizing. He opened his mouth to counter.

"I'll go with you, Your Grace," Sigrid offered.

Pontus whirled on her, clenching the sword-hilt at his side. "My lads and I won't abide a witch!"

"Thou must remain, Sigrid," the Baron declared calmly. "Thou art too valuable to risk losing."

Sigrid flinched before Pontus, but nodded her acceptance.

Was there any "magic" reassurance I could offer before our infiltration plans fizzled out altogether? Digging into my pockets, I came upon a welcome find.

"Sir? I have this charm from Lady Amelia." The jewel-studded khamsa she'd given me days earlier when she'd asked me for food. I held it out for all to see. "If this isn't enough to protect every last one of us, I don't know what is."

Baron Tristan gaped, then held out a hesitant, beckoning hand. "Prithee?"

I passed him the charm, which he squeezed in his fist a moment before pocketing.

Everyone else in attendance seemed convinced we'd be all right. I was sorry I'd never mentioned the thing to Ormyr on our travels. It might've saved us a lot of bickering.

"What about a diversion?" I looked to Pontus. "Maybe some of the soldiers outside could throw something at the keep while we sneak in?"

"Good idea." Pontus looked to our escort. "Fasolt, Logmadr—get topside on the double. Gather some fireworks from the storehouse and sling them at the keep, concentrating on the front door. Counting on you to keep these bastards entertained."

"Aye, sir!" they acknowledged.

"Unseen be with you," Logmadr added.

I shook hands with them. "Be safe."

As they hurried out, Pontus adjusted his gauntlets and looked about the cell. "Right then, lads. I'm taking our Baron upstairs."

The remaining soldiers turned into a pleading mass. "I'll come too, sir! Take me?"

Pontus silenced them by raising his voice again. "I'd take you all if I could, but we have to keep numbers down to avoid detection. Magnus, with me."

"Aye, sir!" Magnus leapt away from the wall, exuberant.

The others wilted from disappointment.

Baron Tristan glared at Ormyr. "Unlock the passage closest to the infirmary, then stay here and wish hard. Wish *very* hard."

Ormyr's gaze, and shoulders, fell in utter defeat.

The infirmary! That seemed a likely place to find Ingvar. Anguish and longing tore at my heart. *Please hold out a little longer,* I urged him mentally.

The Baron then turned to the handmaid, softening. "Sigrid?"

He couldn't bring himself to ask a witch for her blessing, but didn't need to. In plain sight, Sigrid raised her dagger-hand over her head. "Hear me great powers, deciders of fate! Protect our Baron and all in his company as they cast off our oppressors ..."

Eyes narrowed, Ormyr plucked a lantern off one of the soldiers and limped outside. Thordia darted out of his path just in time. Pontus and the other soldiers were quick on Ormyr's heels, even those who weren't accompanying us. Several wary glances strayed toward Thordia, but no one said anything in the interests of a swift escape.

If Pontus had found Holsten's note, Sigrid's meteoric rise in influence would never have happened—but there she was, supporting Baron Tristan at this dark hour. I resolved to talk to my fellow "witch" in private before we separated. She could safeguard Thordia while I was away, and if I didn't make it back, she could persuade the Baron to listen to Thordia's case.

When Sigrid finished chanting, she opened her eyes to find the cell only half as full. The Baron nodded to her in thanks. "Remain here until further notice."

"Yes, Your Grace. Be careful." Sigrid lowered her arm.

"Thou as well, masked one," the Baron told Thordia as he turned to leave.

"Sir, the others are getting ready for our breach," I said. "I'll join you in a moment."

The Baron faced me. "Prithee hurry. Thou art my augury, I would fight at your side."

"I'd be honored, sir."

He strode out.

"I need to speak with these ladies," I told Dag. "Can you wait outside and make sure no one interrupts us?"

Dag frowned. "I still get to go with you?"

"Of course."

He nodded, then ducked out after the Baron.

I remained in the cell with Sigrid and Thordia: all of us real or accused witches. Sigrid remained close to me, while Thordia and the surgical construct had backed against the wall beside the cell door.

Awe flooded the handmaid, as if she were in the presence of two idols. "Is it really Thordia Naustvik?" she chanced.

Thordia stiffened, the fist around one of her satchel straps tightening.

"I'm so glad you're safe! *Sisters!*" Sigrid gushed, grabbing my free hand to crush against her chest. "I can't believe it, you found her! You even charmed Master Ormyr into leaving her alone! I wished hard for your success, but I never imagined how you'd succeed!"

Thordia remained frozen, probably from confusion. She did the smart thing and kept her mouth shut.

"Your success is nothing to sneeze at, either," I said. "I need you to keep Thordia safe, and hide her identity, until we can tell the Baron about all the good she's done within the Harbinger."

"I'll protect her with my life," Sigrid vowed.

I faced Thordia. "You should be safe here," I said, fully aware of the irony. "Assuming I return, we'll discuss our next steps then."

Thordia hesitated, then finally spoke. "I'll cooperate and wait for my audience with Baron Tristan."

Good. "See you both soon, I hope."

I advanced toward the threshold, and nearly reached it, when an icy realization slid down my spine. Unconsciously grasping my side sword tighter, I whirled back on Sigrid.

"Holsten and the adepts helping him are Gyllenfeld loyalists, like you. Why are you aiding the Baron and not them?"

Sigrid's expression frosted over. "You were right about Madam Castor. If she removes Baron Tristan, she'll give Nidaros to Holsten." The ice succumbed to a flaming hatred. "Holsten is no Lord Gyllenfeld. And I'd rather die than bow to any adept."

Her explanation provided only marginal solace. I could only hope her loyalty to fellow witches surpassed all else.

Dag had glued himself to the threshold, digging his thumbnail into the slingshot he'd readied. Behind him loomed Pontus. Once I stepped into the corridor, the lieutenant blocked my path and arrested my gaze with an intense expression.

"Let's get this straight, Lady Knight: I'm glad ye survived the Harbinger," he muttered. "Our Baron's not interested in handing out death penalties, and I'm glad about that, too. But I'm *furious* about you dragging our captain along on your business. Now he's out of a fight in which he's sorely needed. If he lives, Unseen willing, tell him to keep to soldier business from here on out. If ye actually care one shred about him, that's what ye'll do."

An uncomfortable flush rose to my face. Guilt reared up as well, but I didn't let it take hold. "Ingvar made his own choices," I returned firmly. "I never asked Ormyr to show up at the port, and I didn't tell Verahl to lose his temper, either."

Pontus wasn't impressed. "If ye *had* hauled him off to the Harbinger, we'd have lost him for the invasion all the same."

"And if he'd been here, and fell in the first wave of attack, what then? If we're throwing around pretend scenarios now, what about that one?" I stopped myself and took a collecting breath. "Believe me, I'm worried about him, too, but I'm not taking the blame for this. Let's focus on getting him back, and save our anger for anyone who stands in our way."

Pontus didn't seem entirely convinced. I doubted he would be until, or if, he saw Ingvar again. He turned to walk down the dungeon corridor. Several feet away, Baron Tristan and the soldiers congregated outside of a different dungeon cell from which poured the glow of lantern-light.

Dag glanced up at me with conviction. "We'll find the captain. He'll get over it."

I smiled a little. "Thanks."

"Is Thordia safe with that witch?" he asked.

"Sigrid considers Thordia a friend. She'll be fine," I replied. "But if you ever find yourself alone with Sigrid, keep your guard up. She's tougher than she looks."

Dag didn't seem to need any convincing.

I gripped my side sword with resolve. "Let's go."

We approached Baron Tristan and the soldiers. While the Baron had lost himself in sullen thought, the soldiers were a knot of anticipation, offering Magnus plenty of friendly shoves, elbows, and pats on the head. As we drew closer, I caught more of that nervous energy myself.

Pontus raised his voice. "By the Unseen and all who came before us, let's make them regret they ever landed here!"

The Baron drew his sword with grim resolve. "Perchance we are but delivering ourselves into their hands. If so, their fingers shall bleed."

CHAPTER 22

An unusual hope permeated the dark dungeon. The soldiers, Dag, and I gripped and re-gripped our weapons, eager for the mission ahead: infiltrate the adepts' keep and recover Ingvar and Lady Amelia, quietly.

Thoughts of Ingvar made my heart ache desperately. All those hours we'd been away, how had he fared? They hadn't found him in the dungeon at the hands of pro-Gyllenfeld adepts; that was somewhat reassuring. Was he in the infirmary like Baron Tristan suspected, recovering from Verahl's panic? Or had the adepts taken him elsewhere, hoping to thwart any rescue attempts? Was he suffering? Had his wounds received proper care, or had the adepts made things worse?

My love for him brought on a painful worry that eclipsed any injury I'd racked up. I was prepared to do anything to free him and ensure he survived.

Sword drawn, Baron Tristan entered the dungeon cell we stood beside. Pontus and Magnus let me and Dag in first, then followed.

A single lantern huddled in one corner of the cell, its flame struggling to light the whole expanse. Ormyr huddled against the far wall, fiddling with something. A twist of his hand caused

a previously invisible door to slide open. Past it, a ramp led upward into the adept's keep — infested with guild mercenaries,
hostile adepts, and who knew what else.

Days earlier, Ormyr had been the absolute master of this
place. Now, he shook as any of his prisoners might've. "If Your
Grace still refuseth my company, at least permit me to offer a
blessing," he beseeched.

Baron Tristan ignored him. "Soldiers, scout ahead and ensure our path is clear."

"Aye, sir." Pontus and Magnus hurried up the ramp.

Ormyr slumped against the wall, defeated once more.

My strange pity for him intensified. He believed I was a
witch. Together, we'd brought *the* witch, Thordia, into the Baron's
midst. Ormyr could've pointed these things out, tried to sink
me in order to save his drowning self, but he hadn't. Was he
actually serious about his promise? Or was he just waiting for a
better opportunity?

I shook off cynicism and approached Ormyr, Dag straying
up with me. "Be safe, all right?"

Ormyr blinked with surprise. Then the mati amulet reap-
peared in his hand, the one he'd used to track my and Ingvar's
movements. I wondered how much similar surveillance technology was littered throughout the dungeon.

"Keep it," I told him. "Holsten might use it to spy on us."

"It helped us this far. It shall safeguard thee still." Undaunted, Ormyr placed the eye-shaped amulet around my neck,
then tucked it under my armor so it wouldn't escape.

Surprised, and moved, I swallowed hard. "Thanks."

He met my gaze with bare nervousness. "Take care. They
cannot accuse our Baron of murder whilst thou yet livest.
Unseen watch over thee — and thee, whelp." Ormyr stuck out a
hand toward Dag, revealing three smoke bombs cradled within.

Dag brightened and snatched them up.

Moments later, Magnus returned to the secret door's threshold. "The way's clear, Your Grace."

The Baron nodded. "Lady Knight, with me."

I exchanged one last nod with Ormyr. At last, my chance to rescue Ingvar had arrived. All the wounds and fatigue I'd sustained seemed to vanish. I hurried up the passage after Baron Tristan, with Dag close behind.

Magnus led us up to where Pontus waited in tense silence. We found ourselves inside a narrow corridor capped on either end with burgundy curtains. Between the candlelit wall sconces, dripping streaks of green paint covered the words of decorative spells. Perfume filled the air, along with a hint of smoke. Distant, agitated shouts reached us as well.

"That sounds like fighting," I said, then frowned in confusion. "I thought everyone in here was on the same side." Namely, serving Madam Castor, some misguided sentiment for Lord Gyllenfeld, or both.

"Some adepts may have refused to join Adept Holsten." But Pontus' expression made clear he didn't think it likely.

"Whoever remaineth loyal, I welcome their fealty." Baron Tristan pointed down the hall with his sword. "The infirmary lieth in this direction. After me."

"'Tis too dangerous for Your Grace to take point in here," Pontus objected. "Too many opportunities for ambush." Indeed, the curtains could easily hide enemies lying in wait. "I'll go first. Magnus, cover the rear."

Baron Tristan relented, but followed directly after Pontus. I proceeded the Baron, with Dag behind me, and Magnus last. Like almost everyone else, I kept my sword primed. Dag favored his slingshot.

Pontus advanced to the end of the corridor, sneaking a glance past the curtain. "Clear, but watch your step."

Beyond the curtain lay a small circular chamber: the remains of a study, now trashed, reminiscent of what the adepts had done to the Naustviks' house. As we inched around up-ended desks and chairs, torn scroll fragments fluttered between our feet like kicked-up dust.

"Wherefore should they destroy their own keep?" the Baron asked.

These sights made more sense than the strife we'd heard. "The guild mercenaries might be looting," I explained, "and the adepts loyal to Gyllenfeld might be purging the place of Catherwood regalia."

The Baron's eyes narrowed. "I wonder if those Gyllenfeld specters shall ever be put to rest in my lifetime. Let's press on."

Pontus scouted the room's exit, then waved us into another empty corridor. Angry disembodied voices surrounded us again, impossible to pin down. Even so, I heard Baron Tristan's whispering loud and clear. "The infirmary lieth ahead."

At that, we all hurried forward with less discretion than was warranted. My heart and guts twisted into anxious knots. *Please be here. Please be all right,* I willed Ingvar silently.

We tore past the curtain and spilled into a large circular room. The Baron and soldiers halted near the threshold, weapons poised to address any nasty surprises. Caution be damned, I pressed ahead for a better look around.

Beds lined the infirmary's perimeter, much like the flower-shaped layout of the Harbinger's medical ward, but that was where the similarities ended. Here, a candle-studded magic circle marked the room's center. Baskets hung from the ceiling like chandeliers, spilling over with dried herbs and crystals.

Compared to where I'd been, the place was gut-droppingly primitive — and deserted.

Disappointment crushed my insides. Panic threatened to set in next, but I noticed that one of the beds to my left stood out from the others. A rumpled blanket lay on top, as did a basket filled with bloody linens. Had Ingvar been here after all?

I darted toward the bed while the others hung back, possibly discouraged or seeking an ambush. Desperate for clues, I rifled through the blanket and basket, but found nothing to confirm Ingvar's presence or betray his current whereabouts.

The blood was worrying. Were his injuries more severe than I'd thought? Or had he received more wounds *here*?

To the left of the bed stood a wardrobe, partially ajar. I threw open the door. Armor and a burgundy-and-gold tabard were piled on the shelf near my feet. Atop them sat a familiar loop of wishing beads.

He *had* been there. But all that remained was another pile of artifacts, arranged like a memorial.

Trembling with dread, I fell to my knees and set my sword aside to examine Ingvar's belongings. No signs of blood, but nothing that told me where to find him, either. His wishing beads remained laced through my fingers, feeling more futile than ever.

In the absence of concrete evidence, my mind raced with speculation. Had he succumbed to injury or torture, his remains carried out for disposal? If he'd survived, were he and Lady Amelia in the same place now, captives of Holsten and Commander Savidge? *Where?* The keep was huge. Could we possibly find them before anything worse happened? The terrifying uncertainty twisted into me like a dull knife.

"Lady Knight?"

I glanced over my shoulder. Dag stood on the right side of Ingvar's bed, eyes full of urgency.

"Over here," he prompted.

Hope and dread took hold of me at once. Leaving Ingvar's belongings in the wardrobe, I forced myself up and rushed over to join Dag. On the floor at his feet sprawled a young man and woman, both motionless. Their robes were green, bearing the seal of an open hand, palm forward: Gyllenfeld's seal.

A wave of nausea hit me. How did these adepts fit into the picture? They must've intended harm toward Ingvar. A struggle had followed. Ingvar, or whoever might've been helping him, had subdued these two. But how many others might've overpowered and dragged him off?

Grief threatened me almost as much as panic. Forcing away tears, I glanced back, seeking the Baron and soldiers. They huddled in pooled dismay at the foot of the bed: weapons lowered, beads wrapped over their hands. I didn't have to explain our findings.

"Looks to me like Captain Leirfall gave 'em what-for, then got out of here," Dag piped up.

I looked his way, surprised by the optimistic interpretation. Though I wanted to believe it, I feared being horribly disappointed later. All the same, Dag's description brought a weak smile to my face. "Maybe."

Without a body, there was hope. That much I could allow.

Magnus let out a humorless laugh. "Nice thought, but they would've sent more than two adepts for him."

"Why?" Dag faced him. "They thought he was hurt. Mayhap he *wasn't* so hurt."

The Baron blinked, but his gaze remained detached.

"Nice thought indeed, lad," Pontus said. "Too bad it may be a while afore we know for certain. Where to, Your Grace?"

"Hold on. We're not done here," I stated with authority. There was still a whole infirmary to search for clues, and I'd never checked the adepts' vitals, either. I quickly scanned the perimeter. Judging by the curtained spaces, there were four entrances into the infirmary total. Four ways Ingvar might've left, of his own volition or otherwise.

"Dag, let's figure out which way Captain Leirfall was taken," I said. "Can you look for footprints or any other traces?"

"Aye." Dag darted off.

While he tended to that, I knelt before the motionless adepts. Fortunately, their pulses were strong. Why not see what the evidence had to say — literally? Moving carefully so as not to upset my head or sore muscles, I flipped the female adept prone, then dragged her closer to the soldiers and the Baron, who looked on with bewilderment.

"Can someone help me pin her so she can't run?" I asked.

Pontus frowned. "Where d'ye think she's going, lass?"

"We'll see." I straddled the adept, sat on her back, then reached into my first aid kit, pulling out a capsule of smelling salts.

After some hesitation, Magnus laid down his sword and approached to pin the adept's legs.

Once the adept was secure, I cracked the capsule open against the floor, then held it to her nose. Within moments, the adept jerked awake, crying out in confusion.

"Unseen!" The Baron gave a start.

I threw the capsule aside and gave the adept something new to focus on: my dagger blade, inches from her face. Her struggling turned fierce, but Magnus and I held fast.

Frustration left me short on pity. "Sober up!" I snapped. "Captain Leirfall. Where is he?"

"I ... Where ...?" The adept was all confusion.

"Answer!" Baron Tristan demanded, stepping forward.

"I ... I don't know. I was supposed to ... I don't know what happened. I don't remember!" she pleaded. "He was here. I don't know."

Pontus' bitter laugh mocked her confusion. "Sounds like he beat your brains in for you!"

"What of Lady Amelia?" The Baron knelt before the adept with an intense expression.

"The observatory." She screwed her eyes shut. "It's heavily spelled and defended. You'll die before you reach it."

Baron Tristan took a steadying breath. "Our course is decided. Well done, Dame Jessamine."

"Your Grace, let's find something to tie her up with. Both of them." Pontus motioned to the other adept, still out cold.

"Very well. I want witnesses I can question later." The Baron stood. "Doff their robes first. We may wear them instead, and perchance confuse the enemy from a distance."

"Good idea. I leave it to Your Grace." Despite this smooth refusal, I got the feeling Pontus wanted absolutely nothing to do with those colors.

The adepts' plain clothing beneath their robes made them indistinguishable from servants. Making use of the ample bandages within the infirmary, we gagged and tethered them to a heavy wardrobe nearby. The conscious adept's muffled shrieks would be inaudible outside the infirmary.

Baron Tristan replaced his cloak with one of the adept robes, clasping it around his neck and leaving his arms out of the sleeves. When Dag returned, the Baron pointed to the other Gyllenfeld robe with his sword. "Trade thine for this one."

"Aye, Your Grace." Dag got to work on that.

"Did you find anything?" I asked eagerly, recovering my side sword.

"There's blood on the wall over there." Once Dag's head and hands peeked through the new robe, he pointed to one of the infirmary thresholds. "There's another adept in the hallway, out cold."

My heart jumped. Maybe Ingvar had fought his way out after all.

"I bet anything that'll lead to our captain!" Magnus cried.

"We cannot know for certain." Baron Tristan hesitated, strained. "'Tis the opposite direction from the observatory."

My optimism sank like an anchor. I hadn't imagined having to choose between Lady Amelia and Ingvar—if there *were* much choice in the matter. The Baron could force us in any direction he wanted.

Then why hadn't he ordered us toward the observatory immediately, without hesitation? It seemed he was open to having his mind changed. I just hoped we determined the right course of action, not necessarily the one my heart ached for.

"Let's huddle up and figure out where we go from here," I said. In a lower tone, "We don't want the adepts listening in."

We closed together in a tight circle. Apprehension marked everyone's faces. Fortunately, Pontus started before I could. He knew how to reason with superiors, and I couldn't trust myself to be fully rational.

"Both leads are no better than guesses, Your Grace. We don't know whether that adept's telling the truth. If I had to guess who's in greater danger, I'd say Captain Leirfall. If anything happens to Lady Amelia, the guild will earn Lord Catherwood's wrath."

No kidding. In Lord Catherwood's throne room, I'd seen how dearly the young sovereign regarded his aunt.

"Our enemies might see the captain as leverage, sir," I murmured. "Or, they might kill him to weaken and demoralize your army." But I dearly *hoped* they realized Ingvar was worth more to them alive.

"The trail the boy found, let's see how far it leads," Pontus suggested. "If it vanishes, we'll aim for the observatory instead."

With stress chiseled into his expression, the Baron lowered his head over his beads for several moments. "Very well," he finally said. "But as soon as the trail endeth, we abandon it."

"That's fair, Your Grace," Pontus said.

Magnus rolled his shoulders back with a determined look. Dag readied his slingshot, his bright expression betraying approval.

This was understandably rough on the Baron. I wanted to convey my sympathy, but his gaze remained low. I sent a grateful glance Pontus' way instead, which he returned with a nod.

We left the infirmary, most of us galvanized by our new lead.

The third unconscious adept Dag had found was just the start of a chain of adept casualties that we pursued through several more rooms and corridors. Whenever the trail seemed to weaken, we found blood or other evidence suggesting our next move.

"A strange course," the Baron remarked. "It seemeth random, often doubling back upon itself."

"I'm glad Your Grace can tell. I'm completely lost," Pontus admitted.

"Me, too," Magnus said.

I was no wiser than they. If this were Ingvar's path, he was ignorant of the keep's layout, addled from injury, or both. I assumed he sought an exit from the keep, something that remained elusive as we swept through the ground floor.

While we kept finding new leads, there was still hope. It bolstered me more than any medical treatment might've. As we pressed on, the disembodied voices grew louder. A haze of nostril-stinging smoke curled through the candlelight.

"They're burning something now?" I muttered.

"We'll see," Pontus muttered back.

Our trail had been free of conscious adepts thus far — but within a small library, a pretty young woman in burgundy robes darted out from behind a scroll shelf, dodging past Pontus to throw herself at the Baron's feet and sob over bead-covered hands.

"Adept Gunnhilda?" Baron Tristan froze with surprise.

The soldiers quickly grabbed one arm apiece and hauled her away from him.

"I serve Baron Tristan!" Gunnhilda cried, reaching toward him in vain. "Adept Holsten asked me to join him, but I refused!"

The soldiers' scowls made plain their skepticism. Dag looked to me with doubt as well. Before I could reach a conclusion, a different thought hit me like a brick to the face: had *she* been the one creating this body trail?

All my worry for Ingvar flooded back, weakening my knees.

"We can't trust her, Your Grace. She might warn Savidge and Holsten about us," Pontus said.

"I swear upon everything sacred I won't!" Gunnhilda cried. "They're up in the observatory. That's why I'm here, as far away as possible."

Another observatory reference. The enemy might've retreated there with Lady Amelia after all.

"She refrained from attack; we shall return the courtesy. Unhand her," the Baron ordered.

The soldiers complied with clear reluctance.

Baron Tristan's gaze latched onto Gunnhilda's. "Head for the lift, we shall meet thee there. Until then, wish that all obstacles in our path may be lifted."

Gunnhilda bowed to him once released, then took off—sniffling, brushing aside tears.

I'd been too distracted to come up with or voice an opinion. As she fled, I debated whether this run-in would prove helpful, or an awful mistake.

"What's this 'lift?'" Pontus asked.

"The quickest route to the observatory," the Baron replied, "but we require an adept's aid to make use thereof."

"Likely to be well guarded, then," Pontus said. "Shouldn't we have kept her with us?"

"Alone, she can cut a direct path, and shall have an easier time hiding among our enemy," the Baron said.

Neither soldier seemed won over by his reasoning, but neither protested further.

I had no verdict concerning Gunnhilda yet, but figured her absence wouldn't set us back. With two data carriers and recent experience in the Harbinger to rely on, I could probably operate the lift myself—and worry about witchcraft accusations later.

Dag hurried ahead to check the library exits. Burning in my own private hell, I feared our trail would end.

"Over here!" Dag waved.

Heart in my mouth, I got to him first.

Past the curtain lay a short corridor that fed into a large room. The ceiling bore a brilliant rendition of the galaxy, polished crystals suspended at varying heights to augment the painted stars. Powdery magic circles lined the floor. A fight brewed at ground level: a green-robed adept and white-clad mercenary closing in on a single man.

Ingvar!

His name got lost somewhere in my throat. Irrational happiness flooded me upon seeing him alive—irrational because Ingvar was far from safe or healthy. Dried and fresh blood streaked his clothing and skin. His left forearm, wrapped in bandages, rested against his chest. He was unarmed, struggling for balance on a wooden crutch.

Every righteous protective instinct rose to the fore. With no thought of waiting for backup, I charged down the hallway.

Ingvar faced the adept. From several feet outside melee range, the adept threw a fist toward him. More of that awful eye-stinging stuff? Some other horrible surprise?

I never found out. Ingvar went from leaning on his crutch to hefting it like a club. With an upward swing, he struck the adept's fist. He swung downward next, onto his opponent's skull, sending the adept to the floor.

This wasn't so different from my earlier demonstration at the barracks. Ingvar had tricked the adept into underestimating him. But an even more dangerous mercenary closed on him from behind, primed to clobber him with a mace. Ingvar gave no indication that he even knew the merc was there.

I charged into the room, bolting toward the mercenary. Using momentum to my advantage, I rammed the pommel of my side sword into his ribs. He stumbled sideways, stunned. It gave me time to locate a vulnerable spot in his armor and thrust my blade through it.

The mercenary dropped, mace clattering beside him. I braced a foot against him and dislodged my weapon. Dag strayed beside me, slingshot primed.

"Captain! Unseen be praised!"

I turned to see the soldiers swarming Ingvar with hugs. Ingvar threw his crutch aside and returned them with his right arm, wincing at their enthusiasm. Baron Tristan waited patiently close by.

He was alive. Whatever might've happened earlier, he'd escaped it. Relief made me lightheaded and weak all over.

"Gave you grief the last time we spoke, sir," Pontus said, wounded at the memory. "Glad that's not the note we'll end on."

Ingvar laughed. "Ye have every right to question me."

"But ye and Dame Jessamine were right, sir. About everything."

The captain stiffened against Pontus, then turned away to face me. His sharp, insightful gaze was full of longing and disbelief. He pushed past his colleagues, making a beeline toward me.

Overjoyed, I dropped my side sword and darted toward him. Once we met, he pulled me into a one-armed embrace.

I hugged back with everything I had, resting my head on his shoulder. Deep in enemy territory, fear and worry vanished. There was no place safer than where we stood, together.

As I blinked away tears of joy and relief, I noticed the chain around his neck, still bearing my mother's ring. Of all the possessions he'd been forced to leave behind, *this* was the one thing no one had been able to take from him.

My heart raced at an unsafe speed. Not caring who was watching or what rules of decorum I broke, I pulled him into a kiss.

Ingvar tensed against me for just a moment, then kissed back hard, sending me soaring into bliss.

It couldn't last. We were still in danger, and Ingvar needed medical attention. I eased away from him to check for serious bleeding and examine his left arm. At the same time, elation seemed to make my lightheadedness worse. I staggered.

Ingvar caught and steadied me. "Jayce?"

As my head spun, I screwed my eyes shut. "I'm fine, just … it's been a long day, hasn't it? What about you? Your arm?" I struggled to regain composure so I could have a look.

"Later." He reeled me in again. "They told me ye were dead, Jayce."

The pain of that belief leaked out with his words. All this time, he'd mourned me, just as I'd anguished over him. I stayed close, not at all eager to leave his embrace.

"Captain? Thank the Unseen we've found thee alive," the Baron piped up, kindly glossing over our display.

Ingvar separated from me with clear reluctance. I nodded to him reassuringly, having regained my balance.

"Your Grace, am I ever grateful ye're here," Ingvar said. "Damned if I know my way through this gauntlet, or what's going on. I was in the infirmary when a horde of adepts in Gyllenfeld colors tried to haul me off." His gaze landed on Dag.

"Like that one. What're ye doing here, lad—in that traitor getup, no less?"

"Saving your arse," Dag returned, a devilish glint in his eye. He retrieved my sword and handed it to me.

"He's good at it," I said.

Ingvar smirked. "Guess so."

"Captain, there's much to explain. Chiefly, Madam Castor sent an invasion force," Pontus said. "Adept Holsten and most of the cloister are helping them. We've got them pinned down in this keep."

The word "invasion" struck Ingvar in the face like a challenging duelist. Holsten's name followed up to sting the smarting wound. His eyes searched mine, asking if it were all true.

Heart still racing, I nodded. Judging from the path we'd followed, Ingvar had never come across a guild mercenary—not until we'd found him. He must've thought this was purely a pro-Gyllenfeld uprising.

"Lady Amelia is captive here as well," Baron Tristan said, his worried expression returning. "Hast thou seen or heard of her whereabouts?"

Ingvar looked to him with shock. "Nay, Your Grace."

"The observatory is our only lead," the Baron explained. "We believe Adept Holsten and Commander Savidge hold her there. We go now to rescue her."

"I'll go with you." Ingvar straightened to his full height.

"Sure ye're up for it, sir?" Pontus asked.

"*Skíta!* Were my innards half-spilled, I'd not miss the chance to fight with all of you." Ingvar turned to retrieve his crutch.

Part of me wanted to protest as well, but had no room to talk. Knowing us, we'd both fight until we broke down.

"Ye won't need that, sir. Magnus?" Pontus said.

With no further prompting, the younger soldier picked up the fallen mercenary's mace and passed it to Ingvar, who thanked him with a clap on the shoulder.

Still giddy with relief, I approached Ingvar's side again. "I'll stick close, if you don't mind." Though he continued to keep his left arm against himself—I assumed he'd broken it during the fall from *Kepler's Law*—he seemed less hurt than I'd feared. I wanted to keep it that way until I could address his wounds properly.

Ingvar smiled a little. "Ye'll hear no complaint from me, Goose."

"Well! Captain Leirfall, I presume!"

Before we could leave for the observatory, an unfamiliar voice boomed from a different corridor. Guild mercenaries surged into the room, cutting off every avenue of escape. It was clear who led them: a stocky, weathered man with a swagger borne of hundreds of bloody victories. If Linum Dominorum's three-flower seal hadn't covered his fine steel armor, I'd have mistaken him for a Lord's general.

The six of us huddled together, most of us trading uncertain looks. Baron Tristan's expression was more knowing, and worried.

The lead mercenary had eyes only for Ingvar. He advanced toward the captain one unhurried step at a time, grinning. "You've caused a lot of trouble, son. But powers be damned if you didn't just *spare* me a heap of trouble!"

CHAPTER 23

Deep inside the adepts' keep, at least half a dozen mercenaries blocked every exit from the circular chamber in which we'd found Ingvar. Even if we managed to escape, the smoke in the air made me nervous about what we'd be escaping into.

Instinctively, we placed our backs together in the room's center. Ingvar positioned himself at the Baron's right. I stood to Ingvar's right in a weapon-forward stance, while Dag bounded up to my opposite side. His new adept robe offered no hood, so he masked his emotions with a glare instead. Behind us, Pontus and Magnus were surely squaring up as well.

The head mercenary approaching us was older, well equipped, and supremely confident. Still grinning, he halted out of arm's reach, his focus shifting from Ingvar to the Baron. I watched over my left shoulder.

"Journeyman Foster. How's it going?" The mercenary greeted.

"Commander Savidge." I couldn't see the Baron's face, but I heard his contempt. "My title is Baron."

Savidge! Wasn't he supposed to be holed up in the observatory? Apparently not. I recalled Ormyr's trepidation at the mention of his name, and struggled not to let it infect me.

The commander brushed at the side of his nose with a thumb. "It should've taken all of fifteen seconds to lock down this skunk-hole. Sure didn't expect an ex-paper-pusher to put up such a fuss." His tone was congratulatory.

Baron Tristan pointed his sword at him, the blade hovering inches from his adversary's breastplate. "Release my wife, gather up thy forces, and leave."

"But I've *won*, friend!" Savidge returned jovially. "You join the Baroness in custody, and Nidaros is ours. I thought you'd handle defeat with more dignity. Oh well, a corpse is more convenient than a prisoner." He stepped back and drew the longsword from the scabbard at his side.

"He's not either 'til we all lie dead, sellsword!" Ingvar hefted his mace.

I heard Pontus and Magnus tapping their blades against the ground in a taunting manner.

The mercenaries blocking the exits drew their steel as well. Savidge ignored Ingvar to settle into his stance, facing Baron Tristan. I was about to face my most likely dance partner when I noticed the sword-pommel in Savidge's hands. It bore the image of a tesseract.

It couldn't be — but there it was. *Branigan's sigil.*

The air left my lungs. Time slowed down, allowing a decade of grief to seep between seconds. Sir Branigan's sword! Branigan, the friend and mentor I'd loved for years without confessing a word of it. In Gules, Drea and I had found his bloody corpse stripped of everything. The sword specially forged for him, the one he'd never ventured anywhere without, had ended up in this thug's hands.

How?

Lord Catherwood had cursed Gules; his adepts would've carried out the sentence. Had he granted Madam Castor's trade guild permission to assist them? Had Savidge tied Branigan to that post, carved that heretic symbol into his forehead, and left him to die with the same breezy swagger he showed now? Had he helped collect everything of use from the town and left its citizens to freeze or starve, whichever came first? Memories of Gules' corpses, one pile after another, surged back — a town turned mass grave that poor Drea was trapped in still.

Tears blurred my vision, while nausea nearly doubled me over. If Drea and I had just gotten there a little sooner …

No. I might've saved Branigan, or I might've died alongside him. I wasn't to blame for his demise. That bastard wielding his sword, on the other hand …

Anger burned in my heart, crowding out despair. It helped me keep my composure, but it was a dangerous emotion to take into a fight. I struggled to channel it toward a constructive purpose: reclaiming Branigan's sword. I owed my old friend that much.

Clashing blades jarred me out of my thoughts. Savidge, intent on Baron Tristan, never noticed my near-breakdown. As they crossed swords, the mercenaries along the room's perimeter converged on the rest of us.

I had no time to think about a move on Savidge. Somehow, I managed to suppress rage long enough to calmly play my opponent's eagerness against him. Once he got close, I sidestepped and brought my blade down onto his hands like a hammer. As his weapon fell to the floor, I finished with a slash down the side of his throat.

Soon after my attacker dropped, Dag's opponent tripped and landed on top of him, cursing as he lost his sword. Dag had no qualms with nailing him in a sensitive place, then straddling him for a series of punches.

I faced no more immediate threats. My gaze swept the room. Magnus had wrestled his man to the ground. Pontus had locked swords with his. Baron Tristan lay sprawled on the floor.

Worry stabbed into me.

Meanwhile, Ingvar had bested his opponent. With only one good arm, he vied desperately to keep Savidge away from the Baron.

Heart in my mouth, I darted over to help, approaching Savidge from behind.

Ingvar swung at the commander's jaw; one of the mace's spikes grazed his cheek. Savidge stumbled backward, eyes shut. Noticing me closing in, Ingvar used the opportunity to fall back. He dropped his weapon, grabbed the Baron one-handed, and dragged him out of the fray.

As they retreated, my opening slash came down where Savidge's neck met his shoulder.

The commander whirled around in time to block the strike. Our blades locked. His gaze passed over me like a freak blizzard.

Undaunted, I stared him straight in the eye. "That sword belonged to Sir Branigan Cade! What happened to him?"

Realization dawned on Savidge, who laughed in my face. "So, you're Dame Jessamine!" He shoved me away and backed up several paces, avoiding the bodies in his path. "When Adept Holsten couldn't produce a corpse, I worried this might happen. No problem, you'll be dead again soon enough."

"Just try it, you son of a bitch," I replied.

Anger and adrenaline primed me to fight, but also threatened to disrupt my composure at a critical moment. I faced someone stronger, better rested, with a more punishing sword. He could wear me down without breaking a sweat. I'd have to stay mobile and aggressive to have a chance.

I rose to the balls of my feet, shifting weight from foot to foot to avoid planting in any one spot. While remaining in a weapon-forward stance to maximize my reach, I switched to a roof guard, holding my blade horizontally a safe distance over my head.

Savidge dropped back into a solid stance and held Branigan's longsword in a closed guard, the blade standing vertically in front of him. His expression gave away little, but he seemed content to hold still and wait for me to impale myself.

Before launching at him, I chanced a survey of my peripherals. The other mercenaries had been dealt with. To my left, Dag and the soldiers surrounded Baron Tristan. I couldn't tell how hurt he was.

"Get the Baron out of here," I shouted. "I'll catch up!"

Ingvar scrambled to his feet—right hand clenched in a fist, bandaged left arm tucked against his chest. "We're not leaving!"

"Hold on there, son! This is knightly business!" Savidge scolded Ingvar. "She doesn't need some backwater hayseed clodding all over it."

Savidge made a quick thrust at my open torso before he finished speaking.

I dropped my sword-arm and blocked, meeting the weak end of his blade with the strong end of mine. He twisted up from there, aiming for the right side of my head. I stepped forward with my left foot, raised my sword to block, and batted his hands sideways with my open hand. As his blade swung away, I brought mine down on top of his head.

The commander blocked with his vambrace in time, then seized my blade in his steel gauntlet and yanked.

Panic stabbed at me. If he reeled me in, I was finished. My only hope was to let go of my side sword. I released the hilt, but not before stumbling forward a little.

Savidge threw my blade behind himself. His left hand still braced Branigan's longsword. While I was off-balance, he threw its pommel toward my jaw.

I backed several feet away and avoided the strike—safely out of range, but also without a sword. Savidge had time to recover and return to a proper stance. Undaunted, I pulled my dagger, prepared to keep fighting with that.

Before either of us could close on the other, Savidge staggered backward with a surprised cry, clutching his cheek with one hand. A rock tumbled from his face to the floor.

My confusion lasted only half a second. Standing several away to my right, Dag reloaded his slingshot.

"Jayce!" On my left, Ingvar crouched near some fallen men. He'd recovered a longsword from one of them, which he placed on the ground and slid toward me.

With Savidge stunned, I had enough time to sheathe my dagger and pick up the two-handed sword. I then ran toward my opponent, letting momentum build. Once I closed, I rammed the pommel into his sternum with an angry cry.

Unprepared, Savidge stumbled backward and fell, grunting as his back struck the floor. Branigan's longsword jolted out of his hands, clattering to rest at his side.

"Good lass! That's showing the bastard!" Pontus called out.

I planted one foot on Savidge's chest and reversed my grip on the longsword, holding the point several inches above his throat. My heart burned with anticipation for the questioning that'd follow once I caught my breath.

Savidge lay there calmly, one hand grasping the wishing beads on his belt. "I'm ready, Knight. Earn your kill."

"Sir Branigan," I said. "What happened to him?"

"Never heard of him," Savidge replied without any reaction.

"The hell you haven't!" I cried. "You wield his sword!"

"A gift from Madam Castor." Savidge narrowed all-too-perceptive eyes at me. "You know more of its history than she did."

Was he lying? Probably not. If he *had* killed Branigan, he would've been twisting that knife deep under my skin. Frustration spoiled any satisfaction I might've felt from my victory.

"What about Gules? Did Madam Castor help Lord Catherwood with the cursing?" I pressed.

He laughed at a joke that only he understood. "I'd say not."

"Then how'd she come by that blade?"

"Ask her. Now, kill me and get it over with."

"Not getting off that easy," Ingvar cut in, limping up to my left side with a scowl. "Bring him to his feet, lads. He's bound for the dungeon."

Magnus and Pontus approached. Each taking an arm, they hauled Savidge out from under me. Dag darted through the mess to retrieve Branigan's longsword, holding the grip and letting the blade's point rest on the ground.

My arms fell to my sides, but I remained still otherwise. I'd had no interest in killing Savidge. Ingvar probably understood that, but wanted to play it safe, just in case Savidge pushed me too far.

Would that have been possible? I didn't know. I liked to think nothing could make me kill senselessly, but so much anger and vexation filled me then, it was hard to think at all. Somehow, I knew *less* about Branigan's fate than when I'd started. One thing was certain: if I ever returned to Spectra, Madam Castor and I would have words—about this invasion, Gules, and my departed friend.

To my surprise, Baron Tristan approached us next. He nursed his side, his Gyllenfeld robe masking the severity of his injury. "The main dungeon entrance lieth in that direction. Confiscate everything of value and lock him away," he ordered Pontus and Magnus, gesturing toward one of the exits with his sword. "We're not through questioning him."

"Aye," Ingvar said. "He'll tell us what we want to know, then he'll have to cower afore Madam Castor."

Savidge remained expressionless and complacent in the soldiers' grasp.

In contrast, my nerves were fried. A slew of emotions threatened what little composure I had left—but I sure as hell wasn't giving Savidge the satisfaction of seeing me melt down. Trembling, I focused on the floor and forced deep breaths on myself.

Ingvar glanced to the Baron with concern. "Certain ye don't want to lead them to the dungeon yourself, Your Grace?"

"I'm well enough to press on." The Baron spoke convincingly. I wasn't sure to what extent he was lying. "And thee, Captain?"

"I'm fine," Ingvar replied. Definitely a lie to some degree, but no one called him on it. "Jayce?"

I swallowed hard. "I won't rest until the invasion's over." Then I'd have to, at least for a little while, before Drea's rescue.

"Then we four shall storm the observatory and end this," the Baron declared, including Dag in his count.

"Good hunting. Unseen be with you all," Pontus offered as he hauled Savidge away with Magnus' help.

Most of me dreaded further exertion, but it had to be done. I worked on reining in my frustration and gathering myself mentally—but all progress toward that goal evaporated once Dag silently offered me Branigan's longsword.

The longsword in my hands slid from my fingers and hit the ground. Dumbstruck, I cradled Branigan's weapon as though handling a priceless artifact. The shoulder and cross-guard rested in my left palm, while my right hand clenched the grip beneath the pommel. The blade—stained with blood, possibly the Baron's and who knew who else's—nudged against my left side, extending several feet behind me.

Over the years, my old friend had passed this sword to me dozens of times to practice a new counter, or just to admire. Its recovery felt hollow; it was no replacement for the thoughtful, honorable man who'd wielded it. I'd been hoping for vindication and closure, but nothing was resolved. Branigan was gone forever. His misfortune remained a mystery, and Drea was still out there to lose.

The grief would be denied no longer. I fell to my knees with the longsword in my lap. Then I doubled over it, resting my forehead on the floor, and succumbed to racking sobs.

Something rested on my back: a hand, most likely Ingvar's. The sobs kept coming, with me powerless to stop them. My throat and chest ached almost as much as my heart.

"My condolences, Lady Knight." Somehow, even with his wife in danger, the Baron's voice was full of patient sympathy.

"Whenever we travel to Gules for Drea, mayhap we'll learn more," Ingvar muttered close beside me. His hand ran along my back reassuringly.

I hoped like hell it'd be soon, but we still had quite the mess to clean up in Nidaros. I righted myself, sniffling and wiping tears on my sleeve.

Kneeling at my left side, Ingvar pulled me into a one-armed embrace. Meanwhile, Dag lowered himself on my right. "Sure ye can keep fighting? The adepts tortured her, and she got thrown from an ulldyr," he explained for Ingvar's benefit.

"What?!" Ingvar stiffened against me.

I faced his haunted expression, resting my hands on his shoulders. "There was medicine at the Harbinger. I took care of the worst of it." I drew a shuddering breath. "Come on, Lady Amelia needs us."

Ingvar seemed unconvinced on the first point, but couldn't object to the second.

What to do with Branigan's sword? I didn't feel safe leaving it anywhere in the keep, and it wouldn't fit in the scabbard on my back. Ingvar was weaponless; though he was limited to one hand, it made the most sense to give it to him. As with my mother's ring, this was a huge gesture, a level of trust I'd never shown anyone outside my immediate circle. Yet somehow, it felt natural and consequence-free, maybe because this was the right person.

And what would Branigan have thought? Without a doubt, he would've been *much* happier with Ingvar wielding his sword as opposed to Savidge. He would've also been glad I'd found someone trustworthy—someone I loved—to such a degree, even if our time together lasted no longer than my quest in Nidaros.

With calm certainty, I offered the hilt to Ingvar. "Can you use this one-handed?"

Blinking with surprise, Ingvar lifted Branigan's sword reverently from my hands. "This one's lighter than what I'm used to. One hand may be enough. Are ye sure 'tis not ceremonial? Looketh more like a piece for one's mantle."

"Remember how my 'little fencing stick' fared against all those predators in the districts?" I asked, using his phrase. "My mentors forged this sword, too."

"Fair enough." He lowered the weapon long enough to grasp my nearest hand. "I'll try to be worthy of his memory, Jayce."

I choked down another surge of emotion. "So will I."

We were slow to reach our feet, hindered by injuries both mental and physical. Dag retrieved my side sword from where Savidge had dropped it, passing it to me once I was ready to take it. I nodded my thanks.

Baron Tristan waited patiently, still nursing his side. I didn't see any blood on his clothes or the floor around him. That meant it was either a shallow cut or a more serious puncture wound.

"How badly is it bleeding, sir?" I debated offering first aid despite the trouble I'd have to dodge later.

"'Tis no concern. We must proceed to the observatory with all haste," the Baron replied in a commanding tone.

"Where is it?" Ingvar asked.

"At the keep's summit," Baron Tristan answered.

"Blood's oath! Not again," Ingvar groaned.

Unaware of our witch hunt at the top of his estate a night or two ago, the Baron didn't fully understand Ingvar's dread toward another grueling climb, but it didn't weigh on him. "There's a lift we may use to reach it quickly."

"I told you about lifts, remember?" I asked Ingvar.

"It's a box that'll fly us over there," Dag piped up with a nonchalance I would've strained not to laugh at any other time.

"An adept must operate it," the Baron said. "I sent a loyal one there to await us."

Ingvar frowned in confusion. "Can we trust any adepts right now?"

"We have no choice," the Baron replied.

Actually, we did. I might've been able to operate the lift with one of my data carriers, but I'd keep quiet about it unless we became desperate.

"Once we reach the observatory, what then?" Ingvar asked. "How much resistance is up there?"

"We know not," the Baron said.

Ingvar's eyes narrowed. "That's no damned plan, Your Grace."

"We'll tarry no longer! I want my wife back!" the Baron cried.

The urgency in his voice brought Ingvar up short.

I sympathized. Besides, the faster we struck before Holsten and the remaining mercenaries regrouped, the better. "Come on, Adept Gunnhilda can't hold out by herself forever. Once we're headed for the observatory, we can come up with a plan."

CHAPTER 24

Ingvar took point as we returned to the keep corridors, with Baron Tristan providing directions to the lift. Dag covered our rear with his slingshot. Our progress slowed, given all of us but Dag were injured to some degree, but the impending sense of confrontation kept me upright and no doubt bolstered my allies as well. Holsten would have a lot to answer for here. Then, in Spectra, it'd be Madam Castor's turn. I'd see to that eventually.

Though we kept alert for resistance, our path was free of adepts and mercenaries. As we moved through rooms and corridors unimpeded, I could ask about things I'd been too distracted to bring up earlier.

"Sir," I addressed Baron Tristan, "how do you know Commander Savidge?"

His eyes narrowed. "I had frequent dealings with him in Spectra."

The commander had called him "Journeyman" earlier. Then I recalled Ingvar telling me that Baron Tristan had risen to prominence in Spectra—through a *different* trade guild. The Baron's answer likely concealed years of bitter rivalry, but he didn't look eager to elaborate.

"Savidge left a secure position with Holsten in the observatory to come down here. Why?" I wondered aloud.

"He called me a troublemaker," Ingvar said, carrying Branigan's sword one-handed with no difficulty. "Mayhap word of my escape reached them."

"Holsten may be sensing our movements through arcane means," the Baron noted grimly. "He may foresee our arrival."

"There's no chance, Your Grace. We'll be surprising them," Ingvar insisted.

Holsten couldn't track us magically, but these adepts most definitely had Shipbuilder surveillance technology. It'd be foolish to think the amulet around my neck was the only example. "It may be better to assume they'll be ready for us," I said.

The haze in the corridors thickened into nostril-stinging smoke, and the air heated up to sweltering extremes. Eventually, the Baron attempted to lead us down a path, only to find it blocked with smoke and flames. The radiant heat warmed our skin from an impressive distance. Fortunately, the Shipbuilder masonry prevented the fire from spreading.

"'Twas the calefactory," Baron Tristan said with a haunted look.

"*Skíta,*" Ingvar blurted.

I remembered getting alternately blessed and grilled in there by an officious Ormyr days earlier, an Ormyr who'd also disparaged Holsten and his other subordinates. This fire must've been the culmination of a years-long grudge. No grief reached me concerning the place, but I did worry about anyone potentially trapped inside. From our vantage, there was no sight or sound of such. We couldn't risk a closer approach without hurting ourselves. When the Baron turned away, the rest of us followed.

Our alternate route led us to what seemed like the only solid door in the keep. It slid sideways of its own volition, revealing a sunlit box of glass that resembled the Harbinger lifts.

Inside, Adept Gunnhilda stood with her back against the far wall, a dagger in one hand.

"Captain Leirfall! Your Grace!" She held her free hand to her mouth.

It was a relief to find the lift intact. There was no way the Baron, Ingvar, or I would've made it up dozens of flights of stairs.

Ingvar planted himself well outside the car, glancing all around. "No resistance to this point. Seemeth awful convenient."

"Holsten's allies are in the observatory with him," Gunnhilda said.

"Waiting to ambush us?" Ingvar asked.

Gunnhilda wilted. "I don't know!"

"Captain," Baron Tristan chided. He shouldered his way into the lift car first, then leaned against the left wall.

I placed a hand on Ingvar's back and guided him in ahead of me. He maintained a low guard with Branigan's sword despite our close confines, narrowing eyes toward Gunnhilda all the while. Dag slipped in last, preferring the right wall.

Heat from the afternoon sun radiated through our glassy confines. Gunnhilda faced a set of controls mounted on the back wall, murmuring words too soft to hear.

This lift car *lurched* into motion, unlike the smooth gliding of the Harbinger cars. I stumbled and lost my balance, but Dag caught me before I hit the floor.

Lacking a free hand to grab hold of something, Ingvar fell to his knees, crying out when he noticed the floor was transparent also.

The ground fell away from us as the lift traveled up a fixed tunnel. I thanked Dag with a nod, then turned and offered Ingvar a hand. He latched onto it like a buoy in a stormy sea, leaving Branigan's sword on the ground as he returned to his feet. His bandaged left forearm remained tucked against his chest all the while.

"Let's flank the door," Ingvar muttered—rattled, but trying to work past it.

Once I'd fetched the longsword for him, we positioned ourselves on either side of the lift car door. Baron Tristan had pulled away from the left wall, still nursing his side. Under his Gyllenfeld robe, the wound Savidge had dealt him remained a mystery. Concerned, I was about to check him over when Gunnhilda began tending to him with an incantation.

I got ahold of myself. No adept would let me intervene. Besides, I needed time to examine and dress the wound properly, time we didn't have. I could only hope for the best.

Dag remained fastened to the right wall, taking in the view as we rose above the carnage filling the capital. Ingvar also stared out at the violence he'd missed, gaping in horror.

Reassuring words seemed hollow just then. With pained sympathy, I drew closer to Ingvar and placed my free arm around him, hoping to be of comfort. In truth, I was in need of a boost myself; Thordia's protections seemed to be wearing thin. While standing still, the punishment I'd racked up from head to foot, inside and out, became impossible to ignore. I could only imagine the rainbow of bruises that'd develop over the next few days—assuming I made it that long.

I had to. I just had to. Lady Amelia, then Drea, then the ichor.

"Lady Knight?"

Dag's prompt jarred me out of a standing sleep. I hadn't even realized I'd closed my eyes.

Ingvar turned toward me with a worried look. "Are ye sure ye're up to this? What'd the adepts do to you?"

My arm fell back to my side. I was dying to tell him everything and learn more about his stint in the keep, but again, time was short. I shook my head in half-dismissal, half-apology. "Later, I promise. We need to come up with a plan."

Ingvar's eyes narrowed, but he didn't argue. While Gunn-hilda chanted her healing spell, he faced the Baron with a take-charge demeanor. "Hath Your Grace ever been up here? How's this observatory laid out?"

Baron Tristan stared downward, detached. "The lift shall stop within the lower chamber, which is circular. From there, four staircases on the perimeter lead to the sanctum above. I've never set foot within the sanctum. Only adepts may enter."

Ingvar glared at Gunnhilda. "How well fortified are they? Do they have food and weapons?"

The adept paused and flinched, wide-eyed. "I don't know. I stayed on the ground floor this whole time."

"They may've been stocking up for a long time before the invasion," I pointed out. "What sort of magic defenses are in use up there?"

Gunnhilda glanced to me with somewhat less trepidation. "It's heavily warded at all times, surely even more so now."

"With spells? Or Shipbuilder relics?" I feared what physi-cal traps might await us.

"Spells, usually—but they might've taken any of our arti-facts to defend themselves with."

"Like what?"

Gunnhilda's expression turned strained. "I'm not fully ini-tiated yet. I've heard of powerful weapons."

I swallowed hard, unwilling to dismiss anything as rumor. We could be wiped out the instant we arrived—but that line of thinking didn't help us. I glanced to Ingvar. "We should find cover and avoid detection for as long as possible."

"If the enemy's stationed in the lower chamber when we arrive, we may not have a chance." Ingvar paused to deliberate. "If that's the case, we leap upon them afore they alert anyone, then see how things look. If the lower chamber's empty, we stay put, and quiet, 'til we learn more."

Dag primed his slingshot.

I nodded. If they outnumbered and outmatched us, staying mobile and aggressive was our only hope.

The Baron's expression told of mixed feelings. "Lady Amelia is our priority. If we can do no more than convey her to the lift for an immediate withdrawal, so be it. Adept Gunnhilda, stay inside the lift and protect us from all wards and curses."

"Yes, Your Grace." Gunnhilda lowered her head over the charms strung between her hands.

I hoped like hell we wouldn't have to retreat before confronting Holsten, but it wouldn't be the worst setback. If we kept him confined to the observatory, it'd only be a matter of time before the siege ended in our favor.

But the thought of waiting out days, weeks …? I didn't have it in me, not then.

"Let's flank the door, Jayce." Ingvar's words broke through my dread. His eyes fastened onto mine encouragingly. "If they rush us when we arrive, we'll protect the others."

That was a sentiment I could rally my remaining strength behind. But my courage faltered — specifically, the courage to tell Ingvar all the things left unsaid before, things I could lose the chance to say later if this assault went bad. Words of any kind eluded my tired brain. But I did give Ingvar a parting kiss before returning to my side of the lift entrance.

He stared after me, blinking and similarly dumbstruck, before taking up an offensive position with Branigan's longsword.

As my heart raced with fear and anticipation, I took deep breaths, rolling my right shoulder. Not for the last time, I was grateful for a sword I could wield one-handed.

Assaulting a nest of adepts in a sacred space. Most outsiders would've thought we'd lost our damned minds. Back when I was a squire and still believed in "magic," the prospect of opposing adepts had scared the hell out of me. May, my former master, had taught me a simple equalizer: *You just gotta be a little smarter than them for one second.*

I found it worked for a lot more than adepts.

The lift car rose ever higher, revealing Nidaros' sprawling countryside—which vanished as we transitioned into a deep, silent darkness.

CHAPTER 25

As the lift car rose through the adepts' keep, it entered an expanse without light or windows. Darkness swallowed us, offering no clue of what we might face in our bid to rescue Lady Amelia, defeat Holsten, and end the trade guild's invasion.

I went from tense, anxious, and ready for a fight to near panic. Breath lodged in my throat, I braced for an ambush or oblivion itself, but nothing followed. The others with me remained still and silent, maybe also expecting the worst.

The lift car lurched to a stop; I managed to keep my balance. This had to be the observatory's lower chamber. Gripping my side sword tightly, I craned my neck in every direction.

It wasn't completely dark after all. Four points of sunlight surrounded us in a square pattern, each about ten yards away. They illuminated four gleaming staircases that swept upward, presumably into the adepts' sanctum.

There was no sign of immediate resistance, but my nerves refused to settle.

"What dost thou sense, Adept?" Baron Tristan muttered uneasily into the darkness.

"I have no clear picture of our vicinity," Gunnhilda replied under her breath. "But above? Powers help us, the sanctum is terribly warded."

A bright glow burst to life within the lift, aimed at the floor. Behind me, Dag had broken out his light tile, helpfully illuminating our confines — along with the stunned expressions on the Baron's, Ingvar's, and Gunnhilda's faces.

My viscera knotted up with worry. I understood Dag's motivation, but given present company, I wished he'd refrained.

"Thou said thou wert no adept," the Baron said, still aghast.

"He isn't. What is this witchery?" Gunnhilda demanded.

"Master Ormyr discovered his inborn talent on our way to the Harbinger. He wants to train him," I lied in a rush, hoping that would be the end of it. We didn't have time for another witch-hunt.

Dag threw a questioning frown my way. The light tile remained in his grip, not about to be concealed.

"I see. Thy magic might've proven helpful earlier, but if thy power is undisciplined, perchance 'tis best used sparingly," the Baron said, probably rationalizing it to himself as he spoke.

As with Sigrid, he displayed a jaw-dropping openness toward unsanctioned magic. I supposed I may not have to perform much excuse-making for Dag later, assuming we lived through this mess.

Ingvar had seen the light tile in use before. His attention shifted to whatever lay past the lift car, and he raised Branigan's longsword, still clutching his left arm to his chest. "Think I see something," he muttered, then tossed his head in gesture. "Dag, that way."

The light tile's glow passed over empty floor at first. Then a sharp shadow cut into the light's edge: the cast of a skeletal hand. It belonged to an emaciated person in ichor-stained rags, lying on their side, their head hidden behind their other arm.

I gasped.

"*Nidstang*," Dag cursed under his breath.

"Unseen." Gunnhilda placed a hand to her mouth.

Baron Tristan grasped his hammer amulet. Only Ingvar had no open reaction.

Dag swept his light over the floor to find several more such bodies covering the expanse. No furniture or other obstacles, just these unfortunates.

My stomach turned. "They look like prisoners from the dungeon."

"Perchance," the Baron granted.

Dag's brow furrowed in confusion. "Why'd they drag prisoners up here?"

"They're mostly Gyllenfeld dissidents," I said. "They might be friends or family members of the adepts upstairs."

They'd once sought to kill Ormyr, Baron Tristan, Lady Amelia, Ingvar, and many others. Still, a part of me ached for their suffering. Anywhere else in the galaxy, they would've been executed — but better that than *years* underground at Ormyr's mercy. In his bid to stifle further dissent, he'd made them endure the kind of living hell no one deserved. And in the process, he'd deepened the resentment of Holsten and others — like Sigrid — whose kin suffered at his hand.

Like the corpses in Gules, I couldn't help these people no matter how much I wanted to — at least not right then. A bitter pill to swallow, but Lady Amelia and Holsten were still nowhere in sight. They were probably up in the sanctum with Holsten's remaining supporters. We'd have to leave the lift, cross the floor, and climb one of the staircases to find out. The prisoners appeared to be our only obstacle. Unless they had the wherewithal to notice us and call up to the sanctum, they didn't appear to be a threat.

"Ingvar," I prompted under my breath, "maybe someone should scout what's upstairs."

He broke from a sullen reverie, glancing between me and the Baron. "Agreed. Once we have a clearer picture, we'll regroup and plan."

"I'll go," Dag said.

"Nay, lad," Ingvar replied. "Need you to stay here and light the path to the stairwell."

Dag took it in stride, probably because Ingvar had layered a meaningful purpose over the refusal.

"Jayce, ye'll scout. I'll back you up," Ingvar said. "Careful, traps might be anywhere."

I nodded, all too aware of that fact.

Baron Tristan and Gunnhilda clutched at their totems. "Unseen be with you," the Baron said.

The lift car door slid open at our approach, admitting cool air tinged with perfume. Holsten and his followers were probably casting like crazy in the sanctum. There was no indication they were aware of our arrival. With a tilt of his head, Ingvar sent me out first, indicating the nearest stairwell as my destination.

I took a steeling breath, pushing away fatigue, then stepped out with my sword raised to advance slowly, keeping an eye out for hazards. The chamber appeared empty, though, aside from the prisoners. As I approached the closest one, their arms swung up.

I flinched — but the prisoner only cared about shielding him- or herself from Dag's light tile. They wrapped their arms over their face.

Holding my breath, I edged past without incident. From there, I proceeded as though crossing a minefield. Behind me, Ingvar followed, silently placing his feet wherever I had.

Halfway to the staircase, Ingvar's boot scuffed sharply against the ground. I whirled around to find him planted on one foot, struggling to maintain balance. A nearby prisoner had seized hold of his ankle.

With pangs of fear stabbing through me, I grabbed Ingvar's elbow to steady him. I also raised my side sword, prepared to free him that way if necessary.

Ingvar regained his balance and twisted his other leg free. The prisoner let out a screech of protest, a noise that seemed to boom through the chamber.

Had the adepts heard that? We froze; I strained my ears for any reaction from the sanctum above. Back at the lift, the Baron, Gunnhilda, and Dag looked on with wide-eyed horror.

Several seconds ticked past uneventfully. Ingvar gave me a reassuring look and gestured me onward with a tilt of his head.

I didn't quite share his confidence, but pressed on all the same. Fortunately, we reached the staircase with no further difficulty. While Ingvar assumed a guarded stance there, I approached the stairs. They ran in both directions, up to the sanctum and back down into the adepts' keep. The trip upward was short and mostly shielded from sight, but my pounding heart wasn't having any reassurance. Bent double, sword at my side, I crept up one stair at a time, pausing to make certain I hadn't been spotted before taking the next.

The sanctum that crept into view reminded me of a soap bubble: a circular room lined with rainbow-tinted windows and capped with a domed ceiling. Afternoon sun cast shadows across the floor. In the center of the room, Lady Amelia knelt with her hands tied behind her back, eyes closed, murmuring to herself. Surrounding her was a magic circle of ground powder and lit candles. Nothing prevented her from stepping over that circle and running away — nothing physical, at least. She must've believed it was a real obstacle, and that something horrible would happen upon breaking it.

On the sanctum's opposite side, close to windows that likely revealed a dramatic view of the invasion, at least a dozen green-robed adepts huddled over beads and charms. I recognized several from the ambush en route to the Harbinger, but Holsten wasn't visible among them. Maybe he sat in the core of that huddle, leading the devotions. Funny — he'd found yet another way to avoid facing me. No mercenaries. The adepts carried nothing worse than daggers, at least outwardly.

Anger simmered inside my ribcage over all the pain these adepts had caused. The barony's survival was at stake, but drawing out a rotten feud was more important to them. Still, my first instinct would've been to talk sense into Holsten: explain Savidge was in custody, persuade him to surrender. He'd make a devastating witness whenever I returned to Spectra to eviscerate Madam Castor. But Holsten had tried to kill me too many times. If I showed up proposing peace, I knew what I'd earn for my trouble. At least they were grouped together like that. That could work to our advantage.

Swallowing resentment, I retreated into the lower chamber. When Ingvar glanced to me questioningly, I nodded, then pointed toward the lift.

We made much better progress back, entering the lift car safely. The relieved faces awaiting us were a welcome sight. In the glow of Dag's light tile, I explained what I'd seen within the sanctum.

"No Holsten? Don't like that." Ingvar planted the point of Branigan's longsword against the floor.

"I didn't see him, but he has to be there," I said.

"Lady Amelia remaineth our priority," the Baron reminded us.

"I think we can get the drop on them." I gestured to the opposite side of the chamber. "They're crowded near that staircase. If we stage a distraction or ambush there, someone can run up the staircase I just scouted —" I pointed my thumb over my shoulder " — and grab the Baroness."

"I got a distraction!" Dag held up the grenades Ormyr had given him in the dungeon.

I smiled. "Perfect."

Gunnhilda recognized the grenades. Ingvar and the Baron were less certain, but my reaction assuaged them.

"I shall retrieve Lady Amelia." Baron Tristan straightened with a look of brutal resolve.

"But, Your Grace, entering the magic circle would be terribly dangerous," Gunnhilda said.

The Baron produced the jeweled khamsa I'd returned to him and held it out flat in his palm, staring at it with a bitter-sweet expression. "'Twas one of my gifts to her when we were courting."

This stunned Gunnhilda into wide-eyed, reverent silence.

I nodded. "I'm sure she'll appreciate seeing it again, sir."

Ingvar continued with an air of resignation. "When Your Grace ascendeth, the knight and I will run up these other two staircases and contain the adepts. Should give you more time. Lad, return here once your diversion's off. Adept, stay here to animate the lift." He threw a brief glance Gunnhilda's way, less suspicious than before. "Your Grace, once ye bring Lady Amelia here, ye can make a quick escape if needed."

Dag looked ready to protest; I shook my head at him. This was for the best. I wanted him and the nobility to bail if something went wrong.

Baron Tristan hesitated, then lowered his head in assent. "Spare Holsten and his followers for questioning."

Ingvar gave him a dubious look. "Easier said than done, Your Grace. They'll be aiming for Folkvang."

"I know. Try," the Baron said. "We shall wait for thee and Dame Jessamine as long as we can."

"Unseen guide you all," Gunnhilda wished.

I nodded my thanks to her, then to Dag, who returned a look of determination.

Finally, I glanced to Ingvar. My heart sped up, and my nerves fluttered. Before I said or did anything, he pulled me into a one-armed embrace. "Be careful."

I hugged back hard. "You too." The only words I could force past the lump in my throat.

Letting go was the last thing I wanted to do, but the sooner we got going, the sooner this would end. Carefully, everyone but Gunnhilda left the lift car to navigate past the prisoners and toward his or her appointed staircase. Dag positioned himself just beneath the adept cluster, bouncing on the balls of his feet. Clockwise from him stood Ingvar, the Baron, then me. We each raised our hands, signaling readiness. My heart raced with anticipation.

Dag ran up a couple of stairs, threw the bombs Ormyr gave him, then darted back down.

To my surprise, loud reports and a glaring burst of light emanated from upstairs. These weren't smoke bombs, but flashbangs. I wondered if Ormyr had wanted to give Dag something truer to his idiom. Regardless, it'd still have the intended effect.

Dag scurried toward the lift where Gunnhilda was already waiting. "Go!" he shouted.

The Baron launched up his stairs, as did Ingvar and I, charging into the sanctum. The adepts reeled, many bent double with their eyes screwed shut. Lady Amelia, still inside the magic circle, had bolted upright to stare after them.

Ingvar surfaced to my right, on the opposite end of the chamber from me. Behind us, Baron Tristan emerged and rushed up to the magic circle.

With fury and adrenaline, I rushed the closest adepts, not wanting to give anyone a chance to recover or notice the noble pair. Ingvar engaged the adepts on his side of the room. As he'd said, stopping short of lethal force was a tall order. We carried swords, and our opponents were sure to hold nothing back. Still, with the Baron's wishes in mind, I reversed my grip on my sword-hilt to make better use of the pommel, a slightly less deadly implement than the blade.

The first staggering adept in my path received a hook to the temple. The pommel-strike sent him to the floor in a hurry. Without stopping to confirm whether he'd been fully knocked out, I mowed past, preferring targets who faced away from me or remained dazed.

It didn't take long for the other adepts to realize what was happening.

"Triumph or Folkvang!" one of them shouted.

Another adept lunged at me with his dagger, bringing to bear all the ferocity one would expect from a person whose worldly fate, and afterlife, were at stake. With that kind of mentality infecting him, he wasn't thinking of defense. It was easy to dodge and counter with another well-placed strike.

And so it continued. Where my pommel proved inconvenient, my elbow made a handy alternative. When someone refused to stay down, a superficial slash to the leg or arm gave them something more urgent to consider.

One adept winged an unknown object toward my face, which I ducked to avoid. A second adept immediately darted in and shoved hard, sending me falling back toward the wall of windows encircling the room. My brain cruelly reminded me of the glass walls at the top of Baron's estate, how Sigrid had slipped through and nearly plummeted to her demise.

Terror stole the scream out of my lungs. I was too close, and had too much momentum, to be able to stop myself.

My shoulder hit the glass — and stayed there. The wall was solid, keeping me away from the ground below.

Shuddering with relief, I swallowed my heart back down one chamber at a time before returning to the fray, forging a path toward Ingvar's side of the sanctum. When possible, I glanced toward the other half of the room. The magic circle stood empty; Baron Tristan and Lady Amelia had escaped. I indulged in a tiny measure of relief.

Between my and Ingvar's efforts, the entire collection of upstart adepts soon littered the ground. We lowered our arms, gasping for air, glancing all around. There was no sign of Holsten among the casualties. My relief iced over with apprehension.

From the staircase nearest to us, a burst of light below caught our attention. A shout followed, unmistakably Baron Tristan. "Leave! Away!"

Then, a thunderous report, followed by screams.

My heart leapt to my mouth. More concerned with my allies' welfare than anything else, I sprinted toward the staircase.

The lower chamber was now brightly lit. Holsten's small, hunched form lurked near the foot of the stairs; he must've slipped away while his friends had occupied my and Ingvar's attention. Closer to the lift, among the field of ailing prisoners, Baron Tristan lay face-down and motionless.

Alarm paused me for only a second. Then I tore down the stairs, intent on clobbering Holsten. One hit, and I'd finish this.

The booming sound, the distance at which the Baron lay, they didn't add up fast enough in my head. Holsten whirled to stare up at me, green pendulum swaying from one hand. In the other, he raised something compact and familiar.

A handheld laser weapon.

The blinding wrath of a lightning strike burned my eyes. Its fire burned into my chest. I lost my side sword along with my footing, and tumbled down the stairs toward Holsten.

CHAPTER 26

The world was a blur of pain and screams as I tumbled downstairs from the adepts' sanctum toward Holsten. Even after I reached the end of the staircase and sprawled out on solid ground, my brain kept bumping and rolling, defying attempts to focus. New aches cried out all over, none nearly so loud as the fiery agony screaming across my torso.

Holsten's shot should've been fatal. My nanofiber brigandine stopped it from going through me, but couldn't deflect the hit entirely.

I came to rest on my left side in the chamber beneath the adepts' sanctum, facing the stairs, with a partial view of the lift car. Inside the glassy confines, Lady Amelia had collapsed to her knees, leaning against the wall with the haunted look of someone who'd just witnessed an execution. Baron Tristan's motionless body lay just outside the lift car, surrounded by dungeon prisoners.

Behind the Baroness, Gunnhilda struggled to restrain a shrieking Dag, who threw himself toward the lift car door with every ounce of feral energy. The adept, bless her, kept Dag from leaping out into foolish danger. However, she couldn't operate the lift and get away as the Baron had ordered in his final moments.

Was he dead? I sorely hoped not.

Holsten had to be lurking somewhere behind me. My side sword was nowhere in sight. I cursed myself, feeling awfully stupid. But how could I have anticipated a handheld laser *here?* They were damned rare, the sort of thing Lords hoarded.

"*Skíta!*"

Out rang an anguished curse from the top of the stairs. Ingvar raced down, the longsword in his hand almost an afterthought.

I couldn't manage the words to warn him away. My body tensed with horror as I imagined Holsten shooting him next, watching his lifeless body tumble down the stairs …

"Hold still, Captain! I'd rather not hurt anyone, but if you attack me, I'll be forced to defend myself."

Holsten was only audible at my vantage, not visible. I assumed he'd trained his laser weapon up at Ingvar—but, to my relief and confusion, he hadn't taken his shot.

Ingvar halted mid-descent, scowling. "Ye've already crossed that line."

As an adept, I was sure Holsten would have an excuse ready. If he did, he kept it to himself.

I struggled to push aside my worry for Ingvar and focus on redeeming myself somehow, but that damned laser gave me pause. Judging by his voice, Holsten stood a good distance behind me. Surely he could shoot faster than I could reach him.

Then it hit me: the laser was a Shipbuilder device. Might it have an interface?

There were two data carriers in my pockets. The trick would be reaching for them without Holsten noticing. My right arm seemed my best bet, if I could keep it still from shoulder to elbow.

"Dag—hear me?" Ingvar addressed toward the lift. "Stay in that box, lad. Protect everyone with you."

Giving Dag a purpose proved more effective than simply telling him to calm down. The fight drained out of him, freeing up Gunnhilda, who lunged toward the lift controls — but paused there, trembling, glancing toward Baron Tristan.

"Still don't quite have a spine, do you, Gunnhilda?" Holsten's voice held more pity than scorn. "I understand; Ormyr ground us all down for years. It's not too late to join me."

"No, Holsten." Gunnhilda faced Holsten with a pleading gaze, tears pouring down her face. "This is wrong. Please stop."

She must've cared for him, as a friend, mentor, maybe more. I sympathized with how torn she must've felt, and was grateful for her loyalty in the face of that. I was also grateful for the distraction she provided. Once I'd nudged a data carrier out of my left pocket, I worked on slipping it to the floor without making noise.

"I can't. This is the Unseen's will." Holsten's conviction was unshakable. "Tristan Foster and Dame Jessamine had to go."

"The Unseen's will?" Ingvar challenged. "Commander Savidge is in custody. Your friends aren't fighting anymore today. Ye're out of leverage." Pain overtook his anger. "Ye can't put a ghost on the throne. Don't ye get that?"

"You think my family name is Fessel." Holsten paused. "It's Gyllenfeld."

Everyone still standing went wide-eyed and slack-jawed. I was surprised at first, but then suspicious. How many times in my travels had I heard charlatans claiming noble or divine ancestry to get what they wanted?

Ingvar soon leveled his own incredulous scowl at Holsten. "*Gamla skíta!* The Gyllenfelds were killed in the culling of Asgard."

"So you've been told! I'm telling you differently," Holsten replied. "Knowing the truth, do you still oppose me?"

Once I'd rested the data carrier on the floor, a touch of my finger brought its display to life. As I waited for it to detect something, anything, I looked up to Ingvar. To my shock, his expression wavered. Was he actually considering defection? Or had he noticed me, and sought to buy me time?

The uncertainty dug into my racing heart. *Come on, damn it,* I urged the data carrier.

"I care about Nidaros!" Holsten continued. "Unlike the endless line of fools who've just bided their time here until a better position on Spectra opened up. And I'm smarter than they were. Here I am on the verge of becoming Baron without any blood being shed!"

A derisive cry rose in my throat, but went no farther.

"Are ye mad?" Ingvar exclaimed. "D'ye see the carnage here in this chamber, never mind outside? This stopped being blood-less a long time ago!"

"All who died have done so of the Unseen's will," Holsten shot back. "The Unseen are returning Nidaros to her rightful heir. Who are we to question their ways?"

That was some deeply entrenched belief. I remembered Holsten pleading, and failing, to prevent violence during the ambush in the districts. He'd since moved on to rationalizing it so he could keep his treasured delusion intact.

At last, a single device registered on the data carrier. My heart nearly pounded through my burned-up ribcage. I scrolled through the interface, reading the Shipbuilder commands with desperate haste.

"Ye think sneaking behind everyone's backs and plotting with Madam Castor make you enlightened somehow?" Ingvar asked. "Blood's oath! Wherefore would she give *you* Nidaros when she hath a dozen groomed lackeys on Spectra itching to do her bidding?" His scowl deepened into a look of disgust. "Ye're no savior, Holsten. Ye're just a fool who betrayed us."

I found and selected a disabling command. Had it worked? Trial by fire was the only way to tell, and I was the only permissible test subject.

"I? What about you?" Holsten shouted. "You betrayed your blood to put Tristan Foster in power. You made us all slaves of those Catherwood parasites!"

I rolled onto my opposite side to face Holsten. My would-be murderer stood several feet away, weapon and rage trained on Ingvar, so preoccupied that he failed to notice me. I forced myself up to my knees, then pushed off the ground with both feet. It was enough for a sloppy lunge, which brought me close enough to catch the hem of Holsten's green robe in one fist on my way to the ground.

Holsten backed away, struggling to escape my grasp. At the same time, he trained the laser weapon at my skull.

Several gasps went up. I held my breath, in case it was the last.

A click. Then a few more. The trigger failed to deliver.

Footsteps pounded down the stairs behind me. I glanced up in time to witness Ingvar burying Branigan's longsword pommel viciously into Holsten's jaw.

The adept's robe slipped from my fingers as Holsten fell, collapsing onto the dungeon prisoners at his feet.

I went limp with relief, resting my head on my outstretched arm. Lying face-down added unpleasant pressure to the fire on my chest, but I lacked the strength to do anything about it.

A hand took hold of my shoulder and flipped me onto my back. Ingvar hovered overhead with a worried expression. After glancing me over, he struggled with his one good arm to drag me toward the lift.

More footsteps pelted closer. Dag, probably. I pushed against the floor with my arms and legs, convinced I could stand myself up. Hell, I had to. There was still so much to do.

"The Baron. We can heal him," I said. "Thordia's in the dungeon. We brought …"

Adrenaline, drugs, and everything else gave out on me. I trailed off and faded.

CHAPTER 27

My next lucid memory was of waking up in a warm pallet, feeling starved and parched. Ample sunlight streamed through a nearby window, while lavender and cloves laced the air.

I didn't recognize my surroundings at first. Lit candles, ewers of water, and plates loaded with fruit covered the tables arranged on all sides of me. Wishing beads hung from a broken light fixture on the ceiling. Charms and dried flowers littered the floor.

It was as if I were the object of worship in a shrine, and the adulation didn't stop there. On another table rested my polished and gleaming side sword, baldric and belt folded underneath. A chair nearby propped up my nanofiber brigandine, remarkably intact, and a pile of unfamiliar clothing. Beside that, someone had neatly laid out the contents of my coat pockets.

This had to be my room in the Baron's estate, on Nidaros. Further recollections hit me like lightning: our trip to the Harbinger, the ichor's origins, thwarting Holsten and Madam Castor's invasion. After the concussion I'd sustained, it was surprising that I remembered so much.

How long had I been lying here? The Baron, Dag, Ingvar— were they all right?

Overcome with worry, I darted up to a seat, then winced as several aches made their displeasure known. My muscles and joints were sore, but nothing felt broken at least. My mother's ring rested against my bandaged chest; Ormyr's mati had vanished. Strangely, the burns I'd sustained from the laser shot didn't feel as painful as I would've expected.

And what of Ormyr? Thordia? *Drea?* I had to find everybody.

I slipped out from under the covers and stood slowly. My legs weren't happy about it, but tolerated my weight well enough. From there, I dressed myself with careful movements. The linen tunic, trousers, leather gloves, and knee-high boots were all new, and of surprising quality. My pocket items were mostly accounted for: Lord Catherwood's sealed papers, coin purse, cigarillos and fire-making tools, light tile, the ominous vial of ichor from the Naustviks' cellar ... but no data carriers. Thordia had reclaimed them, maybe, or the adepts had seized them.

The door opened. Sigrid entered with eyes lowered, a sprig of dried lavender in her hand. Upon noticing me, she halted, stunned.

I was surprised, too. She'd been outed as a witch, after all. "Hello, sister." I collapsed to a seat on the pallet, waiting for her words or body language to tell me whether we remained allies.

"Thank the Unseen!" Sigrid looked like she'd finally been allowed to drop a heavy burden. She darted to one of the bedside tables, lit the lavender on fire, then rested the burning sprig on a plate.

"How long was I out?" I asked.

"About two days now," she said.

"Hell!" That long? Well, I *had* slogged through ichor, a space station, and an invasion force with little rest in between, to say nothing of how badly I might've crashed from the stimulants I'd taken. "Is everything all right here?"

"The invasion's over," she answered. "Thordia healed you and our Baron with the Shipbuilder relics you brought back from the Harbinger."

Maybe that was why I felt better than I had any right to. It surprised me given Thordia's distrust, but whatever her motives, I was glad. "The Baron survived?"

A dark sadness overtook Sigrid's expression. "Yes. Although ..."

"What?" I demanded, heart lurching with concern.

"His Grace has much recovering to do yet, and Lady Amelia won't let me help." Sigrid's features hardened as she grabbed a stick to stir the lavender ashes.

"Because you're a witch. Right?" I asked. "How are you not in the dungeon right now?" Tossing her in a cell seemed like the first thing Ormyr would've seen to once the invasion had ended.

"Baron Tristan granted me his protection," Sigrid replied.

Then he'd really appreciated her help. It was for the best. The handmaid didn't deserve persecution, and I wasn't interested to learn what might happen if her signals stopped going out to her family-slash-coven in the districts.

"For those too-short hours in the dungeon, His Grace hung upon my every word, as if I were a Vala of old." Sigrid focused wistful eyes on the stirred ashes.

Vala? The reference eluded me; I'd ask what she meant later. "What about Captain Leirfall? Is he all right?" I both feared and longed for her response.

Sigrid smirked knowingly. "He's had some recovering to do himself, but he's visited regularly to check on you."

Of course—my mother's ring. My heart skipped, and a heady elation caused me to lose my train of thought.

This gave Sigrid an opportunity to sit behind me and arrange my hair like she had the first day I'd arrived. She left most of it down, pulling back and braiding a few sections. It was the sort of thing I needed three more pairs of hands and eyes to do myself.

"It's been an awful past few days," she said. "I'm glad you're awake."

"Thanks." Awful how? She was in the Baron's favor—but she'd probably made a lot of enemies upon being exposed. With a stab of worry, I wondered if I'd been similarly outed. Something to dig into later.

"Where's Thordia?" I asked, trying to show the appropriate concern for our "sister."

"She watches over the most injured soldiers, who were moved aboard your ship. My magic has kept her identity hidden."

Right. The veil has nothing to do with it, I thought. I seriously doubted Thordia's identity was a secret to everyone, but it was good she remained free in spite of it. Though my ship was probably the best place for her and the wounded, I couldn't help feeling paranoid about her being there.

"What about Dag Nyvind?" I asked next.

"He's kept with the soldiers," Sigrid replied. "Rumors of his magic talent are all over the capital. The cloister will probably take him in."

Her answer jolted my spine. "But he's under my protection."

But I'd willed him to Ormyr when the Baron had seen his "talent," hadn't I? A nervous knot formed in my gut.

"He is?" Sigrid asked. "Oh, that's good to hear!"

She must've thought I'd train him in witchcraft. I would, after a fashion, if he agreed to be my squire. I had to clear it with his older brother first.

But what if Ormyr *did* want Dag for the cloister now? What if Dag liked the idea? Though I wanted him to follow his preferences, becoming an adept was a waste of his intelligence.

Was I really his best alternative, though? My earlier certainty had holes in it. Did I want a squire? Could I handle it? Could Dag?

Hell, it didn't matter how ready I felt. He *needed* me to do it. There were too many influences looking to shape his "talent." Ormyr, the Naustviks, maybe even Sigrid? No. Dag had to learn not just about Shipbuilder "magic," but also the underlying science, and how to apply it toward helping others while protecting himself from exposure. The Naustviks had gotten him into this mess; I'd get him out of it.

Once Sigrid finished with my hair, I stood gingerly. Far from putting me at ease, her information made me more eager to track everyone down and see how they fared. But there was still so much I didn't know. It'd be best to talk to the Baron first, or whoever was in charge during his recovery. Chances were, I'd have to push off some reunions. Drea was still stuck on Gules, after all.

"Good luck," Sigrid wished me once I shared my intentions. "I'm mending your old clothes and trying to get those awful stains out."

Ichor, I realized with a chill. "Don't bother."

Sigrid waved a hand in dismissal. "It's no trouble, sister. I hope the new clothes are to your liking. I wanted to get you a dress, but I know you prefer masculine fare."

"It's not masculine, it's practical." I threw down a quick glass of water, then left the room.

A soldier stood outside my door, his eyes widening at my appearance. "Lady Knight! Good to see you!"

Had Ingvar stationed him there to stand vigil? Had he feared additional murder attempts while I was unconscious? I fought to ignore my pounding heart.

"Come with me," the soldier said. "Lady Amelia said to bring you to her as soon as ye were up."

Good, just where I'd hoped to head.

Sigrid stepped out behind me. At the sight of her, the soldier's expression darkened. He beckoned me along without another word.

The handmaid threw me a sad look, then turned the other way down the hall.

This marked the first time I'd actually seen the estate's throne room. Burgundy and gold Catherwood tapestries blanketed the perimeter. Hundreds of candles warmed the room in the absence of sun.

At my appearance, Lady Amelia rose from her carved wooden throne, resplendent in her gown. From her wrist dangled a posy of dried flowers, which I remembered from my ill-timed arrival to Nidaros. It was once a spurned gift from Baron Tristan, now enjoying an exalted status. After recent events, she must've rethought her contempt toward him.

To the left of the Baroness stood Adept Gunnhilda, looking well, if troubled. A little farther away, a pair of soldiers flanked the women.

This was nothing like Baron Tristan's humble, no-nonsense audience. It seemed this display of regal dignity was more Lady Amelia's style. I walked down a short velvet runner, through a cloud of that unpleasant Catherwood incense. Gunnhilda nodded in greeting, and the soldiers' eyes lit up at my approach. I nodded to them, then bit my lip while slowly lowering myself to one knee.

"Arise," Lady Amelia commanded. Once I reached my feet, she offered me a faint smile. "Unseen be praised thou art awake. We've all been concerned."

"Thank you, madam," I replied. "How's Baron Tristan?"

Worry cut through the serene facade. "Abed still, but he shall live, thanks to thee … and Thordia Naustvik."

Thordia had been unmasked before Lady Amelia. Was I also out as a "witch," then? Witches seemed to be enjoying the nobility's favor at present, so was that necessarily a bad thing?

Until I had a better grasp of the situation, I wouldn't accept or deny the label.

"The Shipbuilder device Holsten injured us with. Where is it now?" I asked, hoping to ensure it was in a safe place for the time being. It'd have to be dealt with properly later — stored under lock and key, if at all possible.

Lady Amelia darkened. "In my custody, until more urgent matters are addressed."

Tellingly, no longer trusted it in the adepts' care. I couldn't blame her.

"I've assumed my husband's responsibilities whilst he recovereth. There's much to be done in the invasion's wake," she continued, sobering. "Most of the burden hath fallen to our army, given the state of our cloister. Captain Leirfall and Lieutenant Grimsson are both afield at present. I'm certain news of thy recovery shall gladden them."

I struggled to ignore the spike in my pulse. "What *is* the state of the cloister?"

Gunnhilda cast a forlorn look toward the floor.

Lady Amelia narrowed her eyes, smoldering. "Four loyal adepts remain, Master Ormyr included."

My stomach turned. Just four? Had so many defected to Holsten's side?

"I've left Master Ormyr to cleaning up the mess, both literal and figurative, within his keep," Lady Amelia said. "For now."

It was quite the mess. I wondered what Lady Amelia's "for now" meant, but it wasn't important just then.

"Where are the adepts who defected?" I asked. "In the dungeon?"

Lady Amelia's gaze fell, mirroring Gunnhilda's posture. "Dead."

"What?" The news slapped me in the face. Ingvar and I had placed ourselves at risk to avoid killing anyone. "All of them? Even Holsten?"

"Verily. After being taken to the dungeon along with the prisoners they'd dug up, they were found dead shortly thereafter. Some manner of self-inflicted curse, meseemeth."

Some manner of poison, I imagined. Hell, maybe even ichor? They'd known it was in the dirt. Whatever the case, they'd obviously preferred death to captivity.

Frustration welled up in my chest. I'd wanted to get Holsten talking about his collaboration with Madam Castor, even push for him to speak before Lord Catherwood. My resentment over this invasion, Gules, and a certain sword that'd come into Madam Castor's possession hadn't gone anywhere.

"What about Commander Savidge?" I asked.

Lady Amelia glanced up again. "He remaineth in the dungeon with the other captured mercenaries. We shall take them back when we fly to Spectra tomorrow."

"Wha- *tomorrow?*" I repeated, shocked.

"Thou art now well enough to fulfill thy duty to Lord Catherwood. We must inform him of all that occurred here," she explained. "If the court doth not hear it from both of us, I fear the message shan't resonate."

Aversion built up inside me. Yes, this was important, but still …

"I'm not sure I can close out my quest yet," I said. "I'm supposed to wait until Linum Dominorum sends their harvest ships." If Madam Castor's trade guild still had any such intention. That was at least another few days off. In the intervening time, I could hunt down coordinates, fly to Gules, and retrieve Drea. After the harvest, I'd return to Spectra and deal with formalities.

"Thou hast seen our flax in storage," Lady Amelia said. "If thou givest thy vow as a knight errant that we shall deliver it when the harvest cometh, that should be enough to release thee from thine obligation."

Protest lingered in my throat, itching to be let out. However, I recalled Lady Amelia's iciness toward my intention to leave Nidaros for the "wise woman," and that'd been without mentioning Drea was stuck in cursed territory. As much as I wanted to come clean to the Baroness, plead to her as one human being to another, I had to use a less direct approach. "I'll be glad to help, madam, but there's an urgent matter I—"

"Thy duty to Lord Catherwood cometh first." Lady Amelia folded her arms, unmoved. "We shall embark at sunrise tomorrow with my vessel. Captain Leirfall shall accompany us."

His name jolted my spine and trapped the breath in my throat. Ingvar was coming? Hadn't he only left Nidaros once before? This implied he was healthy enough to leave, which was something, but I wondered how he felt about the prospect.

Amusement lightened Lady Amelia's expression. "I hope for us to return within a standard day's time. Once thy quest is over, thou shalt be free to do as thou wilt."

But I'd already squandered days in recovery. How much time did Drea have left? A familiar anguish clenched down on me. I suspected Baron Tristan would've let me fly to Gules first, but I wouldn't be getting an audience with him.

I tamped down as much despair as possible. "A few more questions for you, madam, if I may." She still believed I was still her nephew's trusted emissary. I hoped I could get my way on *something*. "First, has anything been done with the adepts' remains?"

"We've performed rites over them, but naught else," Lady Amelia said. "There've been too many other corpses to burn."

"Good. Please don't move the bodies in the dungeon until I can help out with that. They may be dangerous." I pulled the vial of ichor from my pocket. "I've discovered this poison in the soil throughout Nidaros. It steals water—from crops *and* people."

Lady Amelia's eyes went wide with alarm. She clutched her wishing beads close to her chest.

"It came from the Harbinger. Trust me, there's no witch in the galaxy powerful enough to conjure up something like this," I stated with confidence. "But all isn't lost. The Harbinger's full of Shipbuilder relics. It may contain the solution to the ichor, we just have to find it. That's what Thordia Naustvik's working toward."

Equal parts fear and awe entered Lady Amelia's expression. "I am … uncertain about the wisdom of consorting any further with witches."

"Thordia brought you food and flax, and saved your husband's life," I argued. "And she won't be the only one helping you. When my quest is done, and I've seen to that urgent matter I mentioned, I promise to do all I can to restore Nidaros. However long it takes."

My heart pounded feverishly. This was no trivial offer, but I had no desire to quest anywhere else. I'd see Nidaros through to the best resolution possible, however long it took.

Lady Amelia lowered her head graciously. "We would welcome thine assistance, especially with our cloister weakened."

Did she expect me to aid in "magic" ways as well as mundane ones? I brushed off the thought with a smile. "Just one more thing, madam: let me tell you more about what happened while Master Ormyr and I were away. When we address Lord Catherwood tomorrow, we should have a consistent story."

And there were some details that were best left out.

I felt good about what Lady Amelia and I agreed to tell Lord Catherwood. At the same time, the prospect of prolonging Drea's suffering made me sick to my core. I felt bad enough about being out of action for two days. Heaping on yet another? She had to be struggling, if she were still struggling at all.

But I still lacked the coordinates required to steer back to Gules. Goodness only knew how hard it'd be to obtain them. Even if Ormyr remained willing to help, he might not actually have them. I resolved to keep an eye out for any opportunity to dig through other ships' indexes while in Spectra—although the majority of ships passing through Spectra would be purged of Gules' coordinates, just as mine had been.

"We can head to the barracks from here, if ye like," my escorting soldier offered once I left the throne room. "Our memorial for our fallen is tonight."

His welcome words cut through my anxious thoughts. I hoped to speak to Rigg about Dag as well, assuming Rigg had survived ... and see Ingvar. I trembled, nervous and thrilled at once. "Sure, let's go."

"Lady Knight?"

I turned to find Gunnhilda on my heels. "Friend Adept," I greeted with a nod and smile.

She proffered a drawstring pouch. "Master Ormyr wanted me to give you this when you awakened. He told me to tell you, 'Consult the index.'"

My heart all but stopped. Somehow, I kept my footing and looped the pouch onto my belt. "Thanks. How're you doing?"

Gunnhilda glanced sidelong, wiping away tears with one hand. "I'm sorry. The past few days have been terrible."

"I'm sorry, too." Poor girl. Her whole world had been torn apart. "Do you or Ormyr need help with anything in the keep?"

The offer floored me even as it left my mouth. Helping out in a cloister? Never once in my knightly career. It would've been laughable even a few days earlier.

"There isn't much you can help with, but it's kind of you to offer. See you tomorrow." Gunnhilda returned to the throne room.

Curiosity had the better of me. I faced the soldier. "Go ahead, I'll be at the barracks soon."

Once alone, I ducked around a corner and opened the pouch. Inside was the data carrier Ormyr had taken from me in the "forest" full of constructs. A little browsing revealed he'd copied an entire planetary index onto the device. With trembling hands, I searched for Gules, and found it without a hitch.

My knees went weak. I put my back to the wall and slid to the floor, eyes filling with tears. *Thanks, Ormyr,* I thought.

I had everything necessary to take off for Gules right then, in true knight errant fashion. The thought tempted me for a moment, then reality and guilt swooped in. I couldn't just run off and leave Ingvar and Dag without a thought. The wounded soldiers aboard *Kepler's Law* would have to be moved first. There was also no getting past Spectra, and traveling there with Lady Amelia lent distinct advantages: I'd be shielded from courtly funny business, and have a chance to be with Ingvar for a while. Since I'd just cast my lot with the Nidarans indefinitely, it was best not to upset the local leadership.

Guilt and worry rooted me in place for a while. Finally, I forced myself back to my feet. *It won't be much longer, Drea, I promise. Hang on.*

She'd want me putting Nidaros first. I knew she would.

Before leaving the estate, I stopped by the kitchen to see whether my servant-friends had survived. Apprehension crept up, amplifying the closer I got. Did they now believe I was a witch? The soldier outside my room hadn't given me the glare he'd given Sigrid, and Lady Amelia had been welcoming. It seemed like I hadn't been exposed after all, but there was only one way to find out.

Upon reaching the kitchen, I paused in its threshold. Kofri, Lif, and Alfrun were there, scouring pots. Behind them, a kettle hung over the open fire, covered by a makeshift metal plate that jumped and clattered as steam escaped around it. Earlier, I'd taught them to cover the kettle so the water would boil faster.

The sight filled me with relief and vindication. Even so, I steeled myself. "Hail, friends!"

The trio abandoned their chore to beeline toward me—with smiles, not pitchforks. Alfrun reached me first, greeting me with a strong hug I gladly returned.

"Powers be praised! I feared the worst!" Lif cried as she and Kofri crowded in behind their more reserved counterpart.

"We all did," Kofri seconded.

"I think I found your witch," I told Alfrun.

"I knew you would!" Alfrun pulled away with an outrage that wasn't directed at me. "I can't *believe* Sigrid's gotten away with it!"

Lif mirrored her resentment. "She must be witching our Baron. There's no other explanation!"

"To be fair, Sigrid did help uncover Adept Holsten's plot," I said.

"So?" Kofri challenged. "She lied to us for years! We thought she was our friend. Here she's been working curses on us the whole time!"

"Maybe it wasn't Thordia who caused the drought," Alfrun said. "Maybe it was Sigrid all along!"

Lif and Kofri went pale at this speculation.

Where was their anger toward Holsten? He'd betrayed them in a far worse way. It made me wonder whom they'd rooted for during the invasion. I supposed it didn't matter as long as they hadn't harmed anyone.

Alfrun pushed me into a seat at a nearby table. Lif and Kofri retrieved food and water they placed before me without a word.

I helped myself with a thankful nod. "Neither Sigrid nor Thordia caused the drought."

They surrounded the table, eyes burning with curiosity.

I took advantage of their undivided attention to tell them about the dangerous ichor in the ground: where it'd come from, how it spread. The trio listened with increasing nervousness, but seemed to take the message to heart.

"The Harbinger cursed us, then?" Kofri finally asked.

"Yes—but the Harbinger's full of curses and blessings," I said. "We'll find a way to get rid of the ichor. In the meantime, stick with boiled rainwater." I stood. "Thanks again. I wish I could stay, but I'm heading to the barracks."

"Want some extra food first?" Alfrun gestured toward the larder. The shelves remained sparse, but there were several fresh fruits and vegetables that hadn't been there before. "The veiled woman has been so generous, whoever she is."

"Svana thinks she may be a friendly tree nymph whose beauty is too overwhelming to behold—or maybe the restless ghost of someone who failed to reach the Harbinger," Kofri said with a mischievous look.

"Stop it!" Lif slapped him on the shoulder.

Outside, I was surprised to see the sun so close to the horizon. To my left, the adepts' keep stood as polished and imposing as ever, masking the mess inside. I considered heading there first to thank Ormyr and see how he was doing, but Gunnhilda had seemed to suggest against it. I'd catch back up with him after Spectra. That evening, I wanted to help the soldiers, then attend their memorial.

A familiar scene of carnage stretched between the capital buildings and barracks. Most of the debris around the guild's ships had been cleared away; aside from scorch marks, the ships themselves looked serviceable. I wondered if Ormyr would permit anyone to restore them, or if they'd be "dead" from this point forward.

Several soldiers were still salvaging weapons, armor, possibly even rations they found aboard the ships. That awful burning-flesh smell dominated the air, not just from the fighting. Multiple ash-filled pyres had sent dozens of corpses off to their next purposes.

My stomach knotted up as I thought about all the warm faces I wouldn't find at the barracks. There was some solace in imagining Madam Castor tearing her hair out back in Spectra, dying to have her ships back, wondering how in hell she'd save face.

Kepler's Law remained where I'd landed her, just outside the barracks. I resolved to climb aboard her first and see if I could help with any casualties there. I also needed my jack of plate for my upcoming Lordly audience, along with one of the khamsa amulets I'd received upon being whisked away from Gules. Lord Catherwood's adepts still had to lift my "curse," after all.

Half a dozen unconscious young men occupied the galley. I recognized some of them from my first visit to the barracks—about a week ago at that point, maybe more. I didn't know what their bandages concealed, but burns, fractures, and internal injuries seemed likely. Above the soldiers hovered the surgical construct I'd brought back from the Harbinger.

Sympathy constricted my heart and lungs. Madam Castor's ruthless invasion had been completely uncalled for. I didn't know how yet, but I'd make her pay.

Finally, there was Thordia. The apparition sat in a chair folded down from the starboard bulkhead, her cloak and veil ghoulishly bloodstained—from helping people, not harming them. She stood and assumed her full height as I entered the galley, then pulled back her veil, draping it over her shoulders.

Her expression wasn't quite welcoming or bitter. The ichor-bruises around her artificial eye looked about the same.

A warmer reception than I'd anticipated. I approached her, nodding in greeting. "Thanks for your help."

"Thanks for keeping me out of the dungeon so far," Thordia replied.

I gestured around us. "Will they be all right?"

She nodded. "They just need time to recover."

That was a relief. She wasn't so bad when she remembered her compassion. Maybe the same would be true of Verahl someday, but I was still too angry at him to think about that.

"It seems your concussion cleared up nicely," Thordia remarked. "You're lucky it wasn't worse."

It sounded more like *You're lucky you didn't make it worse*, but I brushed it off. "How're *you* feeling?"

"Well enough, given the circumstances."

I nodded again and broke away to tiptoe aft, past the young men. Once I reached my target storage container, I turned Thordia's way again. She'd since returned to a seat, rummaging through her other satchel. Similarly, I dug through my charm box, sadly bereft of anything that'd help her fight the ichor under her skin.

"I'm warming the Baroness to the idea of negotiating with you," I said, "but she decided we're leaving for Spectra tomorrow. After we get back, I plan to fly out and retrieve my computer expert friend."

Thordia paused her rummaging, glancing my way.

"I hate to do it, but I'll have to relocate all of you then." I gestured through the galley.

"I'll arrange it with the soldiers. Most of them don't know who I am. I'm keeping it that way for now." Thordia retrieved a dermal injector, administering the medicine into her non-robotic arm.

"Most?" I found one of the khamsas I was looking for, and slipped it under my tunic.

"The captain knows. His lieutenant might also."

I retrieved my jack of plate, draping it over my arm, then returned to where Thordia sat with her face buried in a data carrier. Several more such devices peeked out from her satchel, most likely the ones she'd reclaimed from me among others. I couldn't get upset; they'd been hers to begin with. I would've also returned the data carrier in my belt-pouch, but it harbored the coordinates for Gules. Besides, with recent events still fresh in my mind, I never wanted to be without a carrier in either Naustvik's presence.

It was that bit of paranoia that prompted me to ask, "What are you doing?"

"Talking to Verahl," Thordia replied, unfazed. "I've been keeping in touch with him since our arrival."

Fair or not, her answer sent a chill down my spine. "There's an active communications node around here somewhere. Probably in the Harbinger, isn't it?"

"I assume so," Thordia said. "I haven't seen it myself."

"There don't seem to be any others nearby. I mean, within this planetary system." I was half-guessing, half-fishing. For me to message Drea, active nodes would have to exist all the way out to Gules. From my earlier attempt, I'd assumed this wasn't the case. But what if they *had* survived, and I just didn't know how to contact them?

"Not that I've found. Nidaros has been isolated a long time." Thordia's real and false eyes had rolled up my way. She was probably wondering why all this mattered to me. After all, she had all her data carriers back — except for one.

"They need me at the barracks." I made my way to the airlock, suppressing the urge to leap over the soldiers in my path.

CHAPTER 28

I slammed home my ship's stubborn hatch, leaving Thordia with the wounded soldiers.

Behave yourself, little cuss, I thought.

Then I turned with my jack of plate clutched against my side. The last of the day's sun fell on the barracks only a few yards away, a sight both heartening and nerve-racking. I longed to see Ingvar again and talk to Rigg about Dag's future, assuming Rigg had survived the invasion.

Within the barracks, cheery fires burned in both hearths. Aside from cracking firewood, it was quiet. Casualties no longer covered the floor, but a few injured soldiers occupied their bunks.

"Lady Knight!" Ebbe dropped a hand of playing cards to approach me with a grin.

In his wake echoed similar greetings. Also grinning, I tried to return them all around Ebbe's rib-cracking hug.

"How's the leg?" I asked.

"Had worse," he dismissed, pulling away.

"Did Adept Holsten really open the heavens and hurl lightning at you?" another soldier asked.

"He did," Ebbe answered. "And she still got up and crushed him!"

"Your captain helped. Same with Dag," I said.

"Aye, the little Nyvind had all the luck this time!" Ebbe glanced over his shoulder.

I followed his gaze and spotted Dag on a bunk several rows away, sitting up straight with eyes fastened on me. He was barefoot; his ichor-stained boots rested on the floor. His clothes seemed in good shape otherwise. No adept robes in sight.

It was a relief to see him again. Apparently, the feeling was mutual. He darted over to join us, one of his rare smiles beaming full-force. "Ye made it! I wasn't so sure ye would."

I wanted to give Dag a hug or some other friendly physical gesture, but he stopped short of offering one himself. Instead, I steeled myself for a question that wasn't easily asked. "How about Rigg, is he all right?"

"Aye, fine," Dag said, his good mood no less diminished. "Out with the others."

"Everyone should be back soon," Ebbe said.

"Can we talk? Alone?" Dag asked me.

The request surprised me, but I smiled and tried not to let on. "Sure."

"*Still* has all the luck," someone muttered behind me.

Dag turned toward the nearest hearth, weaving a careful path through clothes lying out to dry. Dozens of hasty new offerings — mostly dried grasses woven into knots and other patterns — lay with them.

I draped my jack of plate along the bench before the fire, then sat astride to face Dag. He faced me and tucked in his legs to sit cross-legged. The flames highlighted his many bruises and scars, making his serious young face look older.

All my earlier doubt melted away, leaving only the resolve to squire him right there. The question was on my tongue, itching to jump off so he could accompany me to Spectra. Traveling in a Baroness' retinue to a Lord's court was a once-in-a-lifetime opportunity, after all. Dag could ease into the concept of interplanetary travel before being forced to get used to my less luxurious ship and coarser social circles.

But I hadn't found Rigg yet. Besides, pulling off an appearance in a Lord's court was an awful lot to ask of a brand-new, ill-equipped squire and his mistress. The slightest lapse in etiquette could land us both in trouble. So, I deferred. Dag had already seen a much grander city within the Harbinger, after all, and I also didn't know what path he preferred for himself. Since he'd requested my attention, I kept quiet, allowing him to lead off.

Dag looked me in the eye with determination. "I want to squire for you."

His words sent me reeling backward with laughter—at the timing, at his nerve, and at words that would've panicked me a week earlier. Upon recovering, I leaned closer to him with a smile. "You're supposed to wait until I ask *you*."

"Well?" he asked.

"I should talk to your brother first. It's the honorable thing," I explained. "And trust me, you'll want to wait until after I get back from Spectra. It'll be boring as hell."

Dag's eyes went wide. "Ye're leaving?"

"Tomorrow. I need to escort Lady Amelia and close out my quest. My ship's staying here, though." He might've been worried about Flekka, the little construct he'd found in the Harbinger. She still resided in a closet aboard *Kepler's Law* as far as I knew.

Dag nodded, picking at his sleeve with his disfigured hand.

I wondered if his worry extended further. "I'll only be gone for a day or so." And if I had the opportunity to spend cred anywhere, maybe I'd return with equipment for him. My heart pounded with excitement. So far, this was easier—and more gratifying—than I'd ever imagined.

"So, what've you been up to lately?" I asked.

"Throwing in with the soldiers out in the districts," Dag said. "They're warning people of the ichor, and how to avoid making more of it."

"Oh, good." Ingvar had mentioned doing that. Wonderful that he'd already jumped on it.

"Also took some of Thordia's food out there," Dag continued.

With the cloister devastated, the soldiers must've assumed food distribution duties. "What'd you tell them when they asked where it came from?"

"No one asked," Dag replied. "They were more worried about what happened in the capital. We told them the guild invaded and tried to unseat our Baron."

With no mention of the pro-Gyllenfeld elements involved, I imagined. A wise decision. "I'm sure everyone's looking forward to harvest in a few more days."

"If there is one," Dag said.

A valid concern, one that'd also likely deflected attention away from the source of Thordia's bounty. "When I get to Spectra, I'll do my best to make sure Madam Castor keeps her end of the deal."

And if I were able to confront her, I'd bring up Gules, too. Maybe this trip to Spectra wouldn't be so boring after all.

"Lady Knight!"

Soldiers had filtered into the barracks from outside—among them, Fasolt and Logmadr. The pair threw off their gloves and boots at the door, then ran toward me and Dag at the hearth.

Grinning, I left my jack behind and darted up to meet them halfway.

Logmadr wrapped his arms around my neck with no intention of letting go. "We worried Adept Holsten had you trapped under a sleeping spell!"

"*Ye* worried, fool. I knew she'd be fine." Fasolt halted behind his friend, nodding my way with a smile.

More happy shouts rang out behind us. Additional soldiers piled in from outside, discarding sooty and muddy cleanup gear.

"I was tired," I reassured Logmadr, hugging back. "It's been a rough few days."

"That veiled creature came through here a few times with her healing magic." Logmadr pulled away with trepidation. "Some of the boys think it's Thordia Naustvik. Is it really?"

"Can't be!" a soldier behind him chided. "Thordia's only got one arm!"

"So a valkyrie, maybe?" another soldier theorized, walking past us.

"A norn, I think," Fasolt said. "We didn't give her many dead to lead away, though. Wonder how she'll feel about that?"

These must've been figures from Gyllenfeld's abandoned dogma. The speculation continued with ever more fanciful examples, but fell out of my awareness as I focused on the entrance, searching.

Ingvar stood in the thick of the group. There was no joy to be had from the task they'd been toiling at, and would likely be toiling at for days yet. Nevertheless, the dashing captain bantered with the young men around him in a relaxed, upbeat manner. His left forearm, though still bandaged, seemed to be back in use. Maybe Thordia had also treated him.

My heart traveled up my throat. Jumpiness seized me. For a moment, it felt like those times when Branigan would arrive at the beguinage on a whim. I'd lose all sense of my surroundings and forget to breathe, then run off and wait through minutes, even hours, of grueling solitude until he found and greeted me. I'd always feared intruding on his business, believing I wasn't important enough.

It wasn't a mistake I'd repeat.

"Excuse me, friends." I slipped past Logmadr and Fasolt, smoothing out my tunic and hair as I converged on the entrance.

More happy greetings flew my way. I did my best to answer, but my mind had floated off elsewhere, feverishly entertaining possibilities that hadn't been possibilities a few days earlier.

Alerted by the commotion, Ingvar turned. Then his eyes fastened on me, and lit up in response.

My heart leapt a foot out of my ribcage, but I forced myself to cross the remaining distance at the same measured pace. There was a level of decorum to maintain around his men, after all.

"Good to see you again, Captain." I offered my hand.

Ingvar smiled, returning a firm shake, and strained to be heard over the din. "They finally tossed you out of the estate, then. How're ye feeling?"

"Better than I have any right to," I replied. "You?"

"Fine. The woman ye brought back from the Harbinger's been a great help to us." Ingvar was sincere about it, but his expression also contained a hint of nervousness. "Hope ye'll stay this evening. We're remembering our fallen."

I nodded. "That's what I'm here for."

He tilted his head over his shoulder. "Follow me. I have something for you."

"Me?" I blurted, surprised.

Ingvar glanced aside with amusement. "Mind if I borrow your knight, lad?"

Dag stood beside me. Hell, I hadn't even noticed him there. He didn't seem put out by my inattention, and simply nodded to Ingvar.

From there, the captain guided me past the happy assemblage to his sparse office. Fading sunlight streamed in through the window, just enough to make candles unnecessary. The din quieted behind us once he closed the door. Then he wrapped me up in his arms and kissed me eagerly.

Overjoyed, I returned the gesture, giddy beyond thought.

Eventually, Ingvar parted to speak, but continued to hold me close. "That wasn't what I wanted to give you."

I tensed against him. "It wasn't?"

"Nay. Nay, I mean, it *was*," he quickly reassured me with a laugh, "but I'd been speaking of something else. Hold on."

Ingvar pulled away to round his desk and crouch behind it. A moment later, he stood with Branigan's longsword and scabbard in hand, polished like new.

I gasped. The fight with Commander Savidge came back to me then, along with all the grief I'd carried since Gules.

Once Ingvar brought the weapon before me, I lifted it with trembling hands. It was no replacement for Branigan, but there was some comfort in knowing it'd no longer serve Savidge. I had to return it to the beguinage, then find out who'd killed Branigan for heresy. Whoever it was no longer deserved to be upright and breathing.

Forcing back tears, I ran my thumb over the tesseract—a cube within cubes—engraved on the pommel. "This means a lot to me. Thank you."

"We can speak of him tonight if ye want. Have any stories to tell of him?" Ingvar laughed again, glancing downward. "Look who I'm asking."

I smiled, intending to decline at first. After some thought, I reconsidered. "Maybe. I haven't really had a chance to mourn yet."

Ingvar rubbed at the back of his neck. "Well, tonight's more about laughing than mourning. If that doesn't suit you, ye don't have to join in."

A not-sad memorial? One didn't see many of those around the galaxy. "We'll see." While we were still alone, I had more serious things to say. "For everyone you lost ... I'm sorry."

He hesitated. "As sorry as I am that we didn't travel to the Harbinger together, I'm glad I was here. Not that I did much."

"You didn't have to. You've trained your men well," I said.

Ingvar met my gaze with relief. "Thanks, Jayce."

"I wish you hadn't gotten hurt!" The tears resurfaced against my will. I batted one away with a hand.

"Well, I look forward to Naustvik's apology, right after Ormyr's," Ingvar brushed off with sarcasm. But then he braced my shoulders and arrested my gaze with a pleading look. "Still don't know how Ormyr learned of our intentions. I swear, Jayce, I didn't tip him off."

"I never believed you did," I assured him. "Ormyr could see everything we were doing through those eye-shaped amulets he gave us. They were Shipbuilder artifacts."

"*Skíta!*" Ingvar's expression turned pained. His fingers dug into my shoulders. "Dag told me what happened after. I could kill Ormyr for what he put you both through!"

As much as I tried to keep my emotions in check, my voice quavered. "There were bad parts, but then there were times when we all really helped each other. It surprised the hell out of me, too. When you get Ormyr away from court, he's not so bad." I shifted Branigan's longsword to my right hand, resting the point on the ground, then reached up with my left to cup the side of his face. "We're all still here, right? That's what matters."

Ingvar's expression remained sullen. I longed to cheer him —and I could.

"I'll be staying a while." My heart raced. "I'm not taking any more quests until Nidaros is out of danger. I think we might have a chance to strike up a proper courtship—and I really do want to, Ingvar. I love you."

Ingvar's eyes went wide. He faltered.

An embarrassed flush burned my face. Had I really just blurted it out like that? As silence stretched between us, my panic and shame ratcheted higher. Was this too early? Did he think I was crazy? Should I walk it back?

Oh, to hell with it. What was "too early" when either of us could die on any given day? I'd lost my chance with Branigan, and had nearly lost it with Ingvar. And it wasn't like I didn't mean it.

But he still hadn't said anything. What if he didn't …? Hell—

"I love you, too, Jayce." Ingvar's surprise had transitioned to calm certainty. From there, he pulled me into another kiss.

My elation, and relief, were overwhelming. We stayed close a while, gaining strength from each other, and it felt amazing. *Right.* I'd never expected to find such a kindred spirit, and now that I had, I never wanted to part from him again.

Sadly, reality didn't care about my preferences. I was forced to break the silence eventually. "I have some urgent things to take care of before I can settle in here. Would you wait for me while I get them sorted out?"

He pulled away to look me in the eye. "Drea?"

"Yes. And I'll have to go back to my mentors' beguinage at some point," I said. "That's where Branigan's sword should rest. I'm sure they'll also want to send someone to help with the Harbinger."

While in Spectra, I'd also sent them a note about the trouble Drea and I had run into. Whatever happened next, I had to inform them before they dispatched anyone to chase after us.

"I'll ask to accompany you to Gules. Ye shouldn't be alone then. Sorry this Spectra nonsense got in the way first." Annoyance flared in Ingvar's expression, not directed at me. "From now on, whatever ye need of me, ye have."

He couldn't make a promise like that with the demands of his position, but practicality was the last thing on my mind. "I'm … really glad," I managed, an understatement. "Just be patient with me. I don't have much experience with formal courtship." My former master May had been a tornado, not a suitor.

Ingvar laughed. "I'm no expert, either. Let's just enjoy our time together, aye?"

Candles and lanterns lit the barracks proper, revealing a congregation by the hearth. As Ingvar and I pushed into the crowd, soldiers offered hugs, handshakes, and well wishes. Ale cups, too. I hugged Branigan's sword close and did my best to return the flurry of greetings one-handed.

Pontus plowed through the gathering to crush me in a bear-hug. "'Twas an honor fighting with you. Good to see you here."

He'd dropped his resentment toward me, or had at least put it aside for the evening. Either way, I welcomed his friendliness. "Likewise," I replied, hugging back.

Magnus exchanged a similar hug with me. Dag resurfaced to stick to my side. I didn't see Rigg anywhere, but resolved to find him before the night ended.

After losing me in the commotion, Ingvar gently took me by the arm and pressed on until we reached a bench a comfortable distance from the hearth. He invited me to sit, but remained standing himself. Dag dropped by my left side. I rested Branigan's longsword at my feet.

"Quiet!" Pontus bellowed.

The soldiers scrambled to seats on benches and the floor in a semicircle around the hearth. Dag and I were front and center, with Ingvar close beside us. A hand shot out toward the captain, bearing ale. He took the cup, then stepped into the center of the formation. The battered shields on the hearth flanked him to either side.

Ingvar waited until he had the soldiers' attention, glancing over the crowd with a pained look. "Had a few days to think … still hard to know what to say. We just learned again how much we stand to lose from dividing ourselves. Catherwood or Gyllenfeld or whatever else—enough of that. We're *Nidaran*." He threw back his ale in one go, and let the empty cup hang at his side.

Affirming shouts went up, and others drank along with him. It was an admirable sentiment, potentially a dangerous one, but he'd expressed it as carefully as possible.

"We're a family despite our differences," Ingvar continued. "With the cloister disabled, Nidaros needeth us more than ever. We'll teach the rest of the barony what we already know about comradeship. These past few days, ye've done me proud. Hard to find words to tell you just *how* proud. I know this is only the beginning."

Shouts rang out again. I basked in pride.

"However ye choose to grieve is up to you, as long as ye respect your brothers in the process," Ingvar continued. "Tonight, together, we celebrate the lads we were lucky enough to know. Ulfarr Mord, Sefi Lindberg …"

And so on. A short list, thank goodness, but pangs of unpleasant surprise shot through me upon recognizing some of the names. I glanced to Dag, who'd listened with eyes focused downward the whole time. Had he known any of the deceased? I couldn't tell.

Ingvar took a seat to my right, looking relieved. Someone snagged his empty cup away; in the same instant, another hand stuck out between us and offered a full one. Ingvar tilted his head, gesturing for me to take it.

I accepted with one hand. My other hand slipped stealthily into Ingvar's, giving it a squeeze. He squeezed back with a brief, heart-melting smile my way.

"All right!" Pontus stood and boomed out over the din. "Which of you would testify for Ulfarr?"

"I will!" One of the soldiers toward the back jumped to his feet, waiting for quiet. "So, our mate Ulfarr was as sharp as they come, aye? But sometimes he was also a bit gullible. One day, we're serving watch on the wall, and we all spy this chicken—"

Every soldier present erupted into raucous, stress-clearing laughter. Even Ingvar wasn't immune, though he directed his head toward the floor.

"We all know how that one ends!" Pontus shouted. "Can we at least *pretend* to be gentlemen afore our distinguished visitor this evening? Who else?"

And so it went with tale-telling. Some were bittersweet, others had everyone howling—except for Dag, whom I was beginning to think never laughed. He looked content enough by his own standards, at least: eyes bright, smiling, no fidgeting. No one offered him ale, and he didn't attempt to take any. I wasn't sure whether to let him have any—not that I was his mistress yet, but I had to get used to thinking in those terms.

Pontus led the event, establishing order between one speaker and the next. Ingvar was still very much present, though, offering his own sincere remembrances after others had spoken their minds. Many eyes passed over him and me and our entwined hands. For the most part, I remained tipsy with happiness, ale, camaraderie—some combination thereof.

Then Ingvar leaned in to whisper to me. "Branigan?"

Did I want to speak about him? All through the evening, I'd been wondering the same. These people had done everything possible to make me feel welcome. Warmth toward an outsider wasn't something one found easily in the galaxy. I'd staked my future here, and gladly so, but there was pain in my recent past that I had to let go of before I could move forward here. With the soldiers, I felt safe enough to tell the truth and show my emotional cards without fear of losing face or landing in trouble.

I nodded to Ingvar.

"One more, lads," Ingvar spoke up.

Despite the amount of ale at work on the crowd by then, the soldiers' curious confusion brought them to a quick silence. The confusion only amplified as I stood to face them with Branigan's longsword, resting the point on the ground and bracing the pommel against my sternum.

As the fire warmed my back, I raised my voice. "I lost an old friend of mine recently, and your Captain's been kind enough to let me speak of him here. Sir Branigan Cade of Lirriven, the noblest knight errant I ever knew. I don't know who killed him, but I intend to find out. I owe it to him."

I needed a moment to duck under a wave of tears and gather myself before proceeding. "My former master, Sir Mayweather Stark, told me this story. That means there's almost certainly a lie in it somewhere, but you never know quite where."

Damn May. I didn't just want to let go of the grief he'd given me, I wanted to torch his memory out of existence. After a decade of trying, it seemed impossible. Fortunately, I'd picked up a lot of good from Branigan to balance things out.

I pulled in a deep breath. "May and Branigan were friends a long way back. Sometimes they traveled together, picking up quests if they found any, or just seeing what the galaxy had to offer. One time, while visiting Lord de Fontaine's space, they dropped by Calais. It's a huge city full of tall buildings and busy people, and in every square and street corner are buskers — people who play music or recite poetry, hoping passersby will give them money," I tacked on, realizing they'd probably never seen buskers before.

"Among the performers May and Branigan encountered were three troubadours who, according to my master, were complete garbage. Their verses contained every cliche your grandfathers yawned at, and they couldn't carry a tune with a bucket and a team of mules. Most of the city folk just walked past and ignored them, and May should've done the same, but he couldn't help himself. He started heckling them to their faces. 'Say, friends: when you get near a song, play it!'

"Well, it turned out these weren't troubadours at all. They were disguised de Fontaine *crusaders*: knights attached to a cloister who perform quests for the adepts in that cloister. They're constantly on the lookout for behavior contrary to their native dogma, and when they find it, they punish it. Hard. Those crusaders were probably hoping for someone to happen past and break a rule—or come right up to their faces, like an idiot, and drop scathing insults. May suddenly found himself staring down three swords and charges of heresy.

"Branigan hadn't realized May's intentions, and had no way of stopping him." Hell, had I ever been in that position a million times as May's squire. "He was far enough removed from the scene that he could've just run for it, but he'd never leave any-one to suffer."

Which was probably how he'd gotten in trouble in Gules. I dodged another wave of sorrow.

"He charged right up and got between May and the cru-saders. 'Friends, there's no problem here! My fellow knight errant employed mere words against you, weak-minded ones at that. Does that make him a fool? Yes. A heretic? No.'

"I don't know how well Branigan's pleading moved them, but the odds narrowing from three against one to three against two? That probably moved the crusaders more. They relented, and told May to get out of their faces."

I couldn't help smiling in anticipation of what was com-ing. "It seemed disaster was averted—but sometimes, Branigan was too honest for his own good, and that was one of those times. His mouth kept running. 'However, his disgust isn't en-tirely without merit. If you swapped out that dreadful minor chord for a major one ...'" I shook my head. "So, the fight was back on."

Laughter claimed the barracks. I paused and waited for it to die down.

"Neither May nor Branigan were pushovers in that regard. They dropped two of the crusaders and sent the third running. Then they ran, too, all the way back to Branigan's ship.

"They were certain they'd have trouble traveling through de Fontaine space after that, but they never did. The crusaders must not have gotten a good look at their sigils, or didn't know how to describe them. That's when adopting a complicated sigil is to your advantage. A lot of times, people don't ever catch names. All they can do is tell guards and port officials something like, 'If you see a knight errant with a sun sigil, arrest him!'

"This was Branigan's sigil. See here?" I held the sword and scabbard aloft to all sides of the audience, pointing. "That's called a tesseract. How would you even start to describe that?"

There was some head-shaking and chuckling from those who had the best vantage of the four-dimensional object.

"On Branigan's advice, May adopted an even more abstract sigil. Then May had me do the same." May had selected the Shipbuilder symbol for a transistor, an electronic component. I'd followed the same theme—it'd seemed fitting—and chosen the variable resistor.

"So you see, Branigan was too smart to ever worry about catching trouble. He was more afraid of not doing all he could for others. There are plenty of selfish, no-good charlatan knights errant out there. Branigan was one of the few who lived up to the tales you hear. I'm sure he went down helping people, unflinchingly at that."

He wouldn't have wanted anything different. And he wouldn't want me feeling guilty about anything—even things left unsaid.

Relief washed over me. A mental burden had lifted, for the moment at least. Grief could strike again at any time or place, but it wouldn't have quite the same sting. I sat back down with Ingvar and Dag.

"Sir Branigan!" someone shouted.

"Sir Branigan!" a number of others seconded.

There were cheers, drinks, a flurry of pats on the back. Ingvar pulled me into a hug, which I gladly returned.

"One hour 'til lights out!" Pontus shouted.

A good thing it was delayed, as no one was about to fall asleep anytime soon. The party broke up into smaller groups, commiserating with more ale, laughter, and sweeping gestures.

I got separated from Ingvar and Dag when Pontus pulled me aside. "Condolences, Lady Knight. I'd been wondering what all that was about when we faced Commander Savidge."

"Thanks," I said.

Pontus leaned into my ear to whisper bitterly. "Be careful in Spectra, and watch over our captain. He's never afore stepped in that viper's nest. Don't know why he has to now."

Strange ... I didn't know, either. Nevertheless, I gave Pontus a reassuring nod.

As we parted ways, there stood Rigg: arms folded, frowning. "Dag said ye wanted to talk to me."

A quick glance around showed Dag to be nowhere in sight. I beckoned Rigg to follow me away from the hearth, where we could speak in relative privacy. As I laid out my intentions, they became increasingly real and daunting. My heart pounded with trepidation at the task I was taking on for as many years as necessary.

"I'll provide for him and educate him as long as he's in my service. I can't exactly call what I do 'safe,' but he'll be safe *with me*, I promise you that much. Are you all right with that?" I was taking away the only family member he had a good relationship with, the one he'd looked after until recently.

"Aye. *Skíta*, I'm envious, even." Rigg waved a hand dismissively, his expression as difficult to read as ever. "It'll be good for him, though."

"Is there anything I should know? Anything you want to ask?"

"Just keep it quiet," Rigg said. "Wouldn't want our folks to find out afore ye can leave the planet."

I blinked. "Well, actually … barring a few trips, we'll be staying in Nidaros for a while."

Worry seeped into Rigg's eyes. "Then don't ever send him to the Low North alone, all right? He knows enough hiding places, but still."

"I won't." Worry edged in. Should I keep probing the matter? Maybe not now. If the possibility ever came up, we could address it then. "If you ever think of anything else, come find me, all right?"

"Sure." Rigg parted to rejoin the crowd.

Ingvar insisted on walking me back to the estate. The night-time chill made me miss my coat, but while I remained glowingly light-headed, I didn't feel its absence as much as I might've.

Carrying a lantern in his right hand, Ingvar closed up the barracks behind us, then turned and offered me his left arm.

I stood there, puzzled.

"I'm not throwing an elbow, Goose," he reassured me with amusement. "Trying to be a gentleman."

With a self-deprecating laugh, I looped my right arm through his.

Ingvar smiled and set off at a confident stride. It made me ridiculously happy to walk with him again after all the uncertainty I'd lived through. Hugging Branigan's sword and my jack of plate against my side, I glanced up at a starry sky that was destined to become more familiar than I'd ever imagined.

"What was that just now with Rigg?" Ingvar asked.

It took me a while to descend from the clouds enough to answer. "I'm squiring Dag."

Ingvar's eyes widened. "Aye? I'd have grabbed him up if ye hadn't."

"That's good to hear. He might need that fallback option," I said. "I've never done this before, and I didn't have the best example to learn from, but Dag needs help. People know he's a 'magic wielder' now. I'm sure as hell not giving him up to anyone else."

Sigrid might try to lure him into her coven. Ormyr sought to repopulate his cloister. And the Naustviks couldn't agree on whether to keep Dag in the dark or grant him power without knowledge.

Ingvar stared forward, thoughtful. "Never pried into Rigg's business. Knew he was taking care of his brother, guessed much of the rest. Rigg had trouble early on acquiring discipline and trusting others. Still unsure of himself at times, but he's one of the family now otherwise. If Dag's anything like him, and he seemeth that way, have patience. Explain the wherefore of every order. If something frustrateth him, let him vent, show him ye understand, then get him back to trying. It'll take time, but ye can help him build confidence."

I nodded. "That helps."

"Ye'll be fine. Dag hath respect for you already." Ingvar's gaze lowered. "Still have trouble believing what he told me about the Harbinger. Ye may have to tell me again."

"We'll have plenty of time tomorrow during the flight to Spectra," I said. "How *did* you get roped into that? Not that I'm complaining, I'm just curious."

"Our Baron's insistence," Ingvar said. "His Grace can't go himself and is worried for Lady Amelia. I'm to shadow her, keep an eye out for trouble." He glanced to me with a concerned look. "I have a feeling ye'll need me more. I'll let you know if anything seemeth out of sorts. In turn, ye might help me avoid the sort of mistakes that'll get us all beheaded."

I smiled. "I'm not worried about that. I'm glad you'll be there. How're you feeling about the trip?"

Ingvar laughed. "Nervous as anything. Trying to remind myself ye do it all the time."

"It's fine to be nervous," I said, eager to reassure him. "When you think about it, it *is* completely terrifying: leaving a nice comfortable planet to shoot through a void with no gravity, or air, or *anything* for millions of miles in every direction—"

"Not helping, Goose."

"I'm not done yet!" I insisted around laughter. "It's scary, but there are ways to get past that. When I squired for May, he'd load me up with so many chores around his ship, I never had time to be afraid. At the beguinage, Drea taught me about turning fear into respect—learning the physics and history of space travel, understanding how amazing it all is. And Branigan, he *owned* being alone, out in the middle of nothing. Sometimes he'd think about what good things lay ahead of him, but mostly, he'd just clear his mind and enjoy the quiet."

I choked up, having trouble with the last few words. It didn't help that walking to the estate forced us past the battlefield again. Darkness concealed it, and we swung a wide arc around it, but still.

"Keep focusing on what Branigan taught you, aye?" Ingvar said soothingly. "That much is yours. It'll always stay with you."

I nodded. Drea had encouraged me in a similar way after May's abandonment: ensuring me his hurtful behavior didn't diminish the good things he'd done and taught me. It was a lesson that hadn't quite sunk in yet, as May still got under my

skin on a regular basis. But Branigan's example offset all that
—and I'd make sure it lived on in Dag's training.

By the time we reached the estate and ascended the stairs
to my room, I felt better. Outside my door, Ingvar set his lantern
on the ground, then faced me. "I'll return at sunrise tomorrow."

"You don't have to. It's out of your way to swing here, then
the port," I said.

"'Tis worth it. Now stop dodging my romantic gestures,"
he chided with a smile.

I laughed and grasped his hands while my heart pounded
at an irresponsible speed. "What I mean is, it's easier for you
to just stay here."

Ingvar's eyes widened.

"I mean, if you want. If it's all right," I gunned out. "Every
place has different rules about timing and the order in which
things happen, and I'm willing to respect that. But from my perspective, I never know my next minute, so it doesn't make sense
to—"

He cupped my face in his hands and silenced me with a kiss.
I kissed back, going weak-kneed and lightheaded in the process.

"We can make our own rules," he proposed quietly.

"I'm fine with that." I showed him inside, dragged his
lantern in after, then shoved a side table against the door to bar-
ricade it.

CHAPTER 29

Everything felt new and deliriously thrilling that evening. I dreaded the morning, the return to duty and obligation, and was desperate to appreciate each minute alone with Ingvar. I hoped this would be just the beginning of our time together, but I knew not to take anything for granted.

It was hard to fall asleep while so emotionally charged. Somehow, I'd managed it. I woke up when Ingvar gently moved to free himself from my embrace and rise from my pallet. A bleary-eyed glance toward the window confirmed that sunrise had arrived.

"Don't leave," I blurted, still half-asleep.

He laughed a little, running a hand through my hair. "I don't want to, but there are things to tend to afore we fly. Meet me down in the foyer when ye're ready."

I reeled him into a final kiss, then collapsed on the pallet again, not quite ready to face the galaxy yet.

Sometime after Ingvar had dressed and left my room, Sigrid arrived to shoo my dozing carcass out of bed. I shouldn't have stayed there so long, but the soreness and fatigue from my Harbinger trip still lingered to some degree.

As more of my brain woke up, all the exhilarating emotions of the night before returned. A sense of wonder and excitement settled over everything. While dressing and equipping, I could barely keep the familiar steps straight in my head; it was a good thing Sigrid was there to supervise. She almost certainly understood the source of my odd behavior, but was kind enough not to say anything about it.

Wearing my jack of plate, khamsa amulet, and weapons, I looked almost as I had during my first court appearance, with some differences. First, Sigrid had insisted on sweeping my hair up as nicely as Lady Amelia's. Second, I carried two swords: my own over my shoulder, and Branigan's longsword at my hip, hanging from my belt by a frog. I had to keep a hand on the hilt to prevent the blade from dragging on the ground.

"A witch in Milord's court! I wish I could see it!" Sigrid shook her head in awe. "Good luck, sister."

"Stay safe," I replied.

On my way to the foyer, I struggled to sober up long enough to remember my purpose in Spectra and anticipate what hazards might lie between us and Lord Catherwood's throne room. However, the negatives seemed distant and unlikely, while the positives shined brightly. I'd get to close out my quest, possibly earn closure for Branigan and deliver comeuppance to Madam Castor—all while spending hours in Ingvar's company.

Speaking of Ingvar, my heart leapt upon finding him in the cavernous estate foyer. He wore the same doublet and trousers he'd worn the day of my arrival, with his longsword at his hip. But his eyes flitted about nervously, as though he never expected to see these confines again.

Anxiety overshadowed my optimism. I hurried over, stopping a respectful distance away so as not to breach any etiquette rules. "Is everything all right?" I asked under my breath, not wanting our conversation to echo.

Ingvar waved his hand in dismissal. "Reality hitting me, I suppose."

He was probably nervous about the flight and his first appearance before Lord Catherwood. As if that weren't enough, his only previous travel away from Nidaros had involved pointless war, the deaths of friends and family. No doubt those memories plagued him.

My heart ached in response. I couldn't offer any physical reassurance there, but made an attempt with words. "If your Baron's ship flies half as nice as she looks, this'll be an easy trip. We'll have time to talk about what we missed the past few days — and about anything that's bothering you."

He nodded distractedly, then gestured me ahead of himself.

We stepped into the cool morning air and walked toward the port. Ingvar threw nervous glances over the ship- and pyre-strewn landscape, seizing his longsword's grip in his fist. We'd walked past it all before, but in darkness, it'd been easier not to think about.

"Everything's changed, Jayce," Ingvar blurted. "Everything."

I glanced his way, concerned. "Hopefully not all for worse?"

"Not all, nay." He managed a weak smile in my direction, but there was something big on his mind that he wasn't talking about, something beyond this trip and his past. Something too difficult to talk about, apparently.

My worry surged back. I looked away before it showed on my face, hoping I could get him alone, and soon, to resolve this mystery.

We passed the barracks and *Kepler's Law*, approaching the wall. The soldiers stationed at the gate sent us off with enthusiastic well wishes.

"Sock Madam Castor in the face for us!" one of them called.

"We'll see what we can do!" I returned, forcing a smile.

Ingvar waved to them, his troubles momentarily vanishing behind a grin. "Be well, lads! Don't give Pontus a hard time!"

His second-in-command was back at the estate, effectively in charge of Nidaros until we returned—though any instructions Baron Tristan issued during his convalescence were valid, as I'd learned in Sigrid's case.

At the port, we approached the Baron's ship without any fear of an arrow to the back. The hatch stood open. Ingvar beckoned me aboard first with a tilt of his head.

The Baron's ship had no airlock. I stepped directly into a parlor loud with Catherwood glory: rugs, overstuffed chairs, carved tables and scroll-shelves, with not one bolt pinning anything down. No safety harnesses, either. The air held lingering traces of incense, which probably did a number on the filtration system. On a couch in front of me sat Lady Amelia, working embroidery on a hoop. The familiar posy of dried flowers rested on a glass side table at her elbow.

This was all *too* nice. Jitters seized me—not from flying, but from finding myself light-years out of my league. I dropped to one knee; Ingvar followed suit beside me.

"Arise," the Baroness said. "Adept Gunnhilda, we're ready to depart."

Obediently, Gunnhilda emerged from the curtained cockpit to close the hatch.

Even as Ingvar and I exchanged friendly looks with her, it surprised me to see her instead of Ormyr. Such an important trip, and Lady Amelia was making her master adept stay home? Well, I'd seen firsthand how much she disliked him.

Gunnhilda returned to the cockpit to launch into a spell. "Open now thine ears, O vessel!"

Lady Amelia put aside her embroidery and stood, beckoning me and Ingvar to follow her aft.

We both hesitated before complying. Ingvar managed a neutral expression, but kept his fist clenched around his long-sword's grip. I did the same with Branigan's out of necessity.

"It shall be many hours ere we reach Spectra." Lady Amelia drifted toward the burgundy and gold damask covering the parlor's aft wall, pulling back one side to reveal a door. There she waited for one of us to open it.

I volunteered — then stifled a gasp. Beyond lay another room nearly the size of the parlor. A carved table and chairs sat beside a wide window. Two small beds rested against the far wall. Everywhere lay objects that rattled my nerves to see aboard a ship: an ewer of water, an ashtray, a platter of sliced fruit, decorative statuettes.

"Make yourselves comfortable," the Baroness invited.

Comfortable amid such careless wealth? Not likely. I sure hoped we didn't lose gravity at any point, because no one needed that brassy ewer upside the head.

I shook off the thought. This was another chance to enjoy Ingvar's company, and that was all that mattered. "This is most generous, madam. Thank you."

"Baron Tristan sent me for Milady's protection," Ingvar piped up. "Tell me if there's anything I can do."

Lady Amelia nodded. "Caution is reasonable, but I share not my husband's fears. We are quite safe in Milord's palace."

Ingvar looked far from assuaged. The Baroness waved us into the room, then closed the door behind us.

Once we were alone, my first goal was putting Ingvar at ease. "Here, let's gear down and have a seat." I gestured toward the table beside the window.

"Not sure I want to see us leaving," Ingvar muttered.

"You do," I said.

After stowing our swords in a chest nearby, we approached the table. Ingvar was only too happy to cede the window seat to me. I had a view of the port to my left, Ingvar on my right, staring down at the arms he'd folded upon the table. He looked one jolt of turbulence shy of burying his head into his arms.

He'd been fine in my ship's cockpit the other day — at least until Verahl had started throwing us around. With sympathy, I leaned closer and draped my arm over his tense shoulders. "This takeoff will probably be much smoother than what my rig can manage."

Moments later, the ship's thrusters surged to life. Out the window, the port began to fall away from us, but I didn't feel a thing.

"Here, look — we're airborne!" I said.

Ingvar chanced a glance toward the window, then blinked in confusion.

"On a ship this nice, you don't feel movement." It was like the lift cars in the Harbinger, which canceled out inertia somehow. No wonder nobles hoarded these gravity-endowed ships. I kept the explanation to myself this time, taking Ingvar's hand in mine before sitting back to watch our ascent into space.

As the ship rose ever higher, Nidaros' districts scattered beneath us. Then an unmistakable purplish blotch appeared, a huge blight on the landscape.

"That's the Harbinger." I pointed, tamping down dread. "It's sitting in a gigantic lake of ichor."

Ingvar darted out of his chair, leaning in for a closer look. "Dag told me as much, but to *see* it!" He trailed off helplessly.

I stood up beside him. The landscape was barren for miles around the Harbinger, a brown scar on the planet's surface that engulfed tiny Nidaros. The scar marked the ichor's spread through the soil. Past that boundary, everything became verdant again.

Then, our scenery erupted in a flash of light that faded to black. Ingvar jumped with a startled cry.

"We've gone to faster-than-light travel," I hurried to explain. "That'll be the last of our view until we reach Spectra." To my pleasant surprise, we remained attached to the floor, the room around us beautifully arrayed. Part of me had expected zero-gee mayhem.

Ingvar took a deep breath, then turned to survey the room as though seeing it for the first time.

I rested a hand on his back. "It seems like there's a lot on your mind. It'd be better to get it out now than spend hours stewing over it."

Ingvar turned back to pull me into an embrace. "There's a lot, but the ichor's foremost now."

"I'm glad you and your men have been out warning the districts," I said, hugging back eagerly.

"Seemed the wise thing," he replied.

"Thordia learned that the ichor came from the Harbinger," I said. "When it crashed, it got loose, and has been spreading ever since."

Ingvar stiffened against me. He had no words, not even a curse.

"We don't know how to stop it, but between me, Thordia, and Drea, we might be able to tease that information out of the Harbinger," I continued. "Thordia will definitely want to help us. Some ichor got into her eye by accident. She needs a cure as badly as Nidaros does."

"*Skíta.*" Ingvar's grip on me tightened. "Feeling more and more like what Dag told me was only a fraction of your suffering. It sure seemeth like Ormyr force-marched you through some kind of horrible underworld."

"The trip there was pretty rough. But once we reached the Harbinger?" I broke away to make eye contact, hoping to show him my enthusiasm. "Some things were showing their age, but that's understandable after centuries. Some were just beautiful, Ingvar. Things that leave you breathless, wondering how they're even possible." I longed to show him someday, and explore to-gether, as part of a larger desire to teach him what I'd been taught.

Ingvar studied my awe with surprise.

"And there's so many Shipbuilder artifacts that we could reclaim for our own use, like that surgical construct Thordia's been putting through its paces," I continued. "Ichor aside, the worst things we found at the Harbinger were Verahl and Thor-dia." I struggled against a surge of disgust. "I'm still not close to forgiving Verahl for what he did to you, but Thordia might be redeemable. I talked her into supplying Nidaros with food and flax while we address the ichor. She just has to formalize an arrangement with the Baron."

"Fine for now, I suppose." Ingvar sobered. "I may not always understand, but I'll do what's in my power to help. Ye give me hope that we might really tame the Harbinger. Ye sur-vived it, ye understand all that Shipbuilder magic—"

"It's not magic," I said.

"Whatever ye call it. Ye see hope where most see doom and ruin." He smiled. "'Twould be nice if we conquered the Harbinger's mysteries, or at least enough of them that no one else need grow up in fear of the thing."

I grinned with out-of-control elation. "That's a really nice goal to have."

There was always something to talk about. First, we were curious about each other's fates during our separation. I learned Ingvar had spent most of the time in the infirmary with a broken arm and other impact-related trauma, despair-ing over my rumored demise. He'd worried whether he was bound for the dungeon next, but hadn't been able to summon the strength to escape—until Holsten's adepts had come for him.

In return, I explained more about the journey to the Harbinger, the struggle to survive long enough to reach the Naustviks and my ship, all the while desperate to save Ingvar from whatever fate he'd met. He could hardly believe a word of it, but Thordia and the surgical construct provided some proof. After witnessing her success, many soldiers had accepted the "veiled creature's" aid, including Ingvar. Dag had made him wise to her identity; Ingvar kept it secret for the time being.

I tried to coax out what else bothered Ingvar, but he deflected my attempts toward lighter matters. There was still so much to learn about each other, after all, and it was an intoxicating discovery process. Telling him about my travels, hearing about his experiences with assembling a family that also happened to be an army—the more we shared, the more there was to fall in love with.

May had always kept me on pins and needles, fearing my own mistakes and his wandering eye. There was nothing like that with Ingvar. We had mutual trust and respect from the outset, a bond between equals. It was a triumph and a joy.

The lulls in conversation were nice, too. We had pleasant ways of filling them.

All too soon, the ship entered her final approach, turbulence-free this time. Streaks of light shot past our window like tiny meteors as we breached the planet's atmosphere. Then came the transition from space to sky, the vast ocean glittering beneath fading daylight.

Ingvar stared outside with his face inches from the window. "That much water in one place! Ye'd never worry about drought again!"

"With some oceans, maybe," I said, "but many of them are loaded with salt—"

"*Salt?*" he repeated.

"Or other things that make them no good for drinking, let alone crops," I finished.

"How'd that happen?" he asked.

"Mostly, it happened the same time the oceans formed," I said. "In some cases, it's pollution. People might dump all sorts of horrible things in the water and contaminate it."

Ingvar frowned in confusion. "Who'd be fool enough to poison their own water supply? Though with that much water, I suppose 'tis easy to think it won't make a difference."

"Denial is a huge problem everywhere," I said. "My friends and I have gone places where we just could not convince anyone. They refused to believe they were making themselves sick. Usually, an adept had them convinced of an angry spirit or something." I tried not to dwell on the worst of those illnesses.

On the horizon, we caught a glimpse of the island-city we were gunning for. Massive crystal towers punctuated the skyline.

"That's Spectra," I said. Beautiful from a distance, but only from a distance. I refrained from saying as much, not wanting to intimidate Ingvar.

Too late. He reared away from the window like he'd seen a ghost.

The skyline slowly consumed our view. Soon, we flew among the city spires. Ingvar remained silent and stunned. For him, this had to be the most alien part of this alien world: buildings everywhere, not an inch of open field. Nidaros' capital could've fit inside the city limits dozens of times over.

I squeezed his hand, marveling at how his baseline reality differed from mine. I'd grown up in Freemont, Lord Turinger's capital. Bustling cities, towns, and ports were the sorts of places I frequented in search of quests. To me, Nidaros was a sleepy little outlier.

We approached Lord Catherwood's palace, the most commanding spire in the skyline, before our descent commenced. I broke away to retrieve our weapons, looking forward to some closure.

Ingvar inspected his garb from head to foot. Whatever he felt, he masked with a serious, in-control demeanor.

We geared up in silence. Just before we left, I leaned in for a quick last kiss, still aware of my failure to fully reassure him. "I'll have your back."

He returned the kiss. "And I'll have yours."

In the parlor, Lady Amelia stood by the hatch with the bearing of a queen, posy dangling from her wrist. Gunnhilda left the cockpit soon after, her smile tinged with anxiety. I couldn't blame her. Lady Amelia's company should prove beneficial, and I was also Lord Catherwood's emissary up to the point he dismissed me. But until we disembarked, we had no idea what kind of reception awaited us.

Once Gunnhilda chanted a blessing over all of us, out we went.

We'd landed in a port adjacent to Lord Catherwood's palace. A flock of pages hurried toward our ship with what looked like barely contained fear.

Lady Amelia stood tall, chin tilted upward. "There are prisoners aboard," she addressed the crowd. "Take them away."

The pages opened the ship's cargo bay, where several mercenaries, bound hand and foot, had spent the entire trip in darkness. The mercs blinked and averted their gazes from the artificial light outlining the port. Hesitantly, the pages brought each captive to his feet and guided him out. A few mercs glowered, but none spoke. Savidge was handled last, and with the greatest hesitation. The entire time, he kept his head down and mouth shut.

Resentment from our earlier confrontation surged back. It was a relief not to have to make eye contact, because I didn't know what my expression might've betrayed. My grip on Branigan's longsword tightened.

Lady Amelia turned to Gunnhilda. "Retrieve the flax."

With the mercs gone, all that remained in the cargo hold was a single bushel of flax. Gunnhilda gathered it into her arms.

More adepts arrived to swarm over the Baron's ship for blessings. If she had Gules' coordinates, she'd soon lose them. Fortunate that those coordinates waited safely for me back in Nidaros, on the data carrier I'd hidden in Ingvar's office for safekeeping.

Lady Amelia turned to walk toward the palace with poise. The rest of us trailed behind her, technically part of a noble procession — not something I'd never imagined myself in before.

Ingvar and Gunnhilda craned their necks at our towering confines. They'd probably never experienced that feeling of being completely surrounded by looming buildings. Whether they found the prospect awe-inspiring or daunting was hard to tell.

Gunnhilda shifted and re-shifted the flax in her arms.

"Need help with that?" Ingvar offered just before I did.

"I've got it, Captain," she replied. "Thank you, though."

The four of us walked an uncelebrated fifty yards beneath Spectra's evening sky to the palace entrance.

"I'll see Lord Catherwood at once," Lady Amelia told a stunned guard.

Seconds later, we navigated the rainbow palace like we owned it. One of us practically did. Ingvar and I moved up to flank Lady Amelia. Gunnhilda trailed behind, desperately trying not to shed flax all over the floor.

Lady Amelia, Baroness of Nidaros and heir presumptive to the throne of Catherwood, made statues of every courtier in our path. They all regained their senses to bow low, kindnesses pouring from their lips. She strode past without acknowledgement, for which I was grateful — and tickled. It wasn't every day I got to bypass so much red tape.

Ingvar was a blank, staring dead ahead. I wondered what he thought of this place.

Despite what was surely a full schedule for the teenaged Lord and his master adept, we had no trouble gaining entry to the pungent, sweltering throne room. This was almost *déjà vu* for me, except for the dozens of courtiers packing the chamber's fringes in whispery anticipation.

At our appearance, the sleepy Lord bolted from his throne and ran toward us. Everyone froze as though a boulder careened downhill toward them — everyone but Lady Amelia. Grinning, she caught up Lord Catherwood in an embrace he returned just as fiercely.

Master Ethan, Lord Catherwood's chief adept, left his perch by the thrones to chase after the young sovereign, looking like he'd lost circulation above the neck. I joined the rest of the audience in hastening to one knee, keeping my gaze locked on the floor.

"Albion! Powers be praised," gushed Lady Amelia. "Thou art twice as tall as when I saw thee last."

"Aunt Amelia! We scarcely recognize thee!" Lord Catherwood cried. "Art thou ill?"

"All of Nidaros is ill, my dear," was the Baroness' grim reply. "The land is barren and we starve, victims of a witch's plague."

This was the beginning of our agreed-upon story. Murmurs rose among the courtiers.

The young Lord had no response.

"Dame Jessamine Irless of Freemont!" barked Master Ethan. "Arise!"

It sounded like an invitation to have my head chopped off, but I stood anyway and clasped my hands behind my back. Though Branigan's longsword dragged on the ground, I avoided taking the grip in hand, not wanting to project any hint of aggression. Lady Amelia braced the shoulders of an agape Lord Catherwood. Master Ethan hovered close, focusing a less-than-charitable glare my way.

"Thou hast returned without completing thy quest," the adept accused.

"I beg to differ, Master," I replied, undaunted.

His eyes narrowed. "We shall see. For the moment, art thou willing to give thy word as a knight errant that Lady Amelia speaketh the truth?"

Lord Catherwood faced him with fury. "No one shall call our aunt a liar! No one shall even hint at such a thing!"

Master Ethan weathered the tantrum with patience, still facing me. "Art thou willing?"

"Yes, Master. Upon my word, Milady speaks true," I said.

The boy glared at me next. "Hast thou done nothing about this plague, or this witch?!"

I lowered my head. "I ventured to Nidaros as Your Highness requested. After many days of searching and wishing, I tracked the witch to her lair in caverns far removed from the barony. She was adamant the plague would never be lifted, but after much fighting, I slew her. With her death came the end of the curse."

I'd pushed not to mention the Harbinger, and Lady Amelia had agreed. I didn't know whether anyone on Spectra knew of it, but it seemed a bad idea to draw attention there when we hadn't had a chance to fully explore it.

Feverish murmurs overtook the throne room. Lord Catherwood himself was greatly enchanted. "Unseen be praised!"

Master Ethan frowned, arms folded.

"I'm afraid my tale isn't over yet, Milord." My pulse sped up in anticipation. "Just as I was bringing news of my triumph back to Nidaros, I discovered the barony in the grips of an even more dire peril: invasion!"

A deathly hush fell over the room.

"By whom?" Master Ethan demanded. "Doth Lord Lagana peck at our borders anew?"

"No, Master," I answered. "The invasion came at the hands of the Linum Dominorum trade guild."

Shocked outbursts filled the room. Master Ethan bellowed for quiet, but the commotion persisted. It was the most dramatic moment of my nonsense-telling career. I basked in it, feeling flushed and powerful.

Only Lady Amelia's narrow-eyed glance around the throne room was enough to summon quiet. Once things had settled, she resumed gently with Lord Catherwood. "'Tis just as the knight sayeth. We were forced to defend ourselves against those whom we believed were allies. Even worse, there seemeth no justification for the aggression employed against us. Despite all our hardship, we stand ready to deliver our quota. Adept Gunnhilda?"

Gunnhilda took to her feet behind me, lifting the flax bundle for all to see.

"Ere we had the chance, Madam Castor chose swords over harvesters, attacking us without cause!" Lady Amelia's outrage leaked through. "Our cloister is devastated. Many lie dead, others wounded — including my husband, Baron Tristan."

The resultant outburst was even more chaotic than the last. I couldn't help marveling at the spectacle. Still kneeling, Ingvar kept facing the ground, his reaction a mystery.

Lady Amelia waited for silence with a pained look on her face, then continued. "Were it not for Dame Jessamine and the army at Captain Leirfall's command —" she gestured between me and Ingvar " — many more would have fallen, and the rest would be Madam Castor's property."

"Milord, I must protest!" a familiar feminine voice cried out from the back of the throne room.

Everyone spun toward the interruption. There stood Madam Castor, resplendent and terrible. The same introductory plea as last time, with the same impeccable timing.

My true would-be murderer. A rage that'd been building up for days rushed into me with dizzying force. We'd been establishing a strong case against her, but she wouldn't have come if she wasn't confident she could destroy it. What the hell did she have in mind? She couldn't deny sending ships to Nidaros. We still had them, along with Commander Savidge.

The courtiers buzzed with gleeful anticipation, likely thinking along the same lines.

Master Ethan swallowed around a lump in his throat. "Madam Eugenia Castor, Mistress of the Linum Dominorum trade guild," he announced, unable to keep surprise out of his voice.

Madam Castor started down the runner toward our gathering, full of fire. She was dressed as beautifully as before, rivaling Lady Amelia. I couldn't imagine who and how many had died just for those jewels in her hair. Bile rose in my throat. It was a struggle not to betray any anger.

Ingvar sneaked a peek at her, eyes narrowed. Just about everyone on Nidaros feared and despised her, but had never seen her. Even poor Gunnhilda, an adept who believed she had magical power at her disposal, wilted as the Guildmistress approached.

Madam Castor and her wall of perfume swept past without acknowledging our existence, only stopping before the Catherwoods to sweep into a low curtsy.

Lady Amelia openly glared at her.

Lord Catherwood darkened as well. "Guildmistress! We just said we won't tolerate anyone calling our aunt a liar!"

"Hear me, Milord."

Breathless silence overtook the room. Everyone craned necks toward the scene to better see and hear what came next. I felt faint in that stifling chamber.

"There's been a tragic misunderstanding," Madam Castor continued. "It's true, I sent a detachment to Nidaros."

"Against our wishes?" Lord Catherwood cried.

"I had no choice! I was forced to establish order," Madam Castor pleaded. "I had it on good authority that Your Highness' emissary, Dame Jessamine, had been *murdered* within Baron Tristan's estate!"

Gasps filled the air.

Your authority! I died to add, but couldn't. Talking out of turn wouldn't endear me to anyone.

"Murdered?" Lord Catherwood glanced my way with an eyebrow arched. "Thine intelligence leaveth much to be desired, Guildmistress."

I suppressed a smile.

"I had it on good authority," Madam Castor repeated. "Or so I believed."

"Whose?" Lady Amelia demanded.

"Your own adepts, by means of Shipbuilder magic I lack the knowledge to describe adequately." Madam Castor rested a hand on her breast, stricken. "I'm a victim too, Your Highnesses! Too late, I learned the adepts of Nidaros were traitors, adherents of their foul forgotten Lord Gyllenfeld. *That's* why your cloister was devastated, is it not?" she asked Lady Amelia. "The adepts staged a coup and manipulated me into being their unwitting accomplice!"

The strength left my legs, making me wish I was still kneeling like Ingvar. I thought I knew how to lie. This woman's acrobatics left my head spinning.

"What of this letter, bearing thy guild's seal, that was sent to one of our adepts—your agent in Nidaros?" Smoldering, Lady Amelia produced a folded parchment square. It was the note Sigrid had discovered in Holsten's room. "It stateth the invasion is forthcoming, and biddeth the adept kill Dame Jessamine to discredit my husband."

More gasps issued from the crowd.

Lord Catherwood took the note, frowned over it, then raised that frown toward Madam Castor.

A surge of triumph filled me. She couldn't slime her way out of this one.

Madam Castor faltered. "I can't imagine. My seal has fallen into the wrong hands, or someone in my organization has taken it upon himself to act without authority. On my word, I'll figure out who was colluding with this adept and punish them severely!"

Disappointment crashed down hard. Of course, she had a mountain of underlings to absorb the blame. Anyone who'd disappointed her recently was in for a horrible surprise.

Lady Amelia braced the young Lord's shoulders again. "Nephew, seek the truth thyself. *Prithee.*"

Her emphasis seemed to confuse him, but he nodded.

"The plague hath erased our reserves and killed our livestock," Lady Amelia continued. "Nevertheless, our full quota of flax awaiteth in Nidaros. Albion, I believe 'tis fair to release Dame Jessamine from her quest."

Lord Catherwood glanced my way again. "Thy quest is at an end, Lady Knight. Thy vow and virtue have proven true; we are most grateful."

"Please!" Madam Castor cried, exasperated. "One bundle of flax proves nothing!"

"We shall be recovering from thy valiant bid to 'restore order' for some time yet." Lady Amelia shut her down with a poisonous look. "Thou may'st pick up the remainder of our flax *after* thou meetest our demands for reparations. Thou shalt surrender the fleet of invading ships that yet lie within our capital; provide new livestock, armor, ordnance, and ironworks; replenish our granary; and bring triple our previous food allotment per harvest, into perpetuity."

The court was abuzz over these inflated demands. Lady Amelia expected to bargain down from there.

The starting bid took the vinegar out of Madam Castor. "All of those ships!" she shouted over the din. "One, perhaps, not all! You can't bankrupt me over your internal problems!"

"The Unseen shall decide the matter." Master Ethan dug out his throwing sticks with a weary look, probably anticipating the length and ugliness of the arbitration to come. To my everlasting gratitude, he focused on me first. "As agreed, we shall remove the curse of Gules upon thee." He waved over a lesser adept nearby, a young lady about Gunnhilda's age. "Take Dame Jessamine away."

Lady Amelia turned and leaned down to whisper in Ingvar's ear, motioning for him to follow me. Ingvar stood and bowed to her.

She was sending him after me. I was grateful for the backup, and felt confident Lady Amelia and Gunnhilda would be safe within the throne room. Once Ingvar reached my side, we followed the lesser adept out.

Madam Castor tracked Ingvar's departure as carefully as he'd watched her entrance. He didn't seem to notice her scrutinizing attention. It sent a shiver down my spine.

The young adept led me and Ingvar down several twists through the halls, glancing back occasionally to make sure she hadn't lost us. It was a relief to be out of that sweat-box, but despite Ingvar's presence and two swords on my person, my nervousness ratcheted higher. I'd figured we'd be herded into the throne room antechamber I'd been herded into during my first visit, not flushed out to some remote corner of the palace. Then again, de-cursing a no-name, no-longer-useful knight errant probably ranked low on their to-do list. I focused on memorizing our path for backtracking purposes.

After a long walk, the adept finally stopped before a door that slid open at her approach. Beyond lay a closet-sized room, dark but for a handful of candles on stands. A cloud of retch-inducing incense poured into the hall.

The adept bowed to me. "This way, Lady Knight." To Ingvar, "Apologies. This ritual must be conducted in privacy."

"By Lady Amelia's order, I'm not to leave her." Ingvar's expression made clear he wasn't in any mood to be toyed with.

"Thou art still quite with her if thou waitest just outside here," the adept said with warm patience. "Prithee, it shan't take long."

Ingvar cast an uncertain glance my way.

I shared his paranoia. What choice did we have, though? Armed guards filled the halls, and would have no trouble obeying the adept's summons.

"I'll see you soon," I told Ingvar with a forced smile.

As we entered the tiny room, the door slid shut behind us, plunging us into near darkness. The adept grabbed a candle, then turned to me. In her hand appeared a brass vessel that held the dried remnants of blood I'd shed upon accepting my quest.

"Hear me, merciful Unseen! Accept this covenant fulfilled, and release this knight errant from her suffering." The adept applied the candle's flame to the vessel. Her eyes rolled up to mine. "Now I must reclaim the papers Milord gave thee, with his seal thereupon."

Without Lady Amelia and Ingvar, those papers were my last shred of security in Spectra. But again, I had no choice. Suppressing a cringe, I dug through my pockets. By then, my eyes had adjusted to the dimness. Over the adept's shoulder, I spotted the outline of a second door built into the room's back wall, about ten feet away. Footsteps sounded outside, seemingly both ahead and behind me.

People passing through? My nerves swung me toward less innocent conclusions. A knot formed in my ribcage.

Oblivious, the adept took my papers, reducing them to ash within the same vessel. "Send forth this valiant knight errant in peace, and protect her all her days ..."

I tuned out, more interested in figuring out what was happening outside. Greater numbers of footsteps happened along with every passing second. I longed to return to Ingvar. It took enormous effort to hold still and breathe the pungent, stifling air.

"All is well now, Lady Knight. I shall take that amulet," the adept said.

Gratefully, I doffed the khamsa and handed it over.

"Hey! What—?" Ingvar's muffled voice sounded from outside, abruptly silenced.

My paranoia surged past the tipping point. I whirled around to dash outside—only to fall against a door that refused to open.

Heavy footsteps thudded behind me. Breath in my throat, I turned to find several Catherwood guards flooding in through the opposite door, brandishing short swords. The adept flitted away with my khamsa and escaped around them.

Fear braced me. Were these really Lord Catherwood's men, or disguised thugs? Either way, they were going to stay clear and let me rejoin Ingvar, or there'd be problems. Out came my righteous anger—and Branigan's longsword, which I gripped in both hands and hefted over my right shoulder. It'd be tough to wield in cramped confines, especially with the trauma I'd suffered, but I would've been tripping all over it if I'd tried wielding my side sword instead.

The guards halted defensively outside swinging range.

"Now now, you're smarter than that." Madam Castor emerged from the second door, in the company of more armed toughs.

I bit back the gasp and obscenities that nearly flew out of my mouth.

As the door closed behind her, the Guildmistress stared me down from across the room, making no secret of her resentment. The court sycophant was gone. Candlelight glinted off her crown-to-hem jewels, making her resemble a demon fresh out of hell.

"Put a scratch on any of these men, and I'll have you thrown in the dungeon, where I guarantee you'll meet with an unfortunate accident before Lady Amelia even decides whether your freedom is worth her trouble," she warned, eyes narrowed.

Dread paralyzed me at first. How'd she finish up in the throne room so fast? What was she doing here?

"Lower your weapon!" Madam Castor snapped.

Slowly, I complied. The longsword offered little reassurance anyway; I had no hope of escaping. Inches away, behind a locked door, Ingvar had almost certainly met with a similar ambush—and I couldn't help him. The knot in my ribcage tightened painfully.

The Catherwood guards closed in to flank me. Madam Castor had forced the one-on-one confrontation I'd hoped I'd get with her. She didn't wield all the power; I wouldn't let her intimidate me. Returning her stare, I drove the point of Branigan's blade into the floor, clenching the grip tightly in both fists. "I flew here with Lady Amelia. It's safe to say she gives a damn. If I don't fly out with her in the same number of pieces, it'll look awfully suspicious."

Madam Castor waited out several beats in silence, searching my eyes. She rendered no visible verdict, just kept watching me carefully. "After you escort her to Nidaros, where are you headed next?"

"To hell with that!" I cried around my furiously pounding heart. "What about Gules? Did you help Lord Catherwood's adepts kill and loot those people, or was it strictly *your* massacre?"

"Gules?" Madam Castor's eyes flew open in confusion. Then rage swept away her composure. Her fists clenched at her sides. "Why would I have attacked Gules? It was part of my production chain! The adepts cursed it, saying they let some knight errant run off with a Shipbuilder relic too important to lose. Never mind my linseed operation!"

Her only concern was for her business. Not surprising. But a knight errant stealing a relic from Gules? That detail was new — assuming she told the truth.

"I don't believe you," I said. "If you had nothing to do with it, how'd you come by the spoils?" I held up Branigan's longsword. "Does this look familiar?"

Madam Castor blinked. "Damn you, Savidge!" she muttered. After regaining her composure one breath at a time, she stared me down. "I sent my people rooting through the adepts' take, to see if there was anything … *instructive*. I owe the relic thief my *personal* thanks for their interference."

"This sword doesn't belong to your thief," I said. "This knight errant died on Gules — maybe when the adepts came, maybe earlier."

Her expression soured further. "You and your ilk have cost me far too much of late. I'd just as soon never see you again, but you're clearly no idiot. And here you are, in need of a new quest." She folded her arms, assuming an air of innocent speculation. "Why don't you hunt down this thief for me? Perhaps they aren't just a thief. Perhaps they also killed your friend."

Her stab in the dark came awfully close to my heart. I could only hope my face didn't show it. "Or maybe the 'thief' never existed. The adepts cursed Gules for whatever reason, then made up this story afterward." Or Madam Castor had invented it herself.

"I'll take proof of that, if you find it," she said. "Thirty cred for a live thief, or the real reason for Gules' cursing. Twenty cred more for the stolen relic. Are we agreed?"

Given Lord Catherwood's master adept had shown such distress over my ten cred advance at the start of my quest, these must've been astronomical sums. Still, it wasn't hard to arrive at a decision. "No. I won't be beholden to you."

"Then I suggest you leave Catherwood space and never return." She looked at me like she knew I wouldn't, and would savor making me regret it. "Bring in Captain Leirfall."

The door behind me opened. Two more guards entered with Ingvar between them, goading him forward until he stood in line with me. Ingvar glanced downward, avoiding my gaze.

Oh hell, what was this now? I struggled to maintain composure, fearing what might happen if I accidentally bared my heart to the heartless creature across the room from us.

"Captain," Madam Castor addressed him levelly. "Nidaros should be mine right now. I concede defeat. Well done." She let her arms fall at her sides. "You're much too talented to languish in that backwater. Here in Spectra, among my ranks, you have a chance at wealth and renown. I'll set you up with an apartment, salary, and detachment immediately."

I relished imagining the colorful words Ingvar would surely choose for his refusal. His righteous fire failed to surface, however. Heartsick weariness had aged him twenty years.

"Can't leave my homeworld, Guildmistress," Ingvar forced out. "But ... I'm tired of propping up subjugators."

Madam Castor raised an eyebrow.

Panic seized me from top to bottom. Now what the hell was this? *Ingvar, look at me*, I begged mentally as my heart pounded out of control. *What's going on here?*

"Lost family, good soldiers, all so the same fight can resume a few years hence." Ingvar ignored me, caught up in a deep grief I'd only seen traces of before.

My thoughts raced desperately. The rest of me felt weak, helpless, and confused. I couldn't say or do a damned thing without handing Madam Castor the ammunition she needed to make both our lives miserable. While I was forced to stand there like a callous sellsword who no longer had any reason to care about Nidaros, worry gnawed at my stomach from the inside out.

The Guildmistress folded her arms again, studying Ingvar. "Your people still mistrust Catherwood. Another uprising is inevitable."

Ingvar shut his eyes. "Can't do it again. My people deserve better."

"Baron Tristan will never impose peace upon Nidaros," she said. "It must come from within. I think we both know that. You may be just the man to finally bring peace to your people."

Please tell me I'm not seeing this, I thought, fighting back nausea.

Before continuing, Madam Castor motioned for her men to throw me out.

CHAPTER 30

Across the cramped chamber, Madam Castor had already forgotten me. Her narrowed eyes dissected Ingvar, who stood at my side, looking back as though she offered the only escape from his pain.

Shock and nausea rooted me in place. Had Madam Castor really just proposed they collude – and was Ingvar actually entertaining the prospect?

Though the very idea knifed my heart to ribbons, I had to maintain a blank face and pretend I didn't care, that neither Ingvar nor Nidaros meant anything to me now that my quest was over. But how I longed to shake sense into Ingvar. After all the blood the Guildmistress had spilled, how could it even occur to him to serve her?

I witnessed no more of the conversation. Madam Castor's guards seized my elbows and hauled me out of the room to march through the palace corridors. Eventually, they dumped me off at Lord Catherwood's port, sending me outside with strong shoves.

"Good riddance, sellsword!" one called in my wake.

I lost my balance and skidded to my knees on unforgiving pavement. My shadow stretched out before me; the port was well lit at night. Sentries stood watch nearby, whom I had no desire to break down in front of.

The Baron's ship rested in the distance, deserted. It appeared I'd arrived first, and would have to wait for the others. With a heart that weighed tons, I forced myself to my feet for the long walk.

Judging by Lord Catherwood's warm reception, Lady Amelia and Gunnhilda would be fine. But what the hell was Ingvar up to? That brief, awful exchange — could he really have meant any of it? A lot had been bothering him on the flight over. Had he intended to speak with Madam Castor all along? Why hadn't he told me?

What else was he keeping secret?

Upon reaching the ship, I leaned against her hull. A cigarillo craving hit me hard, and I indulged it without a thought. Once I'd burned through the first, I lit up a second. Ashes piled up by my feet while anxiety ate at my insides like acid. Paranoia spun increasingly horrific what-ifs.

Nidaros came first for Ingvar. I understood that, but could not stand the thought of him casting his lot with that monster. Wasn't it obvious she didn't care about anything but business? Ingvar was smarter than that. Had grief blinded him — or had I been the blind one? Had I misjudged him completely? Had I been so desperate for an ally that I'd built up a picture in my head that didn't exist?

I screwed my eyes shut, forcing deep breaths on myself to stave off panic. For sanity's sake, I had to stop speculating and wait for the chance to talk to him. If he refused to level, then at least I'd know what I needed to know.

"Dame Jessamine?"

I gave a start, almost dropping my latest cigarillo. Lady Amelia and Gunnhilda stood before me with concerned looks on their faces.

My emotions were unfiltered, easy for them to read. As embarrassment burned me from head to foot, I dropped to one knee, hoping to save face.

"Nay, prithee," Lady Amelia dismissed. "Where is Captain Leirfall?"

"I don't know. The adepts separated us," I struggled to report in a level tone. I wouldn't mention what I'd witnessed to anyone before I'd spoken to Ingvar about it.

Lady Amelia nodded. "I shall have him fetched at once. In the meantime, do have a look at our cargo."

At her prodding, I headed aft. There, pages hovered over sleds loaded with supply crates.

A small smile battled its way onto my face. It was a welcome sight, though I wasn't in much of a celebratory mood.

Gunnhilda stood at the ship's hatch as I returned. "Is anything else wrong?"

"No, thanks. I'm just tired," I said.

Her concern lingered, but she didn't press me further.

My feet lugged me aboard, past the damask, into the bedchamber. I doffed my side sword and Branigan's longsword, dropped them onto one of the beds, then collapsed beside them at the bed's edge, doubled over. For a while, I stared at my feet, listening to the thumps of cargo being loaded. It wasn't long before anguish refilled my brain, leaving me sick and helpless.

Ages later, the bedchamber door opened and shut. A pause.

"Jayce?" Ingvar chanced. "*Skíta*, I was hoping I'd get back first. Listen—"

"Stow it!" Trembling with relief and fury, I jumped to my feet and glowered at his form lingering by the door, struggling not to raise my voice and attract unwanted attention. "I've been so worried—about not helping you, about whether I even know the first thing about you! What in the actual hell *was* that?"

Ingvar hesitated, contrite. "'Twas a ruse, Jayce. Our Baron ordered me to carry it out if I got the chance to speak with Madam Castor. It must've been hard to watch. I'm sorry."

A ruse? I hoped so — it made more sense than the alternative — but I still simmered over a number of things, like the fact that I'd never been warned.

Ingvar edged closer to brace my shoulders and look me in the eye. "I do worry about more uprisings one day, but I sure don't think Madam Castor's the answer. I'd sooner throw her off a hill than trust her to tell me how tall it is."

"Then why appeal to her like that?" I begged to know.

"She'll be seeking a new inside man on Nidaros," Ingvar explained. "Best if I 'serve' that purpose so we can control exactly what information she receiveth, limit the damage she looketh to deal us. We don't need another Holsten — or someone like Sigrid, powers forbid — helping her cause more problems."

I took a deep breath, but wasn't as relieved as I should've been. Did Ingvar have any idea what he was getting himself into? "I don't like it, but I get it. Why didn't you tell me?"

"Our Baron ordered me to keep the whole thing secret, and I didn't think I'd get the chance," Ingvar replied. "'Twas a long shot, she and I being alone at any point. I never expected she'd try to recruit me." His grip on my shoulders tightened. "Wouldn't have kept it from you, anyway, whatever our Baron's wishes. I don't want there to be any more secrets between us."

His wording stabbed a knife into my spine. "Any *more?* What else is there?" Paranoia brought back fear and frustration. I struggled to keep my voice from turning shrill. "I thought you were above these stupid political games! But that's just idiot wishful thinking on my part, isn't it? You're a high-ranking official in a Baron's court, you *have* to play them. Fine — but if you actually care about me, you'd better lay it out right now. What don't I know about?"

Ingvar glanced sidelong, his grip on my shoulders tightening. His next words, hollow and miserable, seemed difficult to force out of his mouth. "When ye first arrived in Nidaros, our Baron didn't know your reputation or intent. He wanted to keep you safe and out of the way while Ormyr scried for the witch. I had orders to keep you distracted. However I had to."

I stood there numb at first. As realization seeped into me, my head spun, with nausea following soon after. Of course, it all made too much sense in hindsight. I'd thought I'd been handling myself well in a noble court. In reality, I'd gotten played like a fool. They'd wanted to secure the favor of Lord Catherwood's emissary, and their friendly, handsome Captain of the Guard had just been sitting there, stymied during their crisis. Why not leverage him to tug at my heartstrings?

No wonder there'd been so many eyes on my and Ingvar's introduction. No wonder Ingvar had warmed to me so fast, and stuck with me despite all the crazy trouble it'd led to. Keeping tabs on me, getting me to trust him — and *everyone* had been in on it. Baron Tristan, Master Ormyr, even Pontus had done things to nudge us closer together.

Grief and shame crushed my heart. How had I been so stupid? It'd never been about love, it was about what he could take from me. Like May all over again.

"Hell." Head spinning, I pulled free of Ingvar, reeling away with no set direction in mind.

"Jayce?" Ingvar tried to steady me.

I stuck out a hand out to prevent him from following. After some stumbling, I fell into a shadowed corner somewhere, drawing my knees to my chest. Unchecked tears poured down my face. I pressed my forehead against my knees and wrapped both arms over my head.

"Jayce?" Ingvar was close, sounding as hurt as I felt.

"Hell take me, I'm a fool," I muttered with my head still buried.

"Jayce, I'm sorry," he continued, his tone sincere. "Like I said, I didn't want there to be any more secrets between us. Horrible thing to do to our relationship, base it on lies."

"Are you kidding?" My head shot up; I found myself sitting in the corner formed by the aft bulkhead and one of the beds. "The *whole thing* was a lie!"

And it was over. There'd be this monstrous fight to get through, then I'd somehow have to endure the next few weeks and months of helping Nidaros without dwelling on how badly I'd been played.

Ingvar knelt to my right, looking worried. I tried to get my feet under myself and run away from him, desperate to put distance between us. He twisted himself into my path, then leaned forward until our faces were inches apart.

"Ye haven't heard the full truth yet," he said with a pleading expression.

I froze in dread, heart pounding. "Don't tell me there's more?"

"I told you what I was ordered to do, but what actually happened from there was different," Ingvar continued. "I *hated* those orders, Jayce. Remember when we first met? I couldn't fake liking you for anything."

His sincerity reached past my pain, making me consider his words rather than dismiss them. I realized he was right. The forced socializing, his reluctant invitation to the barracks and sour attitude in general. He'd disliked those orders so much, he'd resented me by extension.

"'Twas only after ye called me on it that I dropped the act and swore to forget the whole thing, orders be damned." Ingvar's voice faltered. "That's when I fell for you for real, Jayce. Fell *hard*. I never faked my affections, and with how supportive ye've been, I only love you more." He sat back, resting his elbows on his knees and bracing his temple with one hand. "I'm sorry."

There was still room to run, but the urge had subsided. In the wake of his words, I found myself both stunned and hopeful. I'd expected a shouting match. May had always bristled at times like this, insisting that if I were upset, it was my problem. Ingvar could've lied from the outset, denied any further secrets and avoided the resultant fallout. Instead, he'd been brave enough to come clean. If I could believe he'd been issued those orders, couldn't I also believe he cared about me in spite of them?

I really wanted to believe. I still loved him. But that sort of blind wishful thinking had hurt me before. I sniffled hard, wiping away tears with my forearm. "Is that it? You're not keeping anything else from me?"

"So help me, ye know what I do," he replied.

"I told you about May," I blurted. "About how he squired me after my old life fell apart. I didn't mention that he and I were closer than we should've been." A shamed flush burned my face. "He made me think we'd have a future together. Then one day, he ran off and left me with no warning, no goodbye, just vanished. I haven't seen or heard from him since."

However much I cared about Ingvar, deep down I was terrified of setting myself up for another betrayal. Years of latent pain welled to the surface. I curled back into myself and finally succumbed to the sobs I'd been resisting.

Ingvar drew closer and placed an arm around my shoulders. "Ye're not upset at yourself, are ye?"

His question startled me out of crying. I glanced up with a confused frown. "No. I'm only sorry I trusted that son of a bitch."

"Then ye do blame yourself, at least in part," Ingvar replied. "But your trust wasn't the problem. Ye loved someone who saved you from a bad situation — that's understandable. He exploited his authority over you, then ended things in the most cowardly way possible. That's *his* shame, not yours."

I swallowed hard, startled to hear the situation framed that way, but it made sense.

Ingvar cupped the side of my face in his hand. "Your trust is important to me. I'd never demean it like that. Wish there were a way to prove it right now, but there isn't. It can only happen over time. If … if I still have your trust?" Pain entered his voice.

I was silent for a while, lost in thought. The order to manipulate me had come from the Baron, not Ingvar. Ingvar's words and actions had never struck me as conniving or false. He'd kept me involved in all his planning, revealed more than once that he had a brain and a conscience, and was clearly hurting because I was hurt. This was completely different from May, whose betrayal I might've anticipated if I'd been less naive.

In the end, I felt I had more to lose by pushing Ingvar away than by putting this behind us and working up to the trust he'd talked about. I embraced him, resting my head on his shoulder.

Ingvar hugged back tightly.

"I'm still worried as hell," I said. "If you couldn't play me, how're you going to play double agent with Madam Castor? She's dangerous. I just lost Branigan, I … I can't …" I trailed off, unable to voice the possibility of losing him, too.

"There's good reason to be wary of Madam Castor," Ingvar replied. "It may help to know, she's just as wary of me. We're still a long way from her trusting me to take over for Holsten. It may be nothing ever cometh of our talk." He paused. "Even without that, I haven't the safest profession. Neither do ye. The level of risk ye accept for yourself, can ye accept it for me as well?"

I had accepted it for May. I would've been willing for Branigan.

"Yes," I said. "But please, let's not hold anything back from now on. I need to know we're always on the same page."

"We are now."

I closed my eyes and relaxed in his arms.

"Madam Castor talked to me a while before bringing you in," I mentioned later. We'd since moved back to the table, off the floor. "She claimed she had nothing to do with Gules, that it'd been part of her supply chain, even. Some knight errant ran off with a Shipbuilder artifact, and that led Lord Catherwood's adepts to curse them. She offered me fifty cred for the thief and the artifact."

"Fifty cred!" Ingvar repeated as though I'd named an entire solar system.

I shook my head. "I turned her down."

"Good." His tense posture relaxed. "She's angry about the cursing — or setting a trap for you."

I frowned in reflection. "When Drea and I got to Gules, it was fenced in. A proclamation nailed to the fence said the town had been cursed for failing to protect assets sacred to Catherwood. So there really could be some thief and artifact involved. Drea's my priority, but once she's safe—" I didn't let myself consider any other outcome "—I'd like to spend some time hunting down evidence for or against." There was a possibility it'd shed light on Branigan's fate.

"I'll go with you," Ingvar assured me once more. "If Madam Castor hath any lingering interest in Gules, better we not take chances."

"I want you with me." And I was sincere about that, even though paranoia didn't let me forget what had happened. Hesitations and doubts lingered in the back of my skull. But I was willing to work toward the trust Ingvar had talked about. It'd take time to build, but if we managed it, it'd be well worth our while.

Our return trip wasn't quite as heady. Recent events had dampened that sense of wonder, but our interactions felt more real, and honest, as a result. By the time we landed in Nidaros, it was nighttime there also. Lady Amelia awaited us in the parlor with a garment draped over her arms. I was pretty sure it was what she'd been embroidering on during the trip.

She nodded to me and Ingvar. "As much as I miss Spectra sometimes, 'tis good to be home."

Her assertion surprised me. For a woman accustomed to such high levels of luxury and attention, relocating to Nidaros must've been miserable. Being attacked on arrival had probably been even worse.

"Aye, Milady. I'll second that," Ingvar said.

Gunnhilda exited the cockpit, lowering her head.

The Baroness glanced between all of us. "I was able to extract much from Madam Castor. Aside from the food we carry, she hath been forced to surrender the invasion fleet to us."

My jaw dropped in shock, mirroring Ingvar and Gunnhilda.

"All of those ships are ours now?" the adept managed.

"Even so," Lady Amelia replied. "And when the harvest ships arrive in five standard days' time, they shall bear double our usual food allotment—a permanent increase."

More stunning news. Thordia's food wouldn't be as imperative, though her flax still would be.

"That's great, madam. Exactly how much trouble has Madam Castor caught?" I asked, but didn't hold my breath. Nothing had stopped her from slithering out and antagonizing me personally, after all.

Annoyance crossed Lady Amelia's expression. "'Tis up to my nephew—more likely his advisors, who are eager to preserve the status quo and their ties with Linum Dominorum."

"So, reparations are likely all the punishment she faceth?" Ingvar asked with a frown.

"I would not expect more," the Baroness replied.

"We do know she's our enemy now, outright," Gunnhilda spoke up, hopeful and determined. "We shall be scrying and casting all manner of spells to ensure nothing like this ever happens again."

The poor girl tried, but her words were of zero reassurance to me.

"'Tis been a long day of travel," Lady Amelia said. "Adept, Captain: dismissed. Dame Jessamine, I suppose thou shalt soon leave upon thine urgent errand."

My heart raced with anticipation. Drea, at long last! I just had to squire Dag first, as promised. He'd be coming with me.

"I hope this may aid thee." Lady Amelia offered me the garment draped in her arms.

I unfurled it: a hooded cloak, light brown velvet with burgundy lining. My variable resistor sigil was embroidered on the left breast. I choked on my gasp of shock.

"'Twas one of mine," she explained. "I stitched in thy sigil and shortened the hem so thou shan't go tripping thereupon." She then pressed a clasp into my hand: a pair of gold snake-eating griffins, each holding rubies in their spare talons.

The increasing magnitude of gifts left me weak-kneed and short of breath. "I can't take this."

"I insist," Lady Amelia returned.

It wasn't like I could realistically say no to a Baroness. And though I normally avoided wearing colors lest anyone think I served a particular Lord or organization, I *would* be serving Nidaros of my own volition for an unspecified length of time.

"I'm too stunned to offer proper thanks, madam, but … thank you." I pocketed the clasp and draped the cloak over my left arm. My right hand still had to counter-balance Branigan's longsword.

"One thing more, Milady," Ingvar said. "I request to go with Dame Jessamine on her errand. 'Tis a dangerous rescue mission, not something anyone should be attempting alone."

Lady Amelia's smile faded. "I'm afraid not, Captain. There's much to be done in preparation for the harvest, and we are shorthanded as is. Thy men need thy guidance and support in this time."

Ingvar looked as disappointed as I felt. "Milady — "

"I have spoken," the Baroness shut him down.

"I won't be gone long," I tried. "With Captain Leirfall's help, I can finish and return even faster."

"Apologies. We cannot spare anyone, least of all for dangerous errands." Lady Amelia strode toward the ship's hatch, resolute. "Goodnight, and Unseen guide thee."

Gunnhilda hastened to open the hatch before the Baroness was forced to lift a finger for that purpose. The look she threw me and Ingvar was apologetic.

The captain looked like he wanted to kick himself.

I remained stuck on Lady Amelia's refusal, clenching my fist around the grip of Branigan's sword. Disappointing that despite our earlier talk and her generosity, she still saw me as a knight errant with no real stake in Nidaros' problems, someone who might get Ingvar killed or stranded somewhere. I supposed I wasn't done proving myself to her.

Everyone disembarked into the cool night. Ingvar had one of the port sentries escort Lady Amelia and Gunnhilda back to the estate; unloading cargo could wait until morning. Once another sentry gave us a lantern, Ingvar and I left the port side by side, aiming for the barracks.

Ingvar stared straight ahead with narrowed eyes. I'd forgotten that, for all the power he wielded as Captain of the Guard, his actions were limited in ways mine weren't. That'd been part of the appeal of knight errantry for me. After the forced-marriage-or-orphanage dilemma I'd faced in Freemont as a teenager, I'd never wanted to be boxed in by authority or circumstance ever again.

"She's worried about you not coming back," I told Ingvar. "I understand that." But the realization that he lacked my freedom was surprisingly painful, as was the idea of being separated again for even a short time. My heart was already fretting and sore at the prospect.

"There's plenty to do here, but nothing my lads can't handle. I'll pitch in my fair share and more when I return. What ye've done for us, our Baroness should be willing to repay with more than a cloak." Ingvar cast a pleading glance my way. "If ye must leave now, I understand, but would ye consider leaving in the morning instead? I'll appeal to our Baron, see if he'll grant me leave to join you."

A glimmer of hope brightened my thoughts. Maybe he would. He'd been willing a few days ago. "I'll wait. I should pay my own respects to the Baron before leaving, anyway." I also needed a proper night's rest. Drea didn't need me groggy.

Ingvar brightened, then sobered. "Don't want to delay you any more than ye already have been. If it gets to midday and I've yet to arrive at your vessel, don't wait any longer."

My heart clenched up again, torn, but I managed a nod.

At the barracks, I collected my data carrier containing Gules' coordinates. Dag was nowhere to be found. One of the soldiers informed us he was at the Baron's estate. That was where Ingvar and I headed next.

We walked the empty halls and ascended to the proper floor. Upon leaving the stairwell, I froze at an unexpected sight. Outside the door to my room, Dag sat cross-legged on the ground, back to the wall—with Master Ormyr sitting beside him, legs stretched out into the corridor.

CHAPTER 31

Ormyr had returned to his usual robes and jewelry, a display of dignity that contrasted with his seated position in the estate corridor beside the door to my room. He looked much improved since I'd last seen him, almost as if our dangerous journey had never happened and Thordia had never attacked him. A lantern rested between him and Dag; at that late hour, it was the only light in the corridor. The master adept was showing Dag how to palm a coin-sized charm.

Ingvar and I left the stairwell, then halted in our tracks, trading a stunned glance.

We went undetected for the moment. Ormyr revealed his palm, demonstrated how to grip the object and posture the rest of his hand to conceal its presence, then passed the charm to Dag. Understandably, the young man was less fluid with the technique.

Ormyr adjusted Dag's hand. "Tighten here, relax this—"

"*Skíta!* I can't do it." Dag threw the charm to the floor, glaring at his deformed fingers. "My damned hand—"

"Nonsense, whelp!" Ormyr still used the insult, but it had acquired a strange sense of endearment. "Don't seek excuses, *practice.* In Spectra, I would sit before a mirror and rehearse these movements for hours."

"Hours!" Dag cried, discouraged.

A handful of throwing darts materialized in Ormyr's left hand. He fanned them out with a flourish. "If thou cravest something badly enough, reach within and channel thy will into action. Otherwise, admit thou dost not truly want it and move on."

This instructive moment baffled me. Ormyr had warmed to Dag during our excursion, but since when had he ever been that solicitous and encouraging with anyone? Recent events must've shaken him, if only for a short while.

Beside me, Ingvar held still, eyes narrowed at Ormyr.

"Hey! Ye're back!" Upon noticing us, Dag jumped up to approach me and Ingvar.

His enthusiasm made me forget Ormyr quickly. I smiled and suppressed the urge to pull him into a hug. "It's good to be back."

"Good seeing you, lad," Ingvar seconded.

"Captain. Lady Knight." Ormyr slowly rose to his feet, using the wall for balance.

With a pang of contrition, I recalled the bolt he'd taken to his leg, blunted by armor. In the Harbinger, I'd given him painkillers. Had his leg gone untreated in the days since?

"Unseen be praised for your safe return," Ormyr continued. "How fare Milord and his court?"

"Everything's fine," I said, hoping to avoid an explanation. "Thanks for those coordinates."

Ormyr lowered his head. "May thou findest the wise woman quickly and in good health."

I swallowed hard. "Is your leg still bothering you? I'm sure the surgical construct could take care of that."

"It should heal well enough by mine own ministrations." Ormyr's gaze shifted between me and Ingvar. "I was hoping I might speak with you both."

"Already told you, I'm in no mood to talk to you yet." Ingvar's tone was level, but his demeanor was stony. "And ye've plagued her enough."

Ormyr's questioning gaze focused on me as though to assess the accuracy of Ingvar's statement.

Dag crept out of everyone's reach, placing his back to the wall with fists clenched at his sides. His eyes tracked our exchange carefully.

I also sensed the building tension, and considered asking Dag to wait in my room, but refrained. If he were to be my squire, he'd also have to be my shadow. While I wouldn't have minded hearing Ormyr out, Ingvar was clearly in no mood for it. It seemed best to defuse the situation. I took a step forward. "Could we talk later, Master? We need sleep, we're heading to Gules first thing tomorrow."

Ormyr straightened with determination. "I wish to accompany thee."

"What?!" Ingvar cried.

The request startled me, too. Was it possible that, after everything we'd endured together, Ormyr had actually retained some compassion? Hadn't he kept my "witching" secret, as promised, while also ensuring I got Gules' coordinates? Maybe he did want to help. Or maybe he was looking for a shot of confidence, and a chance to escape the heat he'd been catching lately. If things went well, our success might even return him to favor.

"After the trouble ye caused?" Ingvar leapt into the gap formed by my stunned silence, advancing several steps toward Ormyr himself. "Ye had a duty to your adepts, but ye always acted like it was the other way around! Of course Holsten got it in mind to defect. It meant getting rid of you! How'd ye not see what was happening? I mean with your *eyes*, damn it, not with cards, or stars, or any other trick ye might shove blame upon? And let's not forget how ye almost killed her." He tilted his head in my direction. "Now ye'd fly with her? Over my corpse!"

His fury spent, Ingvar waved a hand dismissively and spun around, returning to my side with a scowl. "Told you I wasn't ready to talk yet," he muttered over his shoulder.

To my astonishment, Ormyr had no haughty counter. He flinched as though Ingvar had sucker-punched him, then trembled while pulling at the sleeves of his robe. "Better to hear thy words ere thou had a chance to censor them."

I found myself hopelessly mired in mixed-up feelings. Pity, and a glimmer of camaraderie, overshadowed my initial low opinion of Ormyr. If he'd really learned some humility, the master adept could be a useful companion, but I wondered if he'd considered how it might look to the rest of court.

"Do you have permission to leave Nidaros?" I asked. After our earlier conversation with Lady Amelia, I doubted it.

Ormyr hesitated tellingly. "Thou needest aid. Gules is cursed territory, and as such shall be perilous."

"The last thing she needeth is help from you," Ingvar snapped, scowling.

Given the blows Ormyr's reputation had suffered, going AWOL probably wasn't the right thing for him to do just then. I took a collecting breath, making a decision for his sake and mine. "I appreciate your offer, but I think it's better if you stay here and not give the impression that you're running from the barony's problems."

Ormyr's eyes went wide, incredulous. "I—"

"Ye heard her." Ingvar's tone suggested Ormyr clear off.

His face fell. "I understand." Ormyr stooped to retrieve his lantern, then approached us and the stairs. He shook my left hand, and as I withdrew it, I felt the weight of charms in my palm.

Then Ormyr's gaze pierced mine, beseeching me and me alone. "Gules was rumored to possess a relic that could reveal the future."

I blinked. Was that what Branigan had found there—the artifact he'd written to the beguinage about, the entire reason Drea and I had traveled to Catherwood space? Ormyr's clue, while intriguing, wasn't enough to tell me what it actually was in Shipbuilder terms. If townspeople, adepts, and the alleged relic thief had believed the rumor, that would've been enough to imbue *anything* with power.

"Seek me out upon thy return, Lady Knight. There's much more to discuss," Ormyr continued, still staring deep into my eyes. "Until then, Unseen keep thee." He entered the stairwell and carefully started down the stairs.

My confusing mixed feelings persisted. I peeked at the charms Ormyr had given me: three identical khamsas attached to chains, similar to the ones Lord Catherwood's people had trusted to protect everyone from Gules' curse. Even though our chances of being caught would be far reduced this time around—I knew to fly in quietly—Ingvar, Dag, and I would want to wear these conspicuously, just in case. I pocketed them for the time being.

Ingvar's scowl eased once we were alone again. He glanced between me and Dag with apology. "Shouldn't have lost my temper like that."

"It's understandable. We weren't expecting him, and the wounds are still raw," I replied sincerely.

Dag's posture eased, though he remained silent, back to the wall.

Ingvar gave him a small smile. "Sure ye have much to talk about with Jayce. I'll let you get to it." He faced me with less certainty. "If I don't see you tomorrow ...?"

"You will," I assured him. "We'll meet outside the Baron's chambers first thing, approach him together." Between the two of us, we'd surely get permission for Ingvar to accompany me to Gules.

His eyes lit up at the suggestion. "Aye. See you then."

A self-conscious flush rose to my cheeks owing to the fact that we had an audience, but I was intent on not leaving important things unsaid. "I love you."

He smiled a little. "Love you, too, Jayce."

Ingvar's gaze lingered on me as he backtracked to the stairwell, bearing his lantern off with him—and half of my heart. The remaining half panicked at the void beside it, anxious about how long it'd take to refill. But I was optimistic of our chances with Baron Tristan. He'd conspired to bring us together, after all.

Bright light flashed behind me. I faced Dag, who wielded his light tile with a strained look. "Ormyr asked if I want to join the cloister," he spoke before I could say anything.

His words formed an arrow that lodged deep into my remaining half-heart. I struggled to keep the pain off my face. "Do you?"

Dag hesitated. "I already said I wanted to squire with you."

"You haven't pledged to me yet. Even if you had, I'd never make you stay if you wanted to be somewhere else." I took a gathering breath, forcing a smile. "So, Ormyr wants to train you as an adept. Captain Leirfall told me he'd accept you as a soldier. You're in high demand, young man. Do you need more time to decide? It doesn't have to be tonight."

It'd hurt me, a lot, if Dag squandered his intelligence and embraced superstition. I also worried Ormyr's nurturing streak might vanish once the sting of Holsten's betrayal dulled. But if Dag wanted to join the cloister, I couldn't realistically stop him. I'd just have to keep close to him, try to be a good friend and indirect mentor.

Dag threw back his shoulders with a rare smile. "Nay. I'm ready to adventure, get out of Nidaros."

Happy relief didn't have time to settle in before another arrow of painful realization shot through me. How intent was he on leaving the planet?

"Well, I plan to be here a while," I confessed. "Just imagine how much adventure's still waiting in the Harbinger. And the ichor? That's quite the beast to be slain. I will leave Nidaros on occasion, though. You'll definitely come with me then."

He sobered, considering my answer. "What else'll I do?"

I laughed at myself. "It'd probably be good to explain the whole knight errant and squire thing first, wouldn't it? Come on." I beckoned toward my door.

Inside my room, a lit candle sputtered amid the shrine-like offerings, but Dag preferred his tile. I gestured for him to sit on my pallet. Once I'd laid aside my swords and the cloak Lady Amelia had given me, I sat beside him and glanced upward, gathering my thoughts.

"All right. Do you remember Ormyr telling us about Hegemon Zander?" I began.

Dag nodded.

"A few hundred years after the Shipbuilders' collapse, he swept across the entire galaxy and conquered it, reuniting it under one rule," I continued. "While all those planets had been apart, they'd come up with different laws, languages, religions, and such. To help everyone work together, Zander created a common law, language, and religion for everyone to follow.

"When Zander died, there was no successor strong enough to keep the galaxy united. It split into separate domains again, but those common things he established still linger in all of them. One of them is the tradition of knights." I glanced toward my and Branigan's swords for a moment. "There are many different kinds of knights; we can talk more about that later. I'm a knight errant: a knight beholden to no master, who travels the galaxy freely in search of quests. I'm allowed to own a spacefaring vessel and all the things I might keep aboard that vessel. That's *my* property, not any Lord's."

It was a big deal, a degree of freedom denied to most of the galaxy. Dag's eyes never left mine, and he seemed to be following along.

"Whenever she wants, a knight can take a squire, someone who'll train to become a knight themselves one day. As my squire, you'll shadow me and do as I ask. It might be boring, it might be fun. I come across plenty of both." I smiled. "Obedience is important, but I'd never expect you to follow orders blindly. If you're ever not sure of something, ask me. You can talk to me about anything, I'm here to listen," I said with emphasis.

Dag continued paying attention, holding still and reacting little.

"In exchange for your service, I'll provide food, clothing, shelter, and equipment." I gestured at the offerings and gear around us, a pretty representative sample. "I'll also train you in reading and writing, sword-fighting, and more Shipbuilder arts."

Dag's eyes widened on that last note. I had every intention of taking him to the beguinage at some point, where he'd be able to learn much more than what I could teach him.

"Whenever I feel you're ready — probably years from now — I'll knight you," I continued. "When that happens, you'll earn the title 'Sir,' and you'll be allowed to own a ship and take quests of your own. I'll probably help you with getting a ship, they're difficult to find intact."

Although, maybe not anymore. Between the Harbinger and the invasion force, Nidaros had lucked into a staggering windfall of ships.

"I'll know how to fly and repair her?" Dag asked.

A grin leapt to my face at his use of the feminine pronoun. "Hell yes! That's part of what I'll teach you. But keep in mind, I've never had a squire before. We're both going to make mistakes." Though hopefully none as serious as the ones May had made with me. "Let's be patient with each other. Also, remember, I won't bind you to my service. You can quit whenever you want, for any reason."

Dag blinked. "Can ye quit me?"

I leaned closer and lowered my voice. "Yes. But I wouldn't be taking you as my squire if I thought that were a possibility." I shrugged and straightened. "I've talked enough. Do you have any questions, or need more time to think it over?"

"Nay. I'm ready." He jumped to his feet.

My heart raced from fear, excitement, and the gravity of the moment, but I smiled as I stood and gently braced his shoulders. "Dagfin Nyvind, do you hereby pledge to serve as my squire?"

He glanced up with a smile. "Aye—but I'd just rather be Dag."

"No problem. In public, you'll call me Mistress. In private, I'm Jessamine—or Jess, for short." Feeling brave amid my excitement, I held my arms open. "May I have a hug?"

Dag cocked his head, frowning. "I guess."

I wrapped my arms around him at a glacial pace. Dag was a statue the whole time, but tolerated it. After a few moments, I released him and drew back. "All right, time for bed. We're flying out early tomorrow to rescue my friend."

Be well, Drea, I begged mentally. It was head-spinning how much had changed in a matter of days. She would love what I had to show her.

As we prepared for sleep, Dag darted about with such enthusiasm that I feared he wouldn't actually get any rest that night. I was ready to give him my pallet, but he insisted on the floor, taking only one blanket to protect against the cold Shipbuilder masonry. Once ready, I blew out the candle and col-lapsed.

Moments later, Dag's voice broke through the dark silence. "Ormyr said he wants to recruit you, too, so ye're not a witch anymore."

I drew in a sharp breath. Was *that* what he'd wanted to talk with me about? From his perspective, it probably seemed like a mutually beneficial arrangement. He could shield me and Dag from accusations of witchery while we helped rebuild his devastated cloister. If that were the case, I appreciated his concern, but there was no way in hell I'd ever pledge my ser-vice to a cloister, not after all the heartache adepts had caused me over time.

"I'm already not a witch," I said.

"I know," Dag replied. "He didn't believe me when I told him."

My racing mind kept me awake for quite a while. It also roused me well before dawn the next morning.

Gules. Drea. I was so excited about leaving, I forgot about the little squire curled up at the foot of my pallet until I'd nearly tripped over him.

My squire. Hell, had that really happened? This would be the first day of years together. I hoped harder than ever that we found Drea alive so we could start off on a positive note.

Tradition dictated that Dag help me prepare and don my gear, but I was far too used to handling these tasks myself. Despite trembling limbs, I got ready, throwing on my new cloak and pinning up my hair for zero-gee flight. Then I knelt to rouse him. "Dag? Time to get going."

He was slow to stir, and seemed confused about where he was.

"This is the Baron's estate," I explained. "We're —"

The door to my room opened, revealing Sigrid. Her gaze riveted to me with surprise. "You're already dressed?"

Dag sat up and pushed the hair out of his eyes. He cast a wary glance in Sigrid's direction, but said nothing.

I stood. "I'm preparing to leave Nidaros again for a little while."

Sigrid's expression brightened. "So I've heard. Rescuing another sister! There'll be a whole coven right here in the capital before we know it!"

Her phrasing made me nervous. "Do people think I'm bringing back a witch?" I'd always used words like "wise woman" and "friend" when referring to Drea, hoping to avoid anyone attaching that label to her.

"No. But I know her true nature." Sigrid straightened the blankets on my pallet. "Don't worry, the secret's safe with me."

I dearly hoped so. "I want to pay respects to Baron Tristan before I leave. Can you show me where to find him?"

Sigrid paused and stared off into a corner with a pained look.

Worried, I side-stepped around Dag to approach her. "What's wrong? Is he all right?"

"As far as I know. But they won't let me tend to him." Sigrid's eyes pleaded with me. "He needs me, sister! My visions tell me of his suffering. I try to work spells from a distance, but I don't know how much it's helping."

She seemed genuinely concerned about his welfare — strange, given her Gyllenfeld leanings. Not knowing the Baron's condition, it was hard to offer any reassurance. "I'm sure he appreciates everyone's support," I said diplomatically.

Sigrid crumpled my blankets in her fists. "You, Thordia, and I have done more good in a few days than the cloister has in years."

Well, I couldn't argue that.

"And they won't let me near him! They're all afraid!" She glanced down at her fists. "Maybe they should be."

Nervousness crept up on me. "We're not in the dungeon, at least. Don't you think we would be if—?"

"Oh, enough of that," Sigrid dismissed with sudden brightness, turning toward Dag. "I hear you're quite the magic-wielder in your own right, brother."

Still sitting on the floor, Dag straightened. "I know some Shipbuilder spells, and I'm gonna learn more."

"Get ready, Dag," I egged him gently, hoping to short-circuit the topic.

Soon after, Sigrid led us out, gluing herself to my side. Dag hung back behind us.

"I see death in your journey, sister, but also triumph." Sigrid clutched her beads and stared at them as we walked. "I'll wish hard for you, and I'll keep protecting Thordia while you're away."

"Thanks." Her conveniently vague prophecy gave me no worry or solace. The important thing was that she wished us well—for now. I'd have to keep juggling Sigrid with kid gloves during my stay in Nidaros. Despite her friendly overtures, something about her made my skin crawl. She saw me as an ally, but I feared that might change at a whim, through no fault of my own.

"I'm also piecing together a new coat for you. The old one won't come clean no matter what I do with it." Mischief lit up Sigrid's features. "You'll get a dress, too, while I'm at it. Captain Leirfall will want to *see* the lady working such charms on him."

I had no hope of hiding my blush. It was only a matter of time before everyone knew about me and Ingvar, but I worried about such knowledge in Sigrid's hands.

Another servant walked down the hall toward us and waved to me with a smile. "Lady Knight!"

"Hail, friend," I returned.

"Hello, Arikur," Sigrid chanced.

Arikur's face hardened. He looked away without acknowledging her.

Rage flashed briefly in Sigrid's eyes before she lowered her dejected gaze.

My discomfort ratcheted higher. It wasn't as bad as the dungeon, but being ostracized was pretty horrible in its own right. Though I felt bad for her, the situation worked in my favor. There was less chance Sigrid would turn against me and my loved ones if she saw us as her only friends.

We rounded a corner. Sigrid didn't have to point out where Baron Tristan rested. About ten feet down the hall stood a set of double doors flanked by soldiers. Between them, Lady Amelia scowled in mid-argument with Ingvar, who was geared up for a physical fight rather than a verbal one. Still, he'd risen to the occasion with arms crossed and eyes narrowed.

I froze in my tracks. *Hell,* I thought, my heart sinking. So much for appealing to the Baron.

Lady Amelia's gaze turned toward us newcomers. Her scowl focused on Sigrid, and deepened. She forgot Ingvar to stalk toward us. "Wretch! Haven't I told thee to keep away?"

A soldier detached himself from guard duty to tail the Baroness, apparently wanting to keep an eye on her while she dealt with the outed witch.

Sigrid ducked back into the previous corridor with fists clenched at her sides, face pinched with worry. "Go on, sister," she urged me under her breath.

She braced herself as though expecting an attack, but I couldn't imagine Lady Amelia doing more than scolding her. I decided to capitalize on the diversion. "Keep her talking if you can," I whispered.

Dag held still behind me, eyes darting about. I beckoned him to follow me, then hurried toward the Baron's door, where

Ingvar and the other soldier stood staring after the pending confrontation. Even as Dag and I slipped past Lady Amelia, she only had eyes for the corner Sigrid had vanished behind.

"Dag, wait out here." He'd have to get used to watching doors for me. "Let's hurry," I told Ingvar.

"Who'll talk?" he asked.

Fair point. The last time we'd approached the Baron in a rush, we'd tripped over each other and squandered our chance. "I will."

Ingvar nodded, then gestured for me to precede him.

I pushed against one of the heavy wooden doors, then hurried inside with Ingvar close behind. As it swung shut behind us, we found ourselves in a stuffy chamber, its windows covered in velvet drapes. Candles surrounded a bed in which Baron Tristan lay under blankets, eyes closed.

Gut-dropping disappointment halted me in my tracks. He didn't look to be in any condition to receive us or give Ingvar his leave.

Ingvar stopped behind me, his reaction a mystery for the moment.

A young bead-clutching adept positioned at the foot of the bed faced us with wide eyes. "Captain. Oh, and you must be Dame Jessamine. Adept Finnar."

"Well met, friend Adept," I said reflexively as my brain puzzled over my next move. Could I rouse the Baron without getting in trouble? I'd have to work up to it slowly. I hoped Sigrid could distract Lady Amelia long enough.

"Sorry for barging in," I continued. "I wanted to pay my respects before leaving the planet."

Finnar nodded. "I'll let our Baron know when he awakens."

"I'm awake now." Baron Tristan's eyes opened a sliver.

I probably did a poor job of concealing the relief that washed over me then.

Finnar clutched his beads to his chest, contrite. "Your Grace! I didn't realize."

"No matter." The Baron's gaze shifted my way. "Mine eternal gratitude, Lady Knight. Farewell."

I wanted to ask him how he felt, but it'd have to wait. "I'll be back again soon, sir. You still face several plights, and I've come to care very much about the people here." Warm blood burned my cheeks and ears. "Especially Captain Leirfall."

Baron Tristan's eyes widened.

I disliked leveraging my feelings this way, but the Baron had originally conspired to put us together. I hoped the glow of success would endear him to our cause.

"Mistress?" Dag's voice sounded from the corridor, muffled and uncertain.

An instant later, Lady Amelia burst into the chamber and stalked toward the Baron's bedside, leveling an acidic expression on me and Ingvar.

My chest tightened with dread. "Would it be too much to ask that we both travel to retrieve the wise woman who can help us with the ichor?" I gunned out in one breath.

"How many times must I refuse?" Lady Amelia demanded to know. "We need Captain Leirfall here!"

I faltered, feeling defeat close in. That was when Ingvar stepped up beside me with a defiant air. "Your Graces, I request the right to court Dame Jessamine."

Silence followed as everyone processed the sudden shift. The flush I'd felt earlier proceeded to set my whole face on fire. What was this, asking to be considered an "official" couple? Why bother with that now, of all times — or ever, really? Weren't we making our own rules? We didn't need anyone's permission.

Baron Tristan lowered his head graciously. "You both have my blessing. Wife?"

Lady Amelia's anger had melted, but she didn't yet have command of words. Her fingers brushed absently against the posy still hanging from her wrist. Eventually, she managed a nod.

Once her demeanor changed, I began to appreciate what Ingvar had done. He'd communicated the depth of our feelings for one another, my commitment to him *and* Nidaros, in terms Lady Amelia understood.

"Let's not separate this pair after all they've done for us," the Baron continued. "Lieutenant Grimsson can command our army in Captain Leirfall's absence."

The Baroness was self-centered, as I'd learned when she'd tried to bribe me for food, but her husband could coax out her empathy. Sure enough, she glanced between me and Ingvar with a new compassion, clutching her beads. "Very well, venture forth together. Be careful and return swiftly."

Somehow, I managed not to leap with joy. "We will. Thank you."

Ingvar held in his reaction, too, but his eyes lit up unmistakably. "As ye command, Milady."

"Unseen guide you," Finnar offered.

"Wife?" Baron Tristan prompted. "Where is Sigrid?"

His simple question paralyzed me and the rest of the room. Lady Amelia's kind aura vanished. "Working about the estate, husband. All our servants are busy."

"I wish to have her blessing," the Baron continued. "We must begin heeding her visions."

This even greater shock nearly rattled my elation to pieces. Did he really intend to keep trusting Sigrid's "guidance" despite the fact that she was a Gyllenfeld-leaning witch? Was this some sort of fever or delirium talking? I glanced toward Ingvar questioningly, but he seemed as surprised as I was. Same for Finnar. Lady Amelia remained bitter, giving me the impression that she'd heard this plea before. It no doubt fueled her hostility toward Sigrid.

I convinced myself it wasn't worth worrying about just then. There was no telling how Baron Tristan's opinion might change while we were abroad. Better to focus on Drea. At long last, nothing stood in my way.

"Rest now, husband. I shall see to everything." Lady Amelia glanced to me and Ingvar with a look that told us to take our leave.

In the corridor, Dag darted up to us. "Coming with?" he asked Ingvar.

Still working through his surprise, the captain needed a moment to manage an "Aye."

My heart pounded with joy and apprehension. "Let's head to my ship."

Kepler's Law remained outside the barracks. As we approached, it was amusing to see someone else excited to see her. Not just someone else, *my squire*. With emotions ranging from awe to terror, I wondered if I'd ever get used to that distinction.

Once her stubborn hatch yielded, Dag bounded aboard. I waved Ingvar in next, then brought up the rear.

We entered a spotless galley. The wounded soldiers had been moved back to the barracks, and Thordia had opted for a room in the estate—more private, and closer to the Baron in case she was needed during his recovery. To my surprise and gratitude, she'd left the surgical construct behind. It was a welcome companion for the journey ahead, though I hoped like hell Drea wouldn't need it.

Dag slipped the knapsack off his shoulders and darted toward the nearby closets. A little rummaging netted him the silver orb he'd found within the Harbinger, which he hugged like an old friend.

"Blood's oath!" Ingvar hung back, tense. "What's that, lad?"

"Her name's Flekka." Dag straightened with pride. "She followed me out of the Harbinger."

"She? *Followed?*" Ingvar repeated dubiously.

I patted Ingvar on the shoulder with a smile. "You'll see."

"Here, lad. Something for you." From his own gear, Ingvar produced a machete-sized sword capped with a leather sheath.

Dag's eyes widened. He shifted Flekka to his left arm so he could grasp the blade's handle with his right hand and shake off the sheath. Beneath it gleamed a short, single-edged blade.

"Say thank you," I prompted.

"Aye, thanks!"

I smiled to Ingvar. "*I'm* supposed provide his equipment."

"We've a surplus." Ingvar didn't have to explain how.

"What else did those mercs drop?" Dag asked.

"Don't worry about that," Ingvar dismissed. "Worry about working up to competence with that blade. 'Tis an easy one to learn with."

"I'll be getting you practice weapons, too," I said. "Wooden ones."

"*Skíta!*" Dag cried in protest. "That doesn't sound fun."

"Says the young man who's never clubbed anyone yet." I grinned. "All right, let's be careful about how we stow everything, or else it'll go floating everywhere." Dag didn't understand what I meant, but he would soon. Ignoring my mounting jitters, I cleaned out a storage bin and designated it fully his.

Dag clutched Flekka tighter. "I have to put her away again?"

"She'll be safer inside until we reach Gules," I explained. "You'll see."

He hesitated at first, but then gently surrendered her, placing his new sword beside her. Afterward, I stowed my own weapons, along with my gifted cloak.

In the meantime, Ingvar had secured his gear. Nervousness dominated his expression, which he was quick to conceal with a smile whenever Dag was looking.

"Head to the cockpit," I told Dag. "Flying will be different this time since we're leaving the planet. I'll explain as we go."

Dag nodded, then darted out of the galley.

As anxious energy built up in my chest, I helped Ingvar pull down and settle into one of the galley chairs. "A lot of flying for you lately," I commented.

"Aye, but this is where I want to be," Ingvar said with conviction.

My heart jumped. "Takeoff will be rougher than it was on the Baron's ship, but we'll be fine. I'll come back here once we're on course."

"One more thing first." Ingvar wrapped his arms around me and reeled me into a kiss.

I returned it, throwing my arms around his neck, then laughed. "So we're *officially* courting now. What does that mean, exactly?"

He shrugged helplessly, smirking. "We'll find out together, Goose. I told you, I'm no expert."

"No, but you're pretty damn good." After one more kiss, I pulled away.

A good thing there was only one path to the cockpit, otherwise I would've gotten lost amid my giddiness. Dag waited in the copilot's chair, all strapped in. Out the windshield, a pleasant morning had dawned, far more inviting than the harsh winter that awaited us on Gules.

"My friend's name is Drea," I told Dag while squeezing into the pilot's chair. "I hope she's all right. She'll really like you."

Dag nodded.

My first order of business was disabling the ship's beacon via the console. "Wherever I go, my ship normally gives off a signal saying who I am. Think of it like carrying a lantern at night," I explained. "Some Lords have Shipbuilder artifacts that let them spot those signals from a distance. I'm silencing my signal for now — shutting off the lantern — because we're headed for cursed territory. We stand to get in a lot of trouble if anyone catches us landing there, but with the signal off, no one should see us."

Dag nodded again, seemingly satisfied with this explanation.

While the thrusters warmed up, I kissed my hand to pat the console. Premature, maybe, but I owed *Kepler's Law* for the one I'd missed after landing in Nidaros mid-invasion. I took a deep breath, then glanced about the Nidaran landscape one last time. "Ready?"

"Let's go."

The Quest Continues!

Will Dame Jessamine and her friends rescue Drea in time? What challenges await on Nidaros as the ichor spreads and the balance of power is disrupted? How will Jess adjust to courtly life and her new obligations — or *will* she? You'll have to wait for Book 3 to find out!

If you'd like to be informed of its release, please visit my website (http://www.ellismorning.com/) to join my mailing list. You'll also receive free short stories and be eligible for occasional giveaways.

I also want to **THANK YOU** for reading *Harbingers!* Your feedback helps to improve my writing, and the more my books are reviewed, the more likely it is that other people will find out about them. If you have a spare moment, I'd really appreciate you leaving me your honest review wherever you purchased this book.

Thanks for joining me on this adventure!

-Ellis

About Ellis

Ellis has always loved staging adventures in her head before going to sleep each night. When she was twelve, she started putting these adventures on paper.

For the next twenty years, she wrote with varying degrees of seriousness, but always as a hobby. In that time, she fell in love with Mark Twain and Kurt Vonnegut, the original *Star Trek* series, and *Mystery Science Theater 3000*. Science fiction became her favorite domain to work in, but she also enjoyed reading fantasy, horror, Western, and detective stories, and incorporating their elements into her work. One of her favorite things to do was make people laugh.

Ellis denied being a writer for decades. But then she sold articles to The Daily WTF, and a short story to Analog Science Fiction and Fact. After quitting her full-time job to finish her first novel, it was time to own up to writing as her calling. She's currently having the time of her life penning original short stories and novels in a variety of fun and thought-provoking genres.

Website: www.ellismorning.com
Email: contact@ellismorning.com
Google Plus: +Ellis Morning
Twitter: @EllisMorning